T0036675

Praise for *Along a Storied Trail*

"Gabhart's skillful use of period details and the Appalachian land-scape lend plenty of atmosphere to accompany the lessons of hope, compassion, and fortitude amid hardship."

Publishers Weekly starred review

"The author excels at crafting her characters with care."

Evangelical Church Library Association

the
SONG *of*
SOURWOOD
MOUNTAIN

Books by Ann H. Gabhart

The Song of Sourwood
Mountain
In the Shadow of the River
When the Meadow Blooms
Along a Storied Trail
An Appalachian Summer
River to Redemption
These Healing Hills
Words Spoken True
The Outsider
The Believer
The Seeker
The Blessed
The Gifted
Christmas at Harmony Hill
The Innocent
The Refuge

HEART OF HOLLYHILL

Scent of Lilacs
Orchard of Hope
Summer of Joy

ROSEY CORNER

Angel Sister
Small Town Girl
Love Comes Home

HIDDEN SPRINGS MYSTERY
AS A. H. GABHART

Murder at the Courthouse
Murder Comes by Mail
Murder Is No Accident

the SONG *of* SOURWOOD MOUNTAIN

ANN H. GABHART

Revell

a division of Baker Publishing Group
Grand Rapids, Michigan

© 2024 by Ann H. Gabhart

Published by Revell
a division of Baker Publishing Group
Grand Rapids, Michigan
RevellBooks.com

Printed in the United States of America

Library of Congress Cataloging-in-Publication Data
Names: Gabhart, Ann H., 1947– author.
Title: The song of Sourwood Mountain / Ann H. Gabhart.
Description: Grand Rapids, Michigan : Revell, a division of Baker Publishing Group, 2024.
Identifiers: LCCN 2023035455 | ISBN 9780800741730 (paperback) | ISBN 9780800745875 (casebound) | ISBN 9781493445547 (ebook)
Subjects: LCGFT: Romance fiction. | Christian fiction. | Novels.
Classification: LCC PS3607.A23 S66 2024 | DDC 813/.6—dc23/eng/20230824
LC record available at https://lccn.loc.gov/2023035455

Scripture used in this book, whether quoted or paraphrased by the characters, is taken from the King James Version of the Bible.

Cover design by Laura Klynstra
Photography © Magdalena Russocka / Trevillion Images
Author photograph © Everlasting Moments Photography by Juanita Jones

Published in association with Books & Such Literary Management, www.booksandsuch.com.

Baker Publishing Group publications use paper produced from sustainable forestry practices and postconsumer waste whenever possible.

24 25 26 27 28 29 30   7 6 5 4 3 2 1

In memory of my mother,
Olga Elizabeth Hawkins Houchin,
who loved stories and bird-watching
as much as I do.

As might be expected of creatures so heavenly in color, the disposition of bluebirds is particularly angelic. Gentleness and amiability are expressed in their soft musical voice. *Tru-al-ly, tru-al-ly*, they sweetly assert when we can scarcely believe that spring is here; *tur-wee, tur-wee* they softly call in autumn when they go roaming through the countryside in flocks of azure.

—Neltje Blanchan, *Birds Worth Knowing*, 1917

1

When Mira Dean left her rooms for church on Sunday morning, she had no idea that she would hear a proposal of marriage before she returned for her midday meal.

"I-I don't know what to say." Her hazel eyes widened with shock at Gordon Covington's words. She barely knew the man watching her with what seemed the polite smile of someone who had said nothing more than "Good day."

Perhaps she misheard him. Surely she had misheard him.

He glanced around at the people lingering in the church and kept his voice low. "I suppose I should not have been so direct."

When she had approached him after his message to compliment him on his work, he pulled her aside for a private word. Had she any idea what he intended those private words to be, she would have smiled, disengaged her arm, and hurried out the door.

Now she stared past him at the stained-glass window and let those words run through her thoughts again. "*Would you consider marriage, Miss Dean? To me.*" She moistened her lips, but he began speaking again before she could give him the only possible answer. No.

"I did not mean to unsettle you, but I have discovered in my time of service to the Lord in the hills of Kentucky that it is nearly always best to plunge forward whenever the Lord prompts me, Miss Dean."

She obviously had not heard wrong. He not only had said the words, he was implying the Lord wanted him to do so.

She pulled her gaze away from the window to peer at him from under the brim of her hat. He was head and shoulders taller than her, but then she did lack appreciable height. Petite, her mother always claimed for her. A prettier word than *short*.

His coat hung loosely on him as if he might have missed too many meals since she'd known him when they were teens. Not well, although they had attended the same school. At the time, she had her life planned out. Marriage to Edward Hamilton. A houseful of children to love. She had no need to consider other pathways then. That was before Edward contracted tuberculosis and went to a sanatorium.

For over two years, she had stormed heaven with prayers for him. The Lord had to heal him, but her prayers weren't answered. Edward had not recovered and instead died without ever leaving the sanatorium. Quite suddenly, or so it seemed to Mira.

This man, Reverend Gordon Covington, with the intense dark blue-gray eyes little resembled the classmate she remembered. That boy was the first out of the schoolhouse to get to the ball-field. She had been interested in seeing him again when she found out he would be visiting their church to talk about his missionary work in the Kentucky Appalachian Mountains. He'd spoken with passion about the church and school he hoped to establish there.

His words touched her heart. When he talked about the mountain children who had no school, tears had filled her eyes. How terrible it would be to have no way to learn to read. She could hardly believe such a thing was possible here in 1910. All children in Louisville had public schools they could attend, were even required to attend.

She had led many students along a learning path since she began teaching while praying for Edward to regain his health so they could marry. When that did not happen, she had given her life to her students with the thought that they would be her only children.

She had no desire to marry. Besides, even if she were so foolish to dream of love again, at her age she would be unlikely to find a husband. After all, she was twenty-five years old. Gordon was a year older than that, but age mattered less to a man when it came to marriage.

Marriage. The word crashed into her thoughts again. This was absurd. But she was a lady. A mature lady. She could handle this with grace.

"Did the Lord prompt you to be so forward, Mr. Covington?"

She didn't know where those words came from. They weren't at all what she had intended to say. She had meant to step away from him with a murmured refusal to end their uncomfortable encounter. At least she was uncomfortable. Her heart pounded so hard it thumped in her ears. He, on the other hand, looked completely at ease.

"Yes, I do believe that is true. I've prayed with diligence and hope for someone to share my work among the people in Sourwood. The children there need a teacher." His eyes on her were intense. "I need a helpmate."

"I will join my prayers to yours that the Lord will answer your prayers." It was time to make her escape from this impossible conversation. As she started to turn away, he caught her arm.

"But can you not believe you already are that answer?" His gaze didn't waver. "I have no doubt the Lord led us both here on this day. At this very moment. The children need you."

He didn't grip her arm, merely touched it, but his words froze her in place. She did feel a tug at her heart. Not for the man staring at her, but for the children he mentioned. Children with no teacher. The force of his calling seemed to go from his hand to her heart.

"I barely know you."

Her head was spinning. If not for his hand on her arm, she might have swooned. She never swooned, but now it seemed his touch was all that kept her grounded. Or perhaps not him. Perhaps his talk of the Lord. Yes, that was what she should cling to. His mission for the Lord. A mission he was inviting her to join.

When he didn't say anything, she added, "You barely know me."

"The Lord knows us both and he knows the need. A need you and I can fill in Sourwood. You wouldn't be a teacher hired by the county. Ours would be a mission school with our own rules for the position of teacher. A teacher chosen by the Lord." Now he did tighten his fingers on her arm the slightest bit. "I think you feel the calling too. Think of the children you will help."

"I already teach here in Louisville."

"City children have many teachers. In Sourwood they have none, but we have faith the Lord will provide the perfect teacher for the schoolhouse we're building." He leaned closer to her. "And here you are."

She felt captured, not only by his hand, but by his mission. "The need for a teacher doesn't explain your—" She hesitated before continuing. "Your proposal. You do know that teachers are required to be single."

A flicker of a frown tightened his face, but only for a moment. "A foolish policy, in my opinion. Don't you agree?"

"I-I have never considered it, as I knew it would not apply to me."

"You never thought of marriage?"

"Not after Edward died." Even now, years later, simply saying the words made her heart clench with sorrow.

"I was sorry to hear of his passing. A good man lost to the world." His face softened as though he understood her grief.

"So much lost," she murmured. This man could not know how

much. The emptiness, the barren feeling that settled deep within her.

"But the Lord has another plan for you now. Come to the mountains with me. As my wife. The mountaineers will accept you sooner that way and trust their children to your instruction."

"I can't marry you. I don't love you." She looked directly into his eyes. "You don't love me."

"But I love the Lord. You love the Lord. I believe he will honor that love, and with a common mission in both our hearts, the Lord will grow love between us as he did so many of those he brought together in the Bible."

"We are not people in the Bible."

For the first time since he'd pulled her aside, he smiled fully to transform his face. He looked more like the boy she remembered from school, someone everyone liked. She felt her own lips turning up in an answering smile despite the complete disarray of her thoughts.

"We are not, but I believe the Lord still works through people in our day the same as Bible times. He knows the plans he has for us and he opens up paths to let us accomplish his purpose. He sent me to the mountains to minister to the people there. Could you have ever believed that possible when you knew me years ago?"

How could she answer him? At that time, she could have never imagined him becoming a preacher. "I don't know. I suppose I could have if I had considered the possibility."

He waved away her words with a laugh. "Now, now, Miss Dean, I think you do know. You can be honest with me. Honesty is important, even vital, in a marital relationship."

If he wanted honesty, she could give him honesty tempered with kindness. "I think it is important not to pretend, Reverend Covington. I am intrigued by the idea of teaching in your mission area. Sourwood, did you say?" When he nodded, she went on. "But I have no intention of marrying you or anyone."

"Nor did I have intentions to be a preacher or, once I did surrender to preach, to go to the mountains. But the Lord can change our intentions."

"The Lord may have spoken to you and given you a mission. He has not spoken to me." When she stepped away from him, he dropped his hand to his side. The strange urge came over her to move back toward him in the hope he might claim her arm again.

"Are you sure? You did come to hear my message. You seem sympathetic to my plea for help."

"This is the church I attend regularly. I put a gift in the collection they took for you." Her words sounded stiff.

"Such funds are much appreciated, but you have so much more to give." He pinned her in place with his gaze. "Will you do me one favor?"

"I cannot marry you." As he had said, honesty was best.

"I have asked that, and it would be a fine favor, but this is a different request."

"Very well. What is it?"

"Will you pray about what I've asked? Will you let the Lord put that intention in your heart if it is meant to be? As I think. As I hope."

"I will pray for you and for your mission." That seemed a reasonable answer to his request.

"I do covet your prayers, but will you also pray to be open to what the Lord wants from you? I do not believe he ever demands more than we are able to give, and I, should you accept my outrageous request, would never demand anything you are not ready to give with an open heart."

"I will pray for you," she repeated.

His eyes looked sad then, as he nodded slightly. "Thank you. Your presence here was a gift and so will be your prayers for me."

As she turned away from him to find her way out of the church, she wondered if she would ever see him again. For some reason, that thought bothered her. Not because of him, she was sure, but because of her sympathy and concern for his mission.

Under her cloak, she touched her arm where his hand had held her. Despite the frosty chill in the January air, her skin still felt warm. She jerked her hand away and pulled on her gloves. She would pray he would find the teacher he sought.

2

*G*ordon Covington watched Mira Dean hurry out of the church as if flames were rising from the pews. He could hope his words had stirred awake a fire in her heart, but more likely he had simply frightened her.

Perhaps he had been too direct. A fault he always had, but one that became even worse once he surrendered to the calling to preach. He had no time for dithering. Not when the Lord had so plainly pointed out Mira Dean as the teacher he needed. And the wife.

The wife part had shocked her. The idea was somewhat shocking to him as well. After all, they hadn't seen each other for years. He was a different person than when she knew him in school. Back then, he thought of little but the next good time with his friends. And girls. But wasn't that always what young men had on their minds at that age? He had even looked on Mira with favor, but she had eyes only for Edward Hamilton. Other girls were there to grab his attention.

But no other girl had sufficiently caught his interest. Friends told him a preacher needed a wife, but he was unbothered by his single life. Such seemed best when he decided to go to the Eastern

Kentucky mountains to ride circuit, preaching wherever ears were ready to hear.

A wife would not want to ride along on the rough trails in all sorts of weather, nor would any of the women he had ever seriously courted wish to stay alone in a mountain cabin while he was away spreading the gospel.

He had faith the Lord would supply his needs, whether of food or shelter, and he had. If the Lord determined Gordon truly needed a wife, he would send the right woman his way. Hadn't Rebekah come to the well to water her sheep at the very hour Abraham's servant was there with a mission to find Isaac a wife?

Gordon sincerely believed in God's provision. So when his heart stirred at the sight of Mira coming into the church, he had no doubt the Lord was doing the stirring. Often in his ministry, the Lord had given him such a poke. Sometimes to stop at this or that cabin or to soften his words in a sermon or to harden them.

Such a nudge was why he had established a mission in Sourwood. That time the Lord hadn't nudged him. Instead, Dugan Foster felt the Lord pushing him to ask Gordon to come minister to his community.

This morning Gordon had been conferring with the pastor here in Louisville when Mira had grabbed his attention. For a moment, the man's words flowed past him unheard. This woman was here for a reason. He was here for a reason. The Lord's plan.

Pastor Watkins noted his distraction. "Do you know our Miss Dean? She's a faithful member here."

"We were classmates in school some time ago." The man's use of "Miss" had felt like another nudge from the Lord. "I haven't seen her since then."

"A lovely lady. She was engaged to a young man several years ago, but sadly, he passed on. Tuberculosis. She turned her energies to teaching and serving here in our church."

"Oh, in what ways?" More nudges.

"Her kindness draws people to her. Whatever is needed, she is not only ready to help but has the necessary skills to do so. My wife claims she's a gift from heaven."

A gift from heaven. Another nudge. In the service that followed, Mira appeared to listen attentively as he spoke of his mission work in the hill regions of Kentucky. Each time he let his gaze touch on her, he became more positive the Lord had brought her to his attention for a reason.

At school, she was a pretty girl with light brown hair that often escaped the combs used to hold it in place. Her hazel eyes had sparkled with a love of life. She was no longer that girl. Her hair was neatly contained in a roll below her proper black hat. Her eyes were more guarded, although they had widened at his surprising proposal.

She'd left girlhood behind and known sorrow now as most people did. Hadn't he recently lost his source of constant support for his spiritual missions when his mother died? While that wasn't the same as losing your intended life partner, it was a sorrow nevertheless.

But time had a way of blunting the sharp edges of grief. Edward had died five years ago. Gordon was surprised Mira hadn't already married someone else. Perhaps it wasn't a surprise at all, but all part of the Lord's plan. Not that he believed Edward's death figured in that plan, but the Lord could make good come from any situation. He might be doing so now. Gordon merely had to convince Mira of that.

No, he wasn't the one to convince her. He had to leave that up to the Lord. But he wasn't taking the train back to Sourwood for two more days. He would share his mission with another church this evening and then take time to gather needed supplies on the morrow. The Lord could work many wonders in two days.

He had asked Mira to pray. He could do the same. He smiled as he followed Pastor Watkins out of the church to share a dinner table with one of his faithful deacons. The air was frigid, but his heart felt warm as he thought of Mira.

The Lord had created people, male and female. While Gordon had left behind his frivolous young days the same as Mira had, he wasn't an old man. Far from it at twenty-six. He had always assumed he would marry. Someday. The idea that someday might be at hand brought a smile to his face. He was a preacher. Once he accepted the Lord's call, he had never regretted his path, but he was still a man with the same need of love and companionship.

Lord, if it can be, open a path to that love for Mira and me.

Sunday was Mira's favorite day. She could take her time dressing for church without the daily rush to get to school before the children began arriving. At church, she enjoyed the hymns and the pastor's sermons that opened her eyes to Bible truths.

She never missed Sunday morning services, save for times when she was under the weather. The outdoor weather never stopped her. She walked through snow and rain, heat and cold the few blocks to her church. A little discomfort was hardly to be noticed when one thought of the Lord's great sacrifice.

Still, on a day like this with its frigid air, she was happy to return to the rooms she rented from Miss Ophelia Vandercleve, an elderly spinster who had been a schoolteacher herself some years before. The old lady had always lived in this house, except for a few years when she boarded in a nearby county while teaching there. Her parents had long since departed life, and her only relative was a brother who mostly ignored Miss Ophelia, which suited the woman fine, or so she claimed.

"He was always the bossy sort," Miss Ophelia said.

That made Mira smile, since Miss Ophelia definitely shared that family trait. While she was not slow to tell Mira what she thought was proper or not, she did have a kind heart under her brusque manner.

Now as Mira approached the two-story brick house, she felt fortunate to have rooms there. Her school and church were nearby. The steps up to a separate entrance gave her some welcome privacy. Miss Ophelia's father had them built for Miss Ophelia when she was younger so she could come and go without disturbing her mother.

Miss Ophelia said her mother was very fragile. "Nerves, you know. The slightest disturbance could knock her off-kilter for weeks. Poor dear. I say that, but actually it was those of us around her who were the poor ones. Father insisted I tiptoe in my upstairs rooms, and heaven forbid were I to drop something. At times, may the Lord forgive me, I would drop something a purpose." She had tilted her head downward and looked over her spectacles at Mira. "I expect better of you. No loud noises. No gentlemen callers. A schoolteacher has to guard her reputation."

Oh yes, guard her reputation. The school administrators allowed no unseemly behavior. A female teacher wore dark-colored skirts with the proper layers of petticoats underneath and high-necked, long-sleeved white blouses. No bright colors allowed. She kept her hair nicely coiffed in rolls or a bun. Heaven forbid a female teacher be seen smoking a cigarette. She would be ousted from her position before the smoke drifted away. And should a woman decide to marry, she was required to resign her teaching position to devote herself to her husband and family.

That was something Mira had been more than ready to do if Edward had recovered. They had such plans. A beautiful house such as Miss Ophelia's. Room for many children. Edward would prosper in business, and she would make their home a warm and loving place.

Instead, she made a different life for herself, teaching other women's children. She had long ago blocked even the passing thought of a baby in her arms. More times than she liked, her mind betrayed her and let a dream of being a mother rise in her sleep, but such impossible dreams faded away before the water was hot for her morning tea.

She couldn't allow Gordon Covington's idiotic proposal to unsettle her. She had a good life teaching young people, and following a hectic school day, the quiet of her small rooms was more than welcome.

After stepping through her door, she hung her coat on a hook and left her boots on a folded newspaper on the floor. She slipped on soft house shoes that barely made a whisper of noise as she walked across to her small paraffin stove to warm her potato soup.

After her meal, she settled into her one easy chair by the window and picked up Jack London's *Call of the Wild*. She had passed many pleasurable Sunday afternoons in just such a way. A book and a cup of tea. She had no reason to let Gordon's talk about his plans for a school destroy her peace.

A marriage proposal! That was more than idiotic. Mira opened her book, but the words were simply black marks. They made no pictures in her head. Instead, she was back at the church hearing Gordon's appeal for help to establish his mission. A mission to not only bring the gospel to the people there but also the opportunity of an education to their children. And why not the adults too, if they showed interest in learning?

What did the Bible say about gifts? Pastor Watkins had preached on that a few Sundays ago. If a man had a gift to preach, he should preach the message the Lord gave him. If the gift was to serve, one should serve well. If to teach, teach well. If to encourage, rejoice in that gift and be a blessing to others. Whatever the gift, the Lord gave it for a purpose.

She remembered feeling somewhat smug listening to the pastor's words, knowing that she was using her gift. She did teach well. Her students learned what would help them live more successful and fuller lives.

But now she wondered if she truly made that much difference. The youngsters at her school had no lack of teachers and would learn regardless of who taught them. But what would it be like to start a child with no schooling on the road to book knowledge? That had to be more challenging. And fulfilling.

She put her book aside and picked up her Bible. Reading that passage in Romans might calm her mind and assure her she was using her gift as the Lord intended.

But when she placed the Bible in her lap, it fell open to Genesis. She was ready to flip to the New Testament when a verse caught her eye. "Sarai was barren; she had no child."

The word "barren" jumped off the page at her. But could she, a woman who had never been married, never known a man, be considered barren? Whenever it was mentioned in the Bible about Sarah, Rebekah, Hannah, Elizabeth, the Scripture spoke of a married woman unable to conceive. Each of those women received the blessing of a child in God's time, but they had husbands.

Mira had no husband. Her barrenness went deeper than simply not having a child, but in not having a husband. She was a spinster. A woman with no hope of a child even if she prayed with the same emotion and sincerity as Hannah.

She looked up from the Bible to glance across the room at the small kitchen area with her one-burner stove, a sink, and a narrow table with two chairs. Rarely was more than one chair needed. The table served as her desk. Next to where she sat by the window was a lamp on a small round table. On the other side of the window, a three-shelf bookcase held her treasured books. An adjoining room had just enough space for a bed little bigger than a cot and a chest of drawers. The furniture was plain but serviceable. She had no need for more.

Her father had been a clerk, and while they always had enough, they never had abundance. Her parents laid aside any extra money for her and her brother's education. Her brother had gone on to Harvard and a career as a lawyer in Boston.

The last time she heard from him he had five children, but she had yet to receive a response from her Christmas letter. That number could very well be six by now. She had never seen any of them. Travel was difficult with young children, and Mira didn't have the funds to travel their way even had she been invited, which she had not. She'd last seen Paul at her mother's funeral six years ago. Their father died the year before that.

Paul had little time for a sister he considered well settled as a teacher. A perfect course for a spinster woman.

Spinster. Barren. The words circled in her head. She almost smiled when she thought it was good she was barren since she was a spinster.

With a sigh, she closed the Bible. She should open it to Psalms. Try to find comfort there, but instead she picked up the ceramic bird from the table beside her. A little of the blue paint had worn off the feathers, and no wonder, as much as she held it.

Her mother had given her the figurine a few months before she died. "I'm coming to the end of my time, and I want to pass on to you the hope I've always felt when I hold this bluebird, my dear Almira. When I see a bluebird, I can't help but think of the love with which the Lord surely formed that first bird. Through that love, the Lord gifted us with joy and hope whenever our eyes delight in its sight. May this little bird help you remember not only my love but the Lord's as well. A bluebird of happiness."

Since her mother passed away before Edward, she had not known how Mira's dreams of marriage and children were shattered.

The ceramic bird seemed to warm in her hands. How long had it been since she'd seen a bluebird outside? Perhaps here in the city such birds were uncommon, or had she simply stopped looking for them? The kind of happiness her mother had wished for her seemed out of reach.

Mira did have times of happiness. She did. Moments when she was drawn into a story to share whatever adventures the characters were living on the page. Moments when her students did things to make her smile. Moments when she was lifted up by a passage of Scripture. One without the word "barren."

The word echoed in her head. *Barren.* Not just her lack of a husband or child. Her whole life seemed barren, with nothing more than another cup of tea to look forward to.

A knock on the door jerked her away from her melancholy thoughts. Her heart began thumping as, for one inane moment, she hoped Gordon Covington would be the one knocking.

3

When Mira opened the door, Gordon Covington wasn't standing on the small stoop at the top of the steps. Of course he wasn't. The very thought he might be had been foolish. However, seeing Miss Ophelia there was every bit as surprising. She was an imposing sight, scowling down at Mira.

"Well, are you going to let me in?" The woman glared at her. "This wind has to be coming straight off an iceberg."

Without waiting for Mira to answer, Miss Ophelia pushed past her.

Mira stepped aside, still holding on to the doorknob. "Is something wrong, Miss Ophelia?"

In the two years Mira had lived on the upper floor of Miss Ophelia's house, the woman had climbed those steps only one time. That was when she showed Mira the accommodations before Mira rented the rooms.

"It will be if you don't close the door. We'll both come down with the grippe."

"Yes. Certainly." Mira closed the door. "Come in."

"I appear to already be in." Miss Ophelia looked around the room. "Neat. As expected."

"Here, let me take your wrap." Mira found her manners.

"Never mind. My old bones need warming." Miss Ophelia pulled her cloak closer around her.

Very little about the woman looked old. At several inches taller than Mira, she was a commanding presence in the small kitchen area. She narrowed her eyes on Mira. "Are you going to invite me to sit down or expect me to keep standing?"

"Please, please do sit." Mira motioned toward the one upholstered chair.

Miss Ophelia pulled out one of the straight chairs from the table. "This will do." She handed Mira a tea towel–wrapped bundle. "Tea cakes."

"Oh, how lovely. I'll heat some water for tea." Mira turned on the paraffin burner under her teakettle, then got out a plate for the cookies.

A gift of food from Miss Ophelia was as unexpected as her visit. Mira was the one who stopped by her door to share this or that bit of food.

"You should have rung your bell. I would have come down." The old lady had a metal school bell she clanged whenever she wanted to talk to Mira. "Or did you ring it and I not hear?"

"I didn't ring it. Wears me out to shake the thing, and with that wind, it would blow the sound who knows where. The neighbors would be complaining."

Not something that had ever seemed to concern Miss Ophelia previously. Mira didn't point that out. She wasn't sorry to have her visit. The cookies looked delicious, and Mira was glad for an excuse to not only have a second cup of tea but to push aside her lonesome thoughts. Still, this was more than a friendly visit. Something was up.

She studied the woman as she set cups and saucers on the table and poured the tea. She hadn't seen Miss Ophelia since before Christmas when she gave her a jar of honey, something she had told Mira she liked.

The woman's eyes looked watery. Perhaps from the cold wind. "Would you like sugar?"

"I drink it as it comes from the pot." Miss Ophelia raised the cup to her lips to sip the hot liquid. The teacup rattled in the saucer when she put it down. She slid her hand under her cloak but not before Mira saw the tremble of her fingers.

"Are you cold? I can get you a lap blanket."

"No, no. That isn't necessary." She pulled out her hand to hold it over the table to show the trembles. "This isn't from cold. It's from old." She frowned. "Such happens with age."

Mira had no idea how old Miss Ophelia was and certainly was not about to ask. She bit into one of the cookies. "I can never make anything that tastes this good."

"One would need an oven, which you do not have." Miss Ophelia looked at the one-burner stove. "A teacher's pay doesn't supply many conveniences. If not for having this house and these rooms to let, my situation would be much more dire."

"I'm very happy here."

"Are you?" Miss Ophelia narrowed her eyes on Mira.

Before Mira could summon up an answer, Miss Ophelia waved her hand to dismiss her question. "A woman does what a woman must at times. And lives by whatever means she's able. I have certainly done such all of my days."

"Yes." Mira didn't know what else to say.

"I don't think you've ever met my brother, have you?"

"No. He lives in Ohio, didn't you say?"

"He does. He has a daughter. Turned twenty last month. Unmarried and without suitors, or so my brother says. I am not sure if he is being completely honest with me."

"Oh?"

"That is neither here nor there. I am not one to share my family's doings, right or wrong."

"I see." Mira thought the less said, the better.

"I doubt if you do, and better if you don't." She took another sip of tea and then spun her cup around in the saucer once and again. "Mrs. Abrams stopped by to see me a bit ago."

"Mrs. Abrams?"

"She goes to your church."

"Yes, I know. She is very faithful."

"As are you, she assures me." Miss Ophelia picked up one of the cookies and broke off a piece, but didn't put it in her mouth. "I already knew that by how you go out every Sunday. Whatever the weather. Very commendable."

Mira had the feeling she had just passed a test she hadn't realized she had taken. "I don't like to miss. I enjoy the singing." When Miss Ophelia gave her a look, she quickly added, "And the sermon too, of course."

"Do you like to sing?"

"Oh yes, it's such a great way to let the joy of the Lord's love fill you."

"I've never heard you singing."

"I wouldn't want to disturb your peace."

"Peace," Miss Ophelia echoed, then sighed. "I think perhaps I have been too concerned about my peace. Please sing something for me now."

"I couldn't do that. I said I liked to sing. Not that I was talented."

"A joyful sound is all the Lord or I want to hear." She looked directly at her with all the sternness of a demanding teacher. Mira almost expected her to pull a ruler from her wrap and tap the table. "Sing one of the songs you sang at church this morning."

Mira took a sip of her tea and cleared her throat. She did sometimes lead her class in song. She could sing a bit of a hymn for Miss Ophelia. "Blessed assurance, Jesus is mine!"

Miss Ophelia joined in on the next line. Her wavering voice showed her age, but as she sang with Mira, a smile softened her wrinkles. When they finished the chorus, she said, "Fanny Crosby wrote that. Did you know she was blind? Since an infant?"

"I have heard that."

"Makes one wobble between appreciating one's own sight and thinking how little one has done in comparison to someone with such challenges as Miss Crosby."

"I'm sure you as a teacher made a difference in many a child's life," Mira said.

Miss Ophelia lifted her eyebrows as she looked across the table at Mira. "And do you think the same about yourself?" Again she didn't wait for an answer. "I suppose all teachers do touch their students' lives for good or bad."

"I would hope for good."

"As would I, but when I think back over my years, I do wonder if I could have done more. Perhaps I should have gone to the frontier and opened a school." She stared down at her cup.

"That would have been brave of you."

"Brave, yes. Unfortunately, the thought of it being foolish as well was stronger in my mind when the opportunity opened to me. There was a young man. He wanted to go west. He did go west."

"Did he not ask you to go along?"

"He asked, but I did the sensible thing and stayed put. I have no regrets." She spoke the words, but a sound of regret seemed to linger, even though this must have been years ago.

"Sensible is often best," Mira murmured.

"Enough about me. I didn't climb those horrendous steps in that bitter wind to talk about me but about you."

"Me?"

"If you have attended church with Mrs. Abrams, you surely know she is a dreadful busybody. Has been ever since I've known her, which has spanned upward to fifty years."

Mira's head was spinning as she tried to keep up with Miss Ophelia's changing subjects. "I've always thought her very nice."

"Busybodies can seem exceptionally nice. They practice the skill. Gives them more chance to poke their noses into other people's business." Miss Ophelia's lips screwed up into a tight, disapproving circle.

"I have little business for her to be interested in, and I wouldn't divulge anything about anyone else even if I knew something of interest to divulge. Which I do not."

"You talk like a schoolteacher. In circles. It took me years to stop that and learn to say what I meant in plain words. My students began to do so much better then." She breathed in and out. "But I do seem to be taking a circuitous route myself to what I came up here to say."

"Please, feel free to speak plainly." Mira peered over the rim of her cup as she took a drink, not at all sure she wanted to hear whatever Miss Ophelia had to say.

"Then, I shall. Two things. First, Mrs. Abrams said she just happened to be within earshot when the visiting preacher pulled you aside after the services this morning."

"I knew him from school years ago." Mira put down her cup. "Gordon Covington. He spoke about the mission he has started in the Eastern Kentucky mountains."

"Anita—Mrs. Abrams, that is—did say he spoke at length about his work." Miss Ophelia's countenance stayed dour. "That was not what she was most interested in telling me."

"Reverend Covington did pull me aside for a few words of private conversation, but we were hardly alone." Surely the fact that she talked to Gordon was no reason for blame. They had not been alone in the church, although Gordon's words had so surprised her, she paid little attention to those around them.

"Not so private, it seems. Mrs. Abrams obviously has excellent hearing, which must be a boon to one who is a busybody." Miss Ophelia ran her finger along the handle of her cup a couple of times before she looked directly at Mira. "She says he is in need of a teacher for his mission school and that he asked you to be that teacher."

"He did ask me that." Among other things. What more had Mrs. Abrams heard? "The challenge sounded interesting and I do feel compassion for those young people with no school. I can't imagine not being able to read."

"But you refused?"

"I did. I have a position here as a teacher. School will open again this week. This is my home." She looked around. "I'm happy here."

Or at least she had thought she was satisfied with her life before Gordon had voiced his impossible proposal. Impossible, that was what it was. She was quite content with things as they were.

"Positions can be resigned." Before Mira could respond to that astounding suggestion, Miss Ophelia went on. "As I said earlier, you haven't met my brother. Bertram can be a pain, but he is my brother. More telling, he has half ownership in this house, although he has never made any claims on it. Until now."

"What does that have to do with me?"

"A great deal, I fear. There is Phyllis. My niece. The one Bertram wants to ship off to Louisville for a while. I offered her one of the rooms downstairs, although the thought of Phyllis constantly underfoot is not pleasant. Unfortunately, she takes after Bertram and is very opinionated about everything and has ridiculously modern thinking." Miss Ophelia finally took a bite of her cookie and solemnly chewed.

Mira stared at her, knowing her words before she spoke them.

"That arrangement was not acceptable to Bertram or Phyllis. They are insistent on her moving into these rooms."

"Here?" For the second time in one day, Mira was nearly rendered speechless.

Miss Ophelia reached across the table to touch Mira's arm. The woman's fingers were cold. "I am sorry. But Bertram leaves me little choice but to ask you to find other accommodations. My brother can be quite demanding."

Mira's mouth had gone dry. "That might prove difficult."

"Yes. I realize that." She pulled her hand back and broke off another bit of the cookie. She studied it for a moment before she went on. "That is why I was so glad Anita came to call today."

"Does she have rooms to let?" Relief at the thought washed through Mira.

"No. Nothing like that." Miss Ophelia huffed out a short breath. "I might as well be out with it. Anita claims she heard the young visiting preacher proposing marriage. To you."

"I hardly know Reverend Covington. I hadn't seen him for years. Perhaps she misheard."

"Did she?" She gave Mira a stare, no doubt practiced often in her years as a schoolteacher. One that made it almost impossible to do anything but answer whatever question truthfully.

"No." Mira clutched her hands together. "But the very idea is ludicrous." Another word to describe the folly of the man's proposal. Ridiculous. Ludicrous. Impossible.

"Anita said he seemed an amenable young man of good appearance."

Mira's voice rose as she threw up her hands. "What difference does that make?"

"I would think very much in a husband."

Mira shut her eyes and massaged her forehead. She felt ill. "I barely know him. He barely knows me."

"One doesn't have to know everything about one's destination when one begins a journey." Miss Ophelia pushed up from the table. She lightly touched Mira's head. "This is your answer."

Mira looked up at her. "This can't be an answer."

Miss Ophelia pulled her hand away from Mira. "Perhaps *answer* is not the correct word. *Opportunity*. A much better word. One you should take. One I feel that if you are honest with yourself, you may even want to take."

"I don't love him. I am just as sure he cannot love me."

"Love? What a perfectly sweet little word to hold such power over us." Miss Ophelia shook her head. "Do you think Joseph loved Mary in the Bible?"

"I would like to believe that. Don't you?"

"You are a romantic. But you surely know most matches in Bible times were made without consulting the bride and oftentimes not even the groom. They were matches made between families. Perhaps when the two intended were mere children."

"The Bible shows Joseph treating Mary with love."

"It only took an angel speaking to him in a dream to have him spare her from a life of shame. Of course he was a decent man who did intend to set her aside quietly so she wouldn't be stoned."

"I believe they had a loving marriage." Mira had read the Christmas story many times. She always felt love in the words.

"I'm sure you are right. But the truth you need to consider is that love surely grew between them as they faced difficulties together. And experienced miracles that had to beg belief. A virgin birth had to be difficult to understand even if they knew it so."

"They had faith."

"So they did." Miss Ophelia's gaze softened on Mira. "And so can you. That the Lord has opened up this opportunity for you and that he will let love grow between you and this young man as you share a common goal, a common mission."

"This is impossible." Definitely the word that most fit this incredulous idea.

"Nothing is impossible with the Lord."

Miss Ophelia seemed to be waiting for Mira to contradict her words, but no one could argue that. The Lord could make anything happen. Mira had no doubt of that. Mary, a virgin, gave birth to Jesus. A camel could go through the eye of a needle. The Lord made the impossible possible in the Bible. But that didn't mean he would change this impossible idea of marriage to Gordon Covington into something possible.

The silence in the small room deepened. The only sounds were the ticking of Mira's clock on top of the bookshelf and the wind rattling the window.

When Mira couldn't stand the silence another second, she said, "I cannot marry Gordon Covington."

"Cannot or will not?" Miss Ophelia tilted her head to consider Mira. "Have you ever wondered if there were some in the Bible who asked a miracle of the Lord and then did not believe enough to try to stand on legs that were paralyzed?"

"No, I believe the Lord healed those he touched and that his touch turned their doubt into wonder."

"I would hope that to be true and that no miracle was missed due to the difficulty of believing such was possible." Miss Ophelia gave Mira a stern look. "Do not miss the Lord working in your life, Mira. All this could be the Lord's doing."

"All what?"

"Young Reverend Covington at your church this morning in need of a teacher. A man who, according to what Anita overheard, felt the Lord's prompting to ask you to be that teacher."

"He asked me to be more than a teacher." Mira stood up to face Miss Ophelia.

"Oh yes." Miss Ophelia lips turned up in a rare smile. "Even better, he wants you as a wife. A partner in his work. It seems the Lord must want that too. That is why busybody Anita eavesdropped on your private conversation. That is why she came bearing tales to me. That is why my niece has a sudden need for these rooms. That is why I climbed up those steps even though my knees will ache all night because of the effort."

"If all that is so, then why hasn't the Lord spoken to me?"

"Are you so sure he hasn't? The Lord can speak to us in sundry ways." Without waiting for an answer, Miss Ophelia turned and went out the door.

Mira stared at the closed door. After a moment, she spoke into the empty air. "Thank you for the tea cakes."

4

*G*ordon Covington approached Ophelia Vandercleve's door with trepidation on Tuesday morning. The sun was bright on the dusting of snow that had fallen during the night and hidden the grime of the city. The air was brisk and bracing.

He wondered how much snow might have fallen in Sourwood. He hoped not so much that he would have a struggle getting home.

Home. He smiled as the word settled in his thoughts. He wasn't sure when the mountains had become home, but he had no doubt they were. At first, after he answered the call to go spread the gospel in the hill country, he'd felt as out of place as a pig at a debutante ball. Slowly that changed as the Lord softened Gordon's edges and opened his eyes to the goodness of the people he met on the mountain trails.

Not that they were all good. Nowhere would you find people who were all good. The Lord was the only one ever able to live that kind of life. Certainly Gordon lacked in many ways in spite of trying to corner good as an example to those who heard him preach. But sins were slippery as snakes and could find a hole in a man's goodness armor to slither through.

In his prayer time early that morning, he had wondered if that had happened with his desire to convince Mira Dean to come to the mountains with him. He had been so sure the Lord was behind his proposal to Mira, but maybe instead, the devil had sneaked in to push Gordon's own will over the Lord's.

A teacher for his Sourwood school would be a wondrous blessing. He had no doubt about that being a proper desire, but what about his desire for a wife? A desire that he hadn't known until the words spilled out of his mouth to ask Mira Dean to consider matrimony. With him.

She was so lovely. He was so lonely. True, he was far from alone in Sourwood. People were continually coming to him, needing something, offering something, filling every waking moment. Yet, he was lonely.

In the Bible, Paul said a man, if able, should give his efforts and thoughts to serving the Lord by embracing the single life. But it wasn't a command. Many other Scriptures encouraged a man to find a good wife and a woman, a good husband. Two as one serving the Lord.

Sometimes a man shoved his own wants and wishes to the forefront and found a way to believe such was the Lord's doing. Was that what Gordon had done when he saw Mira come into the church Sunday? Was he still doing that as he knocked on Miss Vandercleve's door?

As he waited for a response, he stepped back to look at the substantial two-story brick house. It could easily have ten rooms. His cabin in Sourwood had two rooms. The brisk air now pushing through his coat blew through poorly sealed cracks between logs even easier.

The fireplace warmed one if a person stayed near it. Much wintertime activity took place around a cabin's fire. Women did their sewing, churned butter, and cooked over the fire. Men sharpened their knives, repaired their harnesses, or took their ease after their outdoor chores. Children played games or learned their lessons by the light of the fire, or would once they had a school. People entertained one another with stories and songs. Those fortunate enough to be able to do so read God's Word by firelight.

At least his wasn't a blind cabin. He did have windows. Glass windows and not just holes with shutters to block out the cold or open to the spring breezes. Two windows both on the south side of the house. When he had thought to cut another window in the north side, the men building the cabin had stared at him as though he lacked good sense. They wasted no time telling him a window there would let in winter winds.

He had wanted to insist. He liked light. It was his house. He would be the one to suffer if the north window invited in cold air, but they had cut the logs and hauled them from the woods. They had the expertise to notch those logs and pile them into a wall. It was wiser to do without the extra window than to go against their advice.

Miss Vandercleve's house had six windows in the front. Those on the bottom floor of the house were large, set together in pairs. Dark window coverings shut out the light, but he supposed the cold as well. His gaze drifted up to the top floor where Pastor Watkins said Mira Dean lived. The two windows were open to the sunlight, but then no one on the street could peer into those windows.

Could he ask her to give up living in such a fine place to move into his cabin and teach in a school just as roughly built? Or more telling, should he? When he asked the pastor about Mira, he convincingly spoke of how she appeared happy to serve where the Lord had planted her. What matter that Gordon had sensed a deep sadness and perhaps even restlessness behind her calm? At least calm until he had shocked her with his outlandish proposal.

He smiled. His proposal had shaken her settled view of life. He'd had that same sort of feeling when the Lord first awoke the call to preach in his heart. At the time, he'd denied it, even laughed at the ludicrous thought of him, Gordon Covington, a preacher.

He had never been devout. He believed in the Lord. He never doubted the truth of the gospel, but he was a casual church member.

Went when it suited him and then more to please his mother than because of a desire to worship. Often as not, he let his thoughts wander from whatever the preacher might be saying as he impatiently waited for the final amen.

Now when those listening to him did the same, he wondered if any of the young men wishing for his sermon's end might get a seed planted in their hearts that would someday flower into the desire to preach. That was what had surely happened to him. Even though he had never watered that seed, his mother's prayers had.

He hoped that his words Sunday about the need for a teacher had planted such a seed in Mira's heart. A seed watered by his own prayers and perhaps hers if she hadn't simply brushed aside his words without giving them consideration. Somehow, he didn't think that had happened. At least he hoped not. He looked up toward the windows above him again. He would soon see.

A curtain flicked below in the nearest window before the door creaked open a few inches. One eye peered out at him. "Are you that preacher?"

The voice revealed the speaker was not young. Pastor Watkins had warned Gordon that Miss Vandercleve was somewhat acerbic in speech, but he claimed she had a good heart under her contrary manner.

"I am a preacher," Gordon said. "That is true, but I have no idea which preacher you have in mind."

"Don't be impertinent. You know very well which preacher I mean. The one who shocked sweet Mira Dean with a proposal on Sunday." She opened the door several more inches to reveal her entire face. She wore no smile.

"She told you that?" Gordon didn't hide his surprise.

"I did not say she was the one to convey that news to me. As a preacher, you surely know churches have ears and those ears are always ready to hear."

"Yes, ma'am."

"So why are you pecking on my door to disturb my day? She

40

lives up there." The woman pointed toward the steps at the side of the house.

"I didn't want to compromise her reputation by going to her door."

"You came to mine." The old lady lifted her eyebrows and glared at him. "Had you no concern for my reputation?"

Before Gordon could think what to say to that, the woman laughed. "I do think I've shocked you speechless." She pulled the door all the way open then as her laughter cut off like water after a faucet handle was twisted closed. "Come in before every bit of heat in this house escapes to the street." A sly look slid across her face. "If you're not worried about your own reputation."

He stepped inside, and the woman firmly closed the door behind him. "A preacher does need to guard his good name."

"Do you have a good name, Reverend?" The woman pulled a brown shawl tighter around her as she squinted through her spectacles to look him up and down in the dim entryway.

He considered opening the drapes to give her light for her inspection, but he refrained. Instead, he stayed stuck to the floor until she gave him permission to move. In his youth, he had spent many uncomfortable moments in front of a teacher's desk as he awaited the consequences of a wrongdoing. Miss Vandercleve had not lost her teacher authority. Perhaps if Mira couldn't be talked into going to the mountains with him, he could convince this old teacher to give him a few months. She made him think of some of the Sourwood grandmothers who kept their families in line.

She gave a slight nod. "You don't have the look of an ogre. Our Miss Dean could do worse than accept your absurd proposal."

"Why absurd?"

Again her eyebrows lifted as she pinned him with her teacher gaze. "I do believe you hadn't seen Miss Dean for some years. I do believe you mentioned marriage practically before you said how do you do. I do know most young women want a man to come courting before proposing."

"All so true. Regretfully, I don't have time for the niceties of courtship. I am returning to the mountains this afternoon." He thought to pull out his watch to check the hour but did not. He had time, although he hoped Miss Vandercleve would release him to call upon Mira before too many more minutes slid by. "The children there need a teacher."

"And you need a wife?"

"A man often does, and I thought Miss Dean might be accepted more readily in Sourwood if we were married."

"So, merely a marriage of convenience."

"If that is her desire." He hesitated, then added, "With hope that in time the Lord would knit us into a proper marital union."

"My dear young preacher, knitting is for socks." She frowned at him. "I think the Bible speaks of marriage as cleaving to one's wife."

"Yes." He was not going to win any word battles with Miss Vandercleve. Best to surrender without argument. It would be good to have her on his side. Convenience marriage or a cleaving one.

"Are you saying those in this Sourwood don't approve of single females?" The woman went on without giving him a chance to respond. "Sourwood. Doesn't sound like a very appealing place."

"Oh, but it is. Don't let the name fool you. Bees love the beautiful, fragrant blossoms of the sourwood trees."

"And did you find Miss Dean beautiful? Or accommodating to your proposal?"

"Beautiful, yes. I knew her in school and thought her so then as now. But my proposal yesterday was perhaps too rash. I may have been carried away by the feeling that the Lord had brought her to my attention as an answer to prayer."

"You had prayed for a wife?"

"No, but the families in Sourwood are praying for a teacher."

"Teachers who marry are required to resign from their positions."

"A rather unnecessary rule if you ask me. But in Sourwood,

Miss Dean would not be hired by the county or state. She would be a mission teacher helping eager children learn to read while also sharing the gospel with them."

"But what if Miss Dean gets with child? What then?"

He could feel heat rising in his cheeks and was glad for the dim light. Not that he thought anything could escape Miss Vander- cleve's sharp gaze. "Should things proceed in such a blessed way, the Lord would provide answers. But the children in Sourwood are not unfamiliar with a woman in such a condition."

"Such a condition." She echoed his words with a little laugh. "You do have a way with words. I am surprised your talk is not too fancy for your mountain mission people."

"The people are ready to hear the gospel not in my words but the Lord's."

She cocked her head and stared at him a long moment before she said, "I like you, Preacher Whatever Your Name."

His face burned hotter. "I apologize, Miss Vandercleve. I am Gordon Covington. Please forgive me for not introducing myself immediately."

She waved her hand to dismiss his words. "Not a worry. Better to judge a person by his appearance and actions than his name. So what do you want from me, Reverend Covington?"

"I would like to speak again with Miss Dean and hoped you would accompany me as a chaperone."

"You will hardly need a chaperone if you marry."

"I fear she hasn't agreed to that. I have been praying. I asked her to pray, but I don't know what answers she's heard from the Lord."

"My knees are still complaining from the last time I climbed those steps, but I will summon her down to speak with you here."

She picked up a school bell, opened her door, and clanged it with vigor the way she must have once called her class in from recess.

A smile rearranged her wrinkles as she turned to put the bell back on the shelf. "Every teacher needs a bell. They tried to get me to leave this one for the teacher who followed me, but the bell was mine. Is mine."

"I should buy one for our school," Gordon asked.

"The one without a teacher?"

"The Lord will send a teacher. If not Miss Dean, someone else."

"You appear to have given in to defeat already." When he started to deny that, she shook her head at him. "Don't give up so easily. I have added my prayers to yours."

"Why would you do that? You don't even know me or the children in Sourwood."

"Children are children. But I am not praying for Miss Dean as a teacher but as a woman." Her face changed, suddenly looked sad. "I once lacked courage. I pray she will not. But whatever she says today, Reverend, please don't give up. She is the teacher you need."

"I don't know if I should even ask her to give up her comfortable life here."

"Comfort is overrated. I daresay you gave up much when you answered the Lord's call." Her eyes narrowed as she studied him. "Do you regret those losses?"

"Sometimes I miss a strong cup of coffee in the morning and a warm bed at night."

"I like a man who does not pretend what is not true." At the tap on her door, she twisted her mouth to hide a smile before she turned to open it. "Perhaps Miss Dean will agree to warm that bed."

5

The oatmeal in Mira's breakfast bowl had congealed into lumps. She pushed it aside and looked at her account book. The numbers in it were just as unappetizing. She was running low on funds for even the most basic of needs. She should have looked for a tutoring job during Christmas to tide her over. School would be back in session the next day, but she wouldn't get paid until the end of the month.

She had carefully budgeted and saved barely enough for food and her rent. She had not considered the possibility of losing her rooms and needing more rent money before she received her pay. She glanced around and tried to push away the panic that poked at her and tightened her throat.

Miss Ophelia had not said when her niece would arrive. She should have asked that. It might be this week or not for a month. Mira hoped for the month. She fingered the edges of her account book but didn't open it. She knew the figures on the pages by heart. Again, her throat tightened.

She took a breath and whispered words her mother had lived by. "The Lord will provide."

When Gordon Covington's image jumped into her thoughts, she shook her head so forcefully, a pin holding her hair back from her face popped loose. Not bothering with the pin, she shoved the loose strands behind her ear.

Gordon Covington's bizarre proposal was not the Lord's provision, even if he had claimed the Lord had prodded him to invite her into his mission. Nor did it matter that Miss Ophelia thought his ridiculous proposal was the answer she needed for lodging. Mira was not that desperate.

She shut her eyes and leaned her head into her hands. She was tired. Her sleep had been disturbed by visions of youngsters reaching for books she held up high away from them. Eager children begging to be taught. Nothing like her students accustomed to the privilege of learning here.

She pushed her fingers against her forehead in an attempt to erase the memory of the dreams. They meant nothing. They had simply been brought on by the worries of the day. She would find a new place to live, and her life would settle back into its accustomed routine. Gordon could find another teacher, one who might be happy to accept his proposal to both teach and marry. Many women would be glad to be part of his life. To marry him, have his children. That would be best. For him. For her. She had no reason to feel suddenly so empty.

"Oh, Edward, why did you have to die?" she whispered. Tears came to her eyes, but they weren't for Edward. They were for her lost dreams. Lost chances.

The clanging of Miss Ophelia's bell jerked her away from her sorrowful thoughts. Miss Ophelia never rang the bell before noon. The old lady liked to take her time with her morning ablutions. Something must be wrong.

Mira grabbed a wrap off the hook by her door and rushed out into the cold morning air. When she slipped on the snow-covered steps, she grabbed the icy wooden rail. She should have put on proper boots and gloves and not assumed the worst. After all, the bell had clanged loudly. The old lady had not given it a weak shake.

The door opened at Mira's first knock. Miss Ophelia appeared to be fine. Actually looked cheerful. Maybe she had good news and her niece had decided not to come to Louisville after all.

"Did you need something, Miss Ophelia?" Mira asked.

"My heavens, girl. Where are your hat and gloves? Did you not know it snowed?"

"I was concerned something might be wrong when you rang your bell."

"Well, come in before your ears freeze." The woman pulled Mira into the house. "I'm fine, but someone is here to see you. Reverend Covington."

If Miss Ophelia hadn't been gripping her arm, Mira would have turned to flee back up the stairs to her rooms. She had no desire to see Gordon. None at all. Her mad rush down the steps and the cold air were what had her heart thumping and her skin tingling. Not the thought of Gordon Covington seeking her out with who knew what ludicrous ideas now.

"Mira." He looked almost as uncomfortable as she felt standing there under Miss Ophelia's keen stare. "I hope you don't mind me calling on you."

Mira tucked the stray strands of hair behind her ear again. She should have pinned it back. "I thought you were returning to the mountains."

"I leave this afternoon, but I hoped to speak with you first. Miss Vandercleve was gracious enough to summon you down here."

"He was thinking of your reputation," Miss Ophelia said. "As was only right. So come sit in the parlor while I make our young · preacher some coffee. Perhaps tea for you, my dear?"

"I should go back to my rooms. I left things undone." Mira stayed by the door.

"Nonsense. Whatever you were doing can wait. We must be sociable."

Miss Ophelia had never given any sign of concern over social niceties before now. Gordon must have found an ally in his campaign to convince her to go to wherever he had his mission.

To wherever those children haunting her dreams clamored for a teacher.

"Please," Gordon spoke up. "I'd like to tell you about the people in Sourwood."

"Many children too, I should think," Miss Ophelia added as she ushered them toward the parlor. "Now if you'll excuse me, I'll search out my coffee."

"Don't go to any trouble," Gordon said.

"It's my trouble. I'll go to it if I want." Miss Ophelia headed toward her kitchen.

Mira wanted to follow her. Leave Gordon to his own devices. But she didn't want to upset Miss Ophelia. She might need to beg a place on her settee if the niece showed up before Mira found new rooms. She eyed the stiff piece of furniture. No sleeping comfort there.

She pushed aside the thought. Things hadn't gotten that dire yet. Dire was being in the same room with Gordon, who looked ready to explode with whatever he'd come to say. She forced a smile. "Please, won't you sit down?"

"Only if you join me."

"Certainly." She perched on the edge of a wingback chair. Once she was seated, Gordon gingerly lowered himself down on the settee across from her. He leaned forward and clutched his hands between his knees. "I should have sent a card to ask to call upon you today. I fear I have forgotten some of the social niceties."

She acknowledged his apology with a slight nod, but didn't say anything, even though he obviously hoped she would.

He cleared his throat and went on. "Also, on recalling our conversation on Sunday, I owe you an apology for being too forward."

"Yes."

"I don't regret my words or wish them unsaid."

"Nor do I regret my answer." Mira flashed a look at him and then lowered her gaze to her hands in her lap. She clasped one hand over the other to hide her trembling fingers.

"Did you pray as I asked? For the youngsters at Sourwood in need of a school."

"Doesn't the county there provide schools?"

"There are some schools, but none close enough for the children to attend. They have to board with someone miles away. Few have that option."

"Can't their parents teach them?"

"They do teach them much about how to live and work, but book learning is rare among the adults. They could also use a teacher."

"Then perhaps you should be that teacher." There had to be answers other than her.

"I was called to preach. Not teach."

"It appears to me that a man could do both."

"I don't think I am the answer to the prayers of the good people of Sourwood. I believe you are. I believe if you have prayed about it, you are just as sure of that as I am."

She raised her head to look at him without shying away from his direct stare. "I did pray."

She stoutly claimed that, even if it wasn't exactly true. She had prayed, but she had not asked the Lord if it was his will for her to go to the mountains. Instead, she had refused to allow that thought into her mind and certainly not into her prayers.

"Did you get an answer?"

She avoided answering the question he asked. "I've already given you an answer."

"But was it the Lord's answer?"

She lowered her eyes back to her hands. "Sometimes it can be hard to know that."

"And sometimes it isn't."

Without looking up, she knew he leaned toward her, as if he wanted to reach across the room to touch her. "I suppose that's according to the prayer."

"As well as according to the willingness to hear." His voice deepened in intensity to how he'd sounded in the pulpit on Sunday. He appeared to realize this and was silent a moment before he went on in a less impassioned tone. "I still believe you are the answer to the Sourwood children's prayers for a teacher." His tone softened even more. "I believe you are the answer to a prayer I didn't even know I had made, but one that rose from my heart. I need a helpmate in my mission. I need someone by my side."

She looked up to say once more she was not the answer to his prayer, but he held up his hand to stop her from speaking.

"Let me finish. I realize I was wrong to be so impulsive about my proposal. I can be that way at times when I think the Lord is leading me." He smiled a little. "Actually, my sister says I've always been that way. Pushy, she calls it. Such does not always work well. I should have given you the opportunity to get to know the man I am now and not the boy I was. I have changed."

"Time changes us all."

"So it does. I can see in your eyes the desire to answer the need for a teacher and I have spoiled that with my—" He hesitated a second before he continued. "What you considered my outrageous proposal."

"That is a proper word for it." A smile sneaked out from somewhere to surprise not only Gordon but her as well.

His answering smile lit up his face and settled in his eyes. "So it was. Outrageous, but then the Lord's calling can often be outrageous. I must admit I thought that when I first felt the call to preach."

"But you responded."

"I fought it a while, but the Lord has a way of winning a person over to whatever path he has laid out for him." His smile disappeared. "Or for her. I have heard your no. The Lord heard your no. But I think—I hope—I might hear a maybe behind that no. Would you continue to pray and think of the joy of being a teacher in a place where the children need one so desperately?"

She inclined her head slightly. Not a yes or a no.

He went on. "And in time perhaps consider being the wife of a preacher who needs one every bit as much. If that cannot be, I can find you lodging with one of the families. They would take you into their hearts. I know they would, and although the accommodations would be somewhat less comfortable than those you presently have, the Lord would reward you with many new friends."

"And a husband?" Mira whispered the words.

"I'm not sure how much of a reward a preacher for a husband would be, but I would surely feel greatly rewarded to have a beautiful wife and someday perhaps a child to call me Papa."

"Child." The word pierced her heart. She stood up, no longer able to sit. No longer able to listen to another word. "I can't," she said in a strangled voice as she ran from the room.

He didn't call after her, but Miss Ophelia did. "Mira, where are you going? I have your tea."

Mira didn't look around but instead went out the door. She hardly felt the cold air or noted the snow on her slippers as she raced up the steps to her rooms. She slammed the door behind her and leaned against it, breathing hard.

She looked up at the ceiling. "Dear Lord, what am I going to do?"

She hadn't run to escape Gordon's outrageous words about wanting a wife. She had run because the outrageous word *yes* was on the tip of her tongue.

6

*M*ira pushed away from the door and shrugged off her wrap. She would apologize to Miss Ophelia later. If Pastor Watkins had Gordon's address, she would even write him an apology.

As if compelled, she went to the window. The man surely wouldn't come after her. If he did, she would refuse to open the door. The thought came to her that she had already refused to open her heart. But that was ridiculous. She couldn't be expected to open her heart to a man she barely knew.

She had opened her heart fully to Edward and ended up with nothing but sorrow. Still, she had continued on, opening her heart to her students and to the Lord. That had been enough. That would always be enough.

She saw the years stretching out ahead of her until she was like Miss Ophelia. And what would be wrong with that? She would have helped youngsters learn. She would have served her church and improved her mind through reading, without the distraction of children of her own. She closed her eyes for just a second, her heart heavy as she considered that future. She would be old, cantankerous, and lonely.

Miss Ophelia might not agree with that description. But hadn't she been the one to prod Mira to consider the impossible? The ridiculous impossible.

She opened her eyes and stared down at the front walkway. It was empty. As empty as she felt. Gordon must be drinking the coffee Miss Ophelia had brewed. Mira's face burned at the thought of what they must be saying about her. She leaned her forehead against the cold windowpane. It didn't matter. Gordon would go back to this Sourwood he talked about. He would be gone from her life.

She shook her head. He had never been part of her life. And never would be. That child he wished for would not be her child. She clutched her arms in front of her. That was as she wished. But she stayed at the window.

One of the noisy automobiles rattled past out on the street. Already the snow was being colored with the grime of people. What would snow be like in the mountains? Deeper, she imagined. Whiter. The pines that grew so abundantly on the hills would be frosted in white. She had seen pictures. In late spring, rhododendrons would burst into bloom on those hills.

People had flowers in the city. Gardens of flowers in some places. She had promised to help Miss Ophelia clean out her flower beds behind the house when the weather warmed.

So many plans. Perhaps the niece would help her now, and Mira would find flowers in other places. The vision of those flower-covered hills came to mind again, but she didn't let it linger. Instead, she thought of Miss Ophelia's rosebush that so looked like the one beside the porch where she grew up. Before she lost her mother and father. Before she lost Edward.

Stop dwelling on losses, she ordered herself. Better to think about what she needed to do before students returned to school on the morrow. She should go make sure her room was ready. She had lessons to prepare. She had no choice but to search out new accommodations. Life would continue despite whatever troubles came her way. Didn't it always as long as a person kept breathing?

She was still at the window when Gordon came out on Miss Ophelia's walkway. She stepped back when he looked up toward her window, but she didn't turn away. He stood for a long moment before he put his hands in his pockets and turned toward the street.

She moved closer to the window again. His shoulders appeared hunched against the cold. He needed a warmer coat. His first steps away seemed reluctant, but then he began moving with purpose. As he should. He had a train to catch.

She watched until he was out of sight. She might never see him again.

That was no reason for tears to come to her eyes. She hadn't even thought about Gordon Covington once since their school days. Seeing him walk away was no reason to feel suddenly bereft.

She almost expected to hear Miss Ophelia's bell clang to summon her down to apologize. Instead, silence pounded against her ears. Silence she should welcome. With the start of school, the quiet of her rooms would be a treat at the end of each day. At least for as long as she was here. And who was to say that wherever she found to move would not be as silent or as good? Maybe even better, without a woman downstairs clanging a bell to demand her presence. She angrily swiped away the tears on her cheeks. Tears that were immediately replaced by more.

The morning passed slowly. She considered taking a walk, but the snow was melting away and lacked the beauty of the early morning. She needed a dog. If she had a dog, she would be forced to walk it. Probably everybody had a dog in Sourwood. Wherever Sourwood was. And what kind of name was that for a town? If it was even a town.

She pulled her atlas off the bookshelf. No Sourwood was listed in the towns of Kentucky. She shoved the book back into place. It didn't matter where Sourwood was or what it was.

She found a dustcloth and swiped every surface she had. That took only minutes. After settling in her chair, she picked up Jack London's book about the wilds of Alaska, but the words swam in front of her eyes and lacked meaning. Without even marking her place, she shut the book and laid it on the table beside her Bible. Reading Scripture might settle her jumbled thoughts, but what if the word "barren" jumped out at her from the Bible's pages the way it had Sunday? She needed comfort, not more stabs of sorrow.

Instead, she picked up her mother's bluebird. As usual, it warmed in her hands. When Mira was a child, her mother always seemed at peace no matter what hardships they faced. Whenever Mira's father worried if they lacked money for their needs, her mother would take his hands and they would pray. Then she would say the Lord would provide. He always did. Sometimes not plentifully, but adequately. And other times abundantly. For certain, they had abundant love.

"I miss you, Mother," Mira whispered. "You could help me know why I've let Gordon Covington upset me so. My path is set."

Who set your path? The question was in her head, an echo of an answer to something she had asked her mother years before. When Mira had not known what to say, her mother had Mira look up a verse in Proverbs. She tried to remember the verse, but the words had faded from her memory.

She picked up her Bible and turned to Proverbs. She could read every verse until she found the right one. It didn't take long. Chapter 3, verses 5 and 6. *Trust in the LORD with all thine heart; and lean not unto thine own understanding. In all thy ways acknowledge him, and he shall direct thy paths.*

She laid her hand on the Bible page as she remembered reading the verses aloud. Then her mother had assured Mira the Lord would show her the way if she would give up her will and attend the paths the Lord opened to her.

Mira whispered a prayer. "Dear Lord, I do trust you to direct my paths. Help me to know thy will for my future."

The Lord was already directing her paths. He had brought her through the sorrow of loss. He had supplied a teaching job to give her purpose. She had no reason to doubt that path now.

She would put Gordon Covington's words behind her and continue on the path she knew. She was not the teacher, the wife he sought. That was some other woman's path.

As soon as she ate lunch, she would walk to the school to prepare her room for the students' return tomorrow.

The sight of the Sanderson School's brick facade lifted Mira's spirits. The school was a second home, a place she belonged. Mira taught English and history to the older boys and girls. Another teacher covered math and science. Her classes in the private school were small, which gave her the opportunity to give individual attention to each student. She took joy in teaching children eager to learn.

The unknown children in the mountains who had haunted her dreams came to mind, but she shut the vision away. Her prayer earlier had settled her thoughts. The Lord had directed her path to the one she was already on.

When she walked inside, the scent of chalk dust and books settled around her like a welcoming cloak.

In the front hallway, Mr. Martin, the other teacher of the older students, gave her an odd look and hesitated a moment before he spoke. "Miss Dean. I didn't expect to see you."

She frowned a little at his peculiar greeting. "School does start tomorrow, Mr. Martin. Time to get ready, don't you think?"

"Uh, yes." He pushed his spectacles up on his nose and stared at the wall behind her.

Mira had never seen him so at a loss for words. "Is something wrong?"

"Perhaps you should speak with Principal Harrison." He fidgeted with the corners of his suit jacket as he slid his gaze to her face and quickly away.

"Certainly. I will look for him after I go to my room." She headed down the hallway.

"I am sorry," he called after her.

Sorry? She stopped to ask what he meant, but he was walking away in the opposite direction. Not toward his room at all but toward the lower-level classrooms. She started to follow him, then shrugged. Whatever his problem, she could find out about it later.

Her room was not as she'd left it before Christmas. A box sat on the floor by her desk. A few of the student desks were gone. The bookshelf under the window was empty. She had been right to come set things in order before the next day. But where were her things?

She took off her coat and hat to get to work. She needed to make a list of what was missing. She pulled open the drawer where she kept extra paper. Empty. Every drawer was empty.

Her gaze was drawn to the box on the floor. Her name was printed across one side. She pulled up one of the flaps. A pair of gloves, a couple of scarves, a few pens, and her rulers were on top of her dictionary. She didn't dig down into the box. Without looking, she knew it must hold her other personal books and charts of words and pictures that usually adorned the walls.

Her heart felt heavy as she looked up from the box and stared out the window where the sun was as bright as ever.

"Miss Dean." Principal Harrison came into the room and shut the door behind him. "So good of you to come retrieve your belongings, but we did plan to deliver them to you."

"I don't understand." Mira turned toward him.

He ran his hand through his gray hair the way he always did when he was bothered. He was a short man with a generous

57

middle. He fingered his watch chain as if he'd like to pull it out to look at the time and say he had a meeting to attend. He moistened his lips. "Did you not get the letter I sent you after the term ended in December?"

"Letter? I received no letter."

"The mail. So unreliable these days." His gaze slid to the blackboard and across some of the desks that remained. He did not look at Mira or the box in front of her.

Mira stared straight at him without saying anything to help his unease or hers.

Principal Harrison cleared his throat and wobbled from one foot to the other. "I am sorry, but you do understand our enrollment has dropped among the older students. That has necessitated some staff changes. Hard times, you know. Hard times for everyone."

"I fear that no, I do not understand."

He ran his hand through his hair again. "I did want to save you from this embarrassment. That was the purpose of the letter." He finally looked at her then. "We have had to let you go." He rushed on before she could speak. "With great reluctance, of course. You are an excellent teacher. I have no fear you will find another position without difficulty."

"The term starts tomorrow."

"Yes, yes. Well, it would have been better if you'd gotten the letter days ago so you could have begun your search."

"I was given a promise of employment at the beginning of the school year." She managed to keep the quaver out of her voice. "I have a written agreement with your signature."

"Should you read through that agreement, you will note it is subject to cancellation if the school has financial difficulties. I realize this is a shock to you."

"And has Mr. Martin's agreement also been negated?"

"Well, no. We need a teacher for our older students."

"He doesn't teach English or history."

Principal Harrison waved his hand to dismiss that concern. "He has agreed to add those subjects to his teaching schedule."

"I could add algebra and science to my classes."

"Could you?" Doubt sounded in his words.

"I could." Mira spoke with the same firmness she sometimes used on her students. "Plus, I have been teaching here longer than he has. Two years longer."

"Well true, but Mr. Martin has a family to support. A wife and three young children. I'm sure you can understand that we could not jeopardize his family's well-being."

"And my well-being?"

He started to reach for his hair again but stayed his hand. "I'm sure Miss Vandercleve will be understanding until you find a new position. We will supply you with glowing references."

"How very kind." Mira didn't quite keep the sarcasm out of her tone.

Principal Harrison's voice stiffened. "The decision has been made. If you need help with your belongings, I can find someone to assist you." After he turned toward the door, he looked back. "We hope to have an increase in attendance before next school year. Should you wish to do so, you can apply for the position again if we have need for another teacher."

She stared at the door for a long time after he went out and closed it firmly behind him.

He shall direct thy paths. The words slid through her mind. But was he blocking every other path first?

7

*T*he box was heavy. She should have let them deliver it, but she'd allowed her pride to rule. By the time she got back to Miss Ophelia's house, her arms ached. The steps up to her rooms looked like a mountain. To rest a moment, she put the box down on the walkway.

Even after she carried the box up to her rooms, what then? What path was going to be blocked to her next? She fought against the bitterness that gripped her. A person surely sinned if she allowed bitterness against the Lord to be in her heart. But what about that verse in Psalms that she always had her students memorize?

Delight thyself also in the LORD: *and he shall give thee the desires of thine heart.*

Hadn't she always followed the Lord, been faithful in service to the church, tried to be a good example to her students? Was that not a way of delighting in the Lord? But where were the desires of her heart? She had no desire to be homeless without a job. She felt totally adrift.

When she had her students memorize that verse, she told them to ask themselves what they most wanted. Sometimes they asked her the same question: What were the desires of *her* heart?

She had a ready answer. To teach them. To let her light shine. Sometimes she would quote the next verse to them. *Commit thy way unto the* LORD; *trust also in him; and he shall bring it to pass.* That was her way of letting them know that the Lord would, as her mother always said, provide. He would plant the proper desires in their hearts and show them the way to reach those goals in life.

Had she taught that and never truly believed it? She had lost the desires of her heart when Edward died. A family with Edward had been the true desire of her heart, and the Lord had taken it away.

She stared down at the box that held her teaching life. That it was small enough to carry seemed sad. But the rewards of teaching weren't in things but rather in ideas and abilities planted in young people. The chance to do that had been the desire that filled her heart after Edward died.

But that other desire was still there. The one not quenched by death. She did her best not to allow the thought of it to surface, but it lingered. To be a mother.

She pushed those thoughts away and picked up her box again. She would face whatever challenges came. What other choice was there?

Before she could move toward the steps, Miss Ophelia called to her. "Mira, glad I caught you."

Mira turned to her, still holding the box. "I apologize for my behavior earlier, Miss Ophelia. I hope you will forgive me."

"Your conduct was certainly less than exemplary, but your apology is accepted."

"Thank you."

Miss Ophelia took a step toward her. "Whatever is in that box?"

"It's my—" Tears suddenly clogged her throat and choked off her words.

"Well, never mind. Put it down and come inside. I need to speak with you, but I'll get a chill standing out here."

Mira did as she said and set the box down. She pulled a hand-kerchief out of her pocket to staunch the tears, but they kept coming.

When she reached the door, Miss Ophelia grabbed her arm and jerked her inside as though Mira were a contrary student she was determined to set right.

"My soup pot needs stirring." Miss Ophelia hustled Mira down the hall to the kitchen, where she pushed her down into a chair at the table.

Mira slipped off her coat and rubbed her arm. Miss Ophelia might be advanced in age, but she had not lost the strength in her hands.

The old woman didn't stir her soup. Instead, she scooted the pot away from the heat on her stove. Then she turned to stare at Mira trying to mop up her tears with a handkerchief too dainty for the task.

"Here." Miss Ophelia handed her a folded square of white. "Those flimsy lady hankies are of absolutely no use."

The men's kerchief was much better at the mopping-up chore. "Thank you," Mira whispered.

Miss Ophelia sat down at the end of the table. "If I brew us some tea, will you run off before I pour it?"

Mira sniffed. "I am sorry," she said again. She had been rude, but that seemed the least of her problems now. "I'd love some tea."

The woman stood and rummaged in a cabinet for a teapot and cups. The ordinary clatter of dishes was somehow comforting. Mira swallowed the last of her tears and sniffed again.

"For goodness' sake, blow your nose. Else you'll drive me batty with that sniffling. I hated when students in my classes started a chorus of sniffs."

"I suppose they couldn't help it." Mira did as ordered and blew her nose. She felt she'd been crying all day. At least she had managed to stay her tears until after she left the school.

"You would be surprised what you can help when you try. I

tore an old sheet into squares for them to use as hankies. Solved much of the sniffing." She set a saucer and cup in front of Mira.

The steam rising from the tea warmed Mira's face as she lifted it to take a sip.

Miss Ophelia sat down with her cup. "Are you going to tell me what has you so weepy?"

"The school let me go. Said they needed fewer teachers. At least one fewer." To keep from sniffing again, she rubbed her nose with the handkerchief.

"And the box?"

"My things. They were packed up when I got there."

"Humph. Kind of them. At least I'm sure they thought so." Miss Ophelia gave her tea a sour look before she took a drink. The saucer clattered when she set the cup down. "They appear to be somewhat lax in timely informing you that you were no longer employed."

"They sent a letter I did not receive. Principal Harrison blamed the mail service. Had I received it, I would have had a little time to search for other options." Mira sniffed despite her determination not to as more tears threatened. She blew her nose again before she went on. "It appears I will have to look for a new position as well as new rooms."

"I fear I have bad news in regard to the accommodations. My brother has informed me that my niece is to be here on Saturday."

"This Saturday?" Mira's voice squeaked a little on the words.

"Unfortunately, yes."

"I'm not sure I can move that soon."

"I do recognize the difficulty facing you in obtaining a new place that quickly. I won't put you out on the street, but Phyllis won't abide a roommate even if such would be possible in those upper rooms. They are rather small." Miss Ophelia drummed her fingers on the table and pursed her lips. "Do you have any savings to fall back on?"

"No." That truth awakened a flutter of panic inside Mira.

"I thought that might be the case."

They sat in silence then for what seemed to Mira a long time. She should get up and go on to her rooms. Begin packing up her things even though she had nowhere to take them. Perhaps she could get a loan to tide her over until she found work. There were rooming houses down along the river. The ramshackle buildings appeared to be poor shelter, but people did live there. Others like her with no money for better accommodations.

Miss Ophelia's clock ticked away the seconds and then minutes. Mira stared down into her teacup and thought of her mother again. *The Lord will provide.*

As if the older woman heard her thoughts, she said, "You realize this is all the Lord's doing."

A flash of anger shot through Mira. "A loving God would not do this to me." The words were out before she could stop them. She looked down, ashamed to have shown her lack of faith.

"Now, now. Don't let your temper lead you astray." Miss Ophelia rapped her spoon on the table.

"You're right. I shouldn't have said that," she whispered, still without looking up.

"When you're complaining about the Lord, saying it and thinking it are the same. The Lord knows your thoughts." Miss Ophelia reached across the table to touch Mira's hand. "But worry not. The Lord knows the heart under the angry thoughts."

"But why is this happening?" She looked directly at the other woman. "Losing my place here. Losing my teaching position in the middle of the school year. That shouldn't happen."

"And very rarely does. At least, not all at once. But that may show the Lord's hand in this." Miss Ophelia sat back and studied Mira a few seconds. "I am beginning to believe our young pastor friend did feel a prompt from the Lord to invite you into his work." She paused a couple of seconds. "Into his life."

"You think I lost my job because the Lord wants me to accept Gordon's proposal?" Mira shook her head. "I can't believe that."

"Oh? Do you not believe the Lord guides us and gives us good works to do?"

"But I shouldn't have to go to a strange place to do so."

"Missionaries do that very thing all the time. That is what your young man is. A gospel missionary."

"He isn't my young man, and I haven't received a call to be a missionary."

"Are you sure? I think that is why you ran away this morning. You are afraid of the call you are feeling. Fear has a way of paralyzing us, coloring our thoughts, making us want to believe we know more than God."

"The Lord hasn't spoken to me." Mira kept her voice firm.

"Perhaps not in audible tones, but he has put you at a crossroads. A place where you can choose which direction to take. I'm sure that if you do decide to stay here in the city, you will find employment, a place to live. But what would be so bad about going to teach where there is no teacher? The mountains will be strange to you, but you would have the protection of a nice, caring young man. Love doesn't always have to come first. The Lord would bless your union and give you children."

Children. The word made a pang in her heart. "Did you ever want to have a child?"

"Oh yes. Very much when I was younger, but I let the opportunity slip away from me. You should not do the same."

"Do you want me to live out your dream?"

"No." Miss Ophelia shook her head. "I want you to live out *your* dream. One the Lord appears to be pushing you toward."

This time Miss Ophelia, instead of using her spoon, slapped the table with her hand. It was not hard to imagine her in front of a classroom of boys and girls demanding they learn. Now. Nor did Mira have any problem imagining the young people she'd seen in her dreams sitting in a school and looking at her with eager expressions.

But that was a dream. A person could dream anything.

Mira took a drink of her lukewarm tea. Is that how her life had become? Lukewarm. Had she given up on having a dream to live out?

But even if she did want to embrace Gordon's proposal, she could not now. She had no idea where Sourwood was other than somewhere in the eastern part of the state. And even if she had a map pointing out her way straight to it, she had no way to get there. So it mattered not that she was feeling the pull to say yes.

"Well?" Miss Ophelia seemed to demand an answer to an unspoken question.

"I'm not sure what you want me to say."

"It isn't what I want. It's what the Lord wants. Are you going to let fear rule your life? Or trust what the Lord wants for you?"

"Even if I did feel a call to teach those mountain children, I would have no idea of where they are or how to get there. There is no Sourwood listed in my atlas map of Kentucky."

"But once you are there in the East, someone could direct you."

"Gordon might have recruited someone else by now."

Miss Ophelia smiled slightly. "I don't think that has happened. Or will happen, at least until he is sure you will not change your mind. I think he already feels a great affection toward you. One perhaps, as he believes, given to him by the Lord."

"It would be a long walk to Eastern Kentucky."

"Don't be silly. No one has suggested you walk anywhere. You would go by train to the nearest town. I think the boy said that might be Jackson."

Mira breathed in and out. "Trains require tickets, and even if I were so foolish to think I should set off for the other side of the state, I have no money for the fare."

Miss Ophelia suddenly looked so pleased that Mira had to wonder if her admission of lack of funds was exactly what she wanted to hear. She stood up and started out of the kitchen. When Mira moved to stand as well, she waved her back to her chair. "I'll be right back. I just have to get something."

Mira considered escaping out the back door, but she couldn't run away twice in one day.

Miss Ophelia came back carrying a Bible. "Here we have the answer." She sounded almost jubilant. Not a tone Mira had ever heard from the woman.

"The Bible has many answers." Mira warily watched Miss Ophelia sit down and open it.

"Of course, but this answer may surprise you." She lifted an envelope from the pages. "The Lord does provide."

Hearing her mother's words spoken by Miss Ophelia was somehow jarring.

"As I feel sure you know, your young preacher stayed and drank the coffee I made for him this morning." Miss Ophelia fingered the envelope. "He shared his feelings and his calling. I was very impressed with his earnest desire to do the Lord's will. He claims that sometimes the Lord expects a man to step onto a path that is thick with the fog of the unknown. A path where he has to simply take the next step without knowing if there is a firm path there."

"Gordon is obviously a very devout man called by the Lord. However, I don't know what this has to do with my problem."

"You don't have a problem, my dear. You have an opportunity." She handed the envelope across to Mira. "And this is your ticket to that opportunity."

Mira pulled open the flap. Several dollar bills were inside. She looked up at Miss Ophelia. "I don't understand."

"Our young preacher had faith that if you prayed, your no would change to a yes. He left this money for you to buy your train ticket and travel to Sourwood. I think if you will look, he has written directions on exactly how to make the journey."

Mira's heart pounded up into her ears. She pushed the envelope back toward Miss Ophelia. "I can't take this."

"And if you don't, what am I to do with it? Buy tea?"

"Send it back to him. Pastor Watkins will have his address."

Miss Ophelia scooted the envelope across the table toward

Mira. "I did suggest to our young preacher that you might not accept this grand opportunity, and if that turned out to be true, I asked him what to do with the money."

"Then you can do whatever he said."

"Very well." Miss Ophelia gave Mira a stern look. "You still must take it. He instructed me to give you the money no matter your decision, for he had a dreadful feeling you would soon be in need of help. It appears he was right."

She pulled a few bills out of her pocket and pressed them into Mira's hand to add to those in the envelope.

"I can't take this." Mira stared down at the money.

"A return on your rent. My brother demands that you be moved by Saturday." Miss Ophelia stood up and went to the stove to move her pot of soup back onto the heat. "Should you need it, I have a trunk you can borrow to move your belongings. I'll set it out on the step. I think you can manage to drag it up the stairs while it's empty. Once you have it packed, I will see if I can locate the man who does odd jobs around our neighborhood. He can convey it to your new quarters wherever they might be."

Mira heard the dismissal in her voice. She put on her coat and stuffed the envelope in her pocket. She would pay the money back.

When she started out of the kitchen, Miss Ophelia spoke without turning from the stove. "I do hope you will follow the Lord's lead and make the right choice."

"Maybe you should have gone with him."

"Oh, if only that were possible, but our young preacher wants more than a schoolteacher."

"That is what makes the decision impossible."

The old woman turned from the stove to look at Mira. "Not at all impossible. I saw the yearning on your face when you asked if I ever wanted a child."

"But a woman has to give herself to a man to have children."

"So she does. I've been told it's a wondrous gift given to those who marry. A gift I was never able to open." She pointed at Mira. "But you have that gift before you. All you have to do is accept it."

"I'm not sure I can."

"I think the truer statement is that you're not sure you can refuse." A smile slipped across the woman's face. "But I will give you a promise if you choose to go to Sourwood. I will come visit you when the sourwood trees are in bloom. Our young preacher says they have the loveliest scent in spite of their sour name."

ordon was angry. Not at anybody but at everything.
Nothing had gone right since he left Miss Vandercleve's
house two days ago when he had stayed too long drinking the woman's coffee. Her claim that she believed Mira was
conflicted about the opportunity of teaching at his mission had
raised his hopes. Miss Vandercleve felt sure Mira would realize
what an opportunity he had opened up to her. They didn't speak
about Mira joining Gordon's life as his wife, but the thought had
been there between them.

She had raised his hopes so much that when she encouraged
him to do so, he had left directions on how to get to Sourwood.
While he had the feeling it might be an exercise in futility, he
had written out the instructions with as much exactness as he
could about the train and what to do once she got to the end of
the line. He'd left the name of a preacher there who could help
her find an escort to Sourwood, perhaps even bring her himself.
That would be best. Pastor Haskell could perform their marriage ceremony.

Gordon had almost laughed aloud as that thought came to
mind while he was printing the directions. He was playing the
fool. Mira was never going to come to Sourwood, much less

stand before a preacher with him. Still, Miss Vandercleve had him believing the Lord might make such happen. Had him remembering the sure feeling that the Lord had brought him to Mira's church for a special purpose. In fact, he was so convinced at that moment, he had left most of his remaining money with the instructions.

Miss Vandercleve said that showed faith. She assured him the Lord rewarded a person who stepped blindly into the future. And hadn't he done that many times? How many mountain trails had he ridden up with no idea of what he might find? He was not always rewarded with good, but the Lord had continually kept him safe.

Gordon had been so distracted by his thoughts of Mira that he had forgotten he didn't have all his supplies packed and ready to be transported to the railway station. He had also neglected to ask Mr. Bramblett, the man who supplied him room and board while in Louisville, to be available to take his trunk to the depot.

If that was what even thinking about being married could do to him, perhaps it was best that Mira had run from him.

Whatever the cause, by the time he arranged transportation to the depot, he missed his train. With so little money in his pocket, he had not hired conveyance and instead walked the good distance back to the Bramblett house. At least the depot manager had let him leave his trunk, although that added a new worry. Someone might claim it, or it might be loaded onto a train to who knew where.

When he said as much to Mr. Bramblett, the man had questioned Gordon's trust in the Lord. "You have to give over to the Lord what you can't change, son."

Mr. Bramblett was a big man with more of a farmer's appearance than that of the banker he was. His beefy hands looked made to hold a hoe or plow handles instead of a pen, but a pen was his tool of choice and had made him a very successful man. His support of Gordon and his Sourwood Mission Church was a blessing.

He and his wife had been praying with Gordon that he would find the right teacher for his mission school. The people in Sourwood were praying. The adults would understand the difficulties of bringing a teacher to Sourwood and would continue praying, but the children would be disappointed. They expected their prayers to be answered. They wouldn't be happy with a not yet or no, even though those were answers the same as yes. Gordon for certain had not wanted to hear Mira's no.

Missing the train on Tuesday was bad enough, but then more snow fell on Wednesday to disrupt the train schedules. No train left for Jackson again until Friday. The time hung heavy on him.

That was why he was so disgruntled. He was anxious to get back to the mountains, but he seemed to be facing roadblock after roadblock.

Friday he was up early. At breakfast, Mr. Bramblett assured him the newspapers reported the trains were back on schedule and that even with more snow in Eastern Kentucky the rails were now passable. The need to be back in Sourwood had been like an itch Gordon couldn't scratch.

He had work to do, people to help, a school to finish building. Hadn't he believed that if he built a church, the people would come? Might it not be the same with a school? The Lord would send them a teacher in his own good time.

He believed that, but sometimes he tried to wrestle control from the Lord to his own hands. That was an ongoing problem for him. He wanted things to turn out the way he considered best. What he needed to do was pray and trust answers would come. Hadn't the Lord always sent down plentiful blessings on him and the people in Sourwood?

"Your will, Lord." Gordon whispered the prayer as he fastened his case and went out to tell the Brambletts goodbye and thank them.

Mrs. Bramblett gave him a sack of food. "So you won't get hungry on the train."

Her husband handed Gordon a coat. "This thing is too little for me. Looks like it might be right for you."

Gordon was glad to put it on, even if it was more than oversized for his slim frame. He'd given away his coat back in the mountains before he came to Louisville. Someone was always more in need of warmth than he. In time, no doubt he'd meet another man, a bigger man who could use this coat too.

As he set out for the train station, he put a hand in the coat's pocket and wasn't surprised to feel money there. Mr. and Mrs. Bramblett were some of his mission's ardent supporters. They both planned to visit when the weather warmed. By then, he hoped to have his cabin better furnished.

By the time Mira came.

He had no idea why that thought popped into his head. He had no reason to expect Mira to ever come. No reason but the nudge he'd felt from the Lord before he shocked Mira with his proposal.

She might have come to teach if he hadn't been so audacious. She could have roomed with Nicey Jane Callahan, who would love putting up the new teacher. In fact, as soon as he got back to Sourwood, he would sit down and write Mira a letter telling her that very thing.

Just thinking that made Gordon smile as his step got lighter and quicker. He had no need to be in ill humor. He had on a warm coat that he could pass on to someone who needed it more when he got to Sourwood. He had a few dollars in his pocket, when earlier he'd barely had enough for his train ticket. He knew Mira's address. He could woo her by mail.

A woman needed some wooing. If it was meant to be, then the Lord would make it happen. Wasn't that how he felt about his mission in Sourwood? The people had wanted him there. They had built a church and his house. The school would be finished soon if snow didn't slow their progress.

The Sunday before he'd come to Louisville, dozens of people

had come to hear him preach. He wasn't the one pulling them down out of the hills to hear the gospel. That was the Lord's doing. He was the Lord's hands and feet in Sourwood and wherever he was sent.

At the depot, he was relieved that his trunk and other crate of supplies were ready to be loaded when the train arrived. Once in Jackson, he would need a wagon to carry them on across the hills to Sourwood. The crate held the slates he'd bought and books donated by the people at the churches he'd visited. Some old history books and primers. A few novels. Several Bibles. Some picture books and magazines. He'd also packed in a lot of newspapers. The people were always happy to get those, since many of their walls were covered with the papers to keep the cold wind out of their cabins.

People had gathered on the depot platform. He looked around to see if he saw anyone who might be in need of a friendly word. When he noticed a small, slender woman studying a paper she held in her gloved hand, he blinked twice, not sure he could believe his eyes. The woman's black hat was identical to the one Mira had worn at church on Sunday.

Could that really be Mira or did he wish it so fervently that his eyes played tricks on him? Many women surely had hats such as that and dark cloaks. The woman raised her head and looked down the tracks.

Mira stared at the black marks on the paper and tried to make them form words, but they seemed to do a jig in front of her eyes. She could still barely believe she had a ticket to Jackson in her hand, her trunk ready to be loaded on a train, and her carpetbag stuffed with clothes beside her.

She couldn't really be going to Jackson to teach at a school that had promised her nothing. Well, not Jackson. Sourwood. And Miss Ophelia would say that she'd been promised everything.

The dreams were what had done it. The children looking at her with beseeching eyes. Children she did not know but who needed her. In the dream, she stood in the front of the room, not holding a book or a ruler, but a baby instead. Then all the children started singing and the baby laughed in her arms.

She'd awakened to such a feeling of being loved. She didn't know how long it had been since that sweet warmth had wrapped around her. She thought she'd lost everyone who loved her. Her parents. Edward.

Those at her church cared for her. Miss Ophelia, in her own prickly way, seemed to like her. But this feeling was different. God so loved the world. God so loved her.

But more than the dreams, more than that sweet feeling of being loved, everything had pushed her to this spot at the depot. Everything? There was that word again.

She felt a little faint and was glad for the bracing air. She never had the vapors. She was made of sterner stuff than that. A schoolteacher couldn't be some fragile flower that wilted at the slightest touch. Teachers didn't fall apart. Not even when their world did. Miss Ophelia had assured Mira of that. She had convinced Mira she had no choice but to be standing here on this rail platform waiting for a train to take her into the unknown.

Not unknown, she told herself firmly. Whether she had ever been there or not, Sourwood was in Kentucky. Her state. She wasn't traveling across the ocean to Africa or China to be a missionary. She was going to Sourwood, Kentucky, to be a teacher.

And a wife? That question lingered. Such did not seem as outrageously impossible as it had mere days ago. Now, somehow, it felt more and more possible, even intended.

She blinked and the words on the paper came into focus. Nothing Gordon had written mentioned marriage. Only how to get to Sourwood. She pulled in a long breath. She was here. She had nowhere else to go. She shoved the directions into her coat pocket, squared her shoulders, and stared down the tracks.

When the train came, she would climb aboard.

9

Several men stepped in front of Gordon and blocked his view of the woman. He had to be dreaming. It couldn't really be Mira. But he had to be sure.

He pushed past the men. The woman was still there. He walked quickly to her. She was still watching down the tracks and didn't notice him.

"Mira?"

The woman whirled around. Her eyes wide, Mira put a gloved hand flat on her chest and gasped.

Before she could recover, he went on. "Am I dreaming? Are you really here?"

"Maybe we're both dreaming." Her voice was almost too soft to hear.

"A dream come true if that's so." A flame of joy swept through Gordon from head to toes. He wanted to do a jig right there in the middle of everyone or even better a waltz with Mira in his arms. He did neither, simply smiled at her while fervently hoping if this was a dream, he wouldn't wake soon.

"I thought you left Tuesday." She sounded breathless.

"I missed my train and then the snow delayed me more."

"The Lord's doing," she said.

He barely heard the whisper of her words and wasn't sure she meant for him to hear them at all. She wasn't smiling and instead looked ready to run, the way she had from Miss Vandercleve's parlor. He wanted to grasp her arm, to keep her there beside him as a worry woke inside him. The train to Jackson wasn't the only train to leave this station.

"I want to believe you are answering the Lord's calling to come teach the children in Sourwood." He shoved his hands in his pockets to keep from touching her. "Or do you have a ticket to somewhere else?"

"Somewhere else? I have nowhere else to go. The Lord has blocked my every path." For a moment she looked sad, but then she pulled in a breath and lifted her chin. "I hope the directions you left mean I will still be welcomed there."

"More than welcomed. Needed. Wanted."

A train whistle blew and people on the siding pushed forward. Gordon picked up her bag and clasped it under his arm before he grabbed his own bag. He put his hand under her elbow and guided her toward the boarding area. "Come. We need to get aboard before all the seats fill."

Earlier he had been willing to stand if his seat was needed by someone else, but now he wanted to sit with Mira. They needed this chance to get to know each other better on the long train ride. That too could be the Lord's doing, as she said. He was almost certain the feelings awakening in his heart were the Lord's doing.

"My trunk," she said.

Of course she would have more than this small bag with her. "You don't have to worry. It will get loaded in with the freight."

"Worry." She echoed his word. "It seems time to worry."

"Forget worrying. Pray. Achieves much more." He smiled over at her. "You've already made the first step. Every next one will get easier."

"I've never been on a train."

"They're noisy. Dirty. Often crowded, but they get you where you need to go."

"Where I need to go." Again she repeated his words. "Commit thy way unto the LORD."

"'Trust also in him.' Psalm 37." He ushered her down the aisle to the back of the passenger car. He stuffed their bags under the seats and stepped back to let her settle next to the window.

They were silent as other passengers claimed places around them. Gordon had to force himself not to stare at Mira. It seemed too good to be true that she was actually beside him on this train ready to pull out toward Jackson. His new teacher. Dare he hope for more? The rest of that verse in Psalm 37 came to mind. *And he shall bring it to pass.*

Gordon was thankful for all the Lord had already brought to pass in his life. He was very thankful for Mira in the seat beside him, but he would not push her. She still was not smiling as she stared out the window. He could wait for her to talk about this challenge she had accepted from the Lord.

After a few minutes, she looked around at him. "Do you have the Bible memorized?"

"I wish. That would be more than amazing. But I do have some Scripture hidden in my heart. That psalm is one many know about the Lord giving you the desires of your heart if you delight in him."

"Do you believe that is true?"

"I do, but many have a difficult time properly doing the first part of the verse." He studied her eyes to try to see what she believed.

"Delight yourself in the Lord."

"Yes."

"Why do you call that difficult?" Her forehead wrinkled in a frown.

"Because most people are self-seeking. We often think we know the best way and have a sure idea of what should happen, without

79

considering if those ways we want to choose will delight the Lord. What we should do, what I feel the Lord wants us to do, is let him plant those desires in our hearts."

She tilted her head slightly as she studied him. "Has he done that for you?"

"Once I started trying to follow him, I think he has. I do believe he wanted me to start the mission in Sourwood. Well, perhaps not Sourwood but somewhere in the mountains. And then he planted the desire in some men from Sourwood to have that mission near them." He wanted her to see that the Sourwood Mission was more than just his heart's desire but also that of the local people too.

"It must be comforting to be so sure of your path." She looked down at her gloved hands clasped in her lap.

"Comforting." Gordon looked past Mira's bent head out the window at the land rushing by.

Of course, it wasn't the land, but the train rushing by. That was how things could seem. Opposite from what they really were. To Mira, he looked determined and sure of God's purpose. He supposed he was comfortable with the path he was on, but the Lord could change that. Perhaps the Lord was shaking his world a little by having this woman beside him. Nothing seemed sure about that except Gordon was thankful for the brush of her shoulder against his as the train bounced along on the tracks, even if he had no idea of what to expect next.

The silence built between them. Gordon let his gaze slide away from the passing landscape and back to her. She continued to stare down at her hands with no hint of a smile.

"Sometimes it seems to us that others have a surer grasp on what they are meant to do. Where the Lord is leading them. When I first felt the Lord's call, I couldn't believe it. I knew something scratched at my heart, but it couldn't be the Lord wanting me to preach." The memory of his unease brought a smile to

Gordon. "You knew me in school. Admit it. I had to be the last boy in our school you expected to ever see standing in a pulpit."

"I don't know if that's true," Mira said.

"Come, Mira. As I told you in Miss Vandercleve's parlor, let's not have pretense between us." He finally caught the hint of a smile on her face then, although she didn't look up at him.

"All right. I was a little surprised. I remember you being more interested in sports than anything else."

"I don't think I've ever read anything in the Bible that says a preacher can't play ball. I still like to hit a ball way to yonder. In fact, I have a confession to make. I used a bit of the donations for a baseball. Now I hope to get someone to whittle out a bat and then find a place flat enough to play."

She finally looked up at him. "Are there no open fields in Sourwood that you could use for a ballfield?"

"The terrain is nothing like you know. Hills climb up on every side. Any bit of flat ground is needed for a house or corn and gardens to feed their families."

She looked puzzled by that. "Don't they have stores?"

"None close by, and none like you've known in the city. But even if they did, for most of the people there, money is scarce as hen's teeth unless they turn their corn into liquor to sell."

"Isn't that against the law?" Her forehead knitted together in a frown.

He shrugged. "But some do it anyway. They feel they have no choice."

"Don't we all have choices?"

"We do, but sometimes until we walk the same paths as others, we can't understand the choices they make. It's a hard life."

"Why don't they move to somewhere that isn't so hard?" The frown etched lines between her eyes.

Lovely eyes, Gordon thought. Full of concern for these people she didn't even know. He had the thought to smooth away her

81

frown with his thumb, but stayed his hand. Not yet. Maybe someday she'd welcome such a touch, but not yet.

"It's their home," he said. "Mine too now. I hope you will find the Sourwood holler home as well."

"Holler? Do you mean hollow?"

"Nobody says 'hollow' in the hills. They're hollers. Some people build up on the steep hillsides. Others down in the hollers. My home is in the holler. I don't have to worry about the cabin sliding down the hill, just the tides washing it away."

"Tides? You can't be near an ocean."

"Far from it, but near a creek." He laughed. "Tides are what the mountain people call a flood. They have unique ways of saying things that can make you smile. To them, I still sound like a brought-in flatlander. They laugh at how I talk all the time."

"Oh my." She shook her head slightly. "They'll laugh at me for sure then."

"They will give the schoolteacher a pass. You're supposed to talk proper."

"But will they like me?" Her voice sounded wistful.

"Of course they will. They like me. Mostly." No need bringing up those few who thought him a meddler they'd like to see gone.

"Mostly? I suppose that's all a teacher can hope for too. Mostly. If you're too likable, some students take advantage of you."

"The children in Sourwood will be so glad to have a teacher, they will be ready to do whatever you say."

"Come now, Gordon. As you said, we can't have pretense between us."

He had to smile at that. "All right. I admit it. The kids in Sourwood aren't perfect, but some of them are eager to have a school."

She pulled in a breath and let it out slowly as she turned back toward the window. The clatter of the train and the chatter of the people around them suddenly sounded louder since he was no longer so completely focused on her every word and expression.

Perhaps she needed a while of silence to think about what he'd said. He did sometimes have a way of forcing too many words at a person instead of letting them figure out things in their own way.

He shut his eyes and sent up a simple prayer. *Thank you, Lord, for Mira and for the feeling growing in my heart for her. Please, if it be thy will, let some answering feeling awaken in her. Help me control my eagerness to make that happen and depend instead on thee.*

He wondered if Mira was praying too as she sat frozen beside him. Questions swirled in his head, but he didn't let any of them exit his mouth. He was determined to let her say the next words between them.

When she did pull her gaze from the window to stare back down at her clasped hands and speak, her whispered words surprised him.

"I'm afraid."

"Not of me?" he said without thinking.

"No." She looked up at him with tears in her eyes. "Yes. Of you. Of everything. I don't know what I'm doing. I don't know if I can do what the Lord seems to be pushing me toward."

He decided to ignore the thought she might be afraid of him and concentrate on her worry of doing what the Lord wanted. "What is that?"

"Leave everything I know and be on this train to a place I can't even imagine. A place I couldn't even find on the map."

"You were brave to take that first step."

"I could go back."

"You could. But to what?"

"That's just it. To nothing." She looked back down at her hands. "I lost my position at the school. I lost my rooms to Miss Ophelia's niece. I have nothing in this world except what is in the trunk that may or may not be on this train."

"Then don't think about going back. Think of what awaits you in Sourwood." He leaned forward to peer at her down-turned face. "It will be good. An older woman there named Nicey Jane will give you a bed in her cabin. You will like her and she will love you."

"No."

"No?" Was all lost and she would buy a ticket back to Louisville as soon as the train stopped at the next depot?

"No." Her voice sounded firm as she pulled off one of her gloves to brush away her tears. She took a deep breath. "On Sunday you asked me to marry you. You said it would make me more accepted if I came to teach in your school. Did you mean it?"

His heart began beating harder. He could hardly believe what she was saying. "I meant it. I would consider it a great honor if you would be my wife."

"But I am afraid."

"You have no reason to fear me, Mira." He kept his voice gentle. "I promise to give you as much time as you need to accept all the expectations of marriage."

"You're talking about the marriage bed."

Her frankness surprised him again. "Yes." Heat warmed his cheeks to match the blush on hers.

"Do you have two beds at your house?"

"I can sleep on the floor."

"That is not marriage. The Bible says a man is to leave his parents and cleave to his wife and they shall be one flesh. 'Cleave' in that verse means cling to. Isn't that right?"

"Yes."

"Then if we marry, we will marry as the Lord wills."

He didn't know how she could sound so sure and still have a tremble in her voice. But then wasn't a tremble working through him at the thought of her being his wife?

"You say if we marry," he said. "Are you not sure?"

"I am sure. When we marry." Her lips turned up in the smallest of smiles. "Earlier you talked about how the Lord gives us the desires of our heart."

"When we delight in him."

"And commit our way to him. I'm doing that. I'm on this train, ready to be a new person. Ready to have faith that the Lord has put me here. Ready for him to give me the desires of my heart."

"And what is that desire? To teach?"

"I do hope to be a good teacher for the youngsters at your mission, but no. When you knew me before at school, I hadn't even thought about teaching. The desire of my heart was to marry Edward and have a family."

"But then you lost Edward."

"After he went to the sanatorium, I turned to teaching to wait until he was well. I always thought he would be better, but instead he died. That desire of my heart was lost forever, and I accepted my single life as a teacher."

"But not happily."

"That's not true. I have been happy, but I sometimes feel so alone. Forever alone. Like Miss Ophelia." She moistened her lips and pulled in a breath as if she needed to gather courage to go on. "I prayed to be satisfied with the life the Lord had given me. To be glad I could touch so many children's lives and have the opportunity to love the babies at my church. But I struggled to make that enough. The desire to be a mother was always there."

"The Lord knows our unspoken prayers."

"And then you made that absolutely ridiculous and impossible proposal to me."

He couldn't keep a little smile from touching his lips. "It was ridiculous. Impossible. But the Bible does say with God nothing is impossible."

She was silent for several minutes before she spoke in a voice so soft he had to lean closer to hear her. "I was like Jonah. I ran from it. And now here I am, swallowed by this train, ready to be thrown out in a place I can't imagine."

"But the Lord can. He wants to give you the desires of your heart."

Her face was flaming now, but the tears were gone from her eyes when she looked up at him. "A baby needs a father."

A smile warmed Gordon's face. "That is God's design." He reached and captured her ungloved hand in his. She didn't pull away.

10

Mira stiffened when Gordon took her hand. She
wanted to pull free, to run away again as she had
from Miss Ophelia's parlor, but one could not escape from a moving train or take back words spoken. The very
thought of those audacious words kept a fire burning in her cheeks.

She breathed in and out slowly and forced her arm to relax.
When she did, she was surprised to like the feel of her hand in
Gordon's. He had such sureness about him. He didn't seem to be
filled with doubts as she was. But then, hadn't she done her best
to sound absolutely sure of her path into the unknown?

Sourwood would not be unknown long. Gordon was not unknown. They had been friends of a sort in school. They could be
friends of a different sort now. Love might be too much to expect,
although she had heard some claim love at first sight. Such always
seemed unlikely to her, but she could hope they could like one
another.

She could like Gordon. She did like Gordon. He had shocked
her with his proposal. Could that be only last Sunday? In less than
a week her life had been turned upside down. She had never been
impetuous. Yet here she was, her hand in a man's hand she had
just demanded marry her.

He had asked first. She twisted her lips sideways to hide the smile that wanted to pop out on her face. Marriage was no laughing matter. Cleaving together as the Bible said. She eased her thoughts away from the marriage bed. She had admitted to being afraid. Of everything. Even Gordon. She should have never said that. She should have not said anything about cleaving. One flesh. That sounded wayward. What must he think of her? Yet he had taken her hand.

She gave herself over to the warmth of his hold. Her hands were always cold, but now she felt surprisingly warm. Comforted. Maybe a man sure of his path with the Lord had an overflowing well of comfort to share.

Still, it was best to turn her mind to things other than marriage right now. Better to think about the place that would be her home, the children she would teach before she had time to become a mother.

What if it turned out she couldn't conceive? She mentally shook her head to stop her thoughts from shooting off in another wayward direction. Focus. Think about the children in her dreams. Schoolchildren. Think about them.

"Tell me about the school."

He looked as relieved as she felt to talk of something other than their impending marriage. "You will love the children." He tightened his fingers around her hand.

"Have they been to school?"

"A few left Sourwood to stay with relatives where they were close enough to walk to a school. But most have not."

"What ages are they?"

"All ages."

"With one teacher?" A little of her fear reared back up. How would she have lessons for all ages?

"It's a one-room schoolhouse, but don't worry. The older children help teach the younger ones. That makes the teaching easier and the learning better."

"If you know what you're doing."

He smiled. "You are a teacher. You will know what to do."

"Are there books?" Her own books were packed in her trunk that she could only hope was somewhere on this train, but she had no primers for beginning readers. She would have to make word cards and arithmetic cards too.

"The churches donated some schoolbooks. We'll make it work."

She liked how he said "we." So many things they needed to make work. She couldn't worry about what books she had or didn't have until they got to Sourwood. That would be time enough to plan how she would teach. Once she met her students.

"All right. What about the children? Tell me about them."

Gordon's face lit up. "They are much like children anywhere, I suppose. There's this one boy, Joseph, who comes every day to see if he can do something for me. And not in hopes of making a penny. He's only six, but he fetches water from the creek and hunts firewood for me. He likes Bible stories."

"Does he have brothers and sisters?"

"He's one of seven. Two sisters younger than him. Three brothers and a sister older."

"A few families like his will overflow a one-room schoolhouse."

He laughed. "Some families have more children, but they won't all be in school since some are babies and others past school age."

"Yes, of course." Even so, Mira had an unsettling image of how full the school might be. Another worry to leave until later. "All right, I know about Joseph, helper and Bible story lover. Tell me about one of the girls." In Louisville, the girls were generally happier about school than the boys.

"There is Ada June. She is very eager to learn to read."

"Ada June. Does she have a big family too?"

Gordon's smile faded. "She doesn't have any family. Her mother died when Ada June was five. After that, she's sort of been bumped around to first one place, then another. Now she stays with a woman named Dottie Slade if she's not out in the woods. Nobody keeps track of her."

"What about her father?"

"She's never had one of those."

"What do you mean? A child has to have a father."

"True, but some fathers don't accept their responsibilities."

"That's shameful." Mira frowned.

"True, but it happens." Gordon huffed out a breath. "Things weren't easy for Ada June even when her mother was living, or so I've been told. Sarai was always a loner, never cared the first whit what people said. Seemed she just showed up one spring day when she was well along with Ada June. Most people figured she had followed the father to Sourwood, but if so, she never made that known. An old man named Leathers, who was the nearest thing they had to a preacher before I came to Sourwood, let her live in a cabin on his place way up in the hills."

"Perhaps he was Ada June's father."

"All this happened before I came to Sourwood, but from what I've been told, Arvin Leathers was such a Christian man, nobody could believe that."

"But what happened to Ada June's mother?" Mira asked. "Sarai, didn't you say?"

"Yes. From what I've been told, she either stopped eating or perhaps had nothing to eat. That winter was a bad one. I assume Mr. Leathers had been seeing to Sarai and Ada June, but he had passed on the summer before."

"You'd think someone would have checked on them."

"Of course they should have, but for whatever reason, nobody did." Gordon looked grim as he went on. "A man running his traplines one snowy winter morning found Ada June beside her mother's body. The girl was half-frozen, but she still ran from him. He caught her, wrapped her tight in his coat to keep her from fighting him, and carried her down the hill."

"Poor child." Sadness welled up in Mira at the thought of the girl waiting beside her mother in the cold.

"Yes. After her mother died, she stopped talking. Didn't say a word until after I came to Sourwood."

"So you helped her find her voice?"

"Not me. The Lord. The people had sort of given up on her ever talking or at least decided to let her be. She still doesn't talk much."

"You say she wants to learn to read. She must have told you that. What changed for her?"

"I'm not sure. Perhaps the excitement of having a chance to learn pulled her out of her shell. That and having a dog. Bo is always with her and having him has helped Ada June. Then on most Sundays, she slips into the church to stand in the back. When I see her there, I can almost feel the Lord showering down love on her." Gordon paused a moment and then went on. "The Lord can touch a person's heart even when they try to hide from him."

Mira blinked away tears at the thought of how alone the little girl must have felt. Hadn't she felt the same after Edward died? "How could a dog help her start talking again?"

"I don't know. Maybe by giving her more courage. Anyway, she and her dog started showing up whenever I walked to this or that house. At first she'd just trail along behind me. If I stopped, she took off for the woods. So I began to merely slow my steps and sing. Usually 'Jesus Loves Me.' One day she started singing with me." Gordon's voice broke a little. "I wanted to shout hallelujah. I didn't for fear of frightening her, but my heart was full of thanksgiving."

"And that was a beginning." Mira knew the joy of those kinds of beginnings from working with her students.

"Yes, a beginning. She still doesn't talk much to me or anyone else, but she seems to be pulled toward the written word. That's why she keeps asking about a teacher." He looked directly at Mira. "She will be a happy student."

"I think I love her already."

"And she will love you." Gordon turned in his seat toward Mira. "Some people are easy to love."

"And some are not," Mira whispered, but she didn't look away.

"I will pray for ease between us and promise you will never have reason to fear me." He took her other hand.

Her heart began racing and the noise around them seemed to fade away until it was only her and Gordon. When he continued to look at her, waiting as he must have waited for Ada June to speak, she pulled in a breath for the same kind of courage that little girl must have needed. "I will do the same and that you will never be disappointed in me."

A frown flickered across his face. "That could never be. The Lord has put us together for good. Not bad."

She nodded without saying anything, even as she silently prayed he was right.

"We'll be in Jackson soon. I know a preacher there. He can marry us. Not today, but tomorrow before we go on to Sourwood."

She managed not to jerk her hands free and shrink from his words. She had said this was what she wanted. Somehow she would follow it through even if her feet were itching to run.

"We can stay with Pastor Haskell tonight. In the morning, I'll find a wagon to take us on to Sourwood. It's a rough road and, in places, no road at all."

His gaze was intent on her face. She knew her eyes had widened, even as she tried not to look frightened at the plans he was speaking.

"You will like Pastor Haskell and his wife, Stella. I am just as certain you will like the people in Sourwood." He gently caressed her hands. "Can you think of it as an adventure something like the story of Ruth and Naomi in the Bible? Ruth had to be apprehensive going into the unknown to live with a people foreign to her."

"Your people will be my people," Mira murmured.

A smile broke out on Gordon's face, making her remember the schoolboy she'd known. Then he started singing. "Jesus loves me, this I know . . ."

Without thinking about it, Mira joined in. "For the Bible tells me so."

Their voices singing the children's song blended in with all the noise around them as sunshine pushed through the grimy train window and fell on their joined hands. Fear of the future still poked her, but she suddenly knew she had the courage to keep riding this train with Gordon Covington.

11

Ada June Barton liked the snow even if her hands and feet were near to froze. The sun had finally made it up over the hill to shine down through the pines. The snow, not much more than ankle deep, wouldn't last long.

She shouldn't have even bothered with the cast-off boots Aunt Dottie had found her. Ada June had to stuff them with rags so her feet wouldn't slide out of them. Worse, when she slipped off a rock into a creek back a ways, they leaked. Now the rags squished with every step.

Some old socks worked for gloves, but they got wet too when she built a snow dog at the edge of the woods. Bo hiked his leg to add some color to the snow dog and then bit off its nose.

Ada June laughed out loud. She could do that when nobody was around to hear. Bo did his toothy grin and pranced over to her.

"Don't worry. You're my only dog." As she ruffled his ears, she wondered for the hundredth time why a dog's paws didn't freeze in the snow. Bo wasn't the least bothered by the cold. He pranced in a circle around her, his shaggy black-and-white fur bouncing. Aunt Dottie's husband said Bo's nose was too short and his ears too long. That Bo had got the worse of whatever shepherd-hound mix he might be. Ada June didn't care what Mr. Luther said. Bo was fine. More than fine.

Ada June stuck her hands under her arms. She ought to go back to Aunt Dottie's to thaw out by the fire before her fingers and toes broke off. Aunt Dottie probably needed some wood packed in. She wouldn't want to dig wood out of the snow, what with her baby on the way.

This was the first one to come along since they got Ada June to come help Aunt Dottie nearly two years ago. Emmy Lou was already born then. Babies could come along fast unless a woman was like Ada June's ma and didn't want a man around. Aunt Dottie wasn't nothing like Ada June's ma. She doted on Mr. Luther. Ada June couldn't see why, but Aunt Dottie said she'd figure things like that out when she got older.

What Ada June had figured out now was that Mr. Luther was somebody she'd best keep away from whenever he came in from his logging work. He aimed for her to earn her keep, fetching for Aunt Dottie and doing for Emmy Lou, but that weren't enough to please him. He must've thought she was like other girls, ready to say sweet words and not go wandering in the woods.

He got mad as all get out because she never spoke an answer if he asked her something. He took it personal. It wasn't. Back when she first came to Aunt Dottie's, she didn't talk to nobody. Hadn't since her ma died. Didn't seem anything was worth saying.

He tried to make her talk with his razor strop until Aunt Dottie made him stop. He wanted to kick her out. Aunt Dottie wouldn't let him do that either. Claimed it wouldn't look good to the neighbors after saying they'd take her in for good.

Ada June heard them fussing. She didn't rightly care how it turned out. But Aunt Dottie started crying, and Mr. Luther gave in.

She wasn't really her aunt but wanted Ada June to call her that anyway. At least to think of her as aunt since she wasn't calling anybody anything back then. She liked wrapping silence around her. Somehow kept things from hurting so much. But when she went to talking some not long ago, she did speak Aunt Dottie's name now and again. That pleased Aunt Dottie no end.

She thought Ada June ought to call Mr. Luther "uncle" so he might ease up yelling at her. But that wasn't ever going to happen. Her calling him uncle or him not being sorry he'd ever brung Ada June to his cabin, even if she did have a way of making Emmy Lou happy. Ada June sang to her some when they were outside away from any other ears.

Ada June's ma liked to sing. The songs never made much sense, but sometimes those were the best kinds. Her mother told her that.

So, she still had her place at Aunt Dottie's fireplace even if she was more at home in the woods. Right now a place by a fire didn't sound so bad. Bo would be glad enough to plop down in front of a fireplace too, even if somehow the Lord had made dog feet so they didn't freeze, like as how hers were. Mr. Luther was off logging and wouldn't be there to give her trouble. She could warm up a spell before Aunt Dottie named chores for her to do.

But Ada June kept heading down the hill toward where they were building the school. That morning Aunt Dottie said she figured Preacher Gordon would be home from the flatland by now, and Ada June was anxious to see if he brung a teacher with him.

She hesitated when she came to the trail that went over to Elsinore's cabin. She had to do Aunt Dottie's bidding first, but she made sure to go by Elsinore's place regular to see how she and baby Selinda were making out. Elsinore hadn't gotten her strength back from her baby-bearing time. On top of that, she was pining over her husband, Benny, who went off to hunt work and hadn't been heard from since. That was before she knew a baby was coming. Selinda, born back in the fall, would be a surprise if he ever came home.

Selinda was the sweetest little thing and lit up like a lantern whenever she saw Ada June. Elsinore did too, or would if she had the energy. She was droopy. Couldn't do much more than keep her fire fed. She didn't have any family around. Said they all died of the typhoid. Every last one. Same as Ada June, she'd been pitched around some before she married Benny.

Elsinore was the reason Ada June went to letting words escape her mouth. Her and Preacher Gordon and how he was always singing about Jesus. Preaching about him too. Ada June figured he'd told her about how Jesus loved her more times than a dandelion fluff had seeds.

Sometimes she thought it might be true. At least, she wanted it to be. She missed somebody loving her. Not just thinking she was handy because she had a way of making a baby hush crying. Her mother had loved her. She knew rock solid in her heart that was true, but then her mother had laid herself down and died on a day something like this one Ada June was traipsing through today.

More snow had been piled up that day. At least it seemed so whenever she let that time come up in her memories. Something she didn't often do. Seemed better to think on the now. At least, that was what Preacher Gordon said about Elsinore. Him and most everybody else in Sourwood figured Benny had gone down in one of those mines and never come out, and that it was just a matter of time before the news trickled back to Elsinore. But then Preacher had gone on to say some folks have a hard time looking ahead instead of behind.

Ada June didn't think he was talking about her. Preacher Gordon wouldn't know all that much about her past times seeing as her mother froze in the snow before he came to Sourwood. He wouldn't know about how that hunting man left Ma there in the cold and took Ada June off their mountain. Off Pap Leathers' mountain. Pap had died before Ma. He hadn't laid down to die. He was slumped over his Bible on the table in front of him.

When they found him and her mother saw the little bit of candle wax beside the Bible, she said his light had gone out. Ada June guessed that was why that burnt-down candle jumped in front of her brain's eyes whenever she thought about Pap Leathers dying. Her mother had sent her down off the hill to the nearest neighbor.

Ada June was still talking then. She lost her words when she lost her mama.

She wasn't sorry she'd found some of those words now. She still didn't talk to everybody. Elsinore. Aunt Dottie when she had to. Emmy Lou. Selinda. Preacher Gordon. The preacher said she'd have to talk to the teacher whenever he brought one to Sourwood.

When she told him she wasn't sure she could, he told her to ask Jesus for help. He said she didn't have to talk out loud to Jesus, that he heard her whether she spoke the words or not. Jesus knowing what was going on in her head whether she let it out of her mouth or not was sort of scary.

Even though she didn't admit that out loud, Preacher Gordon seemed to know anyway. He had smiled at her. "Don't you let that worry you. Nothing you ever think can change how the Lord loves you."

Aunt Dottie said preachers didn't lie. Elsinore claimed that true too. But Ada June still wasn't all that sure about what the preacher said. Could be he wasn't lying. Just not looking at things straight on. Or maybe he was just so good, he couldn't imagine somebody having the kind of thoughts that might make Jesus shake his head and move on down the way to listen in on somebody with nicer thoughts.

She knew what kind of thoughts she had. Like wishing Connor Rayburn would fall in a well and be there for a spell before anybody came along to rescue him. She never hoped the well had water over his head, and sometimes she let there be a bucket on a rope he might grab to climb out. If he was strong enough.

Since preacher claimed the Lord loved everybody, even Connor Rayburn, she was pretty sure the Lord wouldn't like her wishing Connor trouble like that. Some thoughts were better kept hid under her hat.

Beside her, Bo growled low in his throat before a storm of snowballs came flying out of the bushes along the path. One of them banged into the side of her head so hard her ears rang.

Just thinking about Connor Rayburn must have summoned him up to torment her. Bo started barking like three bears were closing in on them. She wished it was bears instead of Connor. Marv would be with him.

She scooped up snow to fight back but stopped when she heard Marv's ornery hound bark. That big old dog might be itching for a fight. Better not to take the chance. Bo wouldn't have sense enough to know he couldn't outfight the hound.

She touched Bo's head. His ears flattened on his head. He looked up at her, and she could tell he was ready to take on that big old dog if she'd just let him.

"What's the matter? Scared?" Connor jumped from behind the bushes to throw another snowball.

She scooted sideways to let it fly by her.

Marv stood up too. Perfect targets. Waiting to see what she would do. She could forget snowballs and grab some rocks. That would make them think twice before they ambushed her again. She could bean Connor first throw. But Marv's dog was growling and appeared ready for Marv to sic him on Bo.

Thing to do was run before that happened. No shame in running from a fight they couldn't win with two against one for her and huge against small for Bo. She'd find another way to pay back Connor.

Pap Leathers used to tell her that brain beat brawn every time. She didn't doubt she had more sense than the boys, even if they were a year older than her. Even so, she did wish Pap had told her what her brain was supposed to think up to beat Connor Rayburn.

She turned and ran a few steps, with her boots flopping like she had buckets on her feet. She didn't look around, but the boys would come after her. They aimed to scare her.

She weren't scared. Not of them. Just of Marv's old hound. Bo danced around her, whining now, ready to run, but he wouldn't leave her.

"Hey, you," Connor yelled. "Ain't you got nothing to say?"

"I reckon the cat's got her tongue," Marv taunted.

"More like her witch of a mother put a spell on her," Connor said.

That was almost enough to make her forget the big hound and good sense. They didn't know anything about her ma. Nothing. She kicked off the boots. The snow poked icy needles up into her feet. She grabbed the boots and took off up the hill into the trees.

Behind her, the boys laughed, and Connor shot another volley of words at her. "Go hide, woods colt. Maybe you'll find your pa up there in the trees."

Dumb boy. Didn't he even know a girl was a filly? Not a colt. She thought about stopping to tell him so, but she didn't want to give him the chance to say something even dumber. Besides, she needed to keep moving before her feet froze.

She knew the woods better than Connor. Better than any other kid in Sourwood. She knew where a person could crawl under a big rock jutting out of the hill to sleep awhile. She could find blackberries in the summer and hickory nuts and chestnuts in the fall. She had a favorite sitting spot in amongst flowers Ma named trilliums. She knew the best trees for climbing and where springs bubbled up out of the ground. She especially knew the places she shouldn't go, where some man might be turning his corn into moonshine.

She had plenty of hiding spots too, but today she ran straight through the trees and around the rhododendron thickets toward Miss Nicey Jane's house. She thought about running to Elsinore's place, but she worried the boys would keep after her and cause Elsinore worry she didn't need.

Miss Nicey Jane didn't like Ada June much. She was some like Mr. Luther in that it upset her when she wouldn't talk. She wasn't mean like Mr. Luther, but she got some irritated if Ada June just nodded or shook her head when she was asked things.

Preacher said she ought to talk to Miss Nicey Jane, that she was a good Christian woman. Still, something blocked Ada June's words around her.

Didn't even matter that Miss Nicey Jane wouldn't give her a cookie less'n she said please. She didn't need cookies. But she did need Bo safe. Marv's hound started baying like as how he was trailing a raccoon.

Miss Nicey Jane wouldn't turn her away even if she didn't say please when she got to her door. She and Bo could shelter there. The boys would stop chasing after her when they saw where she was headed. Miss Nicey Jane was Connor's granny, and he wouldn't want her to know his meanness.

Miss Nicey Jane had a whole passel of grandkids. So a body could expect a rotten one or two in the bunch. Most of her grandchildren, at least the ones Ada June knew were kin to Miss Nicey Jane, weren't mean to her. They mostly ignored her, like as how she was just extra. Somebody that didn't belong nowhere.

Ada June dropped a boot. It slid down the hill toward where the boys were coming after her. Aunt Dottie would be mad if she lost one of her boots. Bo raced back to grab it to save her that trouble.

Minutes later she pounded on Miss Nicey Jane's door. Maybe Ada June would try to say "please." Her feet were really cold.

Miss Nicey Jane looked her up and down. "Land's sake, child, what in the world is you doing without no boots on?"

Ada June wouldn't have told her about the boys even if seeing Miss Nicey Jane staring down at her didn't steal her words. Folks didn't like hearing bad things about family.

She tried hard to push out a please, but it stuck. So she tried a different one. "Cold." Her teeth chattered to make the word sound all broke up and shaky, but Miss Nicey Jane still almost smiled at the sound of it. Almost.

"I reckon so. Git on over by the fire." She motioned for her to come in.

Bo whimpered and put his paw on Ada June's leg.

"I don't need no wet dog by my fire." Miss Nicey Jane looked down at Bo. "It can wait here on the porch."

Ada June could feel the heat from the fire drifting out toward her, but she couldn't leave Bo. Maybe she should walk on down to the preacher's house. It wasn't too far and she couldn't really feel her feet anymore anyhow. Could be they wouldn't get any colder.

She stepped back without letting Miss Nicey Jane grab her arm. She looked down toward the preacher's cabin, but no smoke curled up from his chimney. He must not be back yet.

Her insides felt all tight when she heard Marv's hound baying. Closer now. They would catch her for sure before she got anywhere else, and Connor would be mad that she went to his granny's house. She looked up at Miss Nicey Jane and pushed out another word. "Please."

Miss Nicey Jane looked out over Ada June's head. Maybe she heard that old hound too. Anyway, she pressed her lips together a second before she said, "Well, I guess this oncet, but it'll have to sit on a towel till you get thawed out." She shook her head. "Ain't no reason for you to be carrying them boots instead of wearing them."

She thought she ought to say thankee, but the two words she'd already said were all she could manage. Miss Nicey Jane studied her like as how she knew more than she was saying too.

"Put those boots by the fire and peel off your socks." She spread a towel by Ada June's chair.

Without being told, Bo sat on it and started licking snow out from between his toes.

"Them boots is man sized." Miss Nicey Jane clucked her tongue. "No wonder you come out of them. I can't fathom how you kept them on at all."

Ada June pulled out the wet rags to drape over the top of the boots.

"Well, times is we have to make do." Miss Nicey Jane wrapped a blanket around Ada June's shoulders. "Good sakes, child. You ought to have stayed in the house with Dottie and helped her keep the fire fed."

Ada June nodded. Could be Miss Nicey Jane was right. She generally was.

The woman sighed. "Your feet and hands is gonna hurt a right smart. I'll heat you up a cup of milk."

Again Ada June thought she ought to say thank you, but instead she stared at the fire, burning brisk like. Her hands and feet did go to aching as they warmed up. She didn't mind that so much. Pain on the outside helped her not feel the pain on the inside that never went away.

12

~

Mira thought she'd be glad to get off the train, but instead, her legs started to tremble as soon as her feet were on the depot's platform. Each step was taking her farther from what she knew into what she didn't.

While Gordon went to see about their trunks, Mira clutched her coat tight around her and huddled against the depot wall. She wanted to hide in its folds from the sideway glances of the people around her. Their unsmiling faces seemed to indicate they were sure she had gotten off the train at the wrong place.

Maybe she had, but she'd told Gordon she wanted to be here. She claimed to be ready to go to his Sourwood. Ready to teach school. Ready to get married.

Married. Perhaps she'd lost her reasoning powers.

To tamp down her panic, she stared out at the snow that was deeper here than in Louisville. Inches deeper. She'd noticed when the countryside along the tracks had changed. Houses farther apart. Big stretches slid by with no houses at all. Just trees or fields with cows and horses, some nothing but skin and bones as if snow had hidden their grass for too many days.

Gordon shared his food with her. She tried to refuse, but he claimed he had more in his poke than he could eat. When she gave him a funny look, he said calling a sack a poke was mountain talk. He claimed such talk would eventually be second nature to her too.

That didn't seem likely, but the closer the train got to Jackson, the more Gordon changed from the preacher she'd heard on Sunday to sounding like the people climbing aboard at the little towns along the tracks.

A few men greeted Gordon like an old friend. Gordon introduced her each time, but she was relieved he didn't share their plans. Even so, the men eyed her and grinned. They seemed to guess without being told and clapped Gordon on the back as they called him Preacher.

She had been so worried about the whole idea of marriage that she hadn't once thought about what it would mean to be a preacher's wife. Pastor Watkins's wife back at her church practically shone with goodness and love for everyone, while getting whatever needed doing done.

Right now, standing next to this depot while daylight dimmed as the sun slid out of sight, Mira couldn't imagine being anything like Mrs. Watkins with her confident smiles and certainty about the Lord's path for her. Mrs. Watkins wouldn't be trembling here in the shadows, hardly able to swallow, much less smile.

In fact, Mira wasn't sure she could even force a smile out on her face. Maybe ever again. At least not a real smile. On the train with Gordon holding her hands, she had started to believe she was doing what the Lord wanted. But now, without Gordon beside her, fear built until each breath took effort.

What if something had happened to Gordon? He'd been gone forever. The train had left. The tracks were empty.

She tried to gather her courage. Gordon wouldn't desert her. He'd hinted that he cared for her. Already. Something the Lord put in his heart. But not in hers. Maybe she should pray that he would, but the very thought seemed unfaithful to Edward.

She shook her head a little. Edward had been gone five years. More than five years. But hadn't she promised him her love forever when they planned their life together? That he died before they could marry didn't wipe that love from her heart.

Had Ruth promised the same kind of love to Naomi's son and that was why she clung to Naomi instead of returning to her people? Perhaps she, like Mira, had no people to take her in, or did she love Naomi that much? Enough to do what Naomi said to make Boaz want to marry her?

Mira had never met Gordon's mother. She should ask him about her. If she ever saw him again. Her heart beat a little faster as the shadows deepened toward evening.

"Stop borrowing trouble." Mira could hear Miss Ophelia's voice in her head. *"Your young preacher will return. Brace up."*

That last command was Miss Ophelia's exact words before Mira left for the train station. She'd squeezed her hands in what was almost an affectionate gesture and told her to brace up.

While a few minutes ago she thought she might never smile again, she did smile as Gordon came toward her. Whether she could imagine loving him right now, she needed him in this unfamiliar world.

He had found a man with a truck to take them to his preacher friend's house.

"You will like the Haskells." He led her around the depot to where the truck waited. "Stella loves everyone and everyone loves her."

Another preacher's wife to expose Mira's shortcomings.

The trunks were already loaded. Gordon helped Mira up into the truck's seat. "This is Mr. Wilson. Mira Dean."

"How do you do, sir," she said.

The man might have smiled, but she couldn't be sure since his face was all but hidden by a bushy red mustache and beard streaked with gray. "Don't know the last time I was ever called sir, but welcome aboard, little lady."

She tried to keep her knees away from the gear shift sticking up from the floorboard. That pressed her legs tight against Gordon.

"You headin' to Preacher Haskell's for him to tie the knot between you'ns?" the man asked.

Gordon touched her arm lightly, perhaps sensing the man's words made her heart want to jump out of her chest. "Thinking on it. Come morning."

"You best let him go ahead and fix you up proper tonight. Gonna be a cold one." He looked over at Mira. "Could be you'll need to do some cuddling to keep warm."

Even though the light had to be too dim for the man to see the flush burning her cheeks, he still let out a raucous laugh. She was relieved when he braked and slid to a stop in front of a white frame house.

They went up the stone pathway to the porch, where Reverend Haskell flung open the door when Gordon knocked.

"Gordon." A smile engulfed his face as he looked from Gordon to Mira. "And you've brought a friend. Your new schoolteacher, I presume."

Again, the smile Mira had thought lost forever at the depot found her face. In his faded blue shirt with red suspenders holding up his pants, the preacher looked like someone's grandfather. Or maybe everyone's grandfather.

Before Gordon said the first word, the man yelled over his shoulder. "Stella, come see who's here. Gordon and his schoolteacher."

A woman, a matching image of a kindly grandmother with a plump waistline and gray hair, hurried into the room, wiping her hands on her apron.

"Well, don't keep them on the step, Bill. Let them in." The woman's smile was even bigger than her husband's.

The man moved back, and Gordon ushered Mira inside. "This is Mira Dean, soon to be Mira Covington."

Mira's smile stiffened as she stared at Gordon, whose smile was almost as big as the Haskells' as he murmured, "Sorry, Mira. I guess I'm just excited."

"I would think." Mrs. Haskell pulled Mira into a hug. "I

couldn't be happier for the both of you." She pushed Mira back but grabbed her hands. "Don't be shy, dearie. We're the same as family."

Mira moistened her lips but couldn't think of the first thing to say. Nobody seemed to note her loss for words.

Mrs. Haskell looked over at her husband. "Best find your marrying Bible."

Reverend Haskell chuckled. "Now, Mama, hadn't we better let them shed their coats before we start the marrying?"

With her face burning like fire, Mira wanted to pull her hands free and run out the door. But where would she run to?

Gordon laughed too. "You can wait to get your marrying Bible until morning, Pastor Bill. Mira and I need time to catch our breath after a long day coming from the city. I hope you can put us up for the night."

"You know you're always welcome here," Reverend Haskell said. "Stella will stir up something tasty for supper."

Mira found her voice. "Don't go to any trouble, Mrs. Haskell."

"Never you mind about that. And no Mrs. Haskell for you. Call me Aunt Stella. Everybody does."

Mira stared at the woman and blurted out, "I don't have any aunts."

"You do now. And I have a new niece." The woman shook Mira's hands a little.

"You have a few dozen nieces and nephews, don't you, Aunt Stella?" Gordon said.

"More like a few hundred," Reverend Haskell put in.

Mrs. Haskell let go of Mira's hands and turned to grab Gordon in a hug. "And this nephew has been too long gone from our house. I'd ask what you've been up to, but I guess I can see that plain enough. Appears you've been some busy." She stepped back to look over at her husband. "Bill, help the boy get his trunks in here while I finish up supper. Then he can tell us where he found his beautiful, blushing bride-to-be."

After Gordon and the preacher headed outside, Mira wasn't sure what she should do, but she needn't have worried. Mrs. Haskell hadn't forgotten about her.

"Throw your coat over the nearest chair, dearie, and come along. You can set the table while I put another potato in the pot."

As Mira followed her toward the kitchen, she thought of how different, yet how alike she was to Miss Ophelia. Both women expected people to do their bidding. Miss Ophelia didn't bother with smiles along with her instructions, while Mrs. Haskell didn't look as if she knew what a frown was.

Smiling must be contagious. Despite being in a strange place with the unsettling prospect of getting married hanging over her head, the corners of Mira's lips turned up. Her heart felt lighter as she went into the warm kitchen with pots bubbling on the stove. A pan of apple peels and a rolling pin rested amid a scattering of flour on a biscuit board on the cabinet.

"You can wash up at the sink. Just pump on that handle there. Soap's in the dish."

After Mira did as told, Mrs. Haskell waved her toward a small china cabinet. "Get the plates with roses. We'll be fancy tonight."

By the time they finished off the last bites of apple cobbler, the Haskells had found out everything worth knowing about her. Except how the thought of being married to Gordon seemed right one minute and a dreadful mistake the next.

But it turned out Mrs. Haskell guessed that too. After Mira helped wash the dishes, the woman showed Mira to a small bedroom. Mrs. Haskell settled in a small rocker by the window and pointed her to a footstool, the only other place to sit other than the bed.

"While the men have preacher talk in the parlor, we can have some woman talk here."

Mira scooted the stool a couple of feet away from the rocker, but she was still right at Mrs. Haskell's knees when she sat down.

The woman smelled of apples and fried ham. She wiped a few

beads of sweat from her forehead with the tail of her apron. "That kitchen gets hot as Hades."

"Everything was delicious."

Mrs. Haskell flapped air toward her face with her apron. "Bill likes to eat and so do I. I guess you can see that." She chuckled. "It's been a while since either one of us had much of a waistline. Maybe you can fatten up young Gordon a bit. He's so skinny he could dodge raindrops."

"I'll do my best."

"They don't have electric over in Sourwood. I'm thinking Gordon doesn't even have a stove yet. You might have to do fireplace cooking."

"Fireplace?"

"Don't fret." Mrs. Haskell patted Mira's knee. "The women there will help you. Folks like helping the preacher and his missus out." She sat back and rocked a minute without saying anything.

Mira let the silence settle around them while she imagined stirring pots hanging over an open fire.

All of a sudden, Mrs. Haskell leaned forward in her chair, closer to Mira. "I have the feeling something more than what to cook for supper might be concerning you some."

"Oh?" Heat warmed Mira's cheeks as she pretended not to know what the woman meant.

The woman sat back again as she peered at Mira. "I'm thinking all this is sort of rushed for you."

"It has been sudden. I hadn't seen Gordon for years before last Sunday." Mira wanted to look away from the woman, but something about her eyes held Mira's gaze.

"And I'm gathering you hadn't given him the first thought through those years. Or even back when."

"I had plans to marry someone else. So I paid the other boys little attention." Mira did look down at her hands then.

"What happened?"

"He died."

110

"Recently?"

"Years ago."

"I see." The woman rocked back and forth a few times before she went on. "I love young Gordon like a son. He's a good man."

"He is." Mira looked up at her again.

"Is that why you agreed to marry him? Because he's a good man?"

"I'm glad for that, but no. The Lord closed every other path to me. This is the one left open." Mira would not speak of how the desire to have a child had pushed her to insist on the marriage she had thought so ridiculous a few days ago. She could have accepted a way to be Sourwood's teacher without marrying Gordon.

"The Lord's will." Mrs. Haskell nodded. "Sometimes the path he picks for us can take courage. I'm sensing you have some trepidation as you think on the days ahead." She stared straight at Mira. "And the nights."

"Yes." Mira could not deny that.

Mrs. Haskell smiled slightly. "I remember feeling some the same, forty-plus years ago on the eve of my marriage to Bill. My mother, dear woman that she was, told me the Lord made man and the Lord made woman and the design was perfect as only the Lord can make perfection. He aimed for two to join in holy matrimony to become as one. It's a blessed union that will grow stronger with every year you share."

"I hope so."

"Do more than hope. Pray." She leaned forward again and cupped Mira's face in her hands. "That is a duty of a preacher's wife. If you will do that, the Lord will put love in your heart and scatter your worries like chaff in the wind."

"I can pray."

"Of course you can." She stood up. "I watched Gordon tonight. Love for you is already tickling his heart. Your union will be blessed."

"Thank you." She hesitated, then added, "Miss Stella."

The woman shook her head with a smile. "I'll pray that someday you'll be ready to claim me as aunt." She gave her a quick hug, said good night, and left her alone.

Once in bed, Mira stared into the dark and repeated Miss Stella's words aloud. "Your union will be blessed." She needed to believe that.

13

*D*o you, Mira Dean, take this man, Gordon Covington, to be your wedded husband, to have and to hold from this day forward, for better, for worse, for richer, for poorer, in sickness and in health, to love, cherish, and to obey, till death do you part, according to God's holy ordinance?"

Reverend Haskell's deep voice seemed to vibrate in Mira's ears as she stood beside Gordon while the preacher read out of a small book he held on top of his open Bible. He had already spoken almost the same list of vows to Gordon about taking her to be his wedded wife. Gordon had looked at Mira and answered without hesitation.

She intended to do the same, but the words played back through her mind. She could do the better or worse, the richer or poorer, in sickness and health, but what about the love and cherish? Should she solemnly promise in front of God something she didn't feel, that she might never truly feel?

Reverend Haskell kept his gaze steady on her. She sensed Gordon afraid to breathe beside her and knew, without looking, that Miss Stella, as their witness, was praying for the expected answer.

She shut her eyes for a moment and changed the vows in her mind to *learn to love and to cherish.*

When she opened her eyes, the preacher watched her with such patient understanding that she was embarrassed not to have answered at once. She pulled in a breath and pushed out the necessary words. "I do."

Nothing more was expected, but before Reverend Haskell went on with the ceremony, she added, "With the Lord's help."

Gordon took her hand in his then. "And I say the same."

"Not a bad addition to the vows," Reverend Haskell said. "Then I, by the power vested in me, pronounce you, Gordon and Mira Covington, man and wife. You may kiss the bride."

This time Gordon was the one who hesitated, obviously unsure if Mira would welcome a kiss. When he seemed ready to turn away, Mira lifted her face toward his, inviting the kiss. She had vowed to be his wife for the rest of their lives. That promise should be sealed with a kiss.

He smiled and brushed his lips softly against hers. Beside them, Miss Stella clapped her hands. Reverend Haskell closed his marrying book and clasped Gordon's shoulder with congratulations.

The deed was done.

"Oh, I do wish you two would stay long enough for me to bake a cake and invite some of our church people in to celebrate with you," Miss Stella said.

"That would be wonderful, Aunt Stella," Gordon said. "But I'm already days late getting back to Sourwood, and tomorrow is Sunday. After being gone last Sunday, I would rather not leave the church dark two weeks in a row."

"I should say not," Reverend Haskell said. "People have a few Sundays without church, they can get slack about remembering the way back to worship."

"Now, Bill, our people are very faithful."

"Because we are, Mama. Because we are. And the people in Sourwood expect the same from our Gordon here." He bent his head and peered up at Gordon through his eyebrows with a smile all too easy to interpret. "Besides, the children here will be ready to get to their new home."

Heat bloomed in Mira's cheeks again. Her face had been flushed so much since she came into the Haskells' house, they might think a red face normal for her. And now she would be going to a new place where more people would be looking at Gordon and her, assuming more than there was to assume between them.

When the wagon arrived to take them to Sourwood, Gordon and Reverend Haskell went out to load their trunks.

"That will keep them busy awhile." Miss Stella took Mira's arm and pulled her back toward the room where she had slept. "Gives me time to get your wedding gift."

"Please, no. You have been so kind already."

"Pshaw. A bride needs a wedding present. 'Course you'll likely get a passel more at Sourwood. Folks do love to give to their pastor. One of your duties as a pastor's wife will be to always show gratitude no matter the gift. I've had some doozies in my time, let me tell you." Miss Stella shook her head with a little laugh. "But I always embraced the joy they felt in giving. You do the same."

"I will try."

"'Course you will. Be sure to top it off with a smile." She opened a cedar chest.

"Really, Miss Stella, you mustn't give me anything. Your kindness is more than I can ever repay."

"You don't have to repay kindness." She didn't look around as she rummaged through the chest. "Such needs to be given on to the next folks you meet. And could be the first one to spend your kind thoughts and deeds on will be that new husband of yours."

"Yes." She could do that. Surely.

"Ah, here it is." The woman lifted out a quilt to spread on the bed. "I finished this up last winter."

"It's beautiful." Mira traced the intersecting rings of blue and dark pink circles with her finger.

"And it's yours." Miss Stella refolded the quilt.

"Oh no." Mira shook her head. "That's too much."

"You have to take it. I made it with you in mind. Not that I knew what you were going to look like at the time, but I was sure our Gordon would find him a wife one of these days. I was saving it for him. Well, not for him." She pushed the quilt into Mira's arms. "For you."

Mira held it close, feeling not only the warmth of the fabric but of the woman's love for Gordon that spilled over to her. The quilt smelled like cedar from the chest where it had been stored until Gordon came with a bride. "I don't know how to thank you."

"Oh, you'll find a way one of these days when you bring a little one to visit his Aunt Stella."

Mira's heart jumped at the thought. If only someday that could be true. "Do you have children, Miss Stella?"

The woman's face lost its smile. "I did. Two little ones. A dear little boy and a sweet baby girl. My precious girl only lived a few days. Bill said heaven must have decided they couldn't get by without our little angel. We had Jacob a little longer." A smile that hid none of her sadness slid across her face. "He was a sturdy little fellow. Looked the image of his pa. He was four years and three months when he took sick with a fever and heaven called him back too."

"I'm so sorry." Mira blinked back the tears that popped into her eyes. She couldn't start weeping when Miss Stella wasn't crying.

"I know. It's sad." The woman patted Mira's arm. "A body can have some heartbreak in life, but the Lord doesn't intend us to dwell on the sorrow but on the joy of loving those he sends our way. And when we lose those loved ones, he walks us through that hard valley and lets us know we still have things to do before he calls us home. Best to remember that."

"Yes."

The woman's smile got brighter. "But enough sorrowing. Nothing but joy should be falling around you today. And you might need that quilt for your trek to Sourwood. It's cold as a wedge out there. Not a bad thing. Better to have frozen wagon ruts than muddy ones, but it can make for breezy travel." She pointed at the quilt. "You can wrap that around you to keep your toes from freezing off."

When she went outside, the wagon's driver didn't look more than fourteen, but he kept a good hold on his horses. The trunks were tied in place, and they made Mira a seat on a wooden crate beside them.

Miss Stella hugged her and then hugged her twice more before she handed her a cloth bag. "Here's a poke with some vittles in case you'uns get peckish on the way."

After she was settled on the makeshift seat, Gordon climbed up by the driver. Arm in arm, Reverend Haskell and Miss Stella watched them off. Mira waved until she couldn't see them anymore. She leaned back against the trunk.

No going back now. She had said vows that promised forever as long as they had the gift of life. She silently prayed for many years for Gordon. She certainly could not imagine being a widow in this wild country.

She grabbed the edges of the box and endured numerous bounces before they left town. When they headed away from any sign of a road around a hill and down into an icy creek bed, she found out why the trunks were tied down so securely. She could have used a rope tying her down. A bad jostle knocked her completely off her crate down in the wagon bed.

The boy looked over his shoulder and laughed as he eased back on the reins to stop the horses.

Gordon climbed over into the wagon to help her up. "Are you all right, Mira?"

"I'm still in one piece. I think." She jerked the quilt up off the wagon bed.

"You best let the missus sit up here with us, Preacher," the boy said. "We ain't to the rough parts yet. Up here you can hold on to her to keep her from bouncin' out."

Gordon glanced at the boy and back at Mira. "John's right. I thought you might not like being squeezed between us on the seat."

John spoke up again. "We ain't so wide. She'll fit with us, but best come along afore the horses get restless."

Gordon tucked the quilt under the rope across one of the trunks. She would just have to take a chance on those frozen toes Miss Stella talked about. Gordon lifted her over into the seat. The boy took a peek when her skirt caught on the back of the seat and hiked up almost to her knees. With a broad smile, he stared out toward the horses.

Her face hot with embarrassment, she yanked at her petticoats and dress tail. Gordon climbed out of the wagon onto some rocks in the creek and waited until she got things back in order before he clambered back onto the seat. They were shoulder to shoulder, thigh to thigh, but that did keep her warmer.

The boy started the horses down the creek.

"Aren't we getting out of the creek?" Mira asked.

The boy gave her a sideways look as if she'd asked why the sky was blue or the sun yellow. "This here crick is how we got to go."

Gordon smiled. "In the hills, creeks are often the best roads."

"Oh."

"The onliest roads," the boy said. "Take a gander around. You see any other way we wouldn't be runnin' into trees?"

Trees did crowd in toward the creek from all sides. "Oh," she said again.

"'Sides, the snow don't build up in cricks. Water washes it down. You just have to hope it don't wash you with it. That's when the tides come."

She remembered Gordon telling her tides were floods. Pokes were sacks. Creeks or cricks were roads. She might have to write all this down. She seemed to have the same as a foreign language to learn.

"We're comin' along to one of them rougher spots," the boy said. "Best hang on, Missus."

She grabbed the edge of the seat. Gordon wrapped his arm

around her and held her close. She felt safe against him and was a little sorry when he took his arm away along a smoother stretch.

To keep from thinking about that, she looked at the boy. "You seem so young to know the country so well."

"I been along here a time or two." The boy kept his gaze on the horses. "My grandpap lives up a holler not far from Preacher Gordon's place." He leaned forward a little to look over at Gordon. "Pap come hear you preach yet?"

"Not yet. But I'm hoping he might soon. Last time I went over to his place he didn't bring his shotgun out with him when he ran me off." Gordon laughed.

"Shotgun?" Again Mira had visions of being a widow in this godforsaken place. "He wouldn't shoot you, would he?"

"He hasn't yet." Gordon didn't sound concerned. "And I've given him several chances. I think he's softening a little."

"If'n I was you, I wouldn't count on Pap goin' soft." The boy laughed and flicked the reins to get the horses out of the creek and onto a trace of a road up through the pines. "He's a mean cuss. Ain't a one of us grandchillun hasn't had him take a stick to us whether we done anything wrong or not. That about not sparin' the rod is the only Bible he will admit to knowing."

"Sounds like someone to stay away from," Mira said.

"Ornery or not, he's family," the boy said. "And I reckon you don't have to worry your head about the preacher, Missus, long as he goes off like as how he's told. I'm thinkin' Pap would sic the dogs on him afore he went to shooting. Lead ain't cheap, and my pap is. Ma says she figures that ev'ry penny he ever come across is hid in his walls somewhere. Says it would serve him right if the rats took a shine to them and carried them off to their rat holes."

"Rats," Mira echoed.

"You ain't got no worry about rats in Sourwood," the boy said. "Plenty of snakes to take care of them in that holler."

Gordon patted her gloved hand. "Don't pay him any mind, Mira. He's trying to pull a rusty on you."

"Rusty?" Mira's head was spinning.

"That's what they call jokes up here. Now behave, John, and quit trying to upset Mrs. Covington."

Mrs. Covington. That sounded every bit as scary as rats and snakes and mountain men with guns. Mira pulled in a little breath to calm down. She was here. She was Gordon's wife. That made her no longer Miss Dean, but Mrs. Covington. She would get used to the name and learn about the place.

After all, she'd been a teacher for years now. She knew about boys and their jokes. Or rusties. In fact, thinking about how the boy was needling her made her feel better. Boys were boys wherever they lived. She'd find a way to teach them and not let them get away with too much.

She sat up straighter and looked around at the snow soft under the pines. It seemed time to change the subject. "It's beautiful up here."

"Ain't nothing but snow and trees," the boy said.

"Beautiful snow and trees," Mira said.

"You'uns brought-in people sure do have funny thinking," John said.

"Fresh eyes. That's all." Gordon squeezed her hand a little. "Just wait until the rhododendron bloom."

"That does sound wonderful." By then she would know the children in her school. By then she might be calling a sack a poke, a joke a rusty, and feeling at home in Sourwood.

She liked looking forward to where they were going instead of seeing where they'd been, the way she had while in the back of the wagon. That was how she should think about her life now. No looking back. Only forward.

14

*G*ordon was usually impatient with the ride from Jackson to Sourwood, but not this time. He liked Mira beside him. They had sat close on the train, but not touching. Now he could feel her next to him. Side by side. That was how a marriage should be. Two people yoked together with common purpose. And love.

Purpose was a good beginning. Love would come. Faster for him than for her. She was still uncertain of this path she'd chosen. And she had chosen it. He hadn't pushed her into it, although he had definitely tried to convince her to come to Sourwood. The Lord had done the pushing for him.

When she shivered, he slipped one arm out of Mr. Bramblett's coat to wrap it around her. When he pulled her close within the warmth of the coat, he was more than a little surprised she gave no resistance.

She was so small, almost fragile, that he felt as though he were sheltering a precious bird. The Lord had put this woman beside him. Gordon did not want to do anything to spoil that.

Mira was his wife in the sight of God and the state once Pastor Haskell recorded their marriage at the courthouse. Gordon could wait until Mira was ready to be his wife in every way.

The Lord taught him patience after he came to the mountains. At first he had been so eager to spread the gospel that he wanted to demand people respond to his sermons. So when they failed to accept the gospel, he had been distraught, sure he had lacked in sharing the Lord's message.

After much prayer, he realized his task was to faithfully sow the seed. Whatever that seed produced was the Lord's doing. Just like John's grandfather. All Gordon could do was show the man he cared enough to share the greatest gift with him. He couldn't force him to open it.

The same was true with Mira. She would have to want to accept the gift of marital love. Gordon was more than ready to embrace that gift. In time, perhaps Mira would feel stirrings of love for him or at least affection.

When they crossed the final creek and topped the last hill, John reined in the horses before going on down into the little valley. The first time the boy had driven him to Sourwood over two years ago, he'd asked him to stop here on the rise to let Gordon peer down at the place. Since then, John always stopped before Gordon asked.

Part of the hill had been logged a few years ago to leave nothing behind but stumps, scattered brush, and scrub pines. The other hillsides rising up from the little settlement of houses along the holler were still covered with trees. Here and there a cabin was visible among them, while other homesites were hidden.

Gordon was thankful the loggers hadn't found their way back to Sourwood, but someday, they would come again with their saws and axes. The standing timber was money, and only the most stubborn landowners like John's grandfather could turn that down forever.

"Seen enough, Preacher?" John asked.

"I never get tired of this view, John." Gordon looked down at Mira. "What do you think of your new home, Mira?"

"Home."

She spoke the word so softly he couldn't tell if her voice held despair, resignation, or wonder.

Gordon had found the mountains full of beauty the first time he'd ridden up into the tree-covered hills. Since then he'd seen some of the ugly too. Many families worked worn-out farms that made it a struggle to feed their children. Some neighbors stayed crossways with each other for some slight or disagreement they might not even remember. Moonshiners were ready to shoot anyone poking around their stills. Typhoid and tuberculosis took an unholy harvest of loved ones. Some in Sourwood had no welcome for the gospel or the man bringing it.

But the beauty of the place never faded in his eyes, and not just of the place, but of the people too. For every person who wished him gone, ten more had held out their hands in welcome. They would welcome Mira too.

"It ain't a bad place, Missus. Plenty worser spots to land on." John grinned over at Gordon. "Whilst I ain't all that ready to wax poetic about it like I've knowed a preacher to do now and again, peppered over with snow like as how it is now does dress it up a mite."

"Oh, but it is beautiful. Which house is yours?" Mira looked at Gordon.

He wished she'd asked which was theirs, but he couldn't expect that before she'd even stepped through the door. "That one toward the middle. The church is right beside it, and the school is going up on the other side of the church." He pointed toward the buildings.

"You oughta get a bell for the church, Preacher," John said. "A church needs a bell."

"That would be fine, John. I'll put it on my prayer list," Gordon said.

"Schoolhouses have bells too," the boy said.

"So they do. Maybe I'll double the bell prayers."

Mira laughed, a sound that made the sun brighter. "You mustn't get greedy."

"The Lord doesn't limit our prayers. He's ready to answer abundantly if it is in his will."

"Yes, his will." Again her voice was barely more than a whisper.

"Don't count Preacher out, Missus. After all, he got them folks down there to build that there church."

"The Lord had more to do with that than me," Gordon said.

Mira kept staring down at the houses. "It all looks so peaceful and warm somehow."

Gordon felt a smile all through him. "Home is supposed to look warm."

John snorted out a short laugh. "You'uns take the cake. Ain't nothin' warm on a froze-up day like this. And I ain't seein' no smoke risin' up out of your chimney, Preacher. You're gonna have a cold house to get home to."

"True." Gordon wished he'd had a way to let someone know when he was coming so they could have had a fire going. Of course, nobody knew he was bringing a wife with him.

"Well, I reckon the two of you will find a way to stay warm until the fire heats up." John grinned and flicked the reins to head the horses down the hill.

Home. Such a beautiful word. And not one that Mira had really known since she left her mother's house six years ago. She had rented accommodations that were never really home, even Miss Ophelia's rooms, a place she liked. She had always considered herself a guest instead of belonging there. Would that be the way she felt here too?

Everything was so different. She couldn't imagine belonging in a log cabin, miles from any town. Other cabins were scattered along the little valley. Smoke did rise from their chimneys to drift up into the blue sky. A few white clouds floated over the hills.

Even though it wasn't that late in the day, the sun was beginning to dip below the tree-lined hills to the west. Night would come early here.

Night. She wouldn't think about that yet.

She had leaned into Gordon's warmth through the long ride and let him cushion the bumps for her. They had shared Miss Stella's ham and biscuits and fried apple pies, with John eating the most. Mira thought that would have made Miss Stella smile. The boy looked so young, more like one of her students back in Louisville instead of someone ferrying people over these rough hills. But perhaps he was older than he looked. He had been ready with his sly remarks about them being newlyweds.

She might as well get used to that. No doubt Gordon's church people would have plenty of teasing remarks for him and many questions about her. After all, he'd left here last week a single man. He couldn't have given them any warning about returning with a wife. Everything was so sudden. Perhaps too sudden.

No sense thinking about that. Better to think about her new home. The cabin might be cold when they got there, but it would warm soon enough with a fire kindled in its fireplace. Where she would be expected to cook. That thought awoke new worries. What in the world would she cook?

Water would have to be carried from somewhere. A well, perhaps. Or a spring. Cool water filtered by mountain rock. That would be better than water from the creek she could see behind the cabin, but that creek would be the only running water in Sourwood. The cabin would have no water closet. Was there an outhouse? The school would need an outhouse. She would insist on that.

One thing at a time. No need to pile up problems that might or might not be there. Well, people did have to eat. A person did have to have water. Did need a water closet or outhouse.

Other people lived in this community. They managed. She took a deep breath. She had faced challenges before. She would face them now.

The boy pulled the wagon up beside the cabin. "Here you be." He tied off the reins and jumped to the ground. Gordon did the same and then helped her down. She climbed up the two steps to a wide porch along the front of the house that had a door and two windows. She hesitated, not sure if the door was locked or, even if it wasn't, whether she should go in before Gordon opened it.

"Best wait a minute, Missus." John caught Gordon's arm and jerked him away from where he had started to untie the trunks. "Ain't you gonna carry your missus into the house, Preacher? My granny says a man has to pack his wife over the threshold so nothing bad happens to the bride."

"Why is that, John?" Gordon asked.

"I don't know. Granny has all kinds of things like that she says keeps away bad spirits."

"I trust in the Lord, not superstition."

John looked troubled by Gordon's words. "You sayin' there ain't no devil to mess with a feller?"

"I didn't say that. But superstitions don't keep the devil or bad spirits away. Trusting in the Lord does that." Gordon's voice had not the slightest shred of doubt.

John shrugged. "Seems to me doin' something simple like knockin' on wood to keep the bad from messing up the good don't hurt nothing."

"Or help anything."

The boy turned toward Mira. "What do you think, Missus?"

Mira had to smile at the look on his face. He obviously believed his granny. Gordon just as obviously thought it was foolish. A believer shouldn't cling to superstition. "Of course, Preacher Gordon is right, but I appreciate your concern for my happiness, John."

She peeked over at Gordon, who had his hands on his hips, watching her. She couldn't quite read his face, but just as she had surprised him on the train by insisting on marriage, she had the audacious desire to surprise him again.

"But . . ." She hesitated, not sure she should let out the words.

A frown creased Gordon's forehead. "But what?"

"I've heard of the tradition of a groom carrying a bride over the threshold with no thought of superstition. Just a fun thing." Her face went hot even in the cold air. Whatever was Gordon going to think of her? She needed to practice swallowing every foolish word that wanted to come out of her mouth.

He did look perplexed for a moment, but then laughed. "Fun is definitely approved by the Lord."

He was on the porch beside her in what seemed like three steps. He shoved open the door and swept her up in his arms. "If the bride wants to be carried over the threshold, then the bride will be carried over the threshold."

Mira hid her face against his shoulder and smothered a giggle. Behind them, John let out a shout. "Whoopee!"

Once through the door, Gordon held her for an extra moment before he carefully set her on her feet and stared down into her eyes.

Mira didn't look away from his gaze. "Thank you, Mr. Covington. I do hope I didn't compound your difficulties in preaching against superstition." Then in yet another audacious move, she tiptoed up to kiss his cheek.

"You are very welcome, Mrs. Covington." His face looked as flushed as hers felt.

"Preacher, you're home!" A little boy ran through the door behind them and skidded to a stop when he saw Mira.

"Joseph." Gordon turned to the boy. "Just the man I want to see."

"She the teacher you been talkin' 'bout?" the boy asked.

"She is. Meet Miss Mira. Miss Mira, meet Joseph, the best fire builder in the hills."

"Hello, Joseph." Mira remembered what Gordon had told her about the boy, but he looked too young to be building fires. What had Gordon said? Six? He was small for that.

Joseph didn't return her greeting as he narrowed his brown eyes and looked Mira over. "She gonna live here?"

"She is," Gordon said. "She's my wife."

"You done gone and got hitched, Preacher?"

The boy sounded so dejected, Mira had to laugh. So did Gordon. "I surely did."

"Aw heck." The boy's lip jutted out. "Now, you won't be no fun no more. Wimmen ruin ever'thing."

Gordon knocked the boy's felt hat off and ruffled his hair. "No talking like that. Who knows? Miss Mira may be out there playing ball with us." He glanced back at Mira. "She's full of surprises."

"Preacher," John called from the porch. "We best get these trunks unloaded. I need to be on my way so's I can make it to Pap's afore the edge of night."

"Be right there, John." Gordon picked Joseph up and lifted him until they were face-to-face. "You haven't gained an ounce since I left. You forget to eat?"

"I et. Some."

"I brought you some peppermints." Gordon put him down. "You get that fire built and I'll dig them out of my trunk." He shook his finger at him. "And you be nice to Miss Mira."

Joseph gave her another unhappy look, but he followed Gordon out. Mira hoped it was to get wood for the big fireplace on the back wall. John was right. The house was cold now that the flush from her audacious behavior had faded.

She twisted her lips to hide a smile. Miss Ophelia would be amazed, and Miss Stella would be proud. Maybe marriage wasn't so bad. She let her gaze slide over to where she could see a bed through an open door.

One worry at a time. First a fire. Then water and food. Before long she'd have to find the outhouse. Best think on necessary things before worrying about nighttime.

15

ira watched as Joseph laid the wood in the grate. Cold ashes covered the stone bottom of the fireplace.

"Don't you need to remove the ashes?" Mira asked.

"Not less'n they's too high." The boy frowned over his shoulder at her. "Don't you know nothin' about startin' a fire?"

She could almost see him wondering what kind of teacher she could be if she didn't even know how to build a fire. "When I was your age, we had a woodstove, but my mother wouldn't let me build the fire."

"Huh. Guess as how you was babied some."

"I did have to carry in wood." Mira hoped that would gain her a little respect.

"Did you chop it too?"

"No."

"Girls. Spoilt like babies." His voice had all the little-boy disgust for girls.

Mira had to smile. "Chopping wood might be more fun than cooking and washing dishes."

"I can reckon so on that. Did your ma cook on that stove you had?"

"She did."

He turned back to ease some bark and wood chips under the bigger log. "Ma heared of them woodstoves you kin cook on. She cut a picture out of a newspaper and pasted it up on the wall. Said it don't hurt to dream some."

"She sounds wise."

"I reckon she's the smartest woman in the hills 'cepting maybe Granny or Aunt Nicey Jane."

"I'll look forward to meeting her," Mira said.

He stacked another small log on the wood in the fireplace.

"Where are the matches?" She straightened up to see if they might be on the split log mantel over the fireplace. Nothing there.

"Don't need no match. I done run over to Mr. Frank's house and he give me some fire."

Joseph went out on the porch and came back holding a smoking iron pot out in front of him. With tongs beside the fireplace, he picked up the coals and stuffed them under the wood. Flames flickered up from the bark and kindling.

He must have seen her ineptitude for fire building because he said, "That there pan is for fetching coals. Preacher has to do it all the time 'cause he wanders here and there in these hills, but be best if you keep the fire going. Makes things a sight easier, but I reckon you could get coals from anybody around, were you to need to. Cheaper than matches."

"Thank you, Joseph. Preacher Gordon said you were a wonderful help to him and I'm sure you will be to me too."

He hung on to his scowl, but Mira could tell her words pleased him. "I reckon I kin help you if'n you need me to."

"I'm sure I will. Especially after school opens."

"I ain't too good at figuring and reading."

"You will be," Mira said. "But I was talking more about helping with the fire at school or with the other children's names before I learn them."

"School will have a stove for heating up the place, Preacher says. We done have one in the church. My grandpa carried over wood for it yesterday."

"That's nice. Thanks to him, the church will be warm tomorrow. Does your grandfather build the fire there on Sundays?"

"No'm. My brother Willard does that, but says he'd be glad to give over the job to me soon's Ma thinks I'm big enough."

"Doesn't she know you build fires here for Preacher Gordon?"

"Yes'm, but she holds more confidence in Willard doing it right for church."

"I think you must have done this fire just right." Mira held her hands out toward the flames. "Thank you."

The boy cocked his head to the side, studying her. "Was the preacher just funnin' about you playin' ball with us'ns?"

"I have been known to pitch a ball a time or two." Mira smiled at him and almost got a smile in return. She looked around. The trunks were beside the door, but Gordon was nowhere to be seen. "But where is Preacher Gordon?"

"Heck, I plumb forgot. I was supposed to tell you he was headin' over to check on what they been doin' to the schoolhouse. Aimed to see if the roof was tight."

"I see." Mira looked toward the window and was surprised to see a girl's face pressed up against the glass. "Oh."

The girl jerked back. Mira rushed to the door, but she was already off the porch and running away. She stopped behind a tree between the cabin and the church to peek back at Mira.

Joseph followed Mira out on the porch. "Don't let her bother you none. That's just Ada June."

"Go tell her to come warm by the fire."

The boy gave Mira a look. "I ain't sure you want me to do that."

"Why not?"

"Well, Ada June, she's liable to track mud in your door and sometimes she ain't too clean. She's half-wild. Lives in the woods about as much as she lives at Aunt Dottie's." He sounded disgusted. "And she'll expect that dog of hers to come in with her. She don't go nowhere without that dog, and he can be a mean one."

"Does the dog bite?"

"It would if she told it to."

"Does she tell it to?"

"Not unless somebody is pokin' fun at her."

"Then we won't poke fun at her." Mira watched the girl and remembered what Gordon said about her on the train. "Go on. Ask her to come in. Tell her the dog can come too."

"I kin tell her." The boy let out a sigh. "But that don't mean she will. And even if she did, she probably won't say nothing. I ain't never heared her say the first word."

"Preacher Gordon told me she talked to him."

"I reckon everybody talks to Preacher Gordon."

"I see, but I want her to come in whether she talks or not. Please, go tell her I want to meet her. And that I'll give her a piece of peppermint." She'd seen Gordon put the sack of candy in the cupboard after he gave Joseph a couple of pieces.

"That's my peppermint." Joseph's scowl was back.

"I think it's Preacher Gordon's peppermint." Mira gave him her teacher look that showed she meant business. "I won't give her all of it unless you keep acting contrary."

Joseph's shoulders drooped, but he climbed down off the porch and went toward the girl. Mira expected her to run, but instead she came out from behind the tree and stood up tall staring first at the boy and then Mira. She must think Mira was sending Joseph to run her off.

She was a head taller than the boy, with long legs that had to be freezing under her loose skirt. Her ragged coat looked too small. A black-and-white shepherd dog leaned against her legs until Joseph got close. Then the dog stood up, its head and tail rigid. Mira couldn't hear the dog, but she had little doubt it was growling.

Joseph stopped several feet away and yelled at the girl. "That dog bites me, my pa will shoot it."

"Joseph!" Mira called to him. "None of that."

The girl stood as still as the dog for a long minute and then put her hand on the dog's head. It sat down beside her.

Joseph took a step closer to Ada June. "Preacher's missus wants you to come to the house. If'n you want to."

She stayed still.

"Tell her about the peppermint," Mira said.

Joseph looked over his shoulder at Mira. He was scowling again before he turned back to the girl. "She aims to give you a piece of my peppermint."

That must have done the trick because Ada June started toward the house. The dog stayed in step with her and paid no attention to Joseph now as the boy scurried ahead of them. He stopped at the edge of the porch and watched the girl's dog with wary eyes.

She didn't even glance his way as, with no hesitation, she came up the steps to stand in front of Mira. Her face was as solemn as a church deacon announcing a funeral service. Mira smiled at her, but her face didn't change.

The girl's boots were crusted with snow. The dog's feet would be wet too. But Mira couldn't worry about that. She could clean floors.

"Stomp the snow off your boots and come in." Mira pushed the door open wide.

Instead of stomping, the girl pulled her feet out of the boots and stood in stocking feet.

"That's fine. You can warm up by the fire while I get you some peppermint." Mira stepped back to let her in.

Ada June didn't move as she pointed at the dog beside her. She didn't say anything, but Mira had no problem knowing her question.

"Your dog can come in too."

A smile slipped across the girl's face as she and the dog moved past Mira into the house. Mira looked at Joseph. "Aren't you coming, Joseph?"

"I ain't going in there with her and that dog."

"Her dog seems to be behaving nicely," Mira said. "Come on in and you can have another peppermint too."

"I ain't no donkey to be led by no carrot." Joseph glared at her.

"All right. You can get more peppermint another time, but I wish you would come in now."

Joseph shook his head. "I ain't a-gonna do it. Things you don't know being a brought-in person."

Brought-in. She supposed that was more than true. "That's why I need your help."

"I reckon I can tell you one thing afore you take up with that Ada June. My big sister says her ma was a witch and that could be Ada June will grow up to be one too. That maybe even now she might render spells or something."

"I'm not listening to talk like that, Joseph. So you'd best head on home until you can stop carrying tales."

He suddenly looked worried. "You won't tell Preacher what I said about her, will you?"

"Not if you promise never to say that kind of thing again."

"I reckon I kin promise that." He turned to start away and then looked back at her. "But you best be careful in there with that dog." He hesitated and then muttered, "And her."

"I like dogs." Mira chose to ignore his muttered words as she kept her voice cheerful. "I'll tell Preacher Gordon how helpful you were building the fire. I hope you'll come back soon."

"I'll come when Preacher's here." He went a few steps before he called back to her. "Best put some more wood on the fire afore it burns down so's he won't get cold."

She watched him trot off. So much for making her first friend here in the hills. She hoped to do better with Ada June.

When she turned to go inside, Ada June was in the doorway. Her face was stiff, not smiling and not frowning. Instead, she had the kind of look a child learned to wear when she put up barriers to any kind of feeling. Her brown eyes narrowed as she peered past Mira at the trees.

The girl seemed poised on the doorstep like a bird unsure of whether to stay perched or fly away. When Mira stepped toward her, she moved to let Mira go in, but she stayed at the door. The dog watched her, as ready to run as she was.

Mira kept her voice cheerful. "Shut the door please, Ada June. We need to keep the cold air out and the warm air in."

The girl whipped her head around to stare at Mira, her eyes wide. She was a pretty girl, but Joseph was right about her not being clean. She had smudges of dirt on her cheeks, and the clumps of nearly black hair poking out below her knit cap needed a shampoo. Her coat had a long rip on one side and had lost all but one button. Her stockings puddled around her ankles, and her knees peeked out below her faded blue skirt. She wore what looked like men's socks on her hands.

"Joseph told me your name." Mira stepped around the girl and closed the door. "Come over to the fire and warm while I find that peppermint."

She wanted to put her hand on Ada June's arm to encourage her to move toward the fire, but she didn't. She feared if she touched her, the girl would be up on her toes and gone. Instead, Mira went toward the cupboard. She had to show some trust, but she held her breath, listening.

The girl must have moved as silently as a cat. When Mira turned back with the peppermint, Ada June and the dog were by the fire.

"Joseph said I should put more wood on the fire," Mira said. "Do you think I should do that now?"

The girl pulled the socks off her hands, picked up the iron poker propped by the fireplace, and poked the logs. The fire crackled and flared up. Then she picked up the chunk of wood Joseph had left on the hearth and laid it on the fire. Sparks flew up the chimney.

"Be careful." Mira didn't like how close the girl's skirt swung toward the flames.

Ada June brushed her hands together and then rubbed them off on her skirt before she held her hand out for the candy. A smile slipped across her face when Mira gave it to her. The dog's ears perked up as he sat down by the girl.

"I'm sorry I don't have anything for your dog. I just got here and don't know what Preacher Gordon might have for a dog to eat." Or them either, but that was a problem for later. Right now, she wanted to see the girl smile again.

The girl shrugged and broke off a piece of the candy stick. When she held it out to the dog, he sat up on his haunches and pulled his lips back to show his teeth.

"Is he grinning?" Mira asked.

Ada June nodded and did better than smile. She giggled as she let the dog have the candy piece. He sat down and wallowed it around in his mouth.

That made Mira laugh. "What's your dog's name?"

The girl's smile vanished as her body stiffened.

"Never mind," Mira said. "Maybe Preacher Gordon can tell me. Does he know?"

With another nod, the girl's shoulders relaxed. She licked the peppermint stick and stared at the fire.

Mira tried to think of something that could be answered with a nod or shake of the head. "Would your dog let me pet him?"

After Ada June studied her a moment, she touched the dog's head and then pointed at Mira. The dog stood up and trotted to Mira. His tail swept back and forth once, then stopped as he seemed to study her as intently as the girl had.

Not sure if she was risking her hand or not, Mira squatted down in front of the dog and stroked him from head to tail. When she scratched him behind the ears, the dog's tail gave a couple more wags before he went back to sit by Ada June.

"Thank you," Mira said. "I've always wanted a dog or a cat, but never had a place for them." She looked out the window. "Until now, I suppose."

The wood popped in the fireplace as Mira let the silence fall between them. The girl seemed content with no talk as she licked the peppermint. The dog lay flat on the floor and huffed out a breath.

Mira tried to be as comfortable with no words in the air as she fought the need to say something. Anything. It wasn't that she didn't know about silence. Other than when she was teaching, her life had mostly been silence. But now everything would be changed. Had already changed.

She needed to find an outhouse and more wood for the fire and to see if they might have something to eat besides peppermint. Joseph's peppermint. She hoped the boy would come back and let them try again to be friends. But she wasn't sorry she had invited Ada June inside.

She looked around for a clock. One sat on a bookcase, but the pendulum wasn't swaying. Run down. She'd have to ask Gordon to wind it.

Where was Gordon? He had carried her over the threshold, hauled in the trunks, and disappeared. At the school, Joseph had said.

School. She could talk about that. "Are you excited about having a school?"

The girl's eyes lit up as she nodded. She seemed ready to smile but then pointed at the dog.

Again, Mira knew what she wanted to know. "I don't think a dog can come to school."

The girl frowned.

"I can tell he's a very nice dog, but if you brought your dog, all the other children would want to bring their dogs, and that might make teaching or learning difficult."

Her face tightened even more, but not from anger. Instead she looked almost sad.

"He can wait for you outside." She wanted to say he could come in the school just as she'd told Joseph the dog could come in the cabin. Paw prints across the floor didn't matter, but the school was different. She couldn't do that. Could she? Maybe Gordon would have an answer.

Ada June put the last of the peppermint in her mouth and pulled the socks back on her hands. The dog was up at once to follow her to the door.

"I hope you'll come back to see me," Mira said as the girl opened the door, stepped out on the porch, and slid her feet into the boots that were much too big. "You and your dog."

She looked around and said, "Bo."

Mira felt she'd been given a gift. "Yes. You and Bo."

Something close to a smile touched the girl's lips before she went off the porch and walked away without looking back. Gordon was headed toward the cabin from the other direction. He called to Ada June. The dog looked back at him, but the girl kept walking without giving the first sign she heard him.

16

Ada June heard Pastor Gordon, but she pretended she didn't. She wasn't sure why. She'd been watching for him to come home for days. But she wasn't ready to talk to him with the teacher woman listening. Not yet.

She had told her Bo's name, but that was a short little word that didn't take much effort. Bo had wagged his tail when the woman patted his head. So, it was only right she knew his name. The woman had known Ada June's name, but she hadn't spoken her own name.

Joseph said she was the preacher's missus. If that was true, then she'd be Missus Covington. A fancy name like that suited her. She was pretty and appeared to like smiling. She hadn't frowned once. Excepting at Joseph when he said those things about Ada June's mother.

She didn't care what Joseph said. He wasn't nobody she had to worry none about. She could flatten him with one punch. She smiled, thinking how Joseph had been afraid to get close to her. He deserved being flattened for what he said about her mother. Or what he said his sister said.

That would be Ruby. She weren't but a year or two older than Ada June, if she was counting right. Her ma had taught her how to count. She'd have taught her how to read too if'n she'd lived long enough.

She bet that ol' Ruby didn't know how to number her fingers or what letter her name started out with. Ada June knew that. *A*, then came *B*. Bo started with *B*. She looked down at her dog matching his steps to hers.

He wagged his tail the way he always did when she was thinking about him. Dogs didn't have to have things said out loud. A dog knew what a person was thinking and whether it was for good or bad.

Pap Leathers had taught her that. He said he didn't even have to whistle up his old hound when he wanted to go hunting. The dog just knew. She wished she could remember that dog better. And Pap too. She couldn't hardly pull up what he looked like anymore. 'Course he'd passed on before her ma did.

She wasn't going to forget her ma. She couldn't ever forget her. She kept telling herself that, but sometimes when she tried to picture her mother, everything went shadowy. Except for the last, that part she sort of wanted to forget.

But one thing for sure, Ruby didn't know nothing about her ma. Nothing. She didn't have no call saying Ada June's mother was a witch just because she liked being off to herself out in the woods. What if she did dig up roots to make concoctions? They weren't witches' brews. Sometimes Ada June sort of wished they were and that her ma had taught her some spells she could throw on such as Ruby and that Connor.

Preacher Gordon would tell her that wasn't right thinking, but she figured he'd never had anybody call his ma a witch or try to chase him down to rub his face in the snow or the mud. And now this teacher woman was telling her that dogs couldn't come in the schoolhouse.

A few tears slipped out of Ada June's eyes. She did so want to learn to read, but she needed Bo with her. She wasn't sure she could make herself walk into the schoolhouse without Bo beside her.

Bo jumped up to try to lick her face. She sat down on a stump without even brushing the snow off and buried her face in his fur. She should have talked to Preacher Gordon. He might have helped her figure out what to do. He was always telling her she shouldn't keep worrying about the bad, but to think on the good.

She raised her head to let Bo lick the tears off her cheeks. The good. Her times with her mother before the end were good. That was what she would think about. A smile edged out on her face as she remembered trailing after her mother through the woods as she pointed out this or that wildflower and spoke their names. The jack-in-the-pulpit always made her mother smile when she lifted up the top of the flower to show the little preacher. If Ada June found one of those flowers this spring, she'd call it Preacher Gordon in the pulpit.

She laughed and Bo did his doggie grin that had surprised the teacher woman. His tail whipped back and forth. Bo was good.

That first summer after her mother died, Ada June had found the pup huddled back under a shelf of rocks. He weren't big as nothing and had beggar lice in his fur and a tear in one ear. Appeared to be pitched aside as worthless. Not a hunting dog. Not a fighting dog. Naught but a runt.

Something like she was. Considered good for nothing except packing in wood and such as that. Back then she was passed around like an unwanted stepchild nobody was glad to see on their doorsteps. So, half the time, she stayed out in the woods.

That day she found Bo, he hadn't give her no welcome either. He'd give out a growl when she reached under the rocks for him. He was too little to hurt her none, but she pulled her hand back anyhow. She didn't want him mad at her from the first. Instead, she stretched out on the ground to wait him out.

She talked to him. Her voice was some rusty, seeing as how she hadn't said one word to anybody since her ma died. But she warmed up her mouth talking to that pup. She told him all about her mother and how she hadn't ever had a pa so far as she knew.

She told him it didn't do no good to always be growling and hating on folks, even if you was thinkin' they were growling and hating on you. She promised never to growl at him. Ever.

After what seemed like forever, he crept out from under the rock and cuddled up next to her like he knew she needed him as much as he needed her. She named him Bo right off. She didn't know why. The name just came to her.

They hid out in the woods for days. Nobody missed her. They were always forgetting whose turn it was to take her in. Whenever she saw Miss Effie or Miss Nicey Jane leave their houses to work in their sass patches or go visiting, she would sneak inside to snatch a hunk of cornbread or a couple of biscuits. She split what she got with Bo.

She was happy. The pup was happy. And she figured them that were passing her around were happy too that they didn't have to worry with her. She might have carried on that way all the summer, but Miss Effie wasn't like Miss Hallie and Miss Nicey Jane. She kept count of when it was her turn to see to Ada June. When she checked with Miss Nicey Jane, who had the turn before her, she found out Ada June hadn't been at nobody's house for some time.

Ada June, lurking around behind Miss Nicey Jane's, aiming to grab some vittles, heard them jawing at one another about it. She hadn't been close enough to hear all they said, but she knew it had to do with her.

She ought to have run back out into the woods, but she didn't have that good of sense then. So wasn't nothing for it but to go on up to the porch when Miss Nicey Jane hollered for her. She could've pretended not to hear, but even then, without good sense, she knew doing something like that generally made things worse.

With Bo hid inside her shirt, she crept on up to the porch something like Bo had crept out from under that rock shelf when she found him. She weren't expectin' to find love like as how Bo had though. She figured Miss Nicey Jane would be making her go find a switch.

Instead, both her and Miss Effie appeared to be struck speechless when they saw her. She smiled a little, remembering the looks on their faces. She had surely been a sight. She hadn't so much as washed her face in the creek for days. They didn't stay speechless long.

"Land's sake, Ada June. What have you been into?" Miss Effie had a way of sounding cross, but Ada June wasn't ever afeared of being at her place.

"I ought to wear you out." Miss Nicey Jane propped her fists on her hips. "Ain't no need you actin' like some kind of wild child."

Ada June had stared down at the ground. She wasn't fearing a whipping. It was what they would make her do with Bo that had her heart thumping as she held him under her shirt.

"I reckon she's my worry right now, Nicey Jane." Miss Effie had come down off the porch. "I'll tend to her."

Ada June peeked up at her. Miss Effie had a way of looking at her like it didn't much matter whether Ada June said anything or not. She already knew what she was thinking.

"Come along." She stalked off down the trail without so much as a fare thee well to Miss Nicey Jane.

When she hurried after her, Bo made a couple of yips. Miss Effie kept walking like she didn't hear. But instead of heading up to the swinging bridge over the creek, she led the way right down to the water.

"Wash the dirt off'n yore face."

After wading out into the creek, Ada June splashed water up on her face.

"Now come on back here and show me what you got hid in your shirt."

Ada June wanted to run the other way, but she knew better. Not that Miss Effie ever took a stick to her, but she expected any young'un to do as she said. Tears mixed with the water that hadn't dried on her face as she stepped out of the creek, pulled Bo out of her shirt, and held him out for Miss Effie to see.

"Well, leastways it ain't a polecat." She took him out of Ada June's hands and held him up to study him.

Bo must have known he needed to act nice. His tail whipped back and forth to make his whole body wiggle. He wasn't much bigger than Miss Effie's hand. Ada June hadn't washed herself, but she had let Bo play in a creek to get the mud off'n his black-and-white fur. So, at least he was clean. Miss Effie set some store on things being clean.

"Ain't much to him." When Miss Effie set Bo on the ground, he ran straight to lay on Ada June's foot.

"You give him a name?" Miss Effie asked like as how she expected an out-loud answer.

Ada June had the feeling Bo's fate rested on whether she could speak his name. Her heart beat up in her ears as the pup nibbled on her big toe.

Miss Effie's voice was soft. Not hardly cross sounding at all. "Can't have no dog around less'n it has a name."

Ada June's jaws felt locked up like she'd just eaten a green persimmon. She stooped down and picked up Bo. Him licking the tears off her cheeks got her mouth loosened up somehow.

"Bo." His name wasn't much more than a whisper of breath, but Miss Effie heard her.

"A good enough name. Bring him on. He can sleep on the porch." She started up toward the swinging bridge.

Ada June didn't follow her.

Miss Effie looked back. "Come on, girl. It's nigh on supper-time."

Ada June stayed where she was. Miss Effie stopped and frowned at her. "All right. Long as we ain't having a thunder boomer, you can sleep out there with him." She shook her head and started walking again. "Lord help me. I must be goin' soft."

After that, Miss Effie didn't make her go anywhere else until

Mr. Luther came beggin' her for Aunt Dottie the next year. Ada June had cried a little. She liked Miss Effie and she was going to miss her knowin' what Ada June was thinking without her saying anything out loud. Fact was, she hadn't ever said another word after saying Bo's name, but she reckoned that was enough.

That had been nigh on four years ago. Thinking back on it, Ada June sort of wished she'd given Miss Effie a hug before she went with Mr. Luther. Not that Miss Effie was much of a hugger, but when Ada June looked back at her, she had the corner of her apron up wiping something out of her eyes.

17

Bo pulled on her sleeve and yipped to bring her away from her memories. He was right. Light was fading fast and she had promised Elsinore she'd pack in wood for her. Besides, she was cold. She stood up and brushed off the back of her skirt. It was wet. She couldn't stay out all night even if she went up the hill to the place under a ledge where she slept some before winter set in. Better there than at Aunt Dottie's if Mr. Luther was around. She wished he'd stay off logging somewhere till spring, but he did come back to the house regular.

Ada June had carried in water and packed in wood aplenty for Aunt Dottie before she grabbed a cornpone and took off that morning. Mr. Luther hadn't been there then, and Aunt Dottie was feeling right pert. She said she could handle Emmy Lou even if her belly was swelled big with another baby coming.

Aunt Dottie wasn't so bad. She never said so, but she understood Ada June was better off staying out of Mr. Luther's way. Could be he was supposed to come home today. If so, best for her to wait and slip in at Aunt Dottie's after dark. That gave her plenty of time to go see if Elsinore had any fixings for supper and scraps for Bo. A peppermint stick didn't keep a girl's or a dog's stomach from grumbling.

Even before she got to Elsinore's front stoop, she could hear the baby's squalls. The door was unlatched, so Ada June pushed it open and hollered a hello.

"Come on in, Ada June." Elsinore's voice was so weak that Ada June barely heard her over the baby crying.

Bo followed her inside. The cabin was just one room, with a ladder up to a loft. A bed was against the wall on one side, and a table and some shelves were on the other. A line was strung down the middle of the room where Elsinore used to hang a quilt to divide off the bed. Now she used it to hang the baby's nappies to dry.

Elsinore had the bedcovers pulled up to her chin, while beside her, on top the covers, Selinda kicked her feet and waved her little arms. Elsinore patted the baby's belly, but Selinda didn't appear to pay that much mind, as she kept screaming.

"What's wrong with Selinda?" Funny how Ada June didn't have no trouble at all letting words out here at Elsinore's, while it had been all she could do to force out Bo's name with the teacher woman listening.

"Wantin' her pa, I expect." Elsinore looked pale in the dim glow of the dying fire across the room.

"Mr. Benny didn't make it home today then." Ada June played along with her pretend.

"He must have got delayed. I imagine he'll make it in tonight."

"That could be."

Ada June went over to the bed and picked up the baby. She opened up her coat and held her close to get her warm. Her wails changed to whimpers as she started sucking on her fist. She needed a new nappy. Ada June didn't know which to do first. Get the baby's bottom dry or build up the fire.

"You shouldn't oughta let your fire burn so low, Elsinore."

"I was gonna get up and poke it in a minute."

Sometimes Ada June felt like the grown-up instead of Elsinore. Of course, Elsinore wasn't all that much older than she was. Sixteen to her ten, but she was a mother and oughta act like one.

Aunt Dottie said Elsinore couldn't help how she was right now. That sometimes a mother got low after a baby came, especially when her man went off to who knew where. She reckoned the girl needed to go back to her ma's. Trouble was, Elsinore was like Ada June and didn't have a ma to go to. Even if she did, likely she wouldn't go. She aimed to be where Benny could find her if he decided to come on home.

Sometimes Ada June wondered if that was how her ma was. Waiting for Ada June's pa to show up. But then her ma had never once mentioned the first thing about her pa. The one time she could remember asking about a pa, her ma told her some things were better not pondered on.

She sighed and put her mind back on what needed to be done here. Best to take care of the baby's bottom first. Wet bottoms weren't good. She knew from how her own bottom still tingled with cold from sitting in the snow a bit ago.

Bo settled over by the fireplace while Ada June took a clean nappy off the line. Elsinore must have come up with enough gumption to do some washing before she took to her bed.

Selinda smiled when Ada June made some clucking sounds at her. She didn't have but a hint of hair, but she had the bluest eyes ever, even bluer than Elsinore's. Blue eyes were always filled with light, while eyes brown like Ada June's looked like a storm might be coming.

"You think she'll have yellow hair like yours?" Ada June handed the baby over to Elsinore. She started whimpering again as she rooted her head against Elsinore's breast.

"Could be, I guess. Or could be brown like Benny's." Elsinore ran her finger over the baby's head.

"I hope it's yellow like yours. You have the prettiest hair."

"Benny always says so." Elsinore pushed a few strands back from her face. "You come around tomorrow we'll have us a hair-washing day. I got a little soap left from the last making."

"Aunt Dottie says washing your hair in the middle of winter will make you catch the grippe."

"I reckon she might know, but I'm thinkin' running 'round out there in the snow with no leggings on till your knees turn purple might do it first." Elsinore made a face. She never liked it when Ada June told her something Aunt Dottie said.

Ada June shrugged. "I don't have no leggings, but I ain't got the grippe. I reckon we could sit by the fire till our hair dried out."

"You'll have to pack in the water. I wore myself out bringing in water for the wash this morning." The baby began fussing louder.

"Looks like Selinda might be hungry." For sure Ada June was, but she'd best fix the fire before she went to searching for any food.

With a heavy sigh, Elsinore opened up her dress and put the baby to her breast. "I'm some worried my milk ain't coming good for her."

"You eatin' anything? Aunt Dottie says a mother has to eat to keep a baby fed."

"Aunt Dottie this. Aunt Dottie that," Elsinore grumbled. "She ain't no Miss Nicey Jane, you know."

Ada June ignored that and went out the back door to get some wood. She was happy to see a big stack of fresh-chopped wood. She picked out a couple of chunks and gathered up a handful of chips off the ground. Back inside, she didn't have any trouble getting the fire going.

Once it was flaming up, she grabbed her skirt, pulled it tight against her legs, and turned her back to the fire to dry out the snow damp. "Mr. Horace bring you the wood?"

"He did. Said it was his Christian duty to see that Selinda didn't freeze, with it so cold right now."

"Did you let him come in?"

"'Course not." Elsinore frowned. "Folks would be talking."

"I reckon so."

Folks were already talking. Horace Perry lived up the hill from Elsinore with his ma still. Aunt Dottie said he had to be forty if a day and far as she knew never did any courting. But now he seemed to be ready to get in line for Elsinore if she ever admitted that her Benny must have gone off and died somewhere. But Ada June wasn't about to tell Elsinore any of that.

The cabin was quiet except for the crackle of the fire behind her and the sound of the baby suckling. Bo looked to be sleeping there beside her. Ada June's stomach growled to remind her she hadn't eaten anything since sunrise and here it was past sunset.

"That Mr. Horace bring any fixings for your supper?"

"He brung some milk over in that bucket on the table and his ma sent a poke of food. I ain't looked in it. Wasn't feeling pert enough to eat." She held up her hand, palm out toward Ada June before she could say anything. "I know. Aunt Dottie says I should eat. Horace said his ma says the same."

She pulled the baby away from her breast and laid her on the bed again. She pulled a corner of the cover over the sleeping baby.

Ada June looked to where the poke sat on the table but didn't say anything. It weren't proper to go into somebody's house and eat their food if they didn't offer, but a glass of milk and one of Mr. Horace's ma's biscuits sounded good. Bo must have read her thoughts again because he lifted his head and whined. His belly was probably doing some growling of its own.

Elsinore must have read her thoughts too, because she smiled. "If'n you rinse out that nappy and bring a bucket of water in from the creek, we can look and see what Granny Perry sent."

Ada June picked up the nappy and headed out. Bo got up to follow her.

"Oh, and Horace brung an extra poke with ham trimmings in case you come by with that dog of your'n." Her smile got wider. "I'm half a mind that he's thinkin' on courtin' you when you add on another year or two."

"I ain't got no mind to be courtin' any man. Especially a feller old enough to be my grandpap." Sometimes Elsinore could say the dumbest things. "But were I to take a courtin' mood, a feller that took to Bo might be in the front of the line."

Elsinore's laugh started a coughing fit.

Ada June frowned back at her. "Your cough don't sound no better. Maybe you oughta go get Miss Nicey Jane to make you a tonic."

Elsinore spit into a handkerchief she pulled from under her pillow. "I might do that if'n I get enough strength to make the trek to her house a-packing Selinda."

"I could carry her for you."

"You are a right smart help, Ada June." Elsinore looked toward the door Ada June had opened a crack. "I'd be plumb grateful if you'd get that water and then some wood packed in afore you have to run on home. Looks to be dark a falling. Yore Aunt Dottie'll be wondering where you've got to."

"She don't waste time worryin' over me. I could stay here with you and keep the fire up."

"No, Benny might come in and he wouldn't want no company at his homecoming."

Ada June knew she'd say that, but she still asked from time to time. Elsinore needed help more than Aunt Dottie, but when a person didn't want you, a person didn't want you. Leastways she had got that Horace to bring Bo some food. Ada June didn't have the first doubt about who had done the asking and who Horace was wanting to court were the door opened up to him.

18

Mira bowed her head as Gordon thanked the Lord for their food after they sat down at the small table. When he said amen, she kept her eyes on her plate and picked up her fork. It was awkward being married to a man one didn't know very well.

Then again, a first night married to any man whether one knew him well or not might feel awkward. She and Edward had spoken of marriage. Illness had stolen those plans, but she had no assurance she would not have felt some of the same apprehension if they had shared a first night together.

Of course, their love would have softened the strangeness of being alone together. Alone together for all time. Sitting across the table from Gordon, somehow the alone felt stronger than the together.

Gordon had brought in a dish of chicken and dumplings he'd gotten somewhere while checking out the schoolhouse. Mira found dishes in the cupboard to set the table while Gordon went to a spring to fetch drinking water. Then he carried in another bucket of creek water for washing up. A round kettle hung over the fire to heat the water. An iron teakettle was on the hearth and a metal coffeepot sat on a trivet.

"For coffee when we have it," Gordon said.

"Do we have it?" Mira had not seen any in the cupboard. After Ada June left, she had taken stock of the kitchen area to find only a few basic necessities.

"I brought some from the city." He motioned toward a trunk by the front door. "Coffee is one of my vices."

She feared asking him what his other vices might be. She mentally shook her head at the foolish thought. That had simply been a turn of phrase. Gordon was a preacher. A fine man. He wouldn't be surprising her with unknown vices.

What of her own vices? She had married Gordon for purely selfish reasons. With no place to live or means of support, she had jumped into this marriage thinking only of herself. And now she was totally unprepared for being a preacher's wife or any man's wife.

The very thought made the few bites she'd eaten churn uneasily in her stomach. She cut a dumpling into two smaller pieces and then cut it again.

"Are the dumplings not to your taste?" Gordon looked across the table at her. He'd cleaned his plate with enthusiasm.

"No, no. They're delicious." She put down her fork. "I suppose I'm just tired."

Why had she said that? When one was tired, the obvious solution was bed. Her heart skipped a beat.

"Mountain cooking might not be fancy, but it's nourishing." He pushed away his plate.

Mira looked toward the fireplace again. "I fear I have no idea how to cook over an open fire."

"Don't worry about that. I've learned a little since being in the mountains. I can cook our meals if need be." He sat back in his chair. "It would be nice to have a cookstove."

"Joseph said his mother cut out a picture of one from the newspaper and hung it up. She told him there was no harm in wishing."

Gordon laughed. "If we do get one, we'll invite her to come cook on it."

The way he said "we" pleased Mira. "But do you think that might make her think we were trying to be above the other people here?" If he could use "we," so could she.

"They will be happy for us. For you. We will never completely fit in. The people here might love us, might be glad we're here, but we will always be flatlanders and a little different."

"Brought-in," Mira said.

"Right." Gordon smiled. "Just like John said."

"And Joseph." Mira pushed her plate away too. She didn't like wasting food, but with all the butterflies in her stomach, she couldn't eat another bite. "I'm afraid Joseph was upset with me when he left. You will have to try to make amends for me."

"Oh? That doesn't sound like Joseph."

"He didn't want me to share his peppermint with Ada June."

"The rascal. I'll have a talk with him."

"Don't do that. He would be even unhappier with me. He already thinks I've ruined any chance of you ever being fun again."

"He's at that age where he'd just as soon all girls lived on the far side of the hill."

Mira had to smile at that. "I suppose so. For a certainty, he was not happy to see Ada June. He acted afraid of her or at least of her dog."

"That doesn't surprise me. Did Ada June come up to the house?"

"I enticed her inside with the promise of the peppermint and the fire. She was half-frozen."

Gordon raised his eyebrows at Mira. "She must have really wanted that candy. Did you let the dog in too?"

"I did. I hope that was all right."

"That's fine. With Ada June, if you get her, you get her dog. I'm sure she was happy to see you, especially if she knew you were the new teacher. I think I told you on the train how excited she is about going to school."

"I know." Mira frowned. "I'm afraid she wasn't happy with me, the same as Joseph, when I told her she couldn't bring her dog to school. I can only imagine how haywire things might go if all the children brought their dogs."

That made Gordon laugh again. "A schoolroom of hounds might be a little unsettling." His smile died away. "But I'm not sure Ada June will come without her dog."

"I did get that feeling."

"I suppose she didn't talk to you and tell you that." He said it as fact.

"No, but she listened and nodded a time or two. And then she told me her dog's name before she left. Bo." Remembering that still made Mira feel good.

"That's wonderful." Gordon reached across the table to touch Mira's hand. "I knew you would be a perfect teacher for our Sourwood children."

Mira pulled her hand away. "I don't know how you can say that after I met two of those children and both left unhappy."

He sat back, not seeming upset she had not welcomed his touch. "A teacher has to let children understand the rules. Joseph will come around, and if Ada June said even one word, that means she likes you. She needs people to reach out to her with affection." He blew out a sigh. "Something few here in Sourwood have tried to do. As if the child bears fault for her mother's odd ways that made her an outcast in the community."

"What odd ways?" Mira thought of Joseph saying the woman was a witch.

"I've heard snatches of gossip, but none of that matters now. Ada June isn't her mother. She wants and needs love." He beamed at Mira. "I'm glad you are ready to offer that to her."

"If she'll let me."

"It's a beginning. Just as we have a beginning together." He studied her face.

"Yes," she murmured as she stood up to clear the table.

She looked at the food still in the pot and then at what she hadn't eaten on her plate and had no idea what to do with either of them. She felt lost. Everything seemed out of her control.

"I don't know what to do," she said.

The despair on Mira's face stabbed Gordon's heart. He wanted to hold her, comfort her as he might an unhappy child.

Instead, he took the plates out of her hands. "Here. Let me."

He dumped the scraps in a bucket by the door. If Ada June came by tomorrow, her dog would be happy to clean them up. After putting the dishes in the dishpan and a top on the dumplings, he looked back at Mira. "We can have the leftovers for breakfast unless you would rather have something else."

She still stood in the middle of the floor as though afraid to take a step in any direction. "What else is there?"

"Eggs. Bacon. Applesauce. Honey." He kept his smile gentle and moved back to stand in front of her. "You will feel more at home soon."

"I'm sorry." She blinked to keep back tears.

"Shh." He touched her lips with his fingers for a second. "You just need to settle in. School won't start until the middle of February. That will give you time to get to know the people."

"But what if I always say the wrong things?"

He searched her face. "Did you say the wrong thing to Joseph?"

"Maybe. I thought it was what had to be said because he wasn't being nice to Ada June. I told him to go home."

"Sounds like the right thing. And what wrong thing do you think you said to Ada June?"

"I don't know if it was a wrong thing, but I made her very unhappy when I said her dog couldn't come to school with her."

"Do you expect to always make your students happy?"

"Of course not." A frown puckered the skin between her eyes.

"I'm glad to hear that, because you will have to be stern to keep some of these children on task. Most have never been to school. They won't know what is expected of them."

"I don't know what's expected of me."

He knew she was talking about more than teaching now. If only he could take her in his arms, but he doubted she would welcome his embrace. He didn't know how love had bloomed in his heart so quickly. He simply knew it had. That had to be a gift from the Lord. He would pray a little love might sneak into her heart for him, but that was too much to expect this night.

"Nothing is expected of you except what you want to freely give," he said. "It has been a long day. You're tired. I'm tired."

She stared down at the floor. "Yes."

He couldn't help himself then. He put his fingers under her chin to tip up her face so she would have to look at him. In the dim light from the kerosene lamp, her eyes were a dark mix of green and brown. She didn't pull back from him. For that he was thankful.

"You can go to bed. I'll fix a pallet out here where I can keep the fire burning."

Relief mixed with doubt on her face. "You can't sleep on the floor."

"I've done it many times. You can't imagine the places I've slept here in the mountains. In barns. On porches. Just about anywhere I had room to lie down before the good people here helped me build this cabin last year."

"Oh," she said. "If you're sure."

"I'm sure. We need a quiet night." He really didn't think they had to worry about anyone bothering them, as was the mountain custom.

He'd witnessed several serenades, or shivarees, where neighbors and relatives showed up in the middle of the night at a newly wedded couple's home to make all manner of noise. Surely they had gotten to Sourwood too late in the day for the news to spread that he had brought home a wife. Besides John, who had hurried on to his grandfather's place, Joseph and Ada June were the only ones to meet Mira. Ada June wouldn't tell anyone anything, and if Joseph worried he'd done something wrong to bring on Mira's scolding, he might not tell anybody either.

"The quiet is peaceful," Mira said.

"And we can hope it stays that way since I haven't told anyone I not only brought a teacher home with me but also a wife." He smiled.

"You didn't tell anyone you got married?" Mira looked confused. "But don't you think you should? What might they think if they see me here at your house?"

"Don't worry. I won't keep you a secret long. I'll introduce you at church tomorrow morning, but I thought it best to wait, with the hope we won't have to worry about a late-night serenade tonight."

"A serenade?"

"Have you ever heard of a shivaree?"

"Oh my. Would they do that?" Her eyes widened. "To their preacher?"

He nodded with a wry smile. "Probably especially to their preacher. They will think it's hilarious. But I can hope they will be somewhat more civilized about it than I have witnessed at other times. For one thing, they won't be expecting any moonshine from me, but I did buy some extra candy in Jackson to hand out should they decide to serenade us."

"Serenade? You mean sing to us?"

"Serenade is what they call a shivaree here in the hills. But no singing. Just noise and plenty of it. They do whatever they can to disturb a honeymoon night. Bang pan lids. Shoot up in the air. Shout. Laugh. But all in good fun."

"Doesn't sound like much fun to me. For us."

"I guess not." He shrugged. "But if they do come serenade us the way they do their relatives when they marry, it will show they think of us as belonging here." He squeezed her shoulder slightly. "Don't look so worried. It will be fine. Besides, I'm sure all will be quiet tonight."

19

Mira had been too nervous to eat. Now she was too nervous to sleep. How would she ever fit in here at Sourwood? With Gordon?

He had lit a candle and led her into the adjoining room, where he took a pillow and cover off the bed, then to her embarrassment, pointed out the chamber pot before he said good night. After he went out and shut the door, the air seemed colder at once. That was to be expected, with the fireplace in the other room.

The only furniture was the bed, a chest, a bench at the foot of the bed, and two wooden boxes. A small pillow on one box indicated it must serve as a chair. Set on its end, the other box made a table. Gordon had placed the candle there. Her trunk was against one wall.

After she spread Miss Stella's quilt on the bed, she traced the connecting rings. A wedding ring quilt, the woman said. Two lives connected by marriage.

She wished Miss Stella was there to tell Mira what to do. Not that she didn't know what was expected. But she was in one room, Gordon in the other. Not exactly the way a wedding night was supposed to be.

Mira pulled her nightgown and robe from her bag. She slipped off her dress, but left the nightgown folded. After she loosened her corset, she pulled on the robe over her petticoats in case Gordon was wrong. Joseph had gone to the neighbor's house for coals. He was bound to have talked about the preacher's missus schoolteacher who didn't even know how to build a fire.

People talked about their preachers. And their teachers.

She pulled off her shoes but left on her stockings for warmth. When she knelt on a small rag rug beside the bed to say her prayers, the cold soaked up through the rug, her petticoats, and her robe.

Her teeth chattered as she whispered, "Dear Lord, forgive my failings and help me be a blessing to the children here. Watch over Gordon and Joseph and Ada June."

She paused as so many needs ran through her mind. *Help me find a way to live here. Help me know how to be a preacher's wife. Give me joy in teaching these children. Show me what you want me to do.* She didn't speak any of them aloud. The Lord knew her thoughts.

After she blew out the candle, she crawled under the covers and sank down into a soft featherbed. With no windows to let in any moonlight, the room was very dark, and she wished for the glow of the candle flame again. The night pressed down on her like an extra-thick blanket.

She took a long breath and then another. She was not afraid of the dark. Besides, the black of the night wasn't total. On the far wall a few rays of moonlight squeezed through cracks in the chinking between the logs. No doubt the cold came in as well.

Still, she should be warm. She had on her thick robe and at least two covers besides Miss Stella's quilt, but she couldn't stop shivering. If only she'd pulled her mother's bluebird out of her bag, she could hold it and not feel so alone.

Her mother's, or perhaps Miss Stella's, words were suddenly sounding in her head. *"You don't have to be cold. You don't have to be alone."*

She could go be by the fire. With Gordon. Where a wife should be.

Shivers continued to shake her. The cold wasn't all coming from the outside. She felt cold inside too. *"Till death do you part."* This would be no way to live forever.

Gordon had given her such a tender look when he assured her things would get better. That she would settle in here in Sourwood. He was so kind.

What if their neighbors did show up in the middle of the night to serenade them as Gordon had said? They might come right through the front door without knocking and find their newly married preacher sleeping on the hearth. She could easily imagine what the people would think about that. What kind of bride made her husband sleep on the hearth? She might turn out to be as much of an outcast as poor Ada June's mother.

"Then do what needs doing." The voice was in her head again. This time it might be Miss Ophelia. Mira had no doubt that she was always ready to do whatever needed doing. Then again, she had not accepted the challenge to go west with the man she loved. Perhaps her voice was demanding Mira accept the realities of this challenge simply because she knew the cost of refusing to accept her own.

Mira had turned down Gordon's offer to let her come teach without accepting what she had earlier called his ridiculous proposal. Instead, she told him she wanted to be married. Ridiculous or not, she had not changed her mind. She did want to be married.

Whether she ever felt the heart-stopping love for Gordon that she had once known for Edward made no difference. She had been so young then. A woman her age now didn't need to be swept away by dreamy romance. She could be glad for kindness. Glad to be tied to a man who loved the Lord. Glad to have a purpose in life through teaching and, yes, being a preacher's wife, even if she wasn't yet sure she could live up to that task.

She folded back the covers and got out of bed. The floor was icy cold under her stocking feet. The tiny slivers of moonlight through the small holes in the chinking had been swallowed by the grainy black of almost total darkness. She felt along the side of the bed to its end, where she banged her knee against the bench.

She stood still and tried to visualize the room. The bed sat in the middle of the back wall. The box chair and her trunk were to her right. The chest was against the other wall. The door was across from the foot of the bed.

Nothing was between her and the door except her hesitation. A faint light shone at the bottom of the door and through the cracks between its boards.

The door groaned on its hinges when she eased it open. The room in front of her glowed with warmth as flames licked up from the log in the fireplace and invited her closer. Gordon was stretched out in front of the fire. Mira waited for him to sit up and look her way, but he didn't move. His breathing sounded relaxed and even. He must be asleep.

A new shiver shook through her as she hesitated again. Then, as if she were being pushed, she moved toward him. She barely kept herself from trying to knock away the hands she imagined propelling her across the room. Miss Stella would be smiling. Miss Ophelia wouldn't be smiling, but perhaps she wouldn't be frowning either. She might have that knowing teacher look when a student met her expectations.

Mira eased down to sit on the floor behind Gordon, who lay on his side facing the fire. She watched him in the flickering firelight. He was a nice-looking man. Not that outward looks mattered. The inner heart was more important. He had shown her that already, with his love for the Lord and the people here at Sourwood.

He must be very tired to sleep so soundly on the hard floor. She'd thought he would wake when she sat down beside him. Maybe that was the Lord's doing to make it all Mira's giving.

She lifted the edge of the wool blanket over him and scooted under it. The floor was cold even this close to the fire, but his warmth drew her as she moved closer to him until their bodies were touching.

Waking then, he turned toward her and murmured, "I must be dreaming."

"I was cold," she said.

He reached to pull her close. She surrendered to his warmth.

He had to be dreaming. Her touch, her whispered words a dream. But if so, he didn't want to wake up. Mira letting him hold her. Her lips looking so inviting in the firelight.

"The bed would be more comfortable than the floor," he said.

"Are you going to carry me over another threshold?" The whisper of her words was sweet against his cheek. "To keep away the bad spirits?"

"We don't need superstitious ways for that. We have our faith in the Lord. But that doesn't mean we couldn't have fun the way we did earlier."

"Fun. It's been so long since I've thought about having fun. It was always what was expected of me. What I needed to do."

He heard something in her voice on those last words. Tears perhaps. He moved a bit to better see her face. "I don't want to be a 'need to do' for you. I hope you will instead think of being with me as a 'want to do.'"

"That does sound best." She shifted her gaze from his face to the ceiling and fell silent.

He couldn't let her end their talk. "Then what is this? This coming to lie beside me. A 'want to do' or something you felt duty bound to do?"

"Duty bound." She echoed his words without looking back at him. "I suppose a wife does have a duty to her husband."

"And a husband to his wife. But being together only as a duty sounds like an unhappy union."

"Till death do us part." The words were whispered almost as if she meant them for her ears only and not his.

A dozen things came to mind for him to say, but he had to let her choose her own words without trying to put his into her mind. The crackle of the fire and the tick of the clock he'd wound earlier were loud in the silence between them.

Finally she spoke. "A week ago, my life was settled. Duty bound, as you say, to my students. I took pleasure in reading, walking out through the neighborhood, and of course, my church."

"All those pleasures can be had here as well as—"

"Let me finish."

"I'm sorry. It is a fault I have. Wanting to encourage others to see things my way. Please say whatever is on your heart."

"Thank you." Another slight pause before she went on. "A week ago, if I had thought of you at all, it would have been as someone I vaguely remembered from school. And now I'm next to you in a cabin in a place I can barely imagine. In one short week, my whole life has been turned upside down."

"Are you sorry?"

"I don't know yet, but I'm hoping not to be."

"Is that why you're here beside me? Because of that hope or because of the feeling of duty to a husband?"

She turned her eyes back to his face then, to look directly into his eyes with something near a smile on her face. "Neither."

"Then what?"

The trace of smile in her eyes slid away. "I told you. I was cold."

"I will gladly offer you my warmth." He tucked the blanket around her and pulled her closer.

She relaxed against him, her head on his shoulder. He almost didn't hear her next words.

"And I felt so very alone."

"I have often felt the same, even in the midst of people. But now we can be two joined as one the way the Scripture says. Whatever you need, I will try to supply."

His pulse was a drumbeat through his body. She was so beautiful in the firelight. So small and fragile feeling in his arms. He would have been more than ready to fight dragons for her. He smiled at his foolish thought. There were no fire-breathing dragons, but he had no doubt other challenges would come her way here in Sourwood. Their way. Those he would meet and, if need be, fight with the Lord's help.

"I want to do the same," she said. "But I have no idea what is expected of a preacher's wife. Of any wife."

"I expect nothing but your willingness to be here beside me."

"I am willing." She put her hand on his cheek then, and he wished he had taken the time to shave the stubble of his whiskers. But he had not expected her to be ready to embrace him so soon.

He stared into her eyes. "May I kiss you, Mrs. Covington?"

She closed her eyes and lifted her face toward his in silent answer. Warmth flooded through him down to his toes as he touched his lips to hers.

At the sound of a gunshot and then banging on the door, Mira's eyes flew open as she jerked back. "Oh!"

He held her for another moment. "Appears I was wrong about the people not disturbing us tonight." He breathed out a disappointed sigh before kissing her forehead and sitting up. "Guess we are going to be serenaded after all."

20

*M*ira wasn't sure if her heart beat so madly because of the pounding on the door or because of the nearness of Gordon. She had given herself over to his embrace when the noise startled her.

He kept his arms around her even after it seemed that any second the door might crash open. Then he brushed his lips across her forehead before, with a disappointed sigh, he sat up and jerked on his shoes. "First thing Monday I'm putting shutters on those windows."

"Windows?" Mira jerked around to see faces pressed against the windowpanes. She scrambled up off the floor and tied the sash of her robe tighter. "They won't hurt us, will they?"

The hammering on the door was joined by clanging noises outside, along with whoops and yells.

"Not intentionally." Gordon stood up beside her. "Actually, being serenaded on your wedding night is a way they show affection for their family and friends. But you might not find any of it enjoyable." He looked worried as he peered down toward her.

"What should I do?"

"Keep smiling even if they bring out the wheelbarrow."

"Wheelbarrow?"

"Sometimes they insist the groom take the bride for a ride down the road in a wheelbarrow."

"You have to be kidding." Outside the yells were louder. Dogs barked and howled.

"Afraid not. But if we can handle it with grace, that might go a long way to you getting a good beginning here. They might understand if you refuse to take part, but they can be more than insistent. Sometimes they don't take no for an answer." He looked from her to the door, where the insistent thumping continued. "I'd better go talk to them before they break in the door."

She hesitated, wanting to trail after him, while at the same time not wanting to be anywhere near whoever was outside. At the last second before Gordon opened the door, she snatched up the blanket and pillow off the floor and ran to pitch them on the bed. If only she could see somewhere to hide, but from the sound of the men storming through the front door, hiding would be futile.

She barely had time to send up a frantic prayer before Gordon was in the bedroom's doorway to bar the way of several men. Even though the light was dim, she had no trouble seeing the men's grins as they peeked past Gordon.

"Come on, Preacher. We gotta see the little woman." The men grabbed Gordon's arms to yank him away from the door. They stared at Mira and whistled. "You done gone and got you a pretty little thing."

Two of the men pushed Gordon back to keep him from stopping two others from coming into the bedroom.

Gordon sent an apologetic look toward Mira as he said, "Easy, boys. She's a city girl and not used to all this rowdy carrying on."

"We ain't aiming on hurtin' her. We just gonna let you take her for a little ride in the moonlight. Be right romantic." One of the men holding Gordon laughed.

The two who confronted Mira didn't look much older than some of the boys she'd taught in Louisville. Time to quit running scared and take some control of what happened. She squared her shoulders and held out her hand to stop them before they reached for her. "Preacher Gordon says you want to serenade us. So which of you is singing?"

She almost laughed as they gave each other a confused look.

One of them said, "I don't know nothing about any singing."

"You do know that is what serenade means." She gave them a stern look and they backed up a step.

A man yelled from the other room. "Come on, boys. Let's get on with it. The sun's liable to be up afore we're done if'n you keep draggin' yore feet."

The two young men moved toward her again, but without enthusiasm. She smiled at them, understanding their dilemma. "Tell you what. You take one arm"—she looked at the boys—"you take the other, and you can escort me outside. Looks like a beautiful night."

The taller boy gingerly put his hand on her arm. "No use you fightin' us."

"Why would I want to fight two strong boys like you?" she said. "But I do wish one of you would sing something. Don't you know any mountain songs?"

"I know plenty," the younger-looking boy said. "My ma, she commences to singing in the morning soon's she gets up and keeps on most of the day."

"I can't wait to hear her. What's her name?" Mira smiled over at Gordon and the two older men as they moved past them toward the front door.

"Hallie. Hallie Shelton."

"And your names? If I'm going to be walking barefoot out into the snow with a couple of boys, I should at least know your names."

The boy who talked about his mother said, "I'm Vernon." He nodded toward the other boy. "That one's Billy Ray."

"All right." Mira stopped at the door. "Since I don't have on any shoes, Vernon and Billy Ray, you two can carry me across the snow to this means of conveyance you intend Preacher Gordon to push me around in."

"Conveyance?" one of the men behind them said. "What kind of word is that?"

Gordon laughed. "She is a schoolteacher."

When the two boys looked unsure of exactly what to do, Mira showed them how to grasp each other's arms to make a way to carry her. They bent over to let her perch on the makeshift seat. She put her arms around their necks. "Let's go, boys. The people are waiting."

The men behind them made a snort of amusement or perhaps irritation. One of them said, "Preacher, I think you might have brung home some trouble for yoreself with this one."

Mira hid her smile when Gordon answered the man. "Trouble can bring with it a blessing sometimes."

Outside, whoops and catcalls greeted them. The waxing moon coupled with the snow-covered ground kept the night light enough to see.

People crowded around the porch. Some boys peered down from a tree and a few men watched on horseback. Children ran helter-skelter around in the snow. Yells came from all sides. In a barking frenzy, two dogs ran up to the boys carrying her. She pulled up her feet to keep away from any snapping teeth.

Mira forced a big smile on her face. While she felt as though she'd landed somewhere on the other side of the world instead of just on the other side of the state, she intended to hide that. She didn't want to lose any chance of gaining her future students' respect or friendship on her first night in Sourwood.

The wooden wheelbarrow, a rickety-looking affair, had a good layer of snow in it. She considered insisting it be dumped but thought that might be pushing the boys' forbearance too much. She wouldn't freeze with her layers of petticoats and the robe before this whole foolish ordeal was over.

Laughs sounded all around when the boys jerked their arms

out from under her and without ceremony dropped her into the wheelbarrow. She supposed they needed to save a little face after transporting her like a princess to her carriage.

She didn't let her smile waver. In fact, when she looked behind her to see the men ushering Gordon off the porch toward her, her smile turned into laughter. It was all so ridiculously silly. The whole week had been one unbelievable thing after another, from Gordon's audacious proposal to her even more audacious insistence later on the train that they marry.

In a few short days, she'd gone from being a prim spinster schoolteacher to a new bride in her petticoats sitting in a wheelbarrow that didn't look sturdy enough to hold the snow in it, much less her. With only her stockings on, her feet were freezing. She laughed about that too. She'd rarely given anyone a glimpse of her ankles, and certainly never her toes.

If only Miss Ophelia could see this. She might join in with the noisemaking. The thought of Miss Ophelia shouting and banging two pan lids together made Mira laugh more. She pulled up the edge of her robe to wipe laughter tears off her cheeks without even thinking about the ankles she might be revealing.

Several women, snuggly wrapped in cloaks, stood a little back from the wheelbarrow. Some were smiling while others stared at Mira as if not quite sure what to make of her.

Mira could say the same of them, but that wasn't really true. She had met many women with children, and while looks, speech, and dress were different, people were people. She wanted to tell them that, but freezing in a pile of petticoats in a wheelbarrow didn't make the best soapbox. So, she just kept laughing.

One of the women frowned. "What's wrong with her?"

An older-looking woman shook her head. "I'm thinking the preacher must have give his missus a swig of moonshine."

Their moonshine had nothing to do with the moonlight falling around her. Thinking that brought a new fit of laughter.

"I'd be a mite surprised were that the case. Preacher can't abide the stuff. Always after the menfolk to pour it out," another woman answered. "Could be she's feelin' merry because she's married."

"True enough," the first woman agreed. "She ain't all that young. Into her twenties, I'm reckoning. Preacher must have took pity on her."

Considered an old maid without hope at twenty-five. Mira tried to stifle her laughter, but another giggle escaped. Hadn't she considered herself a lifelong spinster before last week?

"Are you all right, Mira?" Gordon looked concerned as he leaned close to speak to her. He probably thought she was having hysterics.

Maybe she was. She nodded as she grabbed the sides of the barrow. "I'm ready for a ride."

The road, if one could call it that, was frozen ruts with plenty of even rougher rocks. More than once she thought she might bounce right out of the wheelbarrow as Gordon pushed her past the church and a building he said would be the school.

One room. She looked around at the children trailing them. One room wouldn't hold them all.

Joseph ran along beside Gordon. She looked for Ada June and finally caught sight of her on the other side of the little valley. She and the dog beside her weren't much more than shadows against the trees, but Mira knew it was her. Maybe because the girl looked as alone as Mira had felt earlier.

No way could she feel alone now with all the people needling Gordon as he pushed the wheelbarrow. Mira tucked her feet under her robe in a vain attempt to warm her toes. She kept her smile, but the laughter was gone, frozen out by the cold and the sight of that lone figure.

Back at the house, she hoped everybody would leave after their fun. But even before Gordon lifted her out of the wheelbarrow, several women went up the porch steps and in the door. No invitation needed, it seemed.

Gordon carried her to the porch, which started up a new round of *whoops*. "You're freezing." He set her down on the porch steps. "I'm sorry about this."

"It's all a little strange, but then what hasn't been this last week?" She kept her voice low as another woman pushed past her up the steps to go inside. "Are they all going to go in with us?"

"Just a few women. The men will hang around out here."

When she went up on the porch, he didn't follow her. "Aren't you coming?"

"Not unless you need me to."

She heard the reluctance in his voice. "I guess you are supposed to stay out here while I face the mountain woman jury."

"They all love you already."

"They think I'm definitely odd and that you only married me because you took pity on this hopeless spinster."

Gordon laughed. "You are an old bride by Sourwood standards." He leaned close to whisper. "If they knew the whole story, they might be even more surprised."

"That can be our secret."

Joseph pulled on Gordon's arm. "Preacher, the men are some worried that you ain't givin' them anything to drink."

"If they're thirsty, water will have to do." Gordon looked down at the boy. "They know I don't keep the hard stuff."

"I reckon so, but no cider or nothin'?"

"I bought a load of candy in case this happened. I'll get it and you can hand it out." Gordon gave him a stern look. "But you can't try to keep it all to yourself the way I heard you did your peppermint earlier today."

Joseph peeked over at Mira. "I reckon she done told you ever'thing I done."

"Was there more to tell?" Gordon frowned at the boy, then looked at Mira. "Mira?"

She kept any hint of a smile off her face. She knew what was worrying Joseph, but they did have an agreement. "I did tell him you didn't want to share the peppermint, but I also told him what a fine fire builder you were. Anything else you think he needs to know, you'll have to tell him yourself."

"I don't reckon I know of nothin' else." The boy looked down and shuffled his feet.

"I know if I don't get inside, my toes are going to break off." Mira turned toward the door.

"Hey, Preacher, we're gettin' mighty thirsty," one of the men called.

"The spring's right over there." Gordon pointed.

Another man called out. "You want us to get them wimmen outa there so's you and the little woman can have some lonesome time together?"

That started up all the uproar and laughter again. The way things were going, nobody was going to get any sleep before sunrise.

"Come on, Joseph. I know where he stashed the candy." Mira glanced back at the boy. "You can bring it out to Preacher Gordon. He better stay out here and deal with these scalawags."

And she would just have to deal with whatever the women inside had waiting for her.

21

Mira swallowed down a nervous giggle as she went through the door. She needed to quit acting like a silly schoolgirl.

Inside, three women stood around the table, but where were the other women? She was sure more had gone into the house.

One of the women shook her finger at Joseph. "What you doin' in here, Joseph Oran Foster? This here is woman time and we don't need to have no menfolk spoilin' it."

"He ain't much of a man," another woman said.

"I reckon not, but he still needs to get on out of here." The older woman glared at Joseph. "Your ma oughta kept you home in bed. Or did you sneak out without her knowing?"

Joseph backed up. "No'm, Granny Foster. I ain't wantin' to be in here, but Preacher Gordon told me to get something for him."

"Then get it and be off with you."

"The preacher's missus has to get it for me." He gave Mira a look of near desperation.

The cabin felt warm after the cold outside. The women had put more wood on the fire and lit the lantern on the table. Mira's hands and feet ached as they began to thaw. She fumbled at the cabinet door and pulled out the bag of candy. She had wondered why Gordon had bought so much. If it was meant to sweeten up the people and convince them to head home, she hoped it served its purpose.

But the women had shed their wraps and didn't appear to have any thought of leaving. The hard candy pieces clattered as Mira emptied them into a small tin bucket. She searched for a bowl to keep some for the women, but the shelves were bare. She was almost positive a few dishes were there earlier. Why would Gordon have moved them?

"Has you lost something, dearie?" one of the women said.

She sounded amused, but when Mira turned to look at her, no smile showed on her face that looked to have all hard edges. She was so thin her dress hung loosely on her. She had gray hair tucked up in a bun, as did both the other women watching Mira.

"No, no. I was just going to put some of this in a bowl, but I don't see one." Mira held out the candy.

The woman Joseph had called Granny Foster took the bucket from Mira, spilled a few pieces out on the table, and shoved it at Joseph.

"Now get on out of here," she told him. "And be sure you don't do no lollygagging afore you give that to the preacher." She was tall and spare, without the first sign of grandmother plumpness.

Joseph wasted no time doing as she said, although he did manage to pop a piece of the candy in his mouth before he went out the door.

Another woman took Mira's arm. "Come over to the fire, Missus Covington, so's you can warm yourself whilst we talk." She looked more grandmotherly, with a few plump curves and almost white hair.

"Oh please, call me Mira." She sat in the chair the woman indicated and smiled, even though she thought she might have more to worry about in the midst of these stern older women than when she'd faced down the two boys.

"Is that short for something?" The woman stood over Mira, perhaps to be sure she didn't attempt an escape.

"Almira. I was named after my grandmother." Mira sat back in the chair and hoped all their questions would be as easy to answer.

"On your ma's side or your pa's?" the thin, shorter woman asked.

"My mother's. I never met my grandmother, but Mother said she was a good woman."

"It's a fine thing to come from good stock." The woman beside Mira must have decided Mira was going to stay put. She moved away to settle in the rocking chair.

Two younger women came out of the bedroom to join those around Mira. One of them was obviously in the family way. Both had wide smiles. Mira couldn't imagine what they could have found in the bedroom to be so amusing. Or perhaps she didn't want to imagine what they might be thinking.

The expectant woman lowered herself down into one of the chairs the women had pulled over from the table for this fireplace meeting. The larger white-haired woman, who seemed in charge of the proceedings, rocked back and forth as the others found their places. Joseph's grandmother sat in the only other chair they had. The other young woman plopped down on the floor. That left the thin older woman standing. Mira was sure she was the one who had thought Mira might have been nipping moonshine when they were outside.

Mira stood to offer the woman her chair, but with a shake of her head, the thin little woman squatted down, seeming comfortable with that position. None of them showed any sign of leaving. Outside, the noise had died down except for a burst of laughter now and again.

Inside, the women's stares were more than a little unnerving. With their silence twanging in her ears, she tried to think of something to say. Anything. She pulled in a little breath for courage.

This was her house, whether it seemed like it or not. Time for her to act the hostess instead of a scared stranger.

"You know my name. I'd like to know yours." Smiling, she looked at Joseph's granny. "Are you Mrs. Foster?"

"Effie Foster." No lift of lips softened her face. "Joseph belongs to my oldest boy."

"I reckon telling names is a good place to start." The woman in the rocking chair leaned forward. "I'm Nicey Jane Callahan."

With her smile even brighter, Mira turned to her. "How nice to meet you. Gordon told me how helpful you've been to him."

"I just do what the Lord leads me to do." An answering smile slipped out and settled in comfortable lines on Miss Nicey Jane's face.

The thin, little woman squatted down by the fire spoke up next. "I'm Hallie Shelton. Glad to have you here with Preacher Gordon."

"Mrs. Shelton. Is Vernon your son?" When the woman gave a little nod, Mira went on. "He told me you sing daylight to dusk. I hope you will teach me some mountain songs."

"That Vernon is a talker." She narrowed her eyes and peered at Mira. "Is you a singer?"

"Not a good one, but I enjoy singing hymns at church. And children sometimes learn more quickly if you set something to song." Mira sang the first few letters of the alphabet.

From the puzzled look on her face, she wasn't sure the little woman had ever heard them before. She should have sung *a* is for apple, *b* is for bread, and gone from there. She had so much to learn. Not just about the children but about the adults too.

The woman sitting on the floor smiled at the older woman. "That's the alphabet Miss Mira will be teaching our young'uns." She turned toward Mira. "I'm Mathena Brown. My husband, Frank, and me live just over the way from you."

"Oh yes. Joseph said he got some coals from your husband to start our fire. Thank you. The house was really cold when we got here."

"Folks are good to share what they can," Mathena said. "Joseph told us about Preacher Gordon showing up with a schoolteacher and wife. We wanted a teacher something awful, but it come as some surprise he married to get one."

Mira just smiled. She wasn't about to tell these women how right Mathena was.

The woman went on. "You and Preacher Gordon know each other for a spell?"

"We went to school together years ago." Nothing but truth in those words, even if they did skip over quite a bit about how well they knew each other.

Mira turned toward the other young woman who looked decidedly uncomfortable in the cane-bottomed chair. She had her hands cupped around her unborn baby. "Are you all right, miss?"

"Me?" The woman let out a long sigh. "I will be if'n this babe ever decides he wants to be born."

Mathena reached over and patted her friend's belly. "He's liking it in there." Then she looked at Mira. "This here is Dottie Slade. She's done got one young'un."

"Is Ada June watching Emmy Lou?" Nicey Jane asked.

"No. Luther come in. He's back at the house with my little one." She went on quickly before any of the other women could say anything. "He weren't wantin' nothing to do with serenading, he said, and Emmy Lou, she sleeps the best. Never wakes up once she's tucked in till mornin' comes."

"I saw Ada June across the valley tonight. She looked so alone. I wondered why she didn't come over to be with the other children." The women looked at Mira as if she'd said something odd, perhaps because they wouldn't know she'd met the girl. "She came by the house earlier."

"Ain't no wonder about any of that," Dottie said. "She don't get on with other kids so good. But the girl does set quite a store by Preacher Gordon, and she's been pinin' for a schoolteacher. Never knowed anybody to want to read so bad."

"That could be because she won't talk to nobody," Nicey Jane said. "Leastways not so much."

"She'll say something now and again," Dottie said.

"To you. Not to the rest of us," Mathena said. "Where is she tonight? You didn't leave her up there with Luther, did you?"

A shadow seemed to settle over the women when Mathena said that.

"No, no. She don't come around much when he's about. The two of them don't gee-haw."

A whisper of relief went through the women.

"Awful cold for her to sleep in the woods tonight," Effie Foster said.

"I 'spect she's down there with Elsinore, poor girl. She can't get over the baby doldrums," Dottie said.

"How old's her Selinda now?" Mathena answered her own question. "Three months, I'm guessing. Plenty old enough for Elsinore to pull herself together."

"The baby blues can grab a woman and hang on," Effie said. "Missing Benny like she does makes it harder."

"Took me a while to get back on my feet after Emmy Lou," Dottie said. "That's how come we took in Ada June." She kept stroking her belly. "And I didn't have no worries about Luther going off and forgetting the way home like as how Benny must have done."

"That boy ain't never coming back. He's done gone on to meet his Maker or I miss my guess," Mathena said.

"It's hard when a woman don't know for sure one way or the other." Hallie Shelton shook her head. "I hear Horace Perry is hanging around her place, hoping he might get invited in."

"He's a mite old for her," Dottie said.

"But a good man," Nicey Jane said. "A woman in need can't always be picky."

A woman in need. Those words poked Mira.

"Come, come, girls." Effie Foster frowned. "We aren't here for gossiping. We're here to give Miss Mira a good start."

Hallie grinned at Mira. "You ain't already in the family way, is you?"

The warmth heating Mira's cheeks had nothing to do with the fire. Before she could answer, Nicey Jane spoke up. "Now, Hallie, you know better than that. We're talking about the preacher here."

"He's a man, ain't he? And appears to be still full of vinegar." Hallie laughed. "I'm thinkin' the first song I might need to teach you is a lullaby, Miss Mira."

"I'd love to learn that lullaby, Miss Hallie," Mira said.

"You can teach one to me, Hallie," Dottie said.

"We better wait on the song teaching and get on with things here, else the morning sun will be in our eyes going home," Effie said.

"True enough." Nicey Jane pointed toward the door. "Mathena, will you fetch our bundles over there?"

"Do you need help?" Mira started to get up.

"I can get them." Mathena waved her back to her chair as she got to her feet and headed toward the door. She came back holding several cotton sacks and a bundle. She handed them around to the women.

Nicey Jane took charge again. "You go ahead, Dottie, so's you can get on home if'n you need to."

Dottie handed Mira a small newspaper bundle. "I didn't have much time to get anything together since, as Mathena said, we weren't expectin' Preacher to show up with a bride, but I'm hopin' you'll have some need for these blossom seeds. I collected them from my patch last fall. Mostly zinnias. Not much good for anything but lookin'."

"I love flowers, Miss Dottie." Mira took the package, careful not to let any seeds spill out. "Thank you so much. I hope you'll help me know when to sow them this spring."

Dottie's face bloomed with a smile. "I'd be pleased to do that, Miss Mira. Now I reckon I'd better head on up the hill."

"If Ada June ain't out there to walk with you, you tell Billy Ray I said for him to see you there," Effie said.

"Ain't no need in that," Dottie said.

"You do as she says," Nicey Jane ordered. "We ain't wantin' to be worryin' about you stumblin' and fallin' whilst you're baby carrying."

Effie followed Dottie out to make sure her son went with her. Nicey Jane nodded toward Hallie. Without a word, she jumped up to hand one of the bags to Mira, then ignored the empty chair to squat by the fire the same as before.

"I hope there are songs in this bag," Mira said.

"Ain't no way to put them in a poke," Hallie said, but she was smiling. "But could be it'll sweeten up yore voice."

Mira pulled out a quart jar of honey. "Oh my. This is wonderful."

"You can thank my young'uns when school commences. Them bees left some stingers in the boys."

"I will be sure to thank them. What a special gift." Mira held the jar out. The light from the fire made the honey glow.

Effie came back from the door. "I guess I'm next. I told Nicey Jane we might oughta wait until later when we had more time to get things together."

Nicey Jane shook her head. "Wouldn't have been no serenade that way. Had to be tonight to make sure to give the preacher's bride a proper welcome."

"I ain't saying you weren't right, Nicey Jane, but it did make for a scramble to come up with a proper gift." Effie looked irritated for a second before she shrugged. "But here you go, Miss Mira." She reached into her bag and pulled out a jar to hand to Mira. "Some more sweetening."

Mira set down the honey and held up this jar. "Blackberry jam?" When the woman nodded, Mira went on. "That's wonderful. My favorite. And I suppose you picked the berries yourself and made it."

"That is how it's done," Effie said. "Come July I'll tell Joseph to show you some patches where you can pick some and make your own jam."

"I'd love that. I hope you'll share your recipe."

"You need a recipe to make jam?" Hallie gave her a look. "Kin you cook at all?"

"Some, but I've never cooked in a fireplace."

"Don't you worry none, honey," Nicey Jane said. "We been more or less feedin' Preacher Gordon since he come to Sourwood. We'll keep on helpin' you some till you settle in."

"That's the best gift yet," Mira said. Being called "honey" warmed her heart too.

"We got a couple more." Mathena looked at Nicey Jane. "You wantin' to go last?"

"No matterance to me," Nicey Jane said. "You go on ahead."

"Well, I didn't rightly know what you might need, but here's some butter I just churned and some sorghum from the cook-off last fall." Mathena smiled. "Looks like as how we're all trying to sweeten up Preacher Gordon for you."

"Or you for Preacher Gordon," Hallie said. "Guess as how it's yore turn, Nicey Jane."

"Here you go." Nicey Jane handed Mira a brown crock bowl. "Every bride needs a good mixing bowl, and I had an extra from them Riley brung in after his ma passed on."

"This is too kind." Mira fingered a small cloth bag in the bowl. "And still more."

"Hickory nuts. They make a fine pie."

"Preacher Gordon does love pie," Effie said. "Don't know how he stays skinny as a beanpole."

Mira's eyes filled with tears as she looked at the women. "I can't thank you enough for making me feel so welcome."

Hallie stood up and gave her a look. "You is a puzzle, Miss Mira. Laughin' when you oughter be crying and crying when you oughter be laughing."

Mira brushed away her tears. "Maybe I'll get things straight soon enough with your help. But all this." She motioned at the gifts on the floor beside her. "All this might be worth that wheelbarrow ride."

That made the women chuckle as they grabbed a couple of pieces of candy off the table and headed for the door.

Nicey Jane looked around before she went outside. "Don't you worry. We'll get this party done with and send the preacher in out of the cold."

Mira stood in the doorway and watched the people drift away. The serenade was over without a single song.

Gordon came up the porch steps to stand beside her. "Why the smile?"

"Nobody sang. Strangest serenade ever."

He laughed. "Come on. It's cold out here." He put his arm around her and turned her back into the cabin. He shut the door and pulled the bar down to keep it closed.

"There won't be any more carrying on tonight, will there?" Mira said.

"I think not, but we'll keep the door barred just in case." He went to lay another log on the fire. Then he looked at Mira for a long moment. "Shall we try to get a few hours of sleep before preaching time?"

"Yes." Mira's heart beat a little faster.

He blew out the lamp. Moonlight through the windows, along with the fire, gave light to see their way into the bedroom. The shadows were darker there, but Mira could still see well enough to avoid running into anything. Gordon turned his back to her to take off his shoes and pants.

Mira slipped off her robe and peeled off her stockings. She felt her petticoats. Thank goodness, they had dried out while she sat by the fire with the women. She pulled in a breath and started to crawl into bed. She gasped and jerked back out from under the covers when her feet hit something hard and cold.

"What is it?" Gordon asked.

"There's something in the bed."

He pulled the covers back and started laughing. The dishes and pans from the kitchen were piled under the covers at the end of the bed. "I think the women played a rusty on us."

"Rusty?" she said and then remembered. "Oh, a joke."

"I'll wager they're all snickering even now thinking about us finding their booby trap." He picked up an iron skillet and put it on the floor.

"That's what Mathena and Dottie were up to. They came out of this room when I came inside." Mira laughed too as she picked up the bowls she'd been looking for earlier. She stacked them on the chest.

Once they cleared everything away, Mira was still smiling as she got in bed. Somehow the women's joke took away her nervousness, but walking around on the cold floor had her shivering again.

When Gordon pulled her close to warm her, it felt right. Later, before Mira drifted off to sleep, she sent up a thankful prayer that she could be a wife to a good man. There were all different ways to be serenaded on a woman's honeymoon night.

22

Ada June watched all the commotion at the preacher's place from across the holler. She'd seen serenades before, but this was the preacher and his new missus, a schoolteacher. Ada June did hope all this carryin' on wouldn't make her want to leave already.

She had a feeling about the schoolteacher, even if she did say Bo couldn't come to school. If she stuck to that, Ada June wouldn't go either. In her head she saw books sprouting wings and flying off. She wanted to grab them to not let her dream of learning to read be gone completely. So many things she'd had to give up on ever having.

Like a ma and a pa. She did have a ma for a spell. She reckoned she had a pa too. Everybody did. Even Jesus, Preacher Gordon told her. God up in heaven made it happen somehow. Ada June couldn't figure out how that could be, but Preacher Gordon said you didn't have to figure it out. You just had to have faith and believe it.

She wanted to believe that if she prayed hard enough and had faith enough, the schoolteacher would change her mind about Bo. But she'd prayed hard after her ma died that her pa, whoever he was, might decide he needed a daughter. 'Course that hadn't happened. She reckoned she didn't have the kind of believing faith the preacher said a body had to have to get the Lord's favor, but she did wish he'd pay mind to her prayers about Bo and school.

The sound of laughter drifted over to make her feet itch to head across the holler, but she stayed put. Better to be here alone than over there where folks might stare at her like she didn't have good sense or something. Like maybe she should just go off to some place where they didn't have to look at her and think about who her pa might be.

Back after her ma first went on to heaven, Ada June used to stare at every man she saw, wondering if maybe this one or that one might be her pa. Some folks said her ma had come across the hill to Sourwood chasin' after Ada June's pa, but true or not, it didn't do much good thinkin' on it now. She breathed out a sigh. A puff of her breath hung in the air.

Bo sat on her feet, doing what he could to keep her toes from freezing, but it weren't like they were gonna find much warm tonight. She wasn't about to go back to Aunt Dottie's. She saw Mr. Luther come in. Had barely got to the woods without him spotting her.

She'd already packed in the wood and a bucket of water from the creek, milked the cow, fed the hog and the chickens. She gathered in the eggs, though they were some scarce. Then she'd got Emmy Lou ready for bed.

Aunt Dottie had been in a stir trying to come up with something fine for the preacher's wife. She weren't at all excited about the flower seeds, but Ada June told her it could turn out to be the best present, seeing as how it would keep giving all summer long. That was more words than Ada June usually let out at once, but it had made Aunt Dottie hug her. Well, as much as she could hug anybody with that baby belly.

Aunt Dottie must have done give the schoolteacher her seeds because she came out on the preacher's porch. Ada June started to head over to help her up the hill to her house, but when Effie Foster followed her outside, Ada June stopped.

Miss Effie would make sure Aunt Dottie was took care of. And sure enough, her boy, Billy Ray, broke away from a group of men to go help her. Ada June took another long look over toward the preacher's house before she turned and headed into the woods. Bo ran on in front of her. Aunt Dottie would know she wouldn't be coming back to their house with Mr. Luther there. She said Ada June ought to try to get on his good side, but Ada June didn't think he had a good side. None he was aiming to turn toward her anyhow.

But she was cold. Smoke drifted up out of the chimneys in the holler below her. It would be mighty nice to lay down in front of one of those fires. Like it had been that afternoon when the schoolteacher invited her in to get warm.

She fingered the matches she'd swiped from Aunt Dottie's mantel. Mr. Luther wouldn't be happy if he knew she took them, but he couldn't have no way of knowing how many Aunt Dottie might have used up whilst he was off logging.

Could be that house where she and her mother had lived was still up there on Pap Leathers' hill. If it was, she could get a fire started in the fireplace to get warm. But the way up there was steep, and she'd have to go by that spot where her ma died. Worse, she might see that man. Not the one that had grabbed her and carried her to Miss Nicey Jane's house. That other man. The one they'd run out in the snow to get away from.

She shook her head. He wouldn't be there now after all these years. Could be he'd never been there. Maybe she'd dreamed it all up the way Miss Nicey Jane said she must've done. That was when Ada June quit talking. Didn't seem no use if nobody was gonna believe what she said.

But she best wait to make that climb in the daylight. Instead, she headed to her little cave in the side of the hill. She had put some wood in there before the snow. A fire at the front of the cave would keep her and Bo warm and varmints away. She had some cornpones in her pocket and an egg she'd sneaked for Bo. She'd make sure to break it for him and let him lick it off a rock. Best he didn't figure out he could steal eggs out of hen nests. Nobody could abide an egg-sucking dog.

Come morning she could wash her face in the creek and go to church. She'd smell like smoke but that wasn't such a bad thing. She always stood in the back close to the door anyhow, with Bo behind her being quiet as a cat ready to pounce on a mouse. Preacher Gordon never minded Bo being there in church. Maybe he'd talk the schoolteacher out of thinking Bo was some old hound what didn't know how to behave.

Once she got the fire going, the little cave was right warm. It wasn't a real cave. Just a dug-out place under a ledge some bear might have wintered in back when they wandered about these hills. Pap Leathers told her the bears had moved on down to some big mountains to the south where folks couldn't hunt them. Pap Leathers knew lots about everything. She wished he was there with her, telling some story that was maybe true, maybe not. He wouldn't ever tell her which it was. Always said to ask her ma. Whenever she did, her mother laughed and said sometimes the truth was hard to figure out.

Ada June wished she could remember some of Pap's stories. Remember more about him. She did remember he told her he weren't her pa and not her grandpa either. She didn't ask her ma if that was true. She knew Pap wasn't fooling about that. She did wish he could have been her kin. When she told him that, he said he'd be proud to have a girl like her.

Maybe that was how Joseph was with Jesus when he took him to raise after he married Mary. He was bound to be proud to be his pa. Preacher Gordon said Jesus never done anything wrong. Not one thing. That was hard to imagine being possible, but Preacher said it was written in the Bible and was God's own truth. So Joseph was bound to have been proud to call him son.

Of course, he took over as pa soon as Jesus was born. Even before, what with taking care of Mary and seeing that she did all right having a baby in a barn.

Sometimes that same kind of thing happened up here in the hills too. Not having babies in cow barns, or if they did, she never heard about it, but folks taking in babies to raise when something happened to their ma or pa. Once Pap and then her ma died, it might have happened to Ada June too if she'd been a baby. But nobody much wanted a skinny girl who weren't all that cute.

Of course, folks thought Aunt Dottie and Mr. Luther had took her in to raise, but weren't no truth to that. They give her a plate at the table so long as she packed in wood and such and took care of Emmy Lou when Aunt Dottie weren't feeling pert.

Bo licked Ada June's face before he settled down beside her on pine branches she'd brought in for a bed. She'd found some that weren't so prickly. Bo was right. She needed to go to sleep. She'd have to wake up early to go milk Beulah at Aunt Dottie's if she wanted to get to church. Beulah had to be milked morning and night, and Aunt Dottie would have a struggle doing that with how she was getting burdened down with baby. Mr. Luther was there, but he wouldn't do no milking. That was women's work.

Women's work. She reckoned that if she was doing the work, she could count herself a woman, even if she was only ten going on eleven. Sometimes a girl had to grow up fast if there weren't nobody to want to take her in as family.

The want for family made her heart hurt. She put her arm around Bo and pulled him close against her. He laid his head on her chest and went to sleep. After a while, so did she.

23

A good thing about sleeping high up on the hill was how the morning light showed up early. Down there in the holler it took a while for the sun to show its face. Bo wasn't beside her now. He was at the front of the cave finishing off whatever varmint hadn't been quick enough to hide from him.

Ada June didn't look to see what it was. She didn't want to feel sorrowful for it the way she did sometimes for the hens Aunt Dottie picked for the stew pot. Folks had to eat. So did Bo, and at least she wouldn't have to sneak something out of Aunt Dottie's kitchen for him.

Shivering, she pulled on her boots. The fire wasn't nothing but ashes. Moving would warm her up. And somebody would be building a fire down at the church. She didn't never get near to the stove Preacher had put halfway along the side wall, but with folks crowding in to hear whatever he was preachin' from the Bible, the church heated up all the way to the back.

She wondered where the preacher's missus would sit. Probably clear up on the front row benches with the likes of Miss Nicey Jane and Miss Effie. Ada June didn't intend on letting either of them see her. They'd be chasing Bo out the door, and Miss Nicey Jane would want to pray over Ada June like as how she had a demon or something. Preacher did say Jesus got out demons, but it weren't no demon keeping Ada June from talking. Her ma hadn't had no demon either. She didn't care what folks said.

The water was running in the creek, so it wasn't froze over. Ada June washed her face. That brought on extra shivers. Bo pranced right out in the water to lap up a drink like it wasn't the least bit cold.

When she sneaked inside Aunt Dottie's house to get the milk bucket, she was glad to hear Mr. Luther snoring. She hoped he'd keep on snoring till she wasn't nowhere around and then be gone on his way before milking time came again.

She warmed her hands under her armpits, and Beulah give down her milk without a fuss. After spilling some out in an old pan for the barn cats, she dipped a tin cup full for herself. Aunt Dottie would still have plenty.

The sun still hadn't peeked over the hill when she carried the milk to the house, but Emmy Lou was at the back door.

"Bo." She grabbed Bo's tail.

The dog gave Ada June a pleading look but didn't try to get away from the little girl.

"Emmy Lou." Ada June put the milk bucket on the cabinet and picked up the little girl. She let Bo out the back door to wait on the steps.

"Aie Oon," Emmy Lou said. "Hungie."

On the far side of the room, Aunt Dottie struggled out of bed. Ada June was glad she didn't ask her to pull her up, the way she did sometimes. Mr. Luther turned over, put a pillow over his head, and went back to snoring.

Aunt Dottie hobbled over to the eating table.

"Ma." Emmy Lou reached for her.

"You stay with Aie Oon." Aunt Dottie waved her away. "Your ma ain't feelin' so pert."

Ada June pointed toward Aunt Dottie's belly. "Baby?"

Aunt Dottie rubbed her baby bump and dropped down in one of the chairs. "I ain't thinkin' so, but I couldn't hardly get any comfort last night, what with my back giving me fits. Can you fix the fire?"

Ada June put Emmy Lou down next to Aunt Dottie to keep her from trailing along toward the fire. Once she got the flames built up, she strained the milk through a rag and dipped some out into bowls. Then she crumbled up yesterday's cornbread in the milk. That was faster than cooking mush or eggs. Besides, Mr. Luther would want the eggs when he woke up. She aimed to be gone before then.

Aunt Dottie let Emmy Lou crawl up in her lap. "I ain't hardly got enough lap to sit her these days." She spooned a bite of the milk-soaked cornbread into the little girl's mouth. Emmy Lou took the spoon away from her to feed herself.

"I reckon it's for the best that you ain't wantin' to be baby no more." Aunt Dottie looked over at Ada June. "You get her dressed and carry her to church with you."

"Not you?" Ada June frowned.

"Don't look so put out. I ain't expectin' you to handle her all the day. You can hand her off to Mathena at church. She offered to take her for a spell were I needin' her to." Her eyes narrowed on Ada June as she reached over to tug on a strand of her hair. "You've got rats' nests in your hair. And is that a stick?"

Ada June pulled a little pine branch out of her hair.

"You look like you slept in a tree. Wouldn't Elsinore let you use her comb?" Aunt Dottie frowned. "And how long you been wearing that dress?"

Ada June shrugged. Her other dress hit above her knees, but Aunt Dottie hadn't noticed that to do anything about it.

"I guess it won't matter, but you need to warsh that tomorrow." She left her bowl uneaten and pushed up from the table. "Put something clean on Emmy Lou so's Mathena won't have nothing to talk about. You'll have to wrap her in a kiver to keep her warm going down there. Mr. Luther didn't bring her that coat he promised."

Ada June fed Emmy Lou as much of Aunt Dottie's bowl as she wanted before she took the rest outside to dump on the step for Bo. She got the little girl dressed and banked the fire. She wasn't sure what time it was, but figured it would be nigh on church time when they made it down the hill. Emmy Lou was excited when Ada June wrapped a little blanket around her and went outside.

When she saw Bo, she reached for the dog. "Bo."

Ada June bent to let her pet him but said, "Can't get down."

"Play. Snow."

"Maybe at Aunt Mattie's." Ada June didn't know whether that would happen or not, but it would be Mathena's trouble then and not Ada June's. She shifted the little girl to a better position on her hip.

Packing her all the way down the hill would make her arm hurt, but she didn't want Emmy Lou to get her feet wet and maybe start coughing like Elsinore. She felt a flash of guilt for not going by to check on her and Selinda, but that Horace Perry was probably down there wanting in her door. He'd tell his ma if Elsinore was worse sick.

When she got to the church house, she stayed out by the big oak until she saw Mathena coming with her husband and young'uns. But she didn't have no carrying ones right now. She could see to Emmy Lou.

Ada June gave Bo a look so he'd know to stay by the tree while she carried Emmy Lou to Mathena.

The woman took the little girl. "Is it the baby, Ada June?"

Ada June shook her head. Emmy Lou saved her having to say anything. "Ma sick."

Mr. Frank shook his head at Mathena like he wasn't happy about her having Emmy Lou before he herded their kids on inside.

"What's wrong with her, Ada June?"

Ada June touched her back.

Mathena looked worried. "That could be the baby." Then her face changed. "But Luther's there, ain't he?"

Ada June nodded.

"Drinking, I'm guessing."

Ada June shrugged. She hadn't smelled any spirits in the house.

Mathena's eyes sharpened on Ada June. "Ain't you got anything better to wear to church than that old coat and dress?"

Ada June shrugged again. She had to wear what she had.

"And those boots. Land's sake, child, I don't know how you walk in them."

Ada June just looked at her. Wasn't nothing to say to any of that, even if she did want to let words out of her mouth.

"And what's that in your hair?"

Ada June pulled a pine needle out of her hair. She forgot about finding a comb after she dressed Emmy Lou.

"You gotta try to do better, Ada June, and not live like some kind of animal." Mathena shook her head. "I don't know what we're gonna do with you."

Ada June stared down at the ground. She didn't look up as she muttered, "Try."

"I reckon you can't help how you are, no more'n your ma could." Mathena sighed and turned toward the church. "Don't worry about comin' after Emmy Lou. I'll take her on up so I can check on Dottie."

Ada June went back to the tree to crouch down by Bo. He leaned against her. He always knew when she was hurting inside. She was glad nobody paid her any attention. After most everybody went inside and they were singing, she and Bo slipped in the back door and found a spot in the shadows.

24

*G*ordon loved seeing people file into the church. Today was a double blessing with Mira on the front bench.

That morning she was so nervous, she had pinned her hair up three times before she put down the combs in something near desperation, with her honey-colored curls still escaping them.

He started to tell her it looked fine, but decided it best to appear to not be paying attention. He had gone out of the bedroom to build up the fire and fill the kettle with water while she dressed. But then he returned to get his Bible, where he pretended to look over his Scripture while really stealing looks at her and soaking in her presence. The very sight of her trapping stray curls back with combs had nothing short of joy filling him.

He didn't know how he could love her so completely so quickly. Perhaps that seed of attraction from when they were young in school had simply languished dormant in his heart to be awakened when he met her again. She didn't feel the same. He knew that. Whether she ever would, he could only hope. And pray.

His prayers had already been bountifully answered. A wife. A teacher. A woman who cared about people. He could tell that from how she responded to those who spoke to her before the church service. He had tried to stay by her side, but he kept being pulled away with this or that concern.

She hid her own nervous concern well now. As they ate their breakfast that morning, she had confessed the worry that her unusual laughter during the silliness of the serenade confusion would make everyone think she was foolish.

"A teacher can have no success with her students if their parents decide she lacks proper sense." With her fork, she drew patterns in the honey on the homemade bread that was part of the basket Aunt Stella had packed for them the day before.

Was it only yesterday he had promised love to Mira and she had promised the same to him? After a hesitation. Today he wouldn't worry about the hesitation.

"They will think you're wonderful," he assured her. "And so will the children once school starts. At least most of them."

"Most of them?" Her eyes widened a little. .

He laughed. "A troublemaker or two are bound to show up. Don't they always?"

"I suppose so, but I'm not worried about that now. I'm worried about what people will think this morning. You don't have troublemakers at church, do you?"

"Just like in school, churches can have a few unhappy folks." He saw no reason to talk about those who worried he was bringing too much change to Sourwood. At least not yet. "But none who will want to make trouble for my pretty wife."

That had made Mira blush, which made her even prettier. Sometimes the Lord threw down blessings by the bushels.

That attractive blush continued to color Mira's cheeks as some of the women spoke to her and the men managed to take a good look before they found their accustomed seats.

People had a way of claiming a place in a church. It had been that way at his home church back in Louisville. His mother sat in the same pew every Sunday and had been known to be more than a little peeved if someone took what she considered her seat. His dear, faithful mother, but not perfect even as none of them were, in church or out. He wished she could have welcomed Mira into their family.

At least his sister could do so. Julie would be surprised, more like shocked, when he wrote her his news. Julie thought his chances of finding a suitable wife had been wiped out by his calling to preach in Eastern Kentucky.

Still alive then, his mother had been his biggest supporter of going on the mission field. She had waved away Julie's words and assured her the Lord would provide if Gordon needed a wife. And now the Lord had.

Mathena Brown came into the church carrying Dottie Slade's little girl after her husband and children were already seated. He looked back at the door, but Dottie wasn't following her in. He started to step away from the podium to ask about Dottie, but his watch said it was time for services to begin.

Mira didn't hide her relief when he announced their first song. They only had three hymnals, but the people were learning the hymns by lining—he sang a line and then they sang the same line. Their voices made a joyful sound to the Lord.

Mathena didn't sit down with her children. Instead, she brought Emmy Lou straight to the front pew where she leaned down, whispered something to Mira, and handed her the little girl. Gordon stumbled over two words in the song as he wondered how to rescue Mira and let Mathena know she couldn't just dump a toddler in Mira's lap. The way Mira beamed as she hugged the little girl stopped him. Emmy Lou clapped her hands and added her jabber to the singing.

Emmy Lou was used to being handed around in church. All the youngsters were. Even though Gordon had preached there over two years, he still hadn't gotten all the relationships straight. Everybody appeared to be kin in some way to almost everyone else.

The church benches were nearly full. He hoped to get the men to build pews soon. Once the school was finished. With spring, the men would be busy with planting and such, but some were eager to do whatever was needed at the church. Especially Dugan Foster. He and his wife, Effie, were rocks in the church.

Gordon was glad to see Effie sitting beside Mira. She was on one side and Miss Nicey Jane was on the other. They would help if tending to Emmy Lou overwhelmed Mira. Right now she didn't appear a bit overwhelmed as she settled the little girl on her lap. She kept the child's blanket wrapped around her. The church was still cool, but the stove would warm it up soon enough after people stopped waving the door as they came in.

He kept his face properly solemn, but he wanted to smile when Ada June came in and slid along the back wall to find a spot in the shadows. Her dog slinked along behind her. He'd have to work something out with Mira about school and Ada June's dog. The girl had to get her chance to learn.

Even the thought of a smile disappeared moments later when Cleo Rayburn and two of his boys came in the church. Gordon ought to be glad to see Cleo at church, but from the look on the man's face, he wasn't there to hear the gospel. Cleo didn't think he needed it.

That wasn't fair. Cleo claimed to be fine with the Lord and Gordon had no right to judge the truth of that. Who Cleo felt far from fine with was Gordon. He said if the Lord wanted Sourwood to have a preacher, he would have called a mountain man and not a flatlander to bring in city ways.

Gordon had no intention of bringing anything to Sourwood except the gospel, education for the children, and better health. Cleo wasn't against any of that, but he wanted to be the one who said what Sourwood needed. Not a brought-in preacher. Gordon had tried to win him over, but the man didn't like him. Plain and simple.

Should he decide to, Cleo could make short work of Gordon. He was built so solid and strong that a hurricane wind couldn't blow him off course or make him change his mind.

His older boy, Connor, followed in his footsteps. If Gordon didn't miss his guess, Connor would be one of those troublemakers Mira would have to deal with. If Cleo made him go to school.

Cleo's wife, Lindy, was Nicey Jane's daughter. Nicey Jane was ready to do anything for the church, but she wouldn't say anything against Cleo. Nor would Nicey Jane's husband, Riley.

That man was another puzzler. While Nicey Jane was at every service, Riley never darkened the church door.

Gordon pushed his worries aside. No need to borrow trouble that might never come to call. He had people to serve. A message to deliver. A schoolteacher wife to introduce.

That could wait until after the sermon since Emmy Lou had stopped bouncing on Mira's lap and looked sleepy. With a happy look on her face, Mira stroked the child's hair. No need disturbing that by asking her to stand.

After they sang every verse of "Lily of the Valley," he opened his Bible and began to preach about the seven gifts of the Spirit. Wisdom. Understanding. Counsel. Fortitude. Knowledge. Piety. Fear of the Lord.

From the look on Cleo's face, Gordon had no doubt he would soon need some of those gifts, especially understanding and wisdom. Could be he should grab Mira and make a run for home before Cleo could corner him after the services. But cowardice was not among the blessed gifts. Fortitude was.

Perhaps a better sermon for his first as a married man would have been about the fruits of the Spirit. Love. Joy. Peace. Long-suffering. Gentleness. Goodness. Faith. Meekness. Temperance.

From all appearances, Mira was gifted with each of those. He hoped she had an abundance of the long-suffering fruit. All pastors' wives needed that.

At the end of the sermon, Dugan Foster stepped up to lead the hymn "Just as I Am." Gordon blocked out all his straying thoughts and bent his head in earnest prayer that the words given to him by the Lord had touched hearts.

After the song, Gordon held his hand out to Mira. Miss Effie took Emmy Lou. Mira's face was flushed and her smile a little shaky, but she didn't hesitate to step up beside him.

"I'd like to introduce our new schoolteacher, my wife, Mrs. Mira Covington." Just saying the name stirred up joy in his heart.

They stood together at the front of the church while the people filed past them to welcome Mira. Ada June slipped out the church door. She wouldn't come forward.

When Cleo and his boys came around, Cleo said, "Hope Sourwood suits you, ma'am."

"Thank you." Mira smiled at the two boys. "I look forward to seeing you at school."

"We'll see if that comes about." Cleo nodded at the boys, who took that as permission to head for the door.

"I hope Miss Lindy isn't ill," Gordon said.

"She's fit. Stayed home with the littlest ones." Cleo glanced back at the people waiting to speak to Mira. "Soon's this glad handin' is done, I aim to get a word with you."

"Certainly." Gordon hid his reluctance as he turned to speak to the man behind Cleo.

After the last people shook their hands, Gordon walked Mira to the door where Cleo waited along with Dugan Foster.

Dugan held out a kettle. "The missus brung some chicken soup for your dinner, seeing as how you're just gettin' settled in."

"How kind." Mira took it from him. "Please thank her for us."

Dugan nodded and, with a curious look at Cleo, went out the door. Cleo made no move to follow him.

Mira hesitated before looking at Gordon. "Perhaps I should take this on to the house."

"That might be best." Again Gordon hid his reluctance. "I won't be long."

"Very well." She adjusted her hold on the kettle handle and smiled toward Cleo. "Nice to meet you, Mr. Rayburn."

Cleo inclined his head slightly to acknowledge her words. After

Mira went out, Cleo stared at the door a moment before he said, "She appears to be on the fragile side, Preacher. I'm thinkin' the boys will run her out of school 'fore a week is out."

"Which boys are those?" Gordon kept his expression blank.

"I ain't meaning mine. But you know how boys can be. Little as she is, she couldn't wield a paddle hard enough to keep them kind in line."

"We can pray the children will behave so they can learn to read and figure."

Cleo scowled. "I can figure fine. My ma and pa taught me."

"Wise parents are a blessing." Gordon wished Cleo would get on with whatever was poking him.

"I ain't being late to get on home to talk about learnin' and such."

"Then whatever it is you want to say, go ahead and get it out." Gordon didn't quite keep his impatience out of his voice.

"I heared there was a rowdy carryin' on at your place. I'm thinkin' that ain't no way of doin' for a preacher."

He didn't feel he needed to explain anything to Cleo, but sometimes a man had to work to keep the peace. "Some folks did show up in the night to do a serenade when they heard I brought home a wife."

"A bunch of foolishness."

"Yes, but harmless enough, I suppose."

"I heared you passed out moonshine aplenty."

"Then you heard wrong. If anybody was nipping, they brought their own supply."

"I reckon that could be." Cleo appeared to want to dispute the truth of Gordon's words but stopped short of that. Instead he moved on to more infuriating words. "I heared yore little woman must have found some of that nipping for her own self. That she acted as peculiar as that Sarai Barton used to up on Leathers Hill."

Gordon clamped down on the anger that wanted to explode out of him. He was a man of God, but then even Jesus had shown some righteous anger. This wasn't the time for that. He pulled in a breath and let it out slowly to cool his temper.

"She was a little unsettled by the idea of being jerked from bed and thrust into a wheelbarrow for the amusement of our neighbors. But I can assure you she was entirely sober last night. Your mother-in-law, Miss Nicey Jane, can confirm that, since she and other of the women spoke with Mrs. Covington at length."

"Well, I'm just saying that if you've brung in another witch like that Barton woman, you'll live to regret it, Preacher." Cleo's eyes narrowed on Gordon. "And while we're about it, that girl of Sarai's needs to be told dogs don't have no place in the church."

"The dog doesn't cause any disturbance," Gordon said. "Never bothers anyone."

"Bothers my boy, Connor. He says it snarls at him."

Gordon considered the impact of his words and said them anyway. "Perhaps Connor should stay away from Ada June."

"My boy ain't got nothing to do with that woods colt." The man's face went red as he shook his finger at Gordon. "But upon my word, if that critter bites my boy, I'll shoot it before nightfall."

Gordon did wish his words back. "Maybe we should pray about this, Cleo."

"I don't need no help from you to do my prayin'." Cleo stormed out the door and slammed it so hard the doorframe rattled.

"Then I suppose I need to pray about it on my own," Gordon muttered. He thought of Mira waiting for him, but he went back to kneel at the altar to ask the Lord's forgiveness for his hard feelings toward Cleo and for stoking his anger.

He let silence gather around him a moment before he whispered, "And please protect Ada June and her dog, Bo."

25

The soup kettle was awkward to carry with her cloak blowing against it as she went down the steps and started across the empty churchyard. The cold wind kept anyone from lingering to talk. The sky looked loaded down with gray. More snow could be on the way.

She set the soup pot down to adjust her cloak and pull on her gloves. She wasn't too weak to carry a pot of soup back to Gordon's house. Her house now, she reminded herself.

Before she picked it up, the low growl of a dog caught her attention. Then laughter, but not the good kind. A jeering laugh.

At the far edge of the churchyard, Ada June was hunched over beside a big oak tree as she held on to her dog's neck ruff. Cleo Rayburn's two boys circled her like wolves around prey. The dog wasn't fighting to get loose, but his bared teeth let the boys know he might.

The older boy picked up an acorn and threw it at Ada June. She kept her head down as she pulled her dog back against her. The boys laughed again. Those troublemakers Gordon warned her about.

Mira looked back at the church to see if Gordon and the boys' father were coming out. But the door stayed closed. She could go for them, but she had the feeling their father might be one of those troublemakers Gordon had hinted about in the church. He had been polite enough on the surface, but he looked anything but glad to be there.

Besides, the children in Sourwood needed to know she would not put up with nonsense. She didn't have to wait for school to start to let them know that.

The boys were so busy with their taunts they didn't notice her walking toward them.

"Stop that right now," she ordered.

Her loud tone startled them. The younger one looked guilty as he stared down at the ground.

The older boy, maybe eleven or twelve, put his hands on his hips and glared at her. "Who's gonna make me?"

She stared back at him without a word. A teacher didn't have to argue with a child, merely hold her ground without wavering.

The little boy pulled on his brother's arm. "Come on, Connor. This ain't no fun no more."

Behind them, Ada June kept her head down and held her growling dog.

The boy named Connor slid his gaze away from Mira. He smacked the little boy's hand off his arm.

"You can both go sit on the church steps to wait for your father," Mira said. "He surely won't be proud of you harassing a girl."

Connor scowled at her. "We weren't doing nothing like whatever it is you just said. We was just talkin' to her."

"And throwing things at her."

"I didn't throw nothing at her," the younger boy said.

"Shut up." Connor shoved the little boy.

"Do you want me to get your father?" Mira said.

"You don't know beans. Pa would be on you, not us. He don't care a whit what we do to her." Connor jerked his head toward Ada June. "Nobody in Sourwood wants the likes of her and her dog round about church or anywheres else."

"That's enough, Connor." Mira gave him her sternest look.

"Enough of you tellin' us what to do."

"I'm hungry, Connor. I'm goin' home." The little boy took off in a run.

Connor stared after him, then frowned at Mira. "I'm goin' too, but it ain't your doing. It's cause it's dinnertime."

As soon as the boy started away, Ada June jumped up to take off the other direction.

"Wait, Ada June," Mira called.

The girl slowed, then stopped to look back at Mira. The dog was right against her legs.

"Do you have a few minutes to help me? I have this pot of chicken soup and my cloak keeps catching against it. Could you carry it for me?"

The girl's shoulders drooped, but she turned around and went to pick up the kettle without a word.

Mira chattered to the girl all the way across the yard. "It feels like snow, don't you think?"

The girl shifted the pot to her other hand. The sleeves on her coat showed her wrists. Her dress below the coat looked filthy, and she had on those dreadful boots. The child's hair resembled a brush pile.

"I've been thinking about school," Mira said.

Ada June's shoulders sagged again as she stared down at the ground. Mira knew she was thinking about the "no dogs in the schoolhouse" rule.

"I wondered if you might like to get an early start on learning and come have lessons with me before school opens."

The girl's head jerked around to stare at Mira as though judging whether she could trust Mira's words. Then her eyes lit up as she nodded.

Mira thought about telling her she'd have to talk if they had school together, but that could wait. "Why don't you stay and eat some of Miss Effie's chicken soup with Preacher Gordon and me?

You can help me get the fire going and the soup heated. If you have time."

"Bo?" Ada June spoke the one word she'd said to Mira the day before.

"Of course. He can come in. Any time."

A smile broke out on the girl's face and stayed all the way to the cabin. She went up the steps ahead of Mira and straight to the fireplace, where she hung the pot on one of the hooks over the smoldering fire. Then she went back outside to get wood and had the fire blazing before Mira got her hat off. With a small hook, Ada June moved the pot to the side of the blaze.

The dog settled near the fireplace with a contented puff of breath. Ada June held out her hands toward the flames. She was tall for her age, only a few inches shorter than Mira. One of Mira's dresses might almost fit her. The skirt would be too long, but skirts could be hemmed. Waists could be gathered in.

Mira hesitated, not sure about mountain customs. Maybe she should ask Gordon before she offered the girl a dress.

"Would you like to take off your boots? I've some slippers you can wear."

In answer, Ada June lifted her feet out of her boots. Mira went into the bedroom to dig out the slippers and a pair of stockings from her trunk.

Ada June sat down on the floor in front of the fire and jerked off her stockings with holes in the toes and heels to pull on Mira's. She slid her feet into the slippers, then held her feet out to admire them before she stood up and did a little shuffle dance. Her dog's tail flapped against the floor.

"Looks like they almost fit. You can wear them whenever you're here," Mira said. "Let's wash our hands so we can set the table. Preacher Gordon should be along soon."

After a look at her hands, Ada June shrugged and followed Mira to the little table where there was a wash pan and soap. Mira dipped some lukewarm water out of the kettle on the hearth. Ada

June watched Mira wash her hands first. Then she scrubbed her hands the exact same way.

When Mira adjusted one of the combs in her hair, Ada June pointed to her own head. Mira looked at the girl's hair. No doubt she could use a comb, but what if she had some kind of vermin in her hair?

Well, what if she did? Combs could be washed. She fetched her comb and the small mirror from the bedroom where she had worked with her hair so abjectly that morning. Ada June propped the mirror on the mantel and tried to jerk the comb through her hair.

When it caught on tangles, she made a face and said her second word around Mira. "Ow."

"Looks like you have some birds' nests in that hair," Mira said.

Ada June gave her a funny look and felt her head.

Mira smiled. "Not real ones. Just tangles." She reached for the comb. "Here, let me see if I can work out those knots."

Mira pulled a chair over to the fire and motioned for Ada June to sit on the floor. "If it pulls too much, raise your hand to let me know."

After the girl settled in front of her, Mira worked the comb through a strand of her shoulder-length dark-brown hair. She picked out a few pine needles. "Gracious, child, did you sleep in a tree last night?"

Ada June shook her head. "On."

"On?"

A nod was her only answer. Communicating with one-syllable words wasn't easy, but Mira didn't push for more. She merely added her own short word. "Oh."

Ada June didn't move as Mira worked the comb through her hair. Nothing was in the girl's hair that shouldn't be, except pine needles. She wanted to give the girl a hug but worried she would jerk away.

Worries. She needed to stop worrying over everything. Her first

Sunday morning in Sourwood had been good. In church, sweet little Emmy Lou's warm body in her lap had been a blessing. One that made her believe someday her prayers would be answered and the child she cuddled might be her own.

Hers and Gordon's. A child might be a better bond between them than a burst of romantic foolishness. She smiled a little at the memory of the night before and hoped those at church would give her a chance to prove she didn't lack good sense.

A few had given her an assessing look. That was only natural. As long as they gave her a chance to teach their children. The children had to give her a chance too. For that to happen, she'd have to handle the troublemakers like Connor Rayburn.

But that didn't have to be today. Today she could enjoy combing this child's hair. She could take unexpected pleasure in the dog settled by the fire. She even felt a spark of happiness in knowing Gordon would soon come through the door so they could share their Sunday dinner.

How many dinners had she eaten alone? Too many to count. And today she would have a husband across the table and a dear child guest beside her. She could start counting her blessings instead of lonely dinners.

The only noises in the room as she continued to work the comb through Ada June's hair were the tick of the clock, the crackling of the burning wood, and the dog's snuffling breath as he slept. Contented sounds. Blessings. She had no reason to think the afternoon wouldn't hold more.

She started humming "The Lily of the Valley," the hymn they sang at church. She sent up a joyful prayer when Ada June began humming along with her.

26

When Gordon came through the door, he stopped at the sight of Ada June sitting on the floor in front of Mira by the fire. His heart warmed as he soaked in the scene.

Mira smiled over at him. "Oh, there you are, Gordon. I hope you don't mind that I invited Ada June to eat with us."

Ada June twisted to look around at him. No smile on her face. She looked worried she'd been caught doing something wrong. Her dog got up and licked her cheek.

"Not at all. I'm sure Miss Effie sent plenty enough to share."

Even if she hadn't, Gordon would gladly give his part to Ada June. The girl always looked so hungry. Not just for food but for the love and security a family gave a child.

Her face eased into a smile before she turned back toward the fire. Her dog settled down beside her, his head on his paws, his eyes warily watching Gordon. Maybe the dog sensed his disapproval of dogs indoors. Whenever Ada June came to see him, they talked in the yard or on the porch.

But Mira had let the dog in the day before, and here he was settled in front of the fire again. Obviously, Mira had no objection to dogs in the house if they brought their girls with them.

He decided he didn't either. While he hung up his coat and pulled off his tie, the unpleasant memory of Cleo's words faded away. Better to think about the pleasure of a warm house with the prospect of a midday meal with a beautiful woman he called his wife.

Mira had gone back to combing Ada June's hair. "We're almost through here. I'm just working to get out the nests the birds built in Ada June's hair while she was sleeping in a pine tree."

Ada June giggled. "On."

"Right. Not in the tree. On the tree." Mira shook her head a little. "I'm not exactly sure how she managed that."

Gordon knew exactly what the child meant. She had spent the night in the woods again and had made a bed of pine branches. He went over to the fire and looked down at the girl. "It's too cold for you to sleep in the woods right now, Ada June."

She didn't look up at him.

"Outside?" Mira frowned.

"Not cold," Ada June said. "Bo with me."

"Still too cold," Gordon said.

"Had a fire."

The comb stilled in Mira's hand. She seemed ready to say something, but after a look at Gordon, she pressed her lips together and went back to working out the last tangles in Ada June's hair.

"Mr. Luther at home?" Gordon kept his voice casual.

Ada June kept her eyes downcast as she hunched up her shoulders. After a couple of seconds, she gave a slight nod.

"You must have brought Emmy Lou to church."

She nodded again.

"Miss Dottie wasn't having the baby, was she?" Gordon should have checked with Mathena.

She shook her head.

"Whoa." Mira put her hands on each side of the girl's head to hold her still. "Just one more minute. I've almost got the last nest out."

That made Ada June smile again.

"Tomorrow when you come, I'll show you how to braid your hair so birds can't build those nests when you sleep in trees." Mira held up the comb and peeked around to smile at Ada June. "Or rather on trees."

"I'll get out some bowls. If I can find them." Gordon smiled too as he remembered finding the dishes in the bed last night and how their laughter at that had eased them into sweet embraces.

Mira blushed. "Some are still on the chest."

The soup was good. Even better was sitting across the table from Mira and watching Ada June eat. He ignored the two or three bits of chicken and potato she slipped under the table to Bo. Mira noticed too but only smiled.

Bo was Ada June's best friend. She needed him beside her. That was why he was a church dog and why Gordon might have to talk Mira into letting him be a school dog. He glanced at Mira in time to catch her dropping something on the floor and not by accident. He twisted his lips sideways to hide his smile. He might not have to do much convincing.

Any thought of a smile disappeared as Cleo Rayburn's hateful words and threats about Ada June and her dog came to mind. That couldn't happen. He had to make sure of that. He shut his eyes. Not him. The Lord. The Lord was the one who could change Cleo's thinking. Not Gordon.

But it wasn't only Cleo. Ada June seemed to be an outcast much the same as people said her mother was. Perhaps by her choice. Gordon had heard the stories about Ada June's mother being a witch, as Cleo said, but never anything to give substance to that. She had named no father for Ada June, but no one spoke of Sarai Barton behaving wantonly after she came to Sourwood. Not actually to Sourwood, but up in the hills. Whenever he dared to ask, he was told she never came down to the holler.

He didn't ask often. Whatever had happened was in the past, and the people seemed to want it to stay there. Even Miss Nicey

Jane, always ready to fill him in on everybody near and far, went stiff-lipped when he asked about Ada June's lack of family. She claimed to know nothing more than he'd already heard from others. She certainly hadn't accused Ada June's mother of witchery, but she had given Gordon a hard look and said that some things were better left unstirred. Those unspoken things cast a dense shadow over Ada June.

"Is the soup not to your liking?" Mira looked concerned.

"No, no. It's fine. Why?"

"You were making a terrible face. Wasn't he, Ada June?"

The girl nodded and made a frowning face. "Like you swallowed a tadpole." Then she giggled.

That made Mira laugh, obviously delighted that Ada June had spoken so many words aloud. He felt the same happiness as he pushed aside his worries and laughed with them. "Miss Effie's soup is always tasty. Maybe we can have some cornbread to go with it for supper."

Mira glanced toward the fireplace, and her smile vanished. "I suppose. If one knew how to cook it."

He tried to reassure her. "Folks have been cooking over fires since forever."

"Not this folk."

Ada June touched Mira's arm. "Easy."

"For you maybe." Mira's smile came back as she turned to Ada June. "Not for this city woman."

"I can show you," Ada June said.

"Wonderful. You teach me how to make cornbread and I can teach you to read."

Ada June's face lit up. "*A B C*."

So did Mira's. "You know the alphabet?"

"*A* Ada. *B* Bo."

"That's right. Have you been to school?" Mira sounded excited.

Ada June shook her head. Her smile slid off her face. "Ma told me."

"Was your mother a teacher?" Mira asked.

Without answering, Ada June pulled her hand back and tucked it under the table.

Worry flashed across Mira's face. Then she leaned close to Ada June. "A mother can be the best teacher. I'm glad you know your letters."

That brought a smile back to Ada June's face. "I might not know them all."

"You soon will," Gordon said.

"Yes." Mira stood and began to gather up their empty bowls. "How about a piece of candy to sweeten your tongue, Ada June? We still have a few pieces the women didn't take last night."

That brightened Ada June's face more. "Can I take some to Elsinore?"

"Elsinore? Oh yes. The ladies mentioned her last night. A young mother, I think." She took the bowls to the dishpan on the cabinet.

"Right," Gordon said. "Ada June has been helping her."

"You are a helper." Mira touched the girl's head when she brought back the candy. "There isn't much left."

When she offered the candy to Gordon, he shook his head. "Let the helper have it."

Mira got a mock serious look on her face as she put the sack in front of Ada June. "You can share it with Elsinore, but not Bo. Dogs don't need candy."

With a smile, Ada June nodded as she peered into the sack and then folded the top down without taking a piece.

"How is Elsinore?" Gordon asked.

Again Ada June's smile faded. "Coughing bad."

"How about the baby?" Gordon should go see the young mother, but he had promised Mr. Hanley he would visit his mother, who was not expected to live through the week.

"Don't know. Crying some."

"Does she have food and wood enough?" Gordon said.

"Mr. Horace sees to her."

"That's good." He dared one more question. "She all right with that?"

"He don't come in."

"I see," Gordon said. "You tell her I'll be by to see her before long. I've got to visit the Hanleys today."

Mira spoke up. "I can go this afternoon if Ada June shows me how to get to her house."

"You don't have to do that." Gordon looked at Mira.

"I want to. If that's all right with you. The women were talking about Elsinore last night. I'd love to meet her and see her baby."

"Very well." Gordon pushed out the words.

He felt uneasy about Mira going without him. He had no reason to feel so protective. But she didn't know the people yet. Not that they weren't good people. They were simply different from those in the city. More apt to be curious about her. And not all dogs were friendly. Would she realize that? What about the people who hadn't come to church and wouldn't know who she was? Outsiders were looked upon with suspicion, even if they wore skirts and a lady's hat.

"May I go with you, Ada June?" Mira asked.

Ada June nodded.

"Good. We can take Elsinore some of Miss Effie's soup." She got a jar out of the cabinet to fill with soup and smiled at Ada June. "You won't let me get lost, will you?"

Ada June looked at him and then Mira. "No."

Mira was turning out to be full of surprises. He supposed that was only to be expected, since what did he really know about her except she was beautiful? And courageous. She proved that by not only accepting the challenge of coming to Sourwood but embracing it. For that, he should be thankful and not let his own worries limit her.

27

Ada June slid off her chair so fast Bo had to jump out of her way. This day was turning out better and better. She hadn't had to pack Emmy Lou around for hours or even carry her back to Aunt Dottie's. Miss Mathena was doing that. Her stomach was full, and she had a pocketful of sucking candy.

Now the schoolteacher wanted to go to Elsinore's with her. Elsinore would like that, and maybe the preacher's missus would know what to do for Elsinore's cough. Not that she appeared to know much about that kind of thing, seeing as how she didn't even know how to make cornbread.

But that was all right. She knew how to read and she was going to teach her. Once Preacher Gordon got there, Ada June hadn't had the first bit of trouble talking to his missus the same as she didn't have trouble talking to him anymore. The words came right out without getting choked up in her throat.

Best of all, the teacher made Connor leave her alone after church. She still didn't know how she did that, but she did. That was enough to make Ada June want to hug her.

Then letting her wear her stockings and slippers and combing her hair. The combing yanked enough to bring tears to her eyes, but she hadn't let on.

Now she reluctantly slipped off the schoolteacher's soft shoes and started to peel off the stockings that didn't have even one hole in the toes.

"No, no, Ada June." The preacher's missus held up a hand to stop her. "Those are yours now. Leave the others and I'll wash them for you. But you'll have to put your boots back on. Slippers don't work for outdoors."

Ada June looked at Preacher Gordon to make sure it was all right.

"Whatever Miss Mira says."

When his missus laughed at that, a warm feeling curled up inside Ada June. After she pulled the stockings back up, she peeked over at the schoolteacher. "Thank you, Miss Mira."

When the woman smiled, Ada June knew it would be good to call her that, although she'd still think about her being the schoolteacher.

Preacher Gordon came out on the porch to watch them off like he was scared that his missus would maybe never come back. Like she might get lost in Sourwood. Ada June didn't see how that could happen, but then she remembered about her not knowing how to make cornbread. Same as she could show Miss Mira how to do that, she'd make sure she didn't get lost heading to Elsinore's. It wasn't that far. Just over in the woods a ways.

With Bo alongside her, Ada June stayed in front to lead the way. That let her hide her smile. The schoolteacher might wonder what had her smiling like a possum. She peeked back at Miss Mira to make sure she wasn't walking too fast and was some surprised to see she was smiling too.

Just as well they didn't meet nobody on the path to Elsinore's house. Else folks would wonder about all the grinning. Her ma had smiled a lot. Ada June did remember that about her.

At Elsinore's, she was glad to not hear Selinda crying before they got to the door, like as how she did the last time she came. But then after she opened the door a crack to speak out a hello so Elsinore would know who was coming, she heard the baby whimpering. Somehow that was worse than the squalling.

"Miss Elsinore, you here?"

"Now where else would I be, Ada June?" She sounded cross.

"I brung you company."

"I ain't sure I'm up to no company," Elsinore said. "It ain't that Miss Nicey Jane, is it? I ain't wantin' to hear her preachin' at me."

"It's the preacher's wife. Miss Mira."

"The preacher has him a wife?" Elsinore's voice showed some interest. "Well, bring her on in, seein' as how she's here a'ready."

Ada June pushed the door all the way open and went in. Bo slipped past her and headed for the fireplace. He did love to lay by a fire.

Miss Mira followed them but stopped just inside the door and looked across at Elsinore. She was laying abed like as how she was most of the time whenever Ada June came.

"Miss Elsinore, I'm Mira Dean. I mean Mira Covington. I just got married yesterday and I haven't gotten used to my new name." She looked a mite nervous as she held out the jar of soup. "I brought you some of Miss Effie's soup she gave us at church this morning."

"That's right neighborly of you," Elsinore said. "Miss Effie makes a fine soup."

Miss Mira came on into the room then, but she appeared to still be some hesitant. The cabin was a mess, with ashes spilling out on the hearth and baby Selinda's dirty nappies piled on the floor by the bed. A few clean ones were draped across the line down through the middle of the room. At least the fire was burning. That meant Elsinore had been up to keep it going, unless'n she'd let Horace Perry in the door after all.

She wasn't about to ask if that was so. She took the jar of soup from Miss Mira when she looked like she didn't know what to do with it and put it on the table. A plate of food and a glass of milk looked untouched. The baby was still whimpering.

"What's the matter with Selinda?" Ada June asked.

"I don't have no idee. She just nursed. She never seems happy." Elsinore coughed. "You got any babies, Mrs. Covington?"

"Not yet, but I hope to someday."

"They can be a right smart of trouble. Ain't that right, Ada June?" She didn't wait for Ada June to answer. "Ada June knows from having to take care of that Emmy Lou and sometimes help me see to Selinda."

"What a pretty name," Miss Mira said. "May I hold her?"

"If'n you want." Elsinore waved her hand toward the baby on the bed beside her. "She's fussy, but I just put a new nappy on her afore I laid myself down for a rest."

Miss Mira picked up the baby. "Her little hands and feet feel cold."

"Ain't no wonder. She won't keep on no kivers. Kicks them right off."

"Is there a blanket I can wrap around her?"

Ada June didn't see why Miss Mira didn't just grab up the blanket from right there on the bed. Weren't no need tiptoeing 'round Elsinore. But she reckoned Miss Mira couldn't know that.

"There's that one there I cut out of an old quilt Miss Nicey Jane give me. I didn't aim to be bad mouthin' her earlier. She's a good woman." Elsinore pushed up in the bed and shoved a pillow behind her to lean against the wall. "She just ain't never had to worry 'bout when her husband comes home. Leastways not lately. Last time she was down this way, she did claim as to how once upon a time, Mr. Riley was gone a spell and how she had to carry on takin' care of her young'uns." Elsinore let out a long sigh.

"Oh?"

Miss Mira laid Selinda down on the little blanket to wrap it snug around her. She picked her back up and cuddled her close.

The whimpering stopped, which made Ada June feel better. She didn't like babies fretting.

"Like as how she thought I weren't doin' as good, but I do fine by Selinda. All babies fuss some."

"They do." Miss Mira rocked Selinda in her arms.

Elsinore motioned toward a chair. "Sit yoreself down if'n your feet is tired from shanks' maring over this way."

"Shanks' maring?" Miss Mira turned one of the chairs by the table toward the bed and sat down.

"I reckon you ain't mountain, if'n you never heared that before. Means going afoot when a feller don't have a horse." Elsinore peered over at Miss Mira. "Preacher Gordon ain't got him a horse for going, has he?"

"No. I suppose he does that shanks' maring too." Miss Mira held Selinda out in her lap and babbled some nonsense words at her.

Something about babies made folks talk silly. Ada June did the same, but now she kept her mouth closed as she poked at the fire. It was burning fine, but she needed something to do whilst she listened to Elsinore talking things she'd never heard.

She never knew Miss Nicey Jane had that kind of trouble with her man. That was some hard to believe about Mr. Riley. Not that Ada June had been around him much. He always turned the other way whenever she come across him in the holler. 'Course he weren't the only one to do that. Like they was afraid they might have to say howdy to her.

With her back to the women, she poked at the coals under the log to make sparks scatter up the chimney. A body could find out a lot by staying quiet and out of the way.

"You appear to be fond of little ones," Elsinore said.

"I love babies."

"You're apt to have one yore own self afore long."

Ada June looked over her shoulder at Miss Mira, whose face went a little rosy and not from being too close to the fire like Ada June's.

"If the Lord wills it," she said.

"I reckon as how the Lord does send down the babies he intends us having. I'm hopin' for more, soon's Benny gets home."

Ada June wondered if she ought to say something. Could be she should've told Miss Mira about Benny. How everybody but Elsinore figured Benny wouldn't never come home. That poor Benny had stepped over to the other side and the news just hadn't come calling on Elsinore yet.

But Miss Mira kept her eyes on the baby as she murmured, "More like this sweet child would be nice."

Somebody must have done told her about Elsinore's unlikely hopes. Ada June turned back to drop a chunk of wood on the fire. She'd need to bring more in to stack by the fireplace before she left so's Elsinore would have it handy. But right now, she aimed to keep her ears open to see what else she might hear.

Elsinore had a coughing fit. Worse than yesterday. Ada June might ought to go beg Miss Nicey Jane to come see about Elsinore, even if she didn't like the woman preachin' at her. Or maybe Miss Mira would tell Preacher Gordon and they'd figure out what to do.

"That's a bad cough." Miss Mira sounded concerned.

"I can't seem to shake it."

"Maybe you should call in a doctor."

Elsinore spit in her handkerchief and made a sound that was something like a laugh. "Ain't no doctors around these parts. But no need for you to be worrying. I'll get somebody to make me a tonic if'n I ain't better soon. Having Selinda there just pulled me down some." She motioned with her head toward the baby. "But I ain't wishin' different. Benny's gonna love her when he gets here."

When Miss Mira didn't say anything, Elsinore went on like she had to convince herself. "I wouldn't be a bit surprised were he to show up this very night. Same as Mr. Riley did for Miss Nicey Jane them years ago. I've heared he was gone the better part of a year. Most as long as Benny. But he come back. Benny will too.

Something's just delayed him some, but he'll come. Selinda needs her pa."

"All children do," Miss Mira said.

Her words stabbed right through Ada June. What about her pa? Nobody ever seemed the first bit worried about that. She didn't want to listen to no more. "I best get in some wood."

Bo followed Ada June out the door to where Horace Perry had stacked up a good pile of split wood. 'Twas a shame Elsinore couldn't turn loose her thinkin' about Benny and let Horace Perry be Selinda's pa. True, he weren't much to look at but appeared he knew how to be caring.

If'n he acted a mite friendlier, Ada June wouldn't mind thinkin' on him as a pa. But she reckoned her pa, whoever he was, hadn't ever thought on being friendly with her. Guess it could be Mr. Horace Perry same as anybody else in Sourwood.

28

*S*elinda's sweet baby eyelids fluttered and grew heavy
with sleep as Mira swayed her knees back and forth
to rock her. Holding the precious little one made her
desire for a baby burn in her heart. If the Lord willed, she had
told Elsinore. She would pray for that will, but before that, she
could find ways to help this young mother who definitely wasn't
well with that terrible cough. On top of her obvious illness, she
appeared to be in a deep well of sorrow.

In one short day, two people in Sourwood had already stolen
Mira's heart. Ada June and Selinda. Then there was Elsinore and
Joseph. And Gordon. She should save some of her heart for him.
After all, she had vowed to love him in sickness and health, till
death parted them.

She pushed that thought aside. Right now she could concentrate
on loving this baby and her mother. The mother needed it just as
much as the baby. Perhaps more. Did she not have a mother to
help her?

She couldn't ask about Elsinore's relatives. At least not yet.
But the girl did seem so alone except for Ada June and a neighbor
named Horace.

Mira continued to rock the baby while Ada June packed in wood and water. Elsinore paid her no notice. She appeared to take the girl's help for granted. If that was so, then why did the child have to sleep in the woods instead of here in this cabin with the young mother? That would seem the best solution for both of them.

When Ada June had several chunks of wood stacked by the fireplace and two buckets full of water on the cabinet, she carried a plate of food and a glass of milk to Elsinore. "You gotta eat, Elsinore."

"That food don't look a bit good." Elsinore turned her head away and coughed again.

Ada June stood there and waited until the coughing eased up. "Ain't one thing wrong with this stew." She pushed the plate toward the young woman again.

When she started to say something more, Elsinore held up her palm to stop her. "Don't be giving me any of that Aunt Dottie says."

"Wouldn't hurt you none to listen to Aunt Dottie. Even I know if you don't eat, you won't have milk for Selinda."

Elsinore turned her head away. "Eat it yoreself or give it to Bo over there."

Ada June's dog wagged his tail at the sound of his name, but Ada June didn't dump the plate for him. "I ain't eatin' it and neither is Bo." She sounded like somebody's mother.

"Give me the milk. I'll drink it down."

"Crumble up the cornbread in it. Looks as how Granny Perry makes fine cornbread."

When Ada June peeked over at her, Mira almost laughed. The girl must still be flabbergasted that anybody could not know how to make cornbread.

Elsinore took a little drink of the milk. "I can't eat that cornbread, Ada June. The way I'm coughing, I would choke on it for sure. Do as I say. Bo wants it."

Bo wagged his tail again and perked up his ears. Ada June sighed and gave in. She nibbled at the crusty part of the cornbread before giving the rest to the dog that swallowed it in one gulp. Ada June shoved the plate toward Elsinore again. "You gotta eat the rest of it."

Elsinore lowered the milk glass and looked at Ada June. "Somebody's gettin' a little big for their britches 'round here."

Ada June didn't back down. "You have to eat." She looked a little guilty as she went on. "So's you feel right when Benny gets home."

Mira could tell Ada June didn't believe that would ever happen, but she was ready to say anything to convince Elsinore to eat.

"You fussin' ain't gonna make me do nothing I don't wanna do." Elsinore's eyes narrowed and her face stiffened. "And us carryin' on so ain't no way to act in front of company. You'll have the preacher's wife thinkin' she needs to pray over us."

They both looked over at Mira, and she surprised herself by saying, "I would like to pray with you before we leave."

She didn't know where those words came from. She never prayed in front of anybody except a short prayer to start the school day. But those were practiced words. What in the world made her think she could pray words out loud over this young woman and her baby?

Mira stood up, holding the baby still to keep from waking her. "Pull the chair over close to the bed and set the plate there, Ada June, where Elsinore can reach it when she's ready to eat."

Ada June shrugged and did as Mira said, with a look at her dog to let him know the food wasn't for him.

"Do you want me to lay the baby beside you, Elsinore, or is there a cradle?" Mira looked around.

"She's fine right here." Elsinore scooted over a little and smoothed out a spot on the bed. "I can see to her fine that way and make sure she keeps her kivers on."

"That might help her sleep better." Mira placed the baby where Elsinore pointed. When the baby stirred a little, Mira patted her to settle her back to sleep.

She straightened up and hesitated, but both Elsinore and Ada June seemed to be waiting for her to pray. "Let's join our thoughts in prayer."

She shut her eyes and pulled in a breath for courage. "Dear Lord, thank you for this day and for this mother and baby. Thank you for Ada June and her sweet spirit and how she cares for others. Help your child, Elsinore, feel better and watch over her and this beautiful baby girl. Amen."

Elsinore dabbed her eyes with her handkerchief. "That was nice, Miss Mira. Thankee."

"Thank you for letting me hold Selinda," Mira said. "I hope she sleeps awhile to let you rest."

"That ain't likely. She'll be wantin' to nurse afore long."

"Then, perhaps you should try to eat before she wakes up."

"I reckon I can. If you want to hand me that plate. Granny Perry's stew is kindly worth eatin'." She handed Mira the half-empty glass of milk and took the plate of food. She grinned at Ada June. "Thataway Miss Bossy Pants Ada June can be smilin' and not be carryin' no tales to her Aunt Dottie 'bout me not eatin' like as how she thinks I oughta."

"I don't carry tales." Ada June scrunched up her face.

That made Elsinore laugh and Ada June frown more.

"I'm just a-raggin' on you. You know I 'preciate you, and see, I'm eating." She took a bite. "Now you best git on to milkin' that cow of Miss Dottie's 'fore dark comes on."

After another aggravated look at Elsinore, Ada June turned to Mira. "If'n you're aimin' to take your leave, I'll point you toward Preacher's house."

"I'm ready." Mira looked at Elsinore. "Would it be all right if I come see you again?"

"You come on any old time you want to rock this fussy babe to sleep."

Mira followed Ada June and Bo outside. Clouds were hanging low and daylight was fading.

"I didn't think it was that late," Mira said.

"Dark comes fast in the holler." Ada June pointed at the path away from Elsinore's cabin. "Preacher's house is right over that way. I gotta milk Aunt Dottie's cow." She clicked her tongue at Bo and headed up the hill.

Mira looked the way Ada June pointed. A faint trace led off into the trees. But if she walked straight, she would be fine. She called out to Ada June. "Wait, Ada June."

The girl stopped to look back at her.

"If you can't sleep at Miss Dottie's or Elsinore's, you come on to Preacher Gordon's house. We'll make you a pallet by the fire. That would be better than on trees, wouldn't it?"

Ada June looked down at Bo without saying anything.

"Bo can come in too."

The girl nodded before she went on up the hill.

Poor child, tossed betwixt and between with no place she could depend on to find a true welcome. Not even at Elsinore's for whatever reason. Mira could give her that welcome. She thought Gordon would want to do the same, although she should have asked before she offered. Her heart followed after Ada June as she disappeared into the trees.

She turned back toward Gordon's house. Her house, she reminded herself again. But she couldn't expect to feel at home here so soon. At the same time, she'd had no problem opening her heart to these girls she'd met.

Perhaps Ada June would come tomorrow to give her that cornbread baking lesson. How in the world did you bake something in an open fire? Mira sighed. She had so much to learn about this place and these people.

Right now the smallest things seemed like big problems. How would she have privacy enough to take a bath? And where did they get their food with no markets?

The shadows deepened under the trees. She was no longer sure of the path. She looked back and saw nothing but trees and rocks. She didn't think she'd walked that far from Elsinore's house.

She had no sense of direction. Of course, she knew the sun went down in the west, but the dark clouds overhead hid any sight of it. Besides, she had no idea if the house was south or north, east or west.

Her heart began to beat too fast as night seemed to fall over her like a heavy blanket. Which way? A snowflake drifted down to land on her cloak. Wind moved through the pines overhead. Moments earlier she'd thought the wind sang through the pines, but now it sounded more like moaning as snowflakes swirled around her.

"Calm down." She muttered the words aloud.

She wasn't lost. Yet. Elsinore's house was only a little way behind her, whether she could see it or not. Gordon's house had to be just beyond the trees. In the holler, as Ada June would say. The dark holler right now.

She would not panic. They had climbed up the hill. If she kept going down, she would come out in the clearing and see their house.

Wind blew snow in under the trees. She pulled her cape tighter and held on to her hat as she kept walking. A huge boulder loomed up before her to block her way. They had not passed anything like this on the way to Elsinore's house.

She was lost. In a snowstorm. With night falling around her.

29

She stepped to the side of the rock where she was sheltered from the wind. That helped settle her nerves as she tried to think. She had gone downhill, but somewhere she must have strayed off the right path. Even so, if she continued walking down, she would eventually come out of the trees and find her way to warmth. To Gordon.

If only she had a dog like Bo to lead her home. She almost smiled. At least she'd thought it home instead of Gordon's house.

No sooner had the thought of a dog entered her mind than one bounded around the rock, barking ferociously. Not Bo. The black dog was twice as big as Bo and might have been nearly invisible in the dim light except for the snow collecting on its fur. It hunched down and bared its teeth, ready to spring at her. It stopped barking, but the growl deep in its throat sounded worse.

Mira froze against the rock. Her fiercest teacher stare would be of no use. She took a steadying breath. Dogs could sense fear.

"Get away." She spoke firmly.

The growling rumble stopped, but the animal stayed crouched in front of her. She scooted a small step to the side. The dog jumped up with a loud bark. Mira shrank back, but the rock blocked her escape.

"Down, Reb." A man's voice came from the trees.

The dog dropped to the ground.

Mira waited for the man to come into view and hoped it was someone she'd met at church. Even that Cleo with his fierce eyes would be a welcome sight, but when the man came around the rock, it definitely wasn't Cleo Rayburn.

She couldn't see the man's face below his hat brim, but while he made a broad shape in the dim light, he wasn't much more than a half foot taller than she was. After a long moment, he spoke in a voice that was almost as much a growl as his dog's. "Who are you?"

Mira moistened her lips. "Mira Covington."

"Covington. The woman told me the preacher brung in a fool city girl. What you doing pokin' round here where you ain't got no business?"

"I apologize if I'm trespassing." Mira lifted her chin and kept her voice steady. What gave him the right to call her a fool girl? She saw no reason to explain herself except she was lost and did need his help. "I was visiting Elsinore. After it started snowing, I couldn't see the proper path."

"You could find trouble wanderin' around these parts, missy."

"Yes." She thought she already had.

"Don't know how you found your way to that girl's house if you ain't got no woods' sense."

"Ada June showed me the way."

"Ada June, huh." The man spit on the ground and stepped closer. "Just like her to leave you adrift."

Mira didn't like his tone. "She pointed the way, but she was late to milk her aunt's cow. I thought I could find the way."

"She don't have no aunts in Sourwood that I know of." He blew out a harsh breath.

"Miss Dottie—" Mira started.

The man raised his hand to cut her off. "I knowed who you meant, but that girl lacks good sense. Guess as how it's to be expected with how her ma was. No sense at all there."

"Did you know her mother?"

"I knowed her. Not that it's any of your bother."

"You're right. I don't have to know her mother. I know Ada June and see what a good heart she has."

"You done learned that in one day, have you?"

The man seemed to want to goad her into an argument. She would not let that happen. She decided to start over. "I don't think I met you at church."

"Reckon not. Seeing as how I wasn't there, and don't bother asking why."

She could feel him staring at her, maybe waiting for her to ask anyway, but when she didn't, he went on. "I guess you want to know my name. Folks is always after names, like that will make them friendly like."

Mira could simply walk away. The dog wasn't eyeing her now and instead appeared to be half-asleep. But it would be better if the man would point her in the right direction. She was about to ask his help when he made a sound that might be a laugh.

"I ain't always so ornery, Missus Covington." He stepped closer. "Reckon coming on you unexpected has me forgettin' my manners and actin' worse than Reb there. I'm Riley Callahan." He tipped his hat at her.

"Miss Nicey Jane's husband."

He snorted another laugh but didn't sound amused at all. "I reckon that's how most folks think of ol' Riley Callahan. As the woman's man."

"I'm sorry. I didn't intend to upset you. It's just that I've met your wife and well . . ." She stopped, not sure what else to say.

"No need in lettin' it fret you. Or me. It's just how things are here in Sourwood with my woman tryin' to run things. Does a fair job of it without no help from me nor nobody else."

"Gordon says she's a big help to him." Mira smiled even though the man wouldn't be able to see her face in the dark. "I'm sure you have been as well."

"I don't know what makes you sure of that, but I did help put up his church."

"Are you helping with the schoolhouse too?"

"I've done some."

"Then I thank you for that. I look forward to teaching the children here in Sourwood."

"Now, do you? A preacher's woman and a schoolmarm. A fine trick your man pulled off whilst he was off in the city." He stepped closer until she could almost feel his breath on her face. The dog got up and came close to her other side.

"I suppose so." Mira's teeth chattered, partly from the cold, but more because of Riley Callahan. His words sounded nicer, but she didn't like being hemmed in between him and the dog, with the rock behind her. "If you would be kind enough to point me in the direction of Gordon's house, I'd be grateful."

"I'm thinkin' your house too if'n you married him."

"Yes." She could see the shine of his eyes and the snow on his hat. She wanted to shove past him and run in any direction just to get away from him.

"Preacher shouldn't have trusted his bride to that oddball girl. It can be dangerous wanderin' around in a strange woods. No tellin' what a body might run into."

She sensed he recognized and was amused by her fear. That he might be laughing at her lit a flame of anger in her that burned away some of that fear. "Sometimes a man and his dog not willing to help a stranger." She pushed away from the rock and stepped past the dog. When it growled, she ignored it and kept going.

The man laughed. "A spitfire, are you? Preacher might be wondering what he's got himself into. Womenfolk can be a trial."

She kept walking, hoping against hope she wouldn't slip and fall in the snow. If that happened, the dog might be at her throat.

"Best move some to your right, Missus."

She didn't look back but was relieved he didn't seem to be following her.

"Mira." Her name came floating on the wind.

The dog let loose another of its ferocious barks.

The man hushed the dog with a word before he said, "Appears Preacher has come lookin' for his bride. Best give a holler so's he'll know where you got lost to."

"Gordon," she yelled, but the snow and wind seemed to swallow the sound of her voice.

"That ain't much louder than a mouse squeak." Callahan made a sound of disgust. "Guess I'll have to help you out." He let out a bellow. "Here, Preacher."

"Thank you, Mr. Callahan." Mira looked back at the man by the rock.

"Naught but my pleasure, ma'am, but if'n I was you, I'd just stand where's you are and wait for Preacher to find you. Just yonder is a big sink. Hard to see in the dark, but wouldn't want you to fall in it and break your pretty head."

With that he made a motion at the dog and they both disappeared into the night.

Gordon yelled her name again. He was closer now, and when she called back, he heard her.

When he ran out from under some pines, he knocked off a flurry of snow. He grabbed her in an embrace. "Mira, are you all right?"

Shivers shook through her as she leaned into him. "I thought I was going the right way, but it started snowing and I couldn't see the path."

"Shh. Let's get you to the house to warm up." He kept one arm around her as he turned her back the way he'd come. "Who yelled? And I heard a dog. Not Bo."

"I ran into Riley Callahan and his dog." She didn't know what she should say about the man. It seemed silly now to think how frightened she'd been without any real reason. "I couldn't yell loud enough to make you hear me at first."

"Oh." His voice sounded a little stiff. "I'll have to make a point of thanking him."

"Don't you like him?"

"Riley is Riley. One of a kind, but then that goes for most of those up here in the hills. They probably say the same about me."

The path through the trees was too narrow for them to walk side by side. With reluctance, she stepped away from him. "You go first and I'll stay on your heels."

The way to the house was just as short as she'd thought and not at all hard. She would have to explore during the daylight hours to get her bearings.

The flickering warmth of the fire was more than welcome when they went inside. He helped her out of her cloak and hung it on a peg by the door. When she took off her hat, snow shook down on the floor. She watched it melt. She was so glad to be back inside Gordon's house. Her house.

"Thank you for coming to find me," she said.

He put his hands on her shoulders. The cabin was only dimly lit, but the feeling in his eyes as he stared down at her was easy to see. "Always, Mira. You never have to fear about that. I will always come for you. You're my wife."

Gently, he pulled her closer to him. She didn't resist. Her house. Her husband. His hug. It all felt right.

30

The roof was on, the logs chinked, and the wooden floor down in the school the first week in February. The men made benches for the children. Gordon found a teacher's desk who knew where. The start of school was delayed another week while Dugan Foster and his son, Billy Ray, built the outhouse Mira had insisted was necessary.

Finally on the second Monday in February, she stood in the school door to wait for children to come. At church, Gordon had announced school would begin the next day, but she had no idea how many students to expect. Not only were some in the community unsure about a brought-in teacher, a few inches of snow had fallen during the night.

Gordon got up well before daylight to build a fire in the pot-belly stove that was a gift from one of the mission's supporters in Louisville. Mira knew she should close the door to let the school warm up, but she stayed where she was. She had to be where the children could see her and know how happy she was to be their teacher.

The cold mountain air seemed to give her a burst of energy, or maybe it was the smell of old books behind her. Whatever the reason, excitement stirred inside her. Slates were on the benches ready for the children. Posters with the alphabet and numbers adorned the rough walls. Her clock sat on a shelf beside her desk.

She even had a bell. Miss Ophelia's treasured teacher's bell. Mira cried when she opened that package from Miss Ophelia and shed more tears over the coat and shoes the right size she'd sent for Ada June.

Now Ada June was still at the house. Since Mira hadn't changed her mind about the problems dogs could cause in a schoolroom, she had reluctantly agreed to leave Bo shut up there during school. The place was like home to him now, since Ada June spent most nights on the cot Gordon had put in the corner of their front room.

Mira looked at the path that led past the church toward their house. No sign of the girl yet. Ada June wanted to learn, but Mira still wasn't sure she would come on to school without Bo. The dog somehow gave her courage.

Besides, she knew Mira would keep teaching her at home the way she'd been doing for weeks. Joseph too. When she started reading lessons with Ada June back in January, Joseph hung around, pretending not to be interested. But Ada June's excitement about learning to read was contagious. Soon Joseph sat with them, forming letters and then words on a slate.

If the snow didn't stop him, Joseph would surely come today. No sooner had the thought crossed her mind than Billy Ray Foster rounded the corner of the schoolhouse, followed by Joseph hurrying to keep up. Then other children came down the paths toward the school. Each one who came into sight was a gift that warmed her heart so that she barely felt the cold air blowing in through the door with them.

She was a little surprised when Connor Rayburn and his little brother Jimmy came down the road. She hadn't thought their father, Cleo, would let them come, but here they were. Jimmy raced across the yard and up the steps to slip inside past Mira with a shy smile. Connor followed with a swagger, not wanting to give any appearance of eagerness. His buddy Marv ran down the road to catch up with him in the schoolyard. Marv's hound was right beside him as always, something the same as Bo always with Ada June.

Mira took another look at the path toward her house. Still no Ada June.

Marv and Connor started up the steps. When the hound stopped, Marv grabbed the rope around his neck and pulled him along with them.

"Good morning, boys." Mira used her cheeriest voice. "Glad you're here, but no dogs can come inside, Marv. Your dog will have to stay outside."

"But it's cold, Missus Covington," Marv said.

"His fur coat will keep him warm enough."

"Bet you're gonna let in that girl's dog." Connor gave her a smirk.

Mira kept her smile easy. "You heard me. No dogs in the schoolroom."

Connor poked Marv. "Then I reckon we won't have to be bothered with that woods colt."

"That's enough." Mira held her hand up to stop his words. "We don't talk like that here."

"I reckon I can say whatever I want to say." Connor laughed.

"Yes, as long as you remember to only want to say the right things." She gave him a stern look. "No bad talk here. You have to follow the rules. My rules."

"Your rules, huh. How you aimin' to make me?" His laughter turned to a scowl. "You lay a finger on me, my pa will run you out of Sourwood."

She'd hoped to have a few days to get to know the children before trouble showed up, but perhaps it was best to face it early. She ignored Connor's threat. She had no plans to use brute force on her students. She would lose that battle early. She kept her gaze steady on the boys.

Marv let go of his hound and shuffled his feet. "Come on, Connor. Just go on in."

"You gonna let some brought-in woman tell you what you kin do?" Connor glared at Marv as he turned to go back down the steps. "Let's get out of here."

Marv looked even more uncomfortable. "I gotta go in. I promised Ma I'd learn to read so's I could read the Bible to her." He waved his dog back and, with a guilty look at Connor, stepped past Mira.

Mira didn't smile, although she wanted to as she watched Connor, who didn't seem to know what to do after Marv's desertion. Then she stopped trying to not smile when Ada June ran across the yard to push past Connor on the steps as if she had no worries in the world except getting to school on time.

Inside the clock chimed eight. Mira looked past Connor. No other children were in sight. "Come in when you're ready, Connor. I won't count tardiness today, but from now on students need to be inside before eight."

She moved back and shut the door. Billy Ray Foster stepped up beside her. "Connor givin' you trouble, Miss Mira?"

"He appears to be uncertain about coming in. That's all."

"I reckon I better go talk to him," Billy Ray said.

"If you want, but he needs to make up his own mind."

"If'n you don't care, I'll help him with that."

When Billy Ray's eyes narrowed before he headed out the door, Mira almost felt sorry for Connor. He looked that much like his mother, and Mira had been in Sourwood long enough to know Miss Effie didn't put up with any nonsense. She wasn't surprised when they both came in the door a few minutes later while she was welcoming her students.

Connor found a place on a bench near the door. Billy Ray settled behind him. Ada June perched on the end of a front bench the other children had left empty. Mira would have to assign the children benches, but not today. Today was for getting to know them, for being glad to be in front of a classroom again, and most of all for trusting the Lord to help her meet the challenges of teaching this group of children.

She took a moment to study their faces. Some smiled at her while others looked unsure of what she might expect of them. Two or three appeared to be like Connor and not at all happy to be there.

"Welcome to Sourwood Mission School." Mira smiled at the children watching her so expectantly. "I'm Mrs. Covington, your teacher. I'm here to help you learn and I expect you to help each other as well. But first every morning, we will ask the Lord for his powerful help. Pray with me."

She bowed her head and asked the Lord's blessings on their day and their school. After she said amen, she went on. "This Bible verse will be a guide for our behavior here. 'Therefore all things whatsoever ye would that men should do to you, do ye even so to them: for this is the law and the prophets.' Matthew 7:12. That means to do unto others as you would have them do unto you." She paused a few seconds to look at each child before she went on. "Please repeat that with me. Do unto others as you would have them do unto you."

By the third repetition, most of the children knew the words. Not all said the words with her, but most had. Connor hadn't. Ada June hadn't. At least not out loud. But Joseph and Billy Ray had, and even the littlest girl there who didn't look over five said some of the words. It was a good start.

Gordon came in at the end of the school day with a sack of peppermint candy to make for a sweet ending to the first day for the children. Mira could only hope that would bring them back the next day.

He waited while she straightened the room and put the slates back on the benches. To get them used to the slates, she'd let them draw pictures or copy their names that she wrote across the top of their slates. There were houses, trees, and what might be dogs or cows. She wasn't sure which. A couple of stick figures with an abundance of hair had to be the students' portrait of their teacher.

She laughed and showed them to Gordon.

"Not you." He shook his head and reached to touch her hair. "Not nearly enough curls in that hair."

Mira hooked some of those stray curls behind her ears. "I need more hairpins."

"No hairpins is best." His eyes were intense on her, a warm, loving look.

She looked down to hide her blush. He gently put his fingers under her chin to pull her face up to look at him.

"Do you know what today is?" he asked. "February fourteenth."

"Valentine's Day. But I've never paid that much notice."

"Nor have I. But today I think we should take a walk and consider the blessings of love."

"I don't know. I need to cook our supper and prepare for tomorrow's lessons."

"A walk first. Later I'll find us something to eat while you do your lesson preparations. But snow is falling again in soft, fat flakes. The very best time for a walk." He got her coat off one of the hooks on the wall and held it while she slipped her arms into the sleeves. He pulled her back against him for a moment before he turned her loose to let her put on her hat. "I love your curls."

The snow was as beautiful as Gordon had promised. It covered the ground in a white blanket and muffled the sounds of the community around them.

They walked past the church and their house on to the creek where snowflakes melted in the water to join the rush downhill. Mira held out her hand to let two snowflakes settle softly on her gloved palm.

"Each one unique," she said as she studied the icy designs. "Like the children who came to school today."

"Yes." But Gordon wasn't looking at the snowflakes. He was

looking at her. "Like you." He paused a moment before he added, "Like our marriage. Unique but blessed. Very blessed."

She thought she should turn away, start back toward their house, but she felt captured by his eyes. "Blessed." She echoed his word, and the truth of it warmed her even as snow swirled around them.

"You are the valentine I never knew I needed, but the Lord knew. He has blessed me beyond measure." Gordon put his hands on her shoulders and leaned down to kiss her.

Without even looking around to see if anyone was around to see them, Mira stepped into his embrace.

When he lifted his lips from hers, his voice was husky. "Let's go home, my love."

After they stepped up on the porch, he picked her up in his arms as he had the first day when she had teased him into carrying her over the threshold.

She laughed. "What are you doing?"

"I was pushed into carrying you over the threshold back in January, but not this time. I want you to know that I'll always be here for you. Ready to carry you, love you, help you, and do whatever you need."

"What will Ada June think if she sees us?"

"She told me to let you know she has to stay at Miss Dottie's tonight. The baby is fussy and Emmy Lou has a cold."

"Mr. Luther is gone?"

"Yes."

"I'll miss her."

"She promises to be back before breakfast. But tonight can be ours."

Mira smiled and rested her head on Gordon's shoulder. "Ours" suddenly sounded like a very good word.

31

*O*ver here, Miss Mira. I'm thinkin' you ain't never seen a bloom like this."

Mira tilted her head a little and gave Ada June a teacher look.

"I mean I'm thinking you haven't never seen a bloom like this." Ada June changed her words before she motioned for Mira.

Mira smiled as she followed her. She'd have to take satisfaction in Ada June correcting the use of "ain't." She wouldn't worry about the double negative. One step at a time. Besides, when they were out in the woods, Ada June was the teacher. Not Mira.

Winter had passed into spring in Sourwood. The pinkish purple of redbud blooms looked lovely against the green of pines. Dogwoods had buds that promised more beauty to come. Fragile-looking wildflowers poked up through last fall's leaves.

Ada June and Joseph had waited on the schoolhouse steps until after Mira finished straightening the room to have it ready for Monday. They were excited about taking her wildflower hunting. Now, out in the woods, they ran ahead to find flowers to show her.

Each Friday when she closed the school until Monday, she thanked the Lord for another week of learning and for helping her meet the challenge of teaching a roomful of children of disparate ages and abilities. She had come to love all the children, but these two, Ada June and Joseph, were the closest to her heart.

She had leaned on the Lord to help her love a few determined troublemakers, but she wouldn't think about them this afternoon. Instead, she would push aside all worries about next week's lessons and take joy in the sunshine and her two flower guides.

When she caught up with Ada June, she didn't see any blooms, only a few fan-shaped green leaves. "Where's the flower?"

Ada June giggled and lifted up two of the leaves to reveal a white bloom hiding underneath.

Mira stooped down to get a better look. "Oh, that's wonderful."

Joseph came up behind them, his face in a little pout. "I was going to show you one of them."

Mira smiled at him. "Good. I'd love to see more."

"Did you find a purple or red one? Those are the prettiest." Ada June looked around. Her dog was right beside her as always.

The girl didn't seem at all bothered that Joseph might find a better flower than she had. She had such a generous heart that Mira could not understand why so many of the children excluded her. At least, Joseph had given up that kind of behavior. Despite the difference in their ages, Joseph and Ada June found common ground in stories. He'd even made friends with Bo.

Now Mira softly traced the petals of the bloom under the leaves. The children in Sourwood were something like these flowers with their beauty hidden beneath their rough exteriors.

"Show us the ones you found," Ada June said.

The boy, his pout gone, took off up the trail, with Ada June and Bo on his heels. Mira followed more slowly as she breathed in the fragrance of the woods and listened to the birds singing.

Even after the children went out of sight, she didn't worry about getting lost the way she had her first time in the woods. While she still didn't know every path, she felt at home in Sourwood now.

Rarely did she give more than a fleeting thought to the life she had so fearfully left behind in Louisville, except when she got a letter from Miss Ophelia. Then the thoughts were only of how grateful she was to the woman for pushing her to take the challenge of coming to Sourwood.

In her last letter, Miss Ophelia told Mira to bloom where she was planted. Mira smiled when she noticed a delicate-looking white anemone flower. She hoped to have the same persistence to bloom as these wildflowers that appeared spring after spring.

"Miss Mira, has you done got lost agin?" Joseph came back down the path.

"Not lost. Just woolgathering." Mira walked faster to catch up with him. "Lead the way to those flowers. By the way, what are they called?"

Mira needed to ask Miss Ophelia to send a flower book. Even better, perhaps the children could draw pictures of the flowers and put the names with them to make their own Sourwood flower book. She would need some drawing paper for that.

Joseph looked back over his shoulder at Mira. "Ada June names them bent head something. Don't know how she knows that. Granny Effie would know, but Ada June ain't got a granny to teach her that kind of stuff."

"Maybe Miss Dottie or Miss Elsinore told her." Mira didn't bother correcting his use of "ain't." How people talked was hard to change, and they were in the woods to have fun.

"Nah. They wouldn't know." He sounded very sure of that.

"Why not?"

"You have to be old to know stuff like that."

"I see. But Ada June isn't old."

"That's how come she probably don't know what's she's talkin' about."

Mira laughed. They definitely needed a flower book.

Ada June was on her knees on the side of a steep hill beside a whole patch of the broad-leaved flowers. She flipped some up to reveal rosy-red blooms.

"Just pick one of them and bring it here," Joseph told her. When she hesitated, he went on. "It ain't like there's only one of them. There's probably a hundred, right, Miss Mira?"

He knew his numbers but still hadn't quite embraced the concept of how many one hundred was.

"Perhaps not that many, but if Ada June would rather let them keep growing, I can see from here."

Ada June shrugged and broke off a stem before she scurried across the steep hill to where Mira and Joseph waited. Bo ran ahead of her. He didn't slip in the leaves. Ada June did.

Mira caught her breath, imagining a bone-breaking catastrophe. "Be careful."

Ada June grabbed a sapling to stop her slide and laughed. After she stuck the flower stem down into the top of her blouse, she scuttled the rest of the way to them. She was still smiling when she handed Mira the flower.

"That was a little too steep," Mira said.

"This ain't all that steep," Joseph spoke up. "You oughter see the hill behind Granny Effie's. It about tips a feller backwards whilst he's climbin' it."

Ada June nodded. "A body can make it up most any hill as long as you grab hold of something with roots that will hold. Else you're liable to be at the bottom again and have to start up all over." She pointed down the hill.

"I'll remember that." Mira looked at the flower under the two big leaves. "A very pretty color."

"I was the one what pointed them out to Ada June."

"You have a good eye for flowers." Mira bragged on him.

"You do," Ada June added.

Joseph beamed. "Come on. I know where some are that look like britches."

"Dutchman's britches," Ada June called before she took off after him.

Mira walked faster to keep them in sight. She didn't know why she felt so out of breath. The paths that snaked around the hills were steep, but she had followed Gordon up and down many of them in the last months to talk families into letting their children come to school.

When the going was steep, she got a little winded, but nothing like today. She wanted to stop and lean against a tree to rest.

The fact was, she'd been feeling under the weather all week. Not with a cold but just tired, and the eggs she had for breakfast hadn't set well with her. Maybe she should ask Miss Nicey Jane for a tonic. Not that the tonics she made for Elsinore were doing much good.

The poor girl's cough kept getting worse. She seemed to be fading in front of their eyes even while Selinda grew bigger. Miss Nicey Jane said Elsinore was grieving herself to death, and she didn't know of any tonics to cure that. The news had finally made it through the hills that Elsinore's Benny had been killed in a coal mine accident nearly a year ago.

Everybody said Elsinore should entertain Horace Perry's courtship now, but although Elsinore had unbarred the door and let him come in, she wasn't entertaining anything other than wood for her fire and food for her table.

Mira thought being pushed toward considering a marriage to Horace Perry had Elsinore more ready to take to her bed. Not that he wasn't a good man. Elsinore didn't argue against that, but he was twice as old as her. More than that, he was not her Benny.

The girl needed time to properly grieve. Mira dared to say something of the kind a couple of weeks ago when the women were discussing what to do about Elsinore in the churchyard. Miss Nicey Jane had let Mira know that somebody brought-in couldn't know how things were in the hills. A woman without family had to keep going however best she could, and if a good man was waiting at the door, that woman should be grateful. It didn't matter how he looked or how old he might be.

"What has the girl done already but grieve for nigh on a year?"

Miss Nicey Jane's eyes had tightened in disapproval of not only Elsinore's hesitation to accept the logical solution to her problems but also of Mira speaking up.

When Mira made no answer, Miss Nicey Jane's face softened as she patted Mira's arm. "Things aren't the same up here in the hills as down where you're from. Women have to do whatever they have to do."

Wasn't that what Mira herself had done? But she wasn't about to share that with Miss Nicey Jane or anybody else in Sourwood. No one needed to know she had married Gordon less than a week after seeing him for the first time in years. After she had called his proposal ridiculous. Her face still flushed hot when she thought about how forward she'd been on the train to Jackson.

She had taken advantage of his desire for a teacher for his mission school. In turn, he had taken advantage of her need for a teaching position and for a home. Whatever had put them together, it was working. Not "whatever." Gordon said chance had nothing to do with it. The Lord had put them together for his purpose. For good.

Gordon. He was a gift to the Sourwood people. He was a gift to her. He whispered words of love to her now when they came together and didn't seem concerned that she could not say the same back to him. She was glad to be by his side. Glad he was willing to add his prayers to hers about the schoolchildren. Blessed that he was understanding, and thankful for his kind spirit that loved so freely.

In time, she hoped to answer his love with hers. In time.

The sound of Ada June's and Joseph's yells pulled her away from her thoughts. Bo's barks added to the commotion. Mira took a deep breath and hurried up the hill.

"Just because you're feared of somethin' don't mean you have to kill it," Ada June yelled.

Beside a huge boulder, Joseph had a rock in his hand ready to attack something behind Ada June. "It's a snake." He sounded more than sure that was reason enough to kill it.

"It's not a rattler. Just a little garter snake. Leave it be. It don't hurt nothing."

"I seen it strikin' at you like as how it wanted to bite." Joseph kept his arm up ready to throw the stone.

Snake. That word put chills up Mira's back. She didn't like snakes and had been on the lookout for them ever since Gordon had warned her to watch her step in the woods.

Ada June reached down next to the boulder, grabbed the snake behind its head, and held it out toward Mira. "Miss Mira, tell Joseph this kind of snake won't hurt anybody."

Poisonous or not, it was still a snake. Mira took a step back and held her palm out to keep Ada June from coming closer. "I can see it from here."

"She don't like 'em either." Joseph waved the rock menacingly.

"That's true, Joseph. I don't. But put the rock down. Ada June is right. The snake won't hurt us. Especially if she puts it down to let it go on its way." She managed a smile. "Just think of the stories it will have to tell its friends after being threatened by a giant and saved by another one."

"We ain't giants, and snakes don't have no friends." Joseph made a face but dropped the rock.

"I suppose they have at least one," Mira said. "One named Ada June."

That made Ada June giggle as she stroked the little snake's head while its tongue flickered in and out, and it twisted its body trying to escape her clutches. Bo sat on his haunches and looked as ready as Joseph to grab the snake and put an end to it.

"You might like it, Ada June, but it don't like you." Joseph backed up faster than Mira when Ada June moved toward him.

"All right, scaredy-cat. I'll let it go." When she put it down, Bo jumped for it, but the snake slithered to safety under some rocks.

"Looks like Bo knows more'n you and that snakes ain't meant to be friends," Joseph said.

Ada June put her fists on her hips and glared at Bo. The dog's ears drooped as he hunkered down and whined.

"Maybe we should stick to looking for flowers," Mira said.

"Suits me." Joseph started past the boulders.

"Not that way." Ada June grabbed his arm. "We best go on up the hill or over that way."

Joseph stopped and looked where she pointed. "You wanting to go to Miss Elsinore's house? Won't be no flowers to amount to anything around her place. Ever'thing's all tromped down around there."

"We can find plenty on the hill up to Granny Perry's house or toward Aunt Dottie's." Ada June still held his arm.

"But I'm thinkin' over that way will be more than plenty." Joseph wasn't giving in.

"I can show you a cave up past Elsinore's," Ada June said.

For a moment, he seemed ready to give in, but then his eyes tightened in a stubborn look. "Probably full of rattlers."

Ada June lost her patience. "We can't go that way." She looked at Mira. "Tell him, Miss Mira. It ain't safe." Ada June didn't notice saying "ain't" this time.

Nothing seemed different about one hillside or the other. Then Mira took a better look at the huge boulder behind Ada June and knew this was the very place where she'd ended up lost on that January day after her first visit to Elsinore. The place where Riley Callahan had come out of the shadows to make her want to run from him even if she didn't know which way to go.

Now she felt the same odd chill as if she expected the man and his hound to appear from the other side of the rock the way he had then.

"We better do as Ada June says. We don't have much more time before we'll need to go home." Mira kept her voice light.

"I don't see why she gets to say what we do." Joseph tried to shake her hand off his arm.

Ada June held tight and leaned down to look right in his face. "That's Mr. Riley's place over thataway. You understand?"

He turned around at once. "I reckon there might be rattlers over there."

"Rattlers for sure." Ada June sounded relieved as she followed Joseph along a faint path across the other hill.

Mira had no idea why Ada June was so against going onto Mr. Riley's hillside, but she was glad to leave the boulder behind. She ignored the heaviness in her legs and kept up with the children. She had promised them a wildflower adventure. A little fatigue was no reason to ruin the day.

Sunshine pushed down through the trees. She wondered which tree gave Sourwood its name. Gordon said they were beautiful when they bloomed. She needed to ask when that was. It could be she should also ask why Riley Callahan's hillside wasn't safe.

32

Ada June was sorry the little snake had crawled out from under its rock for some sunshine right in plain view. She didn't want to mess up their fun by fussing with Joseph, but she couldn't let him smash its head just because it was being what it was. A snake.

She liked Joseph, but he was a boy. Boys were always wanting to kill things. Some boys anyway. Some men too. With them, you had to keep away. You had to figure things like that out. The way she knew she was better off not being in the same house as Mr. Luther. The way she knew they didn't want to step over on Mr. Riley's hill.

Some places a person didn't want to come up on where they didn't have no business. And for certain, they didn't have no business at Mr. Riley's place. He might be married to Miss Nicey Jane, but that didn't mean they were exactly alike.

Not that Miss Nicey Jane was ever ready to see Ada June either, but she was fine with Miss Mira most all the time. Nobody could be fine with everybody all the time. Just like her and Joseph. They got along most always. Even Bo had took to Joseph. That didn't mean that sometimes she wasn't ready to wish him off somewhere else. He could be pesky.

But she could talk to him. She kept adding people that didn't make her throat freeze up. She still didn't say anything at the schoolhouse. Unless she was in there alone with Miss Mira.

She did love Miss Mira. She had wanted a schoolteacher to learn her to read. But Preacher Gordon said sometimes the Lord answered prayers you hadn't even thought up. When he preached on such as that, she had the feeling he was thinking some the same as she did about the prayers they'd said for a schoolteacher. The Lord had answered with more. Way more. A wife for Preacher Gordon and, for Ada June, somebody willing—even wanting—to take her in.

Ada June hadn't slept out in the woods for months. She might again with how it was warming up and all, but she liked the cot Miss Mira asked Preacher Gordon to put in his front room. Special for her. She spent most nights there except when Aunt Dottie needed her to stay if the baby was fretful.

Aunt Dottie had borne Luke without the first bit of trouble and got her strength back in no time. Ada June still went and filled her woodbox most days and carried water in for her on washday. But she was some glad Aunt Dottie had took over milking her cow again.

Sometimes when it wasn't a school day, Ada June carried Emmy Lou down to the preacher's house. She played with some blocks Preacher Gordon made whilst Ada June worked on her reading or Miss Mira read to them. Sometimes Emmy Lou, even little as she was, would stop playing to listen, whether the stories were things she could know or not. When Miss Mira was reading, the words sung in the air.

Plenty of times what Miss Mira read were things Ada June didn't know either, but somehow she could imagine them. Miss Mira helped her believe she might someday live some of those kinds of things and not just be a girl folks looked down on because she didn't have a pa. Or a ma anymore.

She did once have a ma, and a good one no matter what others said. But she did so wish for a mother now. So much that while she made sure to say "Miss Mira" when she was speaking aloud, in her heart she sometimes thought *Mama*.

Ada June watched her now as Joseph pointed out some bluebells. She was bragging on Joseph and making him feel like he was thirteen instead of only six. Miss Mira had that way. Her words could make a person feel good. And she didn't just talk. She made things happen.

Ada June had boots and shoes. Boots that fit. Shoes without holes in the soles. She had dresses that hung down below her knees like they were supposed to. Now when the other kids ragged on her, it wasn't because her clothes didn't fit right or that she had rats' nests in her hair. Miss Mira gave her a comb and barred the door and covered up the windows so Ada June could take baths. Ada June had come to like being clean. Most all the time now even her fingernails were clean.

Best of all, she didn't make Ada June feel like she had to earn her supper. A plate was always on the table for her if she wanted it. Bo never had to go hungry either.

Miss Mira hadn't let Bo come in the schoolhouse. Instead, Ada June put Bo in the preacher's house, where he knew he had to stay. At noon, when Miss Mira let out school for the kids to eat the vittles they brung in their dinner pails, Ada June ran over to see to Bo. Miss Mira always left something there for her to eat. She gave half of it to Bo to keep him from whining much when she headed back for the rest of the school day. She didn't like leaving him locked up, but it kept her from worrying about some hound jumping him whilst she wasn't there to make Bo know better than to tear into a dog twice his size.

Now Bo sniffed on across the hill. Probably hunting a rabbit nest. She couldn't fault him for that. Plenty of times back before Miss Mira, he had to find his own eats.

Ada June felt a little teary-eyed just thinking about how she and Bo didn't have to worry about having eats now or a bed. Not the bad kind of tears she had to fight off when she thought about Elsinore and how she wasn't getting any better. These were sweet-feeling tears because of how Miss Mira kept her door open to her, and Joseph was as much of a friend as she'd ever had.

"Hurry up, Ada June," he hollered at her now. "I see a whole patch of them britches flowers."

"Dutchman's britches." She chased after him. Bo barked and came down the hill to run with them. She laughed out loud and looked over her shoulder at Miss Mira. "You coming, Miss Mira?"

"I better stay over here on the path. If there's an abundance of blooms you can bring one for me to see. Then we should head back." She looked up at the sky. "The sun will be dipping behind the hill soon, and we need to go by and see about Elsinore."

"I'll pick one for her too. It might make her smile."

They found all kinds of blooms and picked a few before they headed toward Elsinore's house. Joseph went off toward Miss Effie's house to show her one of the Dutchman's britches blooms.

Elsinore's lips did curl up a little when Ada June gave her the flower, but it wasn't much of a smile. She didn't appear to have energy for more than that.

"Do you need someone to stay with you?" Miss Mira had hold of Selinda the way she always did at Elsinore's.

"Horace is bringing Granny Perry down in a little bit." Saying that much seemed to wear out Elsinore.

All Ada June's happy feelings drained away.

"Do you want me to get Miss Nicey Jane to come?" Miss Mira looked about ready to cry herself.

"Ain't no use. Ain't nothing no use. Them tonics ain't helpin' me breathe a bit easier." She lay back, her face as white as the pillowcase. "And I'm plumb tired, Miss Mira."

"You can't stop trying, Elsinore." Miss Mira's voice sounded funny. "Think of Selinda."

"I been tryin'. I been tryin' for nigh on a year." Elsinore's face softened. "I give her a good start." She looked over at Ada June.

"I'm reckonin' she's gonna be like you, Ada June. No pa and no ma. But you'll see to her, won't you? With Miss Mira's help?"

All Ada June could do was nod as she blinked back tears. Didn't seem right to be crying when Elsinore was dry-eyed.

"Stop that talk. We won't need to see to her because you are going to get better." Miss Mira looked to be having to work to keep from crying too.

"I reckon you can try to pray that down. Your prayers for me has been sweet words I've held in my heart." Elsinore's hand trembled something fierce when she touched her chest.

The back door opened and Horace Perry brung in Granny Perry. She looked to have got halfway to ancient since Ada June saw her last. She patted Elsinore's arm without saying anything and then reached for Selinda.

"You'uns best get on home. It's the edge of night out there," the old woman said.

"Are you sure you won't need help with Selinda?" Miss Mira appeared to tighten her hold on the baby.

Granny Perry made a sound halfway between a snort and a laugh as she took Selinda out of Miss Mira's arms. "I ain't so old I can't tend to a babe like this here one. Horace there"—she nodded toward where he stood by the back door, wringing his hands—"he can be a help, were I to need it."

"It will be fine, Miss Mira. You go on home and fix Preacher Gordon his supper," Elsinore said. "You can come back in the mornin' time if'n your prayers is strong enough."

"That's the idee. Prayers is a good thing." Granny Perry narrowed her eyes as she leaned toward Miss Mira. "Lookin' like as how you need to do some restin' your own self. How long afore your time?"

"My time?" Miss Mira looked puzzled.

"Your layin' in time."

For a second, Ada June thought Miss Mira might have to sit down, but she stayed on her feet. "I-I'm not sure."

"Reckon it's hard to know with the first one." Granny Perry sat down with Selinda, who seemed happy enough to be in her lap. "Now you and the girl be on your way and let Elsie here get some rest."

"Yes. We best go, Ada June."

"Ada June," Elsinore called to her. "Come on over here and give me a hug. You has been my best friend ever."

Ada June went to the bed and leaned down to hug her, feeling naught but skin and bones. When she raised up, she ducked her head so's Elsinore wouldn't see the tears she couldn't keep back now. Elsinore had never asked for a hug before. Ever.

33

Gordon blew out a relieved breath when Ada June and Mira came out of the trees. Ever since Mira had lost her way on that first Sunday in Sourwood, he felt uneasy whenever she ventured out without him. Not that she would get lost like that again. Especially not in the daytime.

He had no real reason to worry about her, but he did. He knew the Bible said prayer could defeat worry. He should trust her comings and goings to the Lord. Cover her with prayer. That he did. Every day.

He had always thought being married would be easy. His parents had a wonderful marriage. His sister, Julie, and her husband seemed made for one another. Pastor Haskell and Aunt Stella were a powerful couple living for the Lord.

But Gordon was beset by doubts. Not about being married himself. He felt blessed continually to have Mira as his wife, but was she happy? Would she have found more happiness in the city? She gave every indication she liked teaching the Sourwood children, but lately she looked so tired at the end of the day. Was teaching such a large group of children ages six to seventeen too much work for her?

He needed to find ways to encourage her and show her more

love, but would love ever kindle in her heart? His thoughts swirled back and forth. His uncertainty about a place in Mira's heart seemed to allow other doubts to poke at him. Were his sermons losing some fire? He studied his Bible. He prayed for inspired messages, but some Sundays he worried his words might be flying out the church windows without stopping to rest in the first person's head.

He surely did fall short at times. All men did. But most of those in Sourwood had embraced him as their pastor. They brought him their troubles, asked his advice, coveted his prayers as he coveted theirs. Best of all, the church benches were a little more crowded every week.

Plus they had a school. They had a teacher. He had a wife. All that was good. He should be on a mountain of joy instead of sinking into a valley of worry. He had no reason to allow doubts to shadow this blessed path the Lord had set him on. Better to trust in the sunshine of the Lord's love to make those shadows vanish. Gordon needed to push his worries aside and not let Mira's hesitation to answer Pastor Haskell when he read the marriage vows linger in his mind. She had answered. Had promised to take him as her wedded husband for better or worse, to love and cherish. With the Lord's help.

Did he doubt the Lord would supply that help after being so sure the Lord was the one who put them in front of Pastor Haskell to say those vows? And hadn't he said the same? With the Lord's help.

Mira gave him no reason for his doubts. She had promised forever. Till death parted them. She was keeping her promise to be his wife, but even when he held her close and his love for her warmed every inch of his body, she seemed to stay apart. She whispered no words of affection.

He expected too much. Just because love had bloomed abundantly in his heart didn't mean it ever would in hers. He couldn't fight her memory of Edward, her one and perhaps only love. He didn't want to replace him. He simply wanted his own small corner of her heart where he could belong. As much as he said he didn't need to hear her words of love, he yearned for them.

Gordon waited on the porch for Mira. Ada June and Bo were with her. They nearly always were. Ada June stayed at their house most all the time now. Nothing for it but to have the dog in the house.

Fact was, he had not only got used to that but liked Bo's company during the school day while he studied for his sermons. His mother would have had a fit, but then she didn't know Ada June. If she had, she might have opened her door to Bo too.

Mira's steps seemed to drag as she came toward the cabin after her wildflower hunt with Ada June and Joseph, who must have headed home. Gordon had spent the last hour wishing he'd gone with them, but he'd had to visit Greg Washburn, who had expressly asked him to come share about Jesus. Then after he got to the Washburn place on the other side of the far hill, a good two-hour walk through rough country, the man didn't recall asking Gordon to come at all.

Some days were like that. Duty before pleasure, but Mira's face showed no sign of pleasure now. Nor did Ada June's. Even Bo was dragging his tail. He always took his mood from Ada June.

Gordon went out to meet them. A wilted flower was stuck in a buttonhole on Mira's blouse. Both Mira and Ada June appeared just as droopy.

"What's wrong?" He moved faster across the yard. "Is one of you hurt?"

"No, no. We're fine." They didn't seem fine as Mira pulled Ada June close to her side. The girl hid her face against Mira's sleeve. "We went by Elsinore's. You need to go see her."

Relief whispered through him. "All right. I'll go first thing tomorrow."

"I think you should go on now." Mira's eyes were sad.

Ada June turned her face toward him. "She's sinking, Preacher Gordon. Don't seem to want to see the sun again."

"Is anyone with her?"

"Mr. Perry and his mother," Mira said. "Mrs. Perry encouraged us to leave."

"I see." He did see. At times the mountain people were ready to close ranks against any they considered outsiders.

Ada June pulled away from Mira to grab his arm. "Please, Preacher Gordon. Jesus could heal her, couldn't he?"

Her cheeks were wet with tears, something he didn't see often with Ada June.

He squatted down in front of her to be eye to eye. "The Lord can do miraculous healings, but that doesn't always happen."

"Why not? Don't you say that if we pray, the Lord will hear?" Her mouth straightened out into a determined line.

Mira put her hands on Ada June's shoulders. Gordon slid his gaze up at her. He could tell she was hoping for the same assurance.

He searched for the right words. "The Lord knows how much you care and he does hear our every prayer. But sometimes his answer isn't what we want."

"But it might be." Ada June seemed to be daring him to deny that.

"You're right. It might be. Let's all three of us pray right now."

Ada June nodded as Mira kept a grip on the girl's shoulders. Gordon stood up and put one arm around Mira and the other around Ada June. Instead of bowing his head, he stared up toward heaven. The sun had gone to the other side of the hill, and the sky was going from the blue of day to deep evening blue.

A silent prayer for wisdom rose from him before he started praying aloud. "Please, Lord, restore the health of our dear sister, Elsinore. Trouble and sickness have laid her low, but you, Lord, have the power to defeat all sorrows of the world." He took a breath and tightened his arm around Ada June before he went on. "Be with those of us who love Elsinore, but your will, Lord, and not ours."

"Why'd you have to say that?" Ada June jerked away from Gordon to glare at him. "Everybody dies when people say that."

She turned and ran away from them.

"Ada June!" Mira's voice was stern.

Ada June slowed for a couple of steps but then ran faster.

When Mira started after her, Gordon put his hand on her arm. "Let her go."

Mira didn't pull away from him as she stared toward where Ada June disappeared into the woods. "She wants to believe in miracles."

"I know. Poor child hasn't had many of those in her life. Other than Bo." Gordon hesitated. "And you."

Mira let out a shaky breath. "But this is so hard for her. I want to help her."

"You already have, and should Elsinore pass on, you'll help her then too. Give her time to think things through." He stroked Mira's cheek. "Go rest. You look exhausted. She will be ready for your hugs again tomorrow."

"Are you sure?"

"I'm sure." He studied her face. She looked pale. He hoped she hadn't caught Elsinore's sickness. She'd been with her almost every day, but she'd shown no sign of illness until the last few days. "Don't worry. Ada June is a tough girl, but I'll try to find her."

He wanted to stay with Mira, comfort her, but others needed him more. He leaned down and kissed her forehead. "Don't wait up. I may be late, according to the need."

Mira watched Gordon walk toward the path that led to Elsinore's cabin. Ada June had gone into the trees at a different place. He'd go pray for Elsinore before he looked for the girl. That was only right.

Mira hesitated. Perhaps she should follow Ada June, try to find her. But what would more likely happen would be that Mira would get lost as night fell faster under the trees.

Gordon was right. She was exhausted. She could barely put one foot in front of the other to move on toward the porch. Once there, she sank down on the top step as darkness crept over the hills and settled around her.

She should fix Gordon's supper. He could be hungry when he came back. If he came back before morning. He might stay to be a comfort to Elsinore. Mira wished she was there to be with the girl. More girl than woman. Only sixteen. And so ready to leave this world. And her baby. Mira felt too sad for more tears.

Dear Lord. She started a prayer, but what could she say more than what Gordon already had. The Lord knew the sadness of her heart. The sadness of Ada June's heart. He knew Selinda needed a mother. Mira wanted to believe he would send down a healing touch.

She needed to go see to the fire. Heat up the leftover beans. The thought of food made her stomach heave.

Pulling in a deep breath, she faced the thought she had been pushing aside since she left Elsinore's house. How could Granny Perry know more about Mira's body than Mira did? More important, could it be true?

Everything had been such a busy whirl since she got to Sourwood. Even before the schoolhouse was completed, she'd started teaching Ada June and Joseph. Some of the time, Emmy Lou was there too. Along with that, she'd been trying to figure out what a preacher's wife should or shouldn't do.

She thought back through her months in Sourwood. If only she had a calendar. The one she'd brought from the city was on the wall at the schoolhouse, but no need to make the trek over to see it. She knew the date. Friday, April 15, 1910. She had come to Sourwood January 8.

Her cycle had never been regular. What with the stress of

adjusting to her new life and getting ready for school, she had paid no notice to missing a month. Or had it been two?

She closed her eyes and thought back. Was it late January or early February that she had to break the ice in the creek to get water to wash her sanitary cloths? She hadn't wanted to ask Gordon for help with that. So many things she felt uncomfortable sharing with him.

She sensed he felt the same. At times, he looked troubled when he came in from visiting, but he never shared about the people other than to mention a name when they prayed together. She looked forward to their prayer time in the mornings before she headed to the school. While she didn't say her own prayers aloud, she united her silent thoughts with his spoken ones.

Was this one of her unspoken prayers being answered? Was her story like some of the Bible stories of barren women blessed with a baby on the way? A smile slipped across her face.

The night was velvet around her now. She didn't always notice the sound of the creek during the day, but now the water tumbling over rocks soothed her. The spring peeper frogs filled the air with their celebration of spring. A whip-poor-will sang its name. The sound tugged at her heart. She stood to go inside. Still weary to the bone, but joyful in the spirit despite her worry about Elsinore and Ada June.

After fixing the fire and lighting a lamp, she picked up her mother's ceramic bluebird off the mantel and sat in the rocking chair.

Would she soon be rocking a baby in this chair? Not Emmy Lou or Selinda, but her own baby. Hers and Gordon's. Would Gordon be happy? He had never mentioned a desire for children. He wouldn't. Not and add to the challenges she already felt being a wife and a teacher. Would she be able to keep teaching? In the city, they didn't allow married teachers, much less teachers in the family way.

The family way. She ran her fingers along the bluebird's wings. The bluebird of happiness. She whispered a prayer of thanksgiving for this new life beginning inside her and a fervent prayer of appeal for Elsinore to have more time with Selinda.

She set the bird back on the mantel and moved the kettle of beans closer to the fire in case Gordon was hungry when he came in. She lacked any appetite, but touched her middle and promised the new life inside her she would eat come morning.

After she blew out the lamp, the fire's glow gave enough light for her to make her way to the bedroom. She left the door open to keep the room from complete darkness.

With no idea of the time, she woke when Gordon came to bed. He patted her shoulder and whispered for her to go back to sleep.

Mira pushed away the grogginess of sleep. "But Elsinore?" She didn't turn toward him as she held her breath and waited for his answer.

"Her breathing seemed a bit easier. I will go back in the morning. The women have gathered with her." His words were a whisper against her hair.

"The women?"

"Miss Nicey Jane and Miss Effie came to sit with Granny Perry. Horace is splitting wood by moonlight."

"Splitting wood?" Surely she heard him wrong.

"The poor man needed to do something and the half moon is up now."

"Oh. Did Ada June come in?" She hadn't heard her, but she often slipped into the house without waking Mira.

"No."

Guilt stabbed Mira. She should have gone after her. "Did you find her?"

"I looked, but no."

"Where could she be?"

"Maybe she went to Miss Dottie's. Or she might want to stay in the woods tonight."

"All alone." Sadness filled her.

Gordon smoothed her hair. "Not alone. Bo is with her. The

Lord is with her. Before you came, she slept out in the woods more than she stayed inside."

"I know, but—"

"Shh. She'll be fine. I'll find her in the morning." He kissed her cheek. "Rest now. You have looked tired this week."

She should have told him then, but she didn't. It didn't seem the right time. Not with her worries about Elsinore and Ada June.

34

*A*da June didn't let Preacher Gordon see her even though she knew he was looking to talk to her. She didn't want to hear more about the Lord's will. That's what she'd heard folks say about Pap Leathers and her ma.

Maybe the Lord had wanted Pap Leathers to come on home. He might've wanted to sit and talk with him a spell. Pap always had something fine to say. He'd know something good to say to her right now if'n he was there with her.

Preacher Gordon might too if she let him see her, but she couldn't be sure of that. Once he went on past her toward Elsinore's cabin, Ada June considered turning back to see about Miss Mira. She hadn't seemed hardly able to make it across the holler, but she might be ready to say those same kinds of things as Preacher Gordon. Ada June couldn't hear that right now.

Her ma freezing in the snow couldn't be something meant to be. Nobody good would will that. And the Lord was good. Ada June wasn't doubting that. She reckoned he wanted folks to get well. Wasn't the preacher always talking about how he healed people right and left in the Bible? One of them the preacher had said came right up to Jesus and told him he could heal him if he wanted to. Right off Jesus said he wanted to.

Elsinore wasn't asking Jesus to heal her, but just a couple of Sundays ago, Preacher told about this pa asking for healing for his daughter. And that happened too. Could be it didn't always happen. Could be the Bible writers only put in the times it did happen. But some folks thought he still did some healing. Wasn't no reason he couldn't send down staying-alive blessings on Elsinore. Or her ma back when she needed it.

She pushed that last thought away. Wouldn't do no good to think about her ma. The only place she could live now was in Ada June's heart.

Ada June trailed along behind Preacher Gordon to Elsinore's house. After he went inside, she crept up to a spot under the side window. Bo settled beside her, like as how he knew she wanted to be hid. Same as when Connor hunted them to do something mean.

The wooden shutters that covered the window were partly open. She reckoned they needed to let in air. Sounded like more folks than Mr. Horace and his ma with Elsinore now. She held her breath and listened. Miss Effie told the preacher to come in, and then Miss Nicey Jane spoke up loud, like a body did when somebody was hard of hearing, to tell Elsinore he was there.

Elsinore never was that. Unless she'd gone past hearing. That thought froze Ada June's heart, but then she heard Elsinore murmuring something. Not loud enough to make out words, but it was her. Maybe she was telling them to stop being so noisy before they woke up Selinda.

The baby must be asleep. Ada June listened close to see if she could hear a gurgle or whimper, but she couldn't. That was good. And Elsinore talking, even if it was weak, had to be good too.

Preacher Gordon was praying over Elsinore. More good happening. Ada June curled her knees up close so she could lean her head down on them. Bo didn't move. She couldn't hear Preacher Gordon's prayer words, but she knew some of her own. *Please, Lord. Selinda needs Elsinore. I need Elsinore.*

Elsinore was her friend. She acted like Ada June was more than just somebody to pack in wood or water. Same as Miss Mira was now. Ada June felt ashamed for running off and not listening when Miss Mira called for her. She should've stopped. Miss Mira would have understood she needed to go see about Elsinore. She wouldn't have fussed.

But now here she was sitting on the outside, scared to go in and see Elsinore so poorly. Better to think on how Miss Nicey Jane would probably shoo her and Bo back out the door. At least here by the window, she could be close enough to listen with Bo beside her.

In the soft murmur of voices, Ada June caught a word now and again, but nothing she could make much sense of. The sound wrapped around her and she dozed off. She had no idea how much time went by before Preacher Gordon saying her name jerked her awake.

For a second, she thought he might have come around the cabin and found her and Bo hiding there. But no, he was still inside.

"I'll tell Ada June, Elsinore." His voice sounded funny. Sort of like he was extra tired.

Ada June held her breath and scooted up on her knees to get closer to the open window to hear better. She touched Bo to let him know to stay still.

"I mean it. I want Ada June to have Selinda," Elsinore said.

Ada June let her breath out as quietly as she could, but it wouldn't have mattered since Miss Nicey Jane was doing some huffing inside. Preacher must have found a way to stop her saying anything, although Ada June didn't think Miss Nicey Jane let anybody keep her from talking. If she wanted to say something, she did.

But it was Preacher Gordon that spoke. "Ada June isn't but ten, Elsinore."

"Plenty of girls has had to take over raising little ones around here when a mother passes on." Elsinore's voice was a little stronger, sounding determined for them to pay mind to her words.

Ada June wondered if she sensed her out there listening, but she couldn't know that.

"Them that have places to live and a pa to provide for them." Miss Nicey Jane didn't stay quiet long.

"She's got Miss Mira and Preacher here," Elsinore said. "You ain't arguin' agin that, are you, Preacher? Miss Mira aims good for Ada June and Selinda too."

Her voice got low and then she coughed. Not like she was coughing before. This wasn't much more than a rattle. Ada June's heart hurt, but Preacher Gordon didn't sound any different when he answered her.

"Miss Mira holds you in great favor, Elsinore. She will come with me to see you in the morning."

"You mind my words, Preacher." Elsinore sounded a little put out.

"You rest now, Elsinore. Try to sleep."

"I am bone weary." Elsinore's voice faded.

After a few minutes of silence, Granny Perry said, "The poor girl's sleeping now."

The chair scooted on the floor, and then Miss Effie said, "Breathing some easier too. Could be our prayers are bearing fruit, Preacher. You go on and see to your missus and Ada June. The child is bound to be overcome with sadness."

Ada June sank back down to the ground and made herself as small as possible. Preacher Gordon wouldn't have any reason to come around to the side of the house, but were he to look back once he went a ways from the steps, he might spot them there. Soon as the preacher stepped out the front door, Bo lifted up his head. He was probably thinking they would go with him, but when she didn't move, he dropped his head back on his paws.

She kept her face down as the preacher moved away from the cabin. For a few seconds, she wanted to jump up and run after him, but she didn't. He might think she shouldn't be hiding out to sneak a listen. Could be he would be right.

For a while, the night was silent except for an owl screeching somewhere off in the woods and the chunk of Mr. Horace's axe on wood behind the cabin. Ada June had about decided the women inside must have nodded off, like as how she had earlier. She shivered and wondered if they would chase her away if she and Bo sneaked in to sit by the fire. She couldn't see how that could bother anything. And Elsinore never cared about Bo coming inside.

She was thinking on standing up when Granny Perry started talking. "My Horace says Elsinore here don't have no family to speak of. I'm reckoning that's why she took so to that Ada June child."

"That could be," Miss Nicey Jane said.

"Ada June has been a help to her since Benny went off to the mines."

Miss Effie's words made Ada June tear up a little. She had tried to be a help to Elsinore and Selinda.

"It's sorrowful. Poor Elsinore losing her folks to the white plague and then poor Benny gettin' kilt dead in the mines." Granny Perry clucked her tongue before she went on. "As to the girl, well, if Ada June's got folks, they's not admitted to it. Hain't never heared of nobody ever claimin' kin to her ma."

"Who would?" Miss Nicey Jane said.

"We claim kin to some as bad or worse, Nicey Jane," Miss Effie said.

"That's a truth," Granny Perry said. "And there's some what always figured her pa must be here in Sourwood. Could be she has folks around these parts somewheres. I heared tell back when they first brung the child down off'n Leathers Hill that the girl claimed a man was after her ma and that's why they was out in the snow. I reckon that was afore she quit talking."

"Nothing but tales." Miss Nicey Jane sounded like she wasn't about to listen to any such nonsense.

"I never knowed Ada June to lie," Miss Effie said.

Miss Nicey Jane made a humph sound. "Can't lie when you ain't talkin' to nobody."

Granny Perry didn't seem bothered by Miss Nicey Jane speaking against tales. "Reckon that feller what was after them mighta been the girl's pa?"

In the cabin, the women fell silent again. She guessed they might be pondering Granny Perry's question. For sure Ada June was. She hadn't ever thought about that man, who wasn't much more than a dark shadow in her memory, being her pa. Why would her ma be running away from Ada June's pa? Scared like.

She shut her eyes tight and tried to pull up that night to bring up that man in her mind's eye. But it was like trying to see what was moving on the far side of a hill when dawn was barely breaking.

Her ma had been sick. She remembered that. Coughing something like Elsinore. Ada June didn't rightly recall if her ma wouldn't eat or if there wasn't nothing to eat. Seemed it might've been the nothing to eat since they went out most days looking for hickory nuts or chestnuts.

After Pap Leathers passed, they never had much on their table. A time or two Ada June sneaked down the hill to steal eggs out of somebody's henhouse or some corn out of the corncrib. Her ma said surely wouldn't nobody shoot a little girl.

Ada June never knew who she was stealing from. Not even after they brought her down from the hill. Everything looked different then. But she'd always thought that man came after them because she'd stole a chicken. Her ma was running just so the man wouldn't get Ada June.

She didn't know how she could remember all that stealing and couldn't remember that much about her ma telling her to hide while she ran on down the hill. Ada June had hid like she said, but after the man left, she crawled out and followed her ma's tracks.

She found her where she fell and rolled down the hill into a tree. She wouldn't answer when Ada June talked to her. Ada June tried to pick her up, but she wasn't strong enough. All she could do was wait for her to wake up. Her mother felt so cold that Ada June lay on top of her to keep her warm. Next thing she knew, another man with traps swinging off his belt had pulled her up and carried her to Miss Nicey Jane's house.

She hadn't asked what they did with her ma. She wouldn't have known what to ask even if she hadn't quit talking by then. She knew they buried Pap Leathers. She'd been there for that, but she hadn't known what to think about her ma. She just knew she was gone.

Some time later, Miss Effie told her they did right by her ma and buried her in the Leathers grave place right next to Pap Leathers. It took a while, but Ada June found the graveyard a couple of years ago. Since nothing marked her mother's grave, she picked flowers and spread them on both sides of where Pap Leathers' grave was marked by a rock sitting up tall at the head of it.

Thinking about her ma's grave made Ada June start shivering. She wanted to go get in her bed at Miss Mira's house, but she couldn't leave Elsinore. Bo scooted closer against her. She could go inside and at least warm up a few minutes. They'd quit talking about her. At least she thought they had.

But then Miss Nicey Jane's voice pricked up her ears again. "Ain't no reason to dredge up all them tales from back when. We did all right for Ada June."

"Didn't always seem so right." Granny Perry wasn't giving in to Miss Nicey Jane how most folks did. "A man should own up to havin' a child."

"If'n he knows 'bout it," Miss Nicey Jane said.

"I figure a man knows when he plants seeds whether he sees the crop come up or not." Granny Perry sounded more than sure about that.

"We ain't talkin' about planting corn." Miss Nicey Jane had her cranky voice that always made Ada June hide out.

Granny Perry didn't appear worried by that. "No'm, we are not. We're talking about a man doin' right 'stead of wrong."

Miss Effie had been quiet so long Ada June had almost forgot she was in there with the others until she spoke up. "Stirring in the past can be like plucking feathers in the wind. You don't end up with nothing you can hold on to whilst bits of story drift around with no way of knowing what chicken it came from. Ada June don't appear to be too burdened down. Leastways not since the preacher's missus has took a shine to her."

"She don't have much to say," Granny Perry said.

"She speaks when she wants to," Miss Nicey Jane said.

Ada June guessed she was remembering her "please" word that day she needed to get Bo away from Marv's big hound.

"That's so. Horace said he heard her singing to the baby here a time or two. Claims the girl has a purty voice. Reckon her ma had a singin' voice?"

Granny Perry's words brought up the memory of Ada June's ma singing to her when they were traipsing out in the woods hunting something. Sometimes food. Sometimes a flower. Her ma did love the flowers and the stars and the birds. Ada June smiled, glad to remember.

"Can't see how that has any matterance now," Miss Nicey Jane said.

"I reckon not," Granny Perry said. "But you know, I did hear my Horace say once that Elsinore here could do some singing now and again when her breath wasn't too labored. Could be Ada June is some kin to her and that's how come they's so close."

Ada June didn't think that was so. Elsinore would've told her if'n it was.

"Figure we can't know 'bout that, with all Elsinore's folks gone past telling," Miss Effie said.

"True enough." Ada June could almost see Granny Perry nodding her head to that. "But that don't change my feelin' that there's some folks in Sourwood that know more than they is wantin' to speak aloud."

"We ain't gathered here for Ada June, but for Elsinore and her sweet baby." Miss Nicey Jane had a way about her of having the last word, and didn't either Miss Effie or Granny Perry say any more.

The sounds of the woods came back to Ada June's ears then. The owl again. A whip-poor-will. Bo breathing against her leg. She didn't hear the chunk of Mr. Horace's axe now.

After a while, she had no idea how long, she stood up and went around the cabin to the back where the wood was stacked. Mr. Horace had enough wood piled up to last a year, maybe longer, and now it was likely Elsinore might not even need the first chunk. Mr. Horace had sunk down on the back step, his head in his hands. The man's shoulders were jerking.

It took Ada June a minute to determine he was crying. She hadn't oft seen any grown-up shedding tears and never a man. She stopped still in front of him. Bo stopped too like he was just as surprised.

She wasn't rightly sure what to do. Maybe she should go on back around to the front door and act like she hadn't seen him. But he raised his head and looked straight at her before she could decide what was best.

"I loved her, Ada June. I knowed I was too old fer her, but I wanted to do for her."

Ada June hadn't ever said the first word to him, but she pushed some out now. "You did fine for her, Mr. Horace."

He sniffed and brushed his overall jacket sleeve across his face. "I did." He pulled in a shaky breath before he said more. "You best go on in and see her. I'm thinkin' she won't make the sunrise."

She wanted to argue that. To tell him how Preacher Gordon had prayed and about all those healings in the Bible, but she didn't. Instead, she just nodded and edged past him to the door. Bo came with her.

The women around Elsinore's bed didn't look the first bit surprised to see her. Miss Effie nodded at her. "Come on in, child."

Ada June pointed Bo toward the fireplace and he settled down there. She brushed off her dress tail to make sure she hadn't brought in any leaves and went to peer down at Elsinore sleeping peaceful like. Ada June took off her shoes and climbed into the bed to cuddle up right against her. Without waking up, Elsinore put her arm over Ada June and whispered something.

"What'd she say?" Granny Perry asked.

Nobody answered her. Guess Miss Effie and Miss Nicey Jane didn't know, but Ada June knew. Elsinore had spoke Benny's name, like as how she thought Ada June was Benny come home to her at last.

Mr. Horace was right. Elsinore slipped away before the sun came up.

35

Mira got out of bed quietly when the first rays of sun pushed through the cracks in the chinks to send slivers of light across the room. Gordon, who was almost always up first, was still sound asleep. She didn't know exactly what time he'd come in from Elsinore's, but it had to be past midnight.

She would have stayed in bed to keep from chancing waking him, but nausea was roiling her stomach. On top of that, she needed to know if Ada June had come in. Mira grabbed her wrap and tiptoed to the door. She looked back before she went out of the room. Gordon showed no sign of stirring.

Ada June's cot wasn't rumpled. Tears came to Mira's eyes when she thought about the girl by herself out in the woods. She had been so sure Gordon would bring her home. Home. That's how she wanted Ada June to think of it. Gordon wouldn't be against that. They hadn't talked about giving Ada June a forever home, but he'd fixed the bed for her. He never looked sorry to see her come in the door or be sitting at their table, whether learning to read or sharing their meal.

He might simply consider Ada June a child he needed to help.

She was more than that to Mira. Much more. Why hadn't Mira made sure Gordon knew that?

And now this. She ran her hand down over her middle. No baby bulge there. That took a while, she supposed. She needed to tell Gordon her news as soon as he woke up. She didn't want him to hear it from Granny Perry's gossip.

If only her stomach would settle. Maybe if she ate something. She wished for a soda cracker, but those were a treat here, where a person had to travel over the hill back toward Jackson to find a store. An apple would be nice. A crisp juicy apple. She pushed away the thought. By the time apples came on, she'd be well along with this baby.

A slice of Miss Nicey Jane's bread would have to do. Somehow Miss Nicey Jane always had flour for bread. She buttered a slice of the bread, but one bite was all it took to make her race for the door. She barely made it to the edge of the porch before heaving up everything in her stomach. The butter. She should have left off the butter.

She breathed in the cool morning air and leaned against a porch post. The sun slid up over the hill to the east and touched the porch.

She shut her eyes and thought of Elsinore and then Ada June. "Please, Lord." She ought to put more words to the prayer, but she didn't seem to need to say more. The Lord knew.

Bo's bark jerked her away from her prayer thoughts. When she opened her eyes, a small procession led by the dog came across the hollow toward her. Ada June was carrying Selinda. Miss Effie was alongside her, and Mr. Horace was bringing up the rear, packing something that looked too big to carry.

Mira pulled her wrap tighter. Barefoot in her nightgown and robe, she wasn't dressed proper to be out on the porch where anyone might see her, but she didn't run inside. She was covered neck to ankle, and with the sun barely up, a person had a right to still be fresh from bed.

When she tried to swallow the sour taste in her mouth, her

stomach lurched. A dry heave brought tears to her eyes. She wiped her mouth on her sleeve and smoothed down her hair before she turned toward them.

"Are you poorly, Miss Mira?" Miss Effie stopped beside the porch and looked up at her. A frown settled between her eyes.

Ada June peered up at Mira too, sorrow written on her face. She didn't say a word, but her carrying Selinda told it all.

"Just a little morning upset. No call for concern." Mira went down the steps, paying no notice of her bare feet on the cool ground. She held her arms out to Ada June and Selinda. "I'm seeing bad news in your face."

Miss Effie took the baby from Ada June before she almost fell into Mira's arms. "I prayed, Miss Mira. I prayed hard, but Elsinore still went on."

Mira tightened her arms around her and kissed her head. "I'm so sorry." She blinked back tears. "You were such a good friend to her."

"She shouldn't have give up like that." Ada June sounded angry.

"Shh, sweetie. Sometimes it's hard to keep fighting when you're so sick." Mira stroked Ada June's hair.

She looked over the girl's head at Miss Effie. Behind her, Mr. Horace shifted the cradle he was carrying and set it on the ground. "I apologize for my appearance," she said.

"Don't fret over that. We come early and you appear to have needed some outdoor air," Miss Effie said.

"Do you need to see Gordon?"

"More to see you, I reckon," Miss Effie said.

Selinda held her little hands out toward Mira, but Mira just smiled at her and kept her arms around Ada June. She was the one who needed the most love right then. The baby was too young to know the sorrow.

Mr. Horace picked up the cradle again and scooted it onto the porch. His face was blotched red. "I need to head on home to see to things. The cows and all."

Miss Effie touched his arm as he moved past her. "Thankee, Horace. Tell Granny I'll be along soon's I finish here to help with what needs doing."

Mr. Horace nodded and turned to shuffle away, his shoulders drooped.

"Poor man." Miss Effie blew out a breath. "Ain't no changin' things now." She glanced down at Mira's bare feet. "We best go in afore you catch a chill."

Mira looked at the cradle. "Do you want me to watch Selinda for a while?"

"A while." Miss Effie's words sounded more like a question than an answer.

Ada June pulled back from Mira. "Elsinore give Selinda to me to raise."

"I see," Mira said, but she didn't see at all. Surely no one would expect a child Ada June's age to take on mothering a baby. But was that how things were here in the hills? A child could just be given to someone?

Miss Effie patted the baby's back and said, "We best talk it out inside."

Mira turned Ada June to go up the steps. Bo was already at the door. Miss Effie followed with Selinda, who babbled as she looked around. Mira wondered how long it had been since the baby had been outside Elsinore's house. Maybe not since she was big enough to take notice of things. What was she now? Seven months. Maybe more like eight. She would barely fit in the cradle.

Inside, all was quiet. Gordon must be still asleep in spite of Bo's bark earlier and the sound of talking out front.

Mira gave Ada June a hug and turned her loose. "I'll go tell Gordon you're here."

"Might be good for us to talk a minute first. Woman to woman." Miss Effie handed the baby to Mira and poked up the fire before she laid a piece of wood on the flames. "Ada June, come on over here and warm yourself."

Ada June stayed where Mira had left her, a lost look on her face. Miss Effie's voice gentled then. "You will get through this, child. Same as you got through all the other sad times you've known."

Without saying anything, Ada June moved toward the fire. When she sat down on the floor, Bo laid his head in her lap.

Miss Effie narrowed her eyes on the girl and went on sternly. "I ain't havin' you go silent agin on me."

Ada June didn't look up at her, but she mumbled, "Yes'm."

"That's good." Miss Effie patted her head and turned her attention to Mira. "You come on over here too, Miss Mira. You look in need of a chair."

Mira almost parroted Ada June's "yes ma'am" as she sat down in the rocker. They were in Mira's house, but Miss Effie was the one in control. Something like Miss Nicey Jane usually was, but despite Miss Effie's lack of smiles, somehow Mira felt easier with her and less judged as coming up lacking. She could say what she was thinking to Miss Effie.

"Expecting Ada June to take care of a baby is expecting too much of someone so young." When Mira rocked the chair, Selinda giggled and rested her head against Mira's chest.

"My ma passed on when I was twelve." Miss Effie stayed standing by the fire. "Left a newborn and three others younger than me. Weren't easy, but we made out till Pa married again. I was about to marry myself by then."

"I'm not sure that compares to Ada June." Mira looked over at the girl, who kept her eyes on Bo as she stroked him head to tail.

"I reckon not. Just sayin' things can be different here in the hills. But Ada June don't have a pa to supply for her." Miss Effie looked straight at Mira. "Elsinore was thinkin' she had you. Was she thinkin' right?"

Doubts bombarded Mira. Could she handle two babies so close together? How would she be able to teach? What would Gordon think? Was it right for them to put the burden of being responsible for an infant on a child?

Selinda put her little hand on Mira's cheek at the same time as Ada June turned begging eyes up to her. That didn't make the potential difficulties disappear, but only one answer had ever been in her heart and mind. "I'll do whatever Ada June and Selinda need."

Ada June scooted over to lean against Mira's legs. "Elsinore knew you would."

"You've got a lovin' heart," Miss Effie said. "A fine thing for a preacher's wife."

Gordon. She shouldn't have answered before she talked to him. After all, she was promising that he would take on two children along with his on the way. But they had already the same as taken in Ada June. Still, she shouldn't have promised for him. She would have no way of caring for Ada June and Selinda without him.

She swallowed down her panic. He wouldn't say no. His heart was more loving than hers. He proved it every day.

Miss Effie, now that she had the answer she needed, moved one of the other chairs over to sit beside Mira. "How far along are you?"

"I . . . I don't know." She mentally shook her head. She needed to come up with a better answer if people kept asking her that. "I hadn't even considered that I could be any along until Granny Perry asked me that yesterday."

For the first time since she'd brought news of Elsinore, Miss Effie's face relaxed in a smile. "I reckon with the first one it can come on as a surprise."

Ada June jumped up so fast Bo yelped. A smile was across her face too. "You're having a baby, Miss Mira?"

What could Mira do but smile along with them? "So it appears."

Sometimes sorrow and joy could show up at the same time in a person's life.

Something woke Gordon. He reached over to Mira's side of the bed. She wasn't there. The sun was up since light was pushing through the cracks in the chinking that he made a mental note to repair every morning. So far that chore hadn't been done. Mira said there wasn't a hurry. She liked how the morning light sneaked in.

The room was dark when the door was shut, the way it was now. He should have insisted on a window in here, even if the men building the cabin said it would let in too much winter cold. A window could be sealed with putty to keep the wind out. He could buy the glass and cut a hole for a window yet. His church people would understand it was for Mira.

Every day he tried to think of something to please her, to make her not sorry she'd come to Sourwood. To make her not want to return to where life was easier. Where water came through a pipe and not out of a bucket from a spring or a creek. Where she didn't have to cook over an open fire in pots hung on hooks. Where she could go to a store and buy food and not be dependent on the charity of neighbors.

He could do that. Take her back to the city. Give up his mission. He had thought bringing a teacher to Sourwood would be the answer to prayer. It was. The school was well attended. The children were learning. But he couldn't stop worrying about that teacher's happiness.

She had never once said she was unhappy. Perhaps because he was afraid to ask, afraid to know for sure that she was sorry she had come to Sourwood. She had embraced the children and the job of teaching, but she was so small and fragile.

Not that she hadn't seemed perfectly fine until the last week. Perhaps her fatigue was due to her worry about Elsinore and her baby. She had become very attached to them.

He berated himself for sleeping past his usual rising time. He always intended to be up first to get the fire going and have water heating before Mira came out of the bedroom. Today she must have gone out in her dressing gown. Her dress was draped over the bench, with her shoes and stockings on the floor beside it. She probably tiptoed out to keep from waking him.

He was adjusting his suspenders when he heard voices in the next room. He sat on the edge of the bed and pulled on his shoes. Perhaps it was only Ada June, but no, that was a woman's voice. Effie Foster. No doubt with news of Elsinore. His heart sank. Early morning visitors rarely brought good news.

He ran a comb through his hair and pulled on his jacket. He had just pulled open the door an inch when he heard Ada June asking about a baby. Not Elsinore's baby. Mira's baby. His baby.

Convoluted feelings swept through him. Surprise. Joy. Unbelief. Worry. The worry overcame the joy. Hadn't he just been thinking about how fragile she seemed? In the mountains, he had been at the bedside of more than one mother losing her life bearing a child.

"Trust in the Lord and have faith." He whispered the words.

God's will. He had to believe in God's will and his love for his children. For Gordon. For Mira. For this baby being knitted by the Lord in Mira's womb.

For certain, he believed in prayer. He would storm heaven with prayers for this woman he loved and the baby they had made together.

But why had she told others before she told him? Did she not trust him to be happy about a baby? Trust him to take care of her?

He needed to quit tormenting himself with questions. He'd ask for answers when they were alone.

As soon as he stepped through the door, Ada June danced toward him, her dog circling her. "You're gonna be a papa." A smile lit up her face.

Miss Effie was smiling too, as much as Miss Effie ever smiled. "Reckon you need to get your sleep whilst you can, Preacher."

"I suppose so." No need letting on that a baby on the way was a surprise.

Mira kept her face down as she rocked Selinda. He kept his gaze on her until at last she peeked up at him, a flush running across her cheeks. She didn't say anything about a baby. Instead, she said, "They brought sad news, Gordon."

Ada June's smile disappeared as her shoulders drooped. "Your prayers weren't good enough, Preacher Gordon. Elsinore passed on."

He put his hand on her shoulder. "She's in a better place."

Anger flashed across Ada June's face. "It don't seem right. Selinda won't have even a whisper of a memory of her ma."

"You can tell her stories about her. Help her remember," Gordon said.

"Nobody ever tells me stories about my ma." She jerked away from him.

"Don't act up, Ada June." Miss Effie called her down.

Ada June glared at her. "Well, it's true. Nobody ever says nothing about my ma 'cepting bad things."

Mira stood up, handed the baby off to Miss Effie, and grabbed Ada June in a hug. "Shh."

Ada June fought her for a couple of seconds and then collapsed against her.

"You can remember the good things and tell them to me," Mira whispered into Ada June's hair. "And we'll remember good things to tell Selinda about her mother. All right?"

Ada June nodded.

Mira looked over at Gordon. "It seems we've been chosen to help Ada June take care of Elsinore's baby."

"Are you sure you're up to it?" Gordon asked.

"I'm up to it," Mira said.

"And teach?"

"The older children will help," Mira said.

Miss Effie looked across the room at him. "Might be I can come down and sit in on the school. I reckon I can listen whilst I tend to Selinda so's Billy Ray won't get so far ahead of me in learning he won't pay me no mind."

Ada June turned toward him. "Elsinore give me her baby to raise, but she aimed for you and Miss Mira to help me."

"She did," Miss Effie said. "You heared her say that very thing, Preacher."

"Please," Mira whispered.

There was never any answer but yes. But at the same time a worry tickled him when he looked at Mira and Ada June. "We can see to her. We'll be more than glad to. But it could be some of her family might come for her."

36

∞

Once Miss Effie left and Ada June settled down on her cot with Selinda, Mira went into the bedroom to get dressed. She was buttoning up her bodice when Gordon carried a lamp into the room and set it on the chest. He shut the door.

She glanced up at him. His face was so solemn that she looked down at the button she was fastening as though it took all her concentration.

"The girls are asleep," he said.

"That's good."

She searched for more to say as an uneasy silence fell between them. No words came except that she was sorry, but she wasn't sorry. Was he? Or angry that she had welcomed Selinda into their house?

She was still sifting through words in her mind when he spoke. "Why didn't you tell me?"

Her gaze flew to his face, surprised to see he looked hurt. "I was going to as soon as you woke. I didn't know, myself. Had not considered it until Mr. Horace's mother asked me how far along

I was when I went to Elsinore's house yesterday afternoon. How did she know when I didn't?"

"Mountain women are tuned in to such things, I suppose." His face was more relaxed now, but still without a smile. "But you could have told me when you came back from Elsinore's yesterday."

"I was so sad about Elsinore then. And I had to have time to consider whether it could be true. Besides, Elsinore and Ada June needed you. Then when you came home so late, I thought to wait until morning." She studied his face. "Are you sorry?"

"Sorry you didn't tell me?"

She shook her head the barest bit. "Sorry about the baby."

"Are you?"

"Oh no." She put her hands over her abdomen. Over her baby. Their baby. "I'm so happy. Happier than I feel I should be with the sorrow of Elsinore gone."

"Sorrows don't erase joys. Nor joys sorrows."

Tears flooded her eyes. Some of sorrow for Elsinore. Some of joy for how she already loved this child barely beginning to grow inside her. "I want you to be glad."

In one stride, he crossed the distance between them to wrap his arms around her and hold her like a fragile piece of china. "I love you, Mrs. Covington, and nothing could make me happier than being the father of your child."

"Our child."

"Praise the Lord from whom all blessings flow."

He kissed the top of her head as she rested it against his shoulder. Here with Gordon she would always find a resting place.

Elsinore was buried the next day. Mira held Selinda, and Ada June leaned against her, while Gordon said the funeral words at the grave.

The next week after the news about Mira being in the family way spread through Sourwood, things settled down. Not her stomach unfortunately, but even losing her breakfast every morning became part of her daily routine.

Awake early each day to get what the mountain people called a soon start. Gordon was up first to do the fire fixing and water carrying, but Mira was out right after him to start breakfast and dress Selinda. The baby had some fussy times, no doubt needing her mother, but Ada June stayed close to comfort Selinda. That somehow comforted Ada June too.

After Selinda was ready for the day, Mira made sure Ada June combed her hair and washed her face and hands before the girl spooned applesauce or mush into Selinda's mouth and helped her drink milk from a cup. Mira kept an eye on Ada June to be sure she ate something herself and didn't give all her eggs and biscuits under the table to Bo.

Most of the time Mira made it until after everybody was fed before she had to go heave out the few bites she'd taken. Miss Nicey Jane made her a tonic, but even though Mira tried to get it down in little sips, she heaved it out too.

Worse than the heaving was her backache. Probably from all the lifting of Selinda, but she couldn't complain about that. Having the baby was a blessing, whether she was in Mira's arms, Ada June's arms, or Gordon's.

Gordon hadn't complained once about having two daughters join their family, although he did continually speak worries about Mira. That's why she rarely mentioned her back pain and did her best to overcome the fatigue that fell over her at times like a heavy blanket draped around her shoulders. Instead, she smiled and told him she hoped to be carrying a boy instead of a girl so he wouldn't be completely outnumbered by females.

That made him laugh, but then he would look into her eyes and tell her he would love their child whether a girl or a boy. That he already did. And he proved it by praying fervently for the baby every night. He made up songs about the baby. Sometimes he said "her" and sometimes he said "him." Ada June loved it when he did that and Selinda would babble along with him.

Whenever Joseph was there, he frowned when Gordon called the baby her. He would look at Mira with puppy-dog eyes and beg her. "You gotta have a boy, Miss Mira. I can't be the only boy around about here."

Joseph came to the house every day after school to see if Gordon needed anything. At least that was what he claimed, but Mira knew he really came to play with Bo.

Almost every day, Joseph asked Ada June if she would give Bo to him. He knew she wouldn't, but sometimes little boys could be filled with hope for the impossible.

"I could never give Bo away, Joseph," Ada June told him over and over. "You got dogs and your granny Effie has dogs."

"Hounds." That came with a little disgust. "Them don't wanta do nothing but chase rabbits or raccoons. They ain't a bit like Bo."

"Maybe you can get one like him to be your dog." Ada June tried to let him down easy.

"But Bo likes me."

"Maybe so, but he likes me most." And that would end the discussion of ownership, even if Bo was licking Joseph's chin.

Mira's heart warmed at how Ada June was glad Bo had taken up with Joseph. That was proof she counted Joseph a friend. She seemed as wary about making friends as Bo. The dog offered tail wags to very few.

When Mira worried about Ada June not making friends at school, Gordon told her that was to be expected. "Ada June hasn't known much kindness in her time, although those in Sourwood might claim different. They'd say they've seen to her. Kept her from going hungry. But nobody put food on the table for her out of sincere caring."

"Miss Effie seems fond of her in her way." Mira had noted

how when Miss Effie was at the school, none of the children ever bothered Ada June as they sometimes were apt to do when Mira turned her back on them.

"Miss Effie might be the one exception. Ada June stayed with her a long while before Luther Slade asked to take her in as help for Dottie."

"That didn't work out so well," Mira muttered.

"Well, no, but Ada June managed."

"If you call sleeping in the woods managing."

"But you forget Ada June likes being out in the woods. She's got her different ways. She might be sleeping out in the woods now if she didn't know it worried you."

"Then I'm glad she knows that." Mira had no doubt a bed in a house was better than a bed in the woods.

"She does want to please you."

"Isn't that good?"

"Of course, it is. We want to please those we love."

Mira thought of all the ways Gordon worked to please her and tried not to wonder if he thought she lacked in doing the same. But she was carrying his child. What better thing could a wife do for her husband?

Gordon went on. "Anyway, her time with Miss Effie was before I came here. By the time Dugan Foster asked me to establish a mission in Sourwood, Ada June was already with Miss Dottie."

"They just passed her around and treated her like a mule for hire." Anger burned inside Mira at the thought.

"The people aimed to do right. Ada June was, maybe I should say is, an unusual child."

"But she has such a good heart."

"You don't have to convince me." Gordon smiled at her. "But you're a teacher. You know how children can sometimes pick on a child who is different. You can't deny Ada June is different, or at least she was before you took her under your wing. Who knows?

In time she might lose that wildness she developed in order to survive after her mother died."

"I just want her to not be afraid to like others. To not have to hear them call her a woods colt. What a dreadful thing for her, as if it's her fault she doesn't have a father." Mira peered up at Gordon. "Do you know who that was?"

"No, I don't." Gordon sighed. "Even if I did, I'm not at all sure telling Ada June would help or simply hurt her more. She's lived without knowing for years."

"She just wants love."

"Everyone does."

The hint of sadness in his eyes when he spoke those last words stabbed Mira. She still hadn't said the words she knew he waited to hear. She should say them. He said them often and she had no doubt he meant them. Yet, she hesitated.

But love, true love, took time, didn't it?

May brought another burst of beauty to Sourwood as the dogwoods bloomed among the trees. As Mira walked to school on the last day of the regular school session, she felt a mixture of regret and relief. She enjoyed the early morning walks to the school, sometimes carrying Selinda. Other days, like this one, Ada June brought the baby later. Mira had started out earlier than usual to prepare for their final day.

Many of the children had already stopped coming since they were needed at home to plant their fields and gardens or sass patches. Mira smiled at the mountain talk she was learning.

She didn't want to shut down school completely. She hoped to have classes a few hours every afternoon for any, young or old, who might want to come practice their reading skills. One of those would be Ada June, who had not lost her excitement about learning to read.

Ada June. What a gift she was to Mira. She and Selinda both. Mira was bountifully blessed.

Ada June had yearned for family ever since her ma died, but she hadn't expected to get it by being a ma at her age. Before Elsinore headed up to heaven, Ada June had been pondering asking Miss Mira if she'd take her on as a daughter. Seemed like Selinda coming to live with Preacher Gordon and Miss Mira put a block to that. Plus with Miss Mira expectin' one of her own, she didn't likely need to take on a half-grown girl.

Ada June missed Elsinore, but she'd never thought about her as a mother. More like sisters could be. Fussing some, but always ready to get done with that and think kindly about one another again.

That was sort of how Ada June felt about Selinda too. More sisterly than what she imagined ma-like would be. Selinda needed a grown-up ma and not somebody who hankered after sleeping in the woods when moonlight fell soft over the trees and critters whispered along their trails in the silvery light.

Before she had Selinda to help see to, Ada June slipped away for a night off to herself now and again. She never told Miss Mira she was sleeping at Aunt Dottie's, but she was pretty sure Miss Mira thought that.

But after Elsinore passed on, Aunt Dottie had waylaid Ada June at church. "I've heared what Elsinore did. What with giving over Selinda to you. So's I know you have to be as busy as a hen with hatchlings to watch. I reckon I can do for my young'uns these days without addin' more burdens on you."

Without the excuse of helping Aunt Dottie, Ada June couldn't slip off to the woods without Miss Mira knowing that was what she was doing. Miss Mira wasn't trying to make Ada June into somebody she wasn't how some others had done in the past, but she worried over her.

Ada June's ma had been gone so long that she had done forgot how it felt to have somebody caring what happened to her. It could be some constraining, but nice at the same time.

That was why most every night she came in and slept in the cot in Preacher Gordon's front room. Selinda still slept in the cradle, even though she didn't hardly have room to wiggle her toes in it. Preacher was working on a bed that would roll right under Ada June's when Selinda wasn't in it. That way the cradle would be ready for Miss Mira's baby.

Seemed like now Miss Mira had babies enough to think about without taking on Ada June. She didn't say that, but Ada June was afraid she might if'n she asked her about being her ma. So, she didn't ask.

Miss Mira seemed happy enough even with heaving up most of what she ate every livelong morning. Ada June heard Miss Effie say she was carrying hard. Sometimes when she thought nobody was paying any notice, Miss Effie got those lines between her eyes that meant something wasn't right when she looked at Miss Mira. But Ada June had learned to most always be paying attention, whether it seemed like she was or not. That gave her a running start if trouble went to brewing.

Connor Rayburn hadn't laid off giving her that trouble. He had got to be some sneakier about it so's Miss Mira wouldn't catch him. But Miss Mira still knew. Preacher Gordon did too. He told her to pay no mind to Connor or any of them others when they shouted out things like "woods colt" and "dumb girl" or whatever worse things they thought up.

That was some easier for her to do than it used to be. She wasn't exactly sure why. Maybe because half the time she was packing Selinda to school to save Miss Mira a load. Seemed like the girls weren't so ready to poke on her with Selinda on her hip and smiling out at them. A time or two, a couple of them offered to take Selinda and give Ada June's arm a rest. Miss Mira said she should let them, but Ada June kept recalling times they didn't appear so nice acting. She wasn't about to take any chances with Selinda.

The older girls did help with entertaining Selinda during the school time. Inside where Miss Mira could make sure nobody did wrong things. Ada June knew how folks were. Sometimes niceness was just a coating like moss on a wet rock that was slippery if a body depended on stepping full on it.

Today when she got to the schoolyard, she spied Connor moving behind a tree. He was probably aiming to scare her, but she wasn't about to run away. Not whilst she was packing Selinda. She didn't even start walking fast. Instead, she held her head up and kept walking, aiming not to pay the first mind to him.

She told herself that, but she did miss Bo beside her. He was back at Preacher Gordon's house like he always was on school days. She kept a smile on like she wasn't worried about the first thing as she come up by the tree. Just like she thought, Connor leaped out in front of her, roaring like some kind of idiot. She only jumped a little, but Selinda let out a wail. Ada June hugged her to calm her down. She didn't say a thing to Connor, or Marv either when he jumped out behind Connor.

They weren't as quiet. Connor danced around her. "Hey, ma. Got your own little woods colt now?"

She wanted to set Selinda down and sock him. But she didn't.

"Where's your pitiful excuse for a dog?" Marv stepped in front of her. He always poked her about Bo. "My old hound could swallow it in one bite." He nodded toward where his dog hunkered down scratching at its ear.

Some of the other kids turned to stare at them. Joseph was over next to the schoolhouse with his head down, pretending he didn't know Connor was pestering her. That didn't bother Ada June.

Joseph was a fine friend when they were off to themselves, but he wasn't but six. He couldn't go against the big boys. He wasn't big enough and he was a boy. Boys had to act like they didn't care about nothing and especially not a girl like her.

Now if Billy Ray was there, he'd put a stop to Connor's nonsense. He was big and not worried about his spot in a schoolhouse yard. She did like Billy Ray. She hoped Joseph would grow up just like him. But Billy Ray was back at Miss Effie's house doing some plowing or planting. That was where she wished Connor and Marv were too.

Now that Selinda had hushed her crying, Ada June decided to get back at Marv. Without saying the first word, she whistled soft like. Marv's hound pricked up his droopy ears and lumbered straight over to Ada June.

She tickled him behind the ears like she'd been doing every time she came across him hanging around the schoolhouse. Dillon and her had become right good friends.

Marv hollered mad like for him to come, but Dillon took his time listening. He liked his ears scratched. Selinda giggled and touched the hound's head. Ada June gave him one more scratch under his chin, ignoring his slobber, before she went on toward the schoolhouse steps.

Connor wasn't through trying to get her goat. "Whose clothesline did you steal that dress off of?"

If it weren't for how she didn't talk to Connor, she'd tell him a few things. After she socked him in the nose. But she guessed she shouldn't think on doing that. Preacher Gordon claimed Connor had the wrong idea that it made him big in other people's eyes when he picked on her. He said Connor's pa was always on him to be tough, and that sometimes the oldest boy in a family had a rough time living up to how a pa thought he ought to be.

Ada June didn't have to worry about that. She wasn't a boy and she didn't have a pa.

A girl named Iva Mae ran over to go up the steps with Ada

June. "I like your dress. If I saw one like it on a clothesline, I'd yank it off for sure."

Then she laughed, but not at Ada June. With her. So Ada June laughed too, and when Iva Mae reached for Selinda, she handed her right off. That made Selinda babble something beyond understanding, and they both laughed again.

37

Gordon had a bad feeling about why Miss Nicey Jane wanted to meet him at the church ever since one of her grandchildren brought her message. More a summons, he thought as he walked to the church on the second Monday in May. A somewhat ominous summons.

Miss Nicey Jane was one of his biggest supporters in Sourwood. She was instrumental in getting the church and school built, even if she never hefted up the first log. But that support came with a price. She expected things to be the way she thought they should be, and she had a very firm idea of how that was.

He pushed away his unsettling worries. A man shouldn't borrow trouble. She might simply want to show him something she wanted done to the building. It wasn't like him to conjure up trouble. And why should he? Wasn't he as happy as he could ever remember being? A baby on the way. A beautiful wife who loved children and opened up her heart and home to them. Ada June and Selinda had brought joy to their house.

Yet the worm of worry threatened to spoil things. Mira was so sick. Even sicker than she admitted. It wasn't only the nausea, although that was certainly enough. He noted how she caught her breath at times and then let her hand go to her back.

Just a few months ago his whole focus was on the people here in Sourwood. But then Mira showed up at that Louisville church and changed everything. An answer to Sourwood's prayer for a teacher, but also an answer to a prayer he had never offered.

His prayers had been all about his service here. Answered prayers as the people had embraced him. Still, in ways, he had felt set apart. Set apart for the Lord's work was good, but he'd also felt a lonesome setting apart. Part of that was the death of his mother and how he missed her letters of support. Part had been because no matter how the people accepted him, he would always be someone brought-in. Not born to the hills.

But now he had Mira. And two daughters. And his own precious baby on the way. He looked up at the sky, blue as only it could be in May. The same blue as the bluebird Mira had set on their mantel. He had been watching for the first bluebirds to return with the warming weather so he could share the sight with Mira. No bluebirds yet, but a mockingbird sang in the top of an oak. The green of the new leaves lifted up to touch the blue sky. Down lower, dogwood blooms speckled the woods with white.

He let go of his worry, but it rushed back when he saw Miss Nicey Jane by the church door and her husband, Riley, leaning against the railing at the bottom of the steps. This wasn't a conference about window curtains or hymnbooks.

If Riley Callahan was at the church, Gordon needed to worry. Not worry. Pray. Fervently. Riley hadn't been in the church since the roof was on. The man didn't withhold his labor. Only his approval.

"Good morning, Miss Nicey Jane. Mr. Riley. The Lord is sending a beautiful day our way." Gordon pretended nothing was unusual about meeting them here.

He held out his hand to Riley, who stepped forward to take it. He didn't bother with a smile, but then Riley rarely did. People claimed Riley was a rounder before Nicey Jane settled him down. Not completely, if the rumors were true about him making the best moonshine this side of Harlan or how once years back he had disappeared from Sourwood for the better part of a year.

He shook away those thoughts. A preacher couldn't put stock in rumors. True or not. He would leave any judgments up to the Lord.

Mr. Riley didn't say anything, but then he generally let Nicey Jane do the talking when they were together.

"Every day is a good day with the Lord, Preacher." Nicey Jane looked around. "But we best go inside for our talk. No need attracting unwarranted attention."

"Very well." He stepped past her to open the door. They never locked the church.

Inside the light was dim after the sunshine. The building had only three windows with glass. The other openings were shuttered until they could get more windowpanes.

He waited until Miss Nicey Jane sat down on the back bench before he asked, "What can I do for the two of you?" He wasn't sure he wanted to hear it, but no need in delaying whatever it was with talk about the weather or spring planting.

Nicey Jane looked at Riley leaning against the back wall instead of sitting down. When he didn't say anything, she twisted her mouth into an aggravated circle and huffed out a breath as she turned back toward Gordon.

He wasn't sure whether she was upset with him or Riley, but he was definitely the one most concerned about it. Riley looked as if he'd rather be up on his hillside doing whatever it was he did that most of the church folks, perhaps especially Nicey Jane, did their best to ignore.

"Well, it's about Elsinore's baby." Nicey Jane's eyes narrowed on Gordon.

"Oh." This might be worse even than he'd imagined.

"You know a child needs to be with her family."

"Elsinore didn't have any family as far as I know. And Elsinore wanted the baby to stay with Ada June."

Another huff, this one sounding even more aggravated. "You

know that was ridiculous, Preacher Gordon. The girl is only ten, without the sense God gave a goose most of the time."

"I can't agree with that." Gordon couldn't let that go by without refuting it. "Ada June is a very intelligent girl. She loves Selinda and Selinda loves her. Ada June has been a wonderful help with the baby."

The woman's eyes tightened. "I'm not disputin' that. But a body can't leave a child to somebody like the baby is no more than a plot of land. You can't deny the truth of that." She pointed her finger at Gordon.

Gordon sank down on the end of a bench in front of Nicey Jane. She was right. "I suppose I should go to Jackson and find a lawyer to do whatever needs to be done to make Selinda legally ours."

Nicey Jane looked down and fingered the edge of her crocheted shawl. Gordon didn't like how her silence pressed down on him. He glanced up at Riley. His eyes were half-closed as if bored by it all.

"That's noble of you. Of your missus too, what with her struggling to carry." She raised her head and peered around at Riley a couple of seconds before she went on. "But whilst Elsinore didn't have family, that don't mean Benny Craig didn't have kin. Living kin."

"Oh?" Dread like a cold hand closed around his heart.

"The mister was off over the hill last week. On business. He run up on Benny's uncle, I think it was." She looked at Riley, who nodded once. "Anyways, he, the uncle, knowed Benny had a wife and he asked the mister how she was gettin' along. Well, we all know she ain't gettin' along at all no more. Come to find out from this uncle—Daniel Craig was his name—it appears that Benny's ma is still living. Not only that, Benny has a sister that don't have any young'uns. Riley says they were right excited to know Benny had left behind a baby. Ain't that right, Riley?"

Riley nodded again.

Gordon's heart sank. More heartache for Ada June. And Mira. Maybe especially Mira.

Nicey Jane must have guessed what he was thinking because she went on. "I know your missus has took to the baby. That's only natural and I'm thinkin' she might not understand how things is up here in the hills. But a child needs to be with blood kin if'n there's any willing to take an orphan in. And Benny's folks appear more than willing. Having his baby to raise will be comfort to them." She stood up. "Riley says they aim to come get the baby soon's they can. We figured it best you knew afore they come up on your porch."

As Gordon got to his feet, his lips trembled as he tried to force a smile. "Yes. Thank you."

Riley stepped away from the wall and spoke for the first time, his voice carrying more than a hint of disapproval. "If'n your woman is gonna live in the hills, she'd best accustom herself to mountain ways."

The man didn't appear to expect Gordon to say anything to that as he headed out the door without waiting for Nicey Jane to go first.

She followed her husband and then stopped on the top step to touch Gordon's arm. "I know you and your missus aimed good taking in Elsinore's baby."

"Yes."

She patted his arm with a little smile. "If'n Mira needs anything, anything at all, you send for me."

He didn't doubt her sincerity as she went down the steps and headed toward the road up to her house. But one of Nicey Jane's tonics wasn't going to be of any help for this.

With the school closed down until the next week when she would welcome any that wanted to keep learning through the summer, Mira enjoyed a relaxed morning where she didn't have to rush to get to school. She even kept down her breakfast.

Selinda giggled as she crawled after Bo. The dog let her touch him and then scampered away again. Ada June laughed as she trailed them to make sure Selinda didn't get too close to the fireplace.

Gordon came in and scooped up Selinda without a word and held her close even though she pushed against him to be let down. And that fast the joy drained out of the day. Ada June's eyes were big as she stared at Gordon. Bo put his tail between his legs and crept over to lean against Ada June.

They were going to lose Selinda. Gordon cried when he told them. His tears touched something deep inside Mira. He was grieved not only for himself but for her. His pain was her pain. Her pain was his. She knew in that moment if she asked him to, he would leave Sourwood and go wherever she wanted. Not that she would ever ask that of him.

Ada June stomped the floor. "They can't take her. Elsinore gave her to me. Me."

Bo growled as he spun around to find the danger.

Gordon handed Selinda to Ada June. She didn't seem to even notice when the baby grabbed a fistful of her hair.

"They can't." Ada June's words weren't much more than a whimper as she stared at Gordon. "Can they?"

"They can." Gordon's shoulders drooped.

Ada June sank down to the floor and clutched Selinda tight against her chest. Bo tried to push his nose in between her and the baby but gave up and leaned against Ada June.

Mira sat down beside them.

Gordon swiped away his tears and dropped to the floor to huddle with them.

The anger in Ada June's eyes must be burning away any tears. Mira's eyes were dry too. In time tears would come, but right now her sorrow went deeper than tears.

"Can't you make it not happen?" Ada June stared at Gordon and then Mira. "Selinda loves us."

"And we love her. We will always love her," Mira said.

"Elsinore wanted me to have her." A few tears finally slid down Ada June's cheeks.

"I know, but she didn't think about Benny's family," Gordon said.

"They didn't think about her." Ada June sounded angry again.

"Shh, sweetie." Mira scooted closer to put her arms around both of these girls she loved so much. She needed to find words to make this easier for Ada June. She moistened her lips. "You know how much Elsinore loved Benny."

Ada June gave a bare nod. "She thought he was coming home every night. But that don't have nothing to do with them taking Selinda."

"They're her family," Gordon said.

"But they never came to act like it," Ada June said. "Family is supposed to help."

"Maybe they didn't know about Selinda." Mira kept her voice gentle as she used the corner of her apron to wipe the tears off Ada June's cheeks. Selinda twisted away from Ada June and crawled into Mira's lap. Bo took her place in Ada June's arms. Mira stroked the baby's head, and she relaxed against her.

"But—" Ada June started, then didn't seem to come up with any more words.

"Don't you remember? Elsinore said Benny went away to find work before he knew a baby was on the way. She grieved that even the promise of Selinda was something he never knew. So it seems reasonable to think his family didn't know either."

Ada June sniffed. "Then how come them to know now?"

"Mr. Riley happened across Benny's uncle wherever he was last week," Gordon said.

"He didn't have to tell him about Selinda." Ada June thrust out her bottom lip.

"But he did," Gordon said. "We can't change that. And maybe it's better while Selinda is so small. It might be easier for her."

"She won't remember me."

"She'll remember in her heart." Mira touched Selinda's chest and then Ada June's. "And we will remember her in ours."

"Yes, always," Gordon said.

Mira swallowed hard and pushed out her next words. "How long before they come?"

"I don't know," Gordon said. "I'd guess not long."

Mira tightened her arms around Selinda. She wanted to keep her there forever, but she couldn't. The Lord gave and the Lord took away.

She kissed the top of Selinda's head. Her fine blond hair was finally growing long enough to comb, but she would never put ribbons in it. No need thinking of what couldn't be. Instead, if they only had this day, they needed to make it good.

Blinking back the tears finally filling her eyes, she managed a smile. "Then today and every day we have before they come, we will love this child completely." She looked at Ada June. "The sun is shining. We'll fix a picnic, and you can show Selinda and us your favorite places in the woods. Selinda needs to see the things you love."

"She won't remember."

"Maybe not, but you will. I will. Preacher Gordon will."

Gordon leaned over and kissed Mira's cheek and then Ada June's forehead. "Miss Mira is right. This is the day the Lord has made. Let us rejoice in it."

Rejoice was a hard word to embrace, but for Ada June, for Selinda, she could try. Gordon reached down to help Mira up. And yes, for Gordon.

38

Ada June didn't see how traipsing around in the woods was going to help anything, but sitting on the floor crying wouldn't change anything either. All it would do was make her head hurt and probably make Miss Mira lose her breakfast, which for the first morning in forever she hadn't.

But for sure Ada June didn't see how Preacher Gordon expected them to do any rejoicing. Somebody, folks she didn't even know, were gonna come and take Selinda away. After Elsinore had plain as day said she wanted her to stay with Ada June and Miss Mira.

She hadn't ever thought about how having a father could make a difference. Made her sort of glad she didn't have one.

Preacher Gordon helped Miss Mira get their fixings for eating in the woods while Ada June lay down on the floor and let Selinda crawl over top her. The baby giggled when Bo jumped over Ada June after her.

Joseph showed up as they headed into the hills. He didn't know about Selinda. Ada June was glad nobody told him. That made it easier to act like this was the same as any other day. Excepting for no school and Preacher Gordon not going off visiting but staying with them.

They ate their food under a dogwood tree. Some petals had

already fallen to dot the ground. Preacher Gordon reached high to pick off a bloom.

"See these petals. They make a cross." He touched the reddish pink on the edge of the petals. "And this bit of color represents the Lord's blood given to pay for our sins. In nature we find many signs of the Lord's love."

He looked at the tree like he almost expected to see an angel perched on one of the limbs like a dove or something. Doves were in the Scriptures too. But a blackbird was all that was there, which seemed about right to Ada June. She was having trouble with that rejoicing stuff. Felt more like a weeping day to her.

"A bluebird would look pretty among the white blossoms." Miss Mira sounded all full of wishing.

Ada June thought of the little bird Miss Mira kept on the fireplace mantel. The bird looked really old with some of its blue faded away, but whenever Miss Mira held it, she always smiled like it was the prettiest thing ever.

Preacher Gordon kept looking around at the trees like as how he hoped to spot one of those bluebirds for Miss Mira. "I've heard them called bluebirds of happiness."

Happiness. None of that was happening today. Selinda was asleep on a blanket Miss Mira brung along. Bo went between her and Ada June, not sure which of them he should spend his loving on. All the sad feeling in the air must have had him addled.

Even Joseph, who didn't know nothing about Mr. Riley going off and finding Selinda's uncle when he didn't need to do anything of the sort, seemed to feel things weren't like they oughta be. So when Miss Mira and Preacher Gordon started looking for birds, he got all excited and jumped up.

"I kin find you a blue bird, Miss Mira. Don't know why you'd want to see one of them noisy jays, but one is sure to be around about somewheres," Joseph said.

Miss Mira smiled. "Not jays, Joseph. This is the Eastern bluebird that has sky-blue feathers on its back and a red breast. My mother used to tell me a story about how it got that red breast something like Preacher Gordon's dogwood flower legend."

"What's that?" Joseph asked, even though he looked some disappointed Miss Mira wasn't wanting him to be off looking for a blue jay.

"The story goes that a bluebird was watching from the rafters in the stable while Joseph built a fire to warm Baby Jesus. When the bluebird flew down to blow on the coals under the kindling to get the flames started, its breast feathers were scorched."

"That's a nice story." Preacher Gordon sat down by Miss Mira and took hold of her hand, gentle like.

Joseph rocked back and forth on his feet. "I might could find one of them too."

Miss Mira smiled. "Then look for one, but don't go off too far."

Bo was up with his tail whipping back and forth. He looked at Ada June, as ready to do some running as Joseph was. So, Ada June went off with Joseph, but she knew they wouldn't find one of Miss Mira's bluebirds. A person couldn't expect to see a bluebird of happiness on a sad day like they were having. She didn't care what Preacher Gordon said about rejoicing.

A week passed. Ada June began to hope she might be doing all this grieving for no reason. Miss Mira put on a good face, but she was grieving too. She didn't even talk about going over to the school. They wanted to both be right there with Selinda, doing whatever they could to make her giggle like as how they could store up that sound.

They didn't talk about it happening, but it was always right there with them, sort of like staring up at a boulder on the side of a cliff that was edging free. It was coming down. A person couldn't know when, but wasn't the first doubt it was gonna happen. So, every step up on the porch, each time Bo lifted up his ears and looked toward the door, they held their breath and waited.

Then the knock came that wasn't somebody come to visit or hunting Preacher Gordon. Something about that peck on the door with nobody hollering out a hello made Ada June freeze where she was. When Bo went to barking like he knew something bad was about to happen, her heart sank.

Miss Mira looked at the door and bent her head for a second. Ada June knew she was praying, but she wouldn't be able to pray them away.

When she raised up her head, her face was white like it was after she heaved up her breakfast. "Make Bo hush, Ada June."

Ada June snapped her fingers. Bo whined and came to sit at her feet. Miss Mira still hadn't moved toward the door. The knock came again, a little louder this time. Selinda started crawling toward the door.

Miss Mira picked her up and kissed both her cheeks. She made a sound that was something like a laugh but more like a sob before she handed Selinda off to Ada June. "Seems she's readier than we are."

By the time she opened the door, Miss Mira had her face back in order. Ada June tried to do the same, but she couldn't. She wanted to run out the back door and carry Selinda up to her cave. But a baby couldn't live thataway.

A woman maybe Miss Mira's age and an old man that looked something like Ada June remembered Benny looking made some noises of greeting. The woman leaned to the side to peer past Miss Mira. Ada June knew what she was looking for, but she didn't step closer.

Then Preacher Gordon was out on the porch sounding all out of breath like as how he'd run from Miss Nicey Jane's house instead of just from the church next door. Miss Mira was trying to smile as she asked them in. Ada June had no intention of smiling.

The woman started crying as soon as she saw Selinda. She

pulled out a handkerchief and wiped at her tears. "Oh, she looks just like Benny."

When she held out her hands toward Selinda, the baby went right to her. That didn't mean anything. She did that with everybody. Ada June kept hold of Selinda's foot, but ducked her head and turned loose when Preacher Gordon looked at her.

Miss Mira asked them to stay for supper, but the man said they needed to get back over the mountain afore dark. So they put Selinda's clothes in a poke, and Miss Mira tried to tell them all the things Selinda liked to eat. Then they kissed her and told her goodbye, like as how they would see her come morning when they might never see her again.

Miss Mira and Preacher Gordon went out on the porch to watch them leave, but Ada June ran out the kitchen door with Bo on her heels. She didn't stop until she was at her cave up on the hill behind some rhododendron bushes. Nobody could see her there. Nobody but Bo.

The dark fell around them. Then she stared up at the stars until the fingernail moon came up. She stayed sitting. Bo poked her with his nose but then huffed out a breath and flopped down beside her. She could practically hear him thinking that they were supposed to be through with these kinds of nights. The kind where she hated everybody because everybody hated her.

She tried not to think about anything. To not let nothing in her head but starshine. But then an owl hooted. A few minutes later a bobcat let out a scream that had Bo's hair on end. She grabbed him before he could run out of their hiding place. He went still, hearing more than she could ever hope to hear, but suddenly the night was so quiet the silence hurt her ears.

A little voice started up inside her head. *Selinda loves you.* She could almost hear one of the baby's giggles she'd hidden in her heart. Even if she never saw her again, she knew without a doubt that Selinda loved her. Preacher Gordon liked her. Even before Miss Mira came, he liked her. Miss Effie didn't hate her. Billy Ray didn't hate her. Joseph didn't hate her. And she didn't hate them. Not even for one night now.

Miss Mira didn't hate her. Miss Mira loved her. She didn't hate Miss Mira. She loved her. And now she'd run away. Miss Mira might not care if she came back after this. She had a baby coming. She didn't need a girl like Ada June who ran away instead of staying and helping. Staying and loving.

She wanted to slip out of the cave and go back right then, but the bobcat made its noise again. Bo trembled in her arms. He knew better than to mess with something like that, but what if he thought Ada June was in danger? He would jump right on that old bobcat even if he couldn't win.

So she stayed where they were until the stars began disappearing in the first gray light of dawn. Then they slipped down the hill back to the preacher's cabin.

She opened the door inch by inch to keep it from making a squeak. Nothing but coals showed in the fireplace, so the light was dimmer in the cabin than outside. She stopped when she heard something. The snuffling sound of somebody crying.

Miss Mira was sitting on Ada June's cot with her head in her hands. She was sobbing. Quiet like. Maybe so Preacher Gordon wouldn't hear.

Ada June stopped still, but Bo went on in. When his toenails clicked on the floor, Miss Mira looked up. "Ada June." She held a hand out toward her. "I'm so glad you're home."

Home. The word wrapped around her and took away some of the chill of the night. She was home.

Ada June went to sit beside her. Miss Mira swiped at her eyes and then covered her face with her hands again as her shoulders shook with more sobs. After a minute, she sniffed and swallowed hard. "I'm sorry, but my tears got started, and I can't seem to stop them."

"You miss Selinda," Ada June said.

"I do. So very much. I know she's going to be fine. Her aunt will love her just as much as I do, but my heart had already claimed her as a daughter."

The words Ada June wanted to say got caught in her throat. For a second she thought maybe she was going to lose her voice again the way she had after her ma died. She couldn't let that happen. She wouldn't let that happen, no matter whether Miss Mira would want to hear her words or not.

"I can be your daughter."

Miss Mira turned to look straight at her. More light had come in the windows, and Ada June could see her face easy, but she couldn't tell if what she saw was surprise or worry or what. She ought to say something else, but she didn't know what.

"Oh, Ada June," Miss Mira whispered. "You are already my daughter. My forever daughter."

She put her arms around Ada June and pulled her close. She kissed the top of her head. "You smell like starshine."

39

Starting on the Monday after Benny's people came for Selinda, Mira opened the school in the afternoons. Not only did she need something to help her not hear the echo of Selinda's giggle in the cabin, Ada June needed a reason not to disappear into the woods and silence again.

The world around them was exploding in green and flowers, but a cloud seemed to follow Mira around. It shouldn't be that way. Selinda was sure to be loved by her aunt. Mira had Ada June to love and the promise of her baby growing inside her. While she still hesitated to speak words of love to Gordon, she was not sorry to be his wife.

Gordon wasn't shy about saying sweet words of love, but she had times when she wondered if he could really love her that much already. Everything had happened so fast between them. Even this baby on the way.

But then he would do something that swept away every doubt. A day after Selinda went to be with Benny's family, he borrowed a horse and made the trip over the mountain to Jackson. He claimed a need to see Reverend Haskell about some church issue, but he came back with a tin of soda crackers. For her.

Even better, Miss Stella sent a bunch of strawberry plants and a start of rhubarb. Ada June and Gordon spent much of the next day digging up a place to plant both. They wouldn't have strawberries this year, but the plants were a promise for the future.

Only a few students came for afternoon school. Even Joseph told Mira a fellow had to have time to look for crawdads. He did show up at least once every day to get his licks and tail wags from Bo. Ada June still left Bo at the cabin instead of bringing him to school.

Mostly young girls came to the classes. The boys were like Joseph with boy things to do if they weren't working in the fields. That didn't stop Mira from encouraging them to come.

Connor laughed when she told him he could use the extra work on his reading. She wasn't bothered by his laughter, but she was ashamed of her relief when he didn't come.

On the last Friday in May, she expected a few extra students since rain had come during the night to muddy the fields. When Ada June headed to the spring for a bucket of drinking water, Mira pushed open the shuttered windows to let the rain-washed air flow into the schoolhouse.

She took a minute to sit behind her teacher's desk. Fatigue still plagued her. She didn't know if it radiated from the pain in her back or from her sorrow over losing Elsinore and then Selinda.

Miss Effie said the tired feeling would get better, just as the nausea was already better. Then she warned that such was generally just replaced by some other baby-carrying ill.

"You're so small there ain't no way you can grow a baby to the proper bornin' size without some complaints from your back."

"I'm stronger than I look," Mira assured her.

"I reckon so or you couldn't make a roomful of young'uns pay you mind."

Now as Mira prayed for each of her students, she almost nodded off.

The sound of ferocious barks jerked her out of her chair. Bo's barks. But it couldn't be him. They'd left him at the cabin.

A scream made Mira's heart jump up in her throat. Ada June's scream.

She stepped out on the little stoop. Bo barked at Connor when he tried to kick him. Ada June ran up from the creek, yelling at Connor and then Bo at almost the same time.

"He's trying to bite me." Connor landed a kick that sent the dog flying.

Bo yelped and collapsed with a whimper. Ada June charged toward Connor, fists flailing. Marv grabbed her and held her back.

"Stop this right now," Mira shouted as she rushed down the steps, but the children paid no attention.

Connor looked at Ada June. "That dog ain't never gonna bite me again." He pulled a pistol out of his overalls pocket.

For a few seconds, Mira was frozen in place as the boy waved the gun around at Ada June, at Marv's dog, at Mira. Then he pointed it straight at Bo. The dog was dragging one of his back legs as he tried to go to Ada June.

"Bo never bit you," Ada June screamed.

Mira forced her feet to move toward Connor. Despite her pounding heart, she tried to sound in control. "Put down that gun."

"Pa told me not to let no little dog get the best of me."

"Connor, look at me." Mira willed him to listen, but he didn't even glance back at her.

Ada June was crying now. "Please, Connor. I'll keep him away from you. I promise."

Although he didn't turn loose of Ada June, even Marv started pleading with Connor. "Come on, Connor. This ain't fun no more."

Connor didn't seem to hear any of them as he stared at Bo. He wasn't going to listen. Mira started running, but she tripped on her skirt and went down hard on one of her knees. She scrambled up as Ada June jerked away from Marv.

"He ain't thinkin' right. He might shoot you." He grabbed for her again, but she knocked his hand away and ran toward Bo.

Mira's heart froze. Marv was right. Connor might pull the trigger and hit Ada June. She yanked up her skirt, ignored her knee, and ran. "Stop, Connor."

"No!" Joseph came from nowhere to tackle Connor.

The force of his leap knocked the bigger boy down. The gun disappeared between them as they rolled on the ground. The gun went off.

Neither boy moved. Then Connor pushed away from Joseph and stood up. He looked dazed as he stared down at Joseph.

Mira brushed past him and knelt beside Joseph. She ignored the pain when her injured knee hit the ground. "Joseph, are you all right?"

"I'm shot, Miss Mira."

He had blood on his side.

"You kilt him, Connor," Marv said.

"I weren't aimin' to shoot him. I weren't. He jumped me." Connor still held the gun. "He ain't kilt dead. He can't be kilt dead."

Mira pulled back Joseph's shirt. She had no idea how badly he might be hurt. She tore a strip off her underskirt and pressed the cloth on the wound to staunch the bleeding.

"Go get Miss Effie," she ordered Marv. He gave Joseph another scared look and took off up the hill.

If only Gordon was there. He'd know what to do, but he was somewhere helping a church member put a roof on a barn. She stared up at Connor. "Put the gun down and go get Miss Nicey Jane." She knew about tonics. Maybe she knew about gunshot wounds too.

He blinked as if he didn't understand her words. She gave him a hard look. "Put the gun down and go get your grandmother."

He finally dropped the gun and took off. He ran toward the woods and not Miss Nicey Jane's house.

"Am I kilt dead, Miss Mira?" Joseph's eyes on her were big.

"No, Joseph. Not killed at all. Just bleeding a little." She prayed her words were true.

She looked around at Ada June beside Bo. "Get Mathena, Ada June."

"Bo's hurt." She held Bo in her arms as tears rolled down her cheeks.

"Put him in the house. Then after you go tell Mathena we need help, go for Miss Nicey Jane. We'll see to Bo later."

"Is Bo kilt too?" Joseph tried to sit up to see the dog.

"Be still." She pushed him down. "Bo will be fine."

He collapsed back to the ground. "I'm sorry, Ada June. I just let him out to play with me a minute. He weren't bothering Connor. He was after followin' you."

"Shh. No more talking." Mira kept the pressure on his wound and brushed his hair back from his face with her other hand.

"It hurts to breathe."

"But you're a tough boy. You can do it." She looked straight into Joseph's eyes and willed that to be true.

Then Mathena was beside her. "Oh, Joey. What in the world happened?"

"I'm kilt," Joseph said. "But not kilt dead."

"'Course not. We'll get you inside and see to you." Mathena stood up to look around. "Frank and the boys are out helping Winston build that barn way over on yonder hill. But I'll fetch a blanket and we can pack the boy into the house. Easy like."

She was gone before Mira could say the first word. Blood was soaking up through the folded cloth.

A shadow fell over her. "What's goin' on here?" A man's voice.

She glanced up. "Cleo." He was the last person Mira wanted to see. But help was help. "Joseph's been shot."

"Shot?" Cleo frowned as he looked around. He picked up the gun. "Connor done this?"

Mira didn't answer him. She'd let him find out the story from Connor.

But Joseph spoke up. "He weren't aimin' to, Uncle Cleo."

The man looked around. "Where is he?"

"I don't know," Mira said.

"What do you mean you don't know?" He narrowed his eyes at her, his voice fierce.

"Just what I said. He ran over that way." She motioned with her head. "He wasn't hurt. But Joseph is. I sent Ada June after Miss Nicey Jane."

"She ain't the one you need. It's Riley you're needing."

"Does Connor know that?" Mira asked. "Or where Mr. Riley might be?"

"Most everybody knows that." He looked toward the hill.

"Then he might have run to get him." At least Mira hoped so. For Joseph's sake and for Connor's too. Running away with a purpose would be better than running away to hide from what he'd done.

Mathena came back, a bunched-up cover in her arms. "Oh, Cleo." She leaned over to catch her breath. "You can carry Joseph inside for us."

Mira pulled her hand away from the bloody cloth over the wound, and Cleo picked the boy up with more gentleness than Mira expected him to have. When Joseph groaned, the man said, "Easy, Joey."

"It hurts, Uncle Cleo."

"I reckon so. Holler out if'n you need to."

After he headed toward the house, Mira bit her lip to keep from crying out as she pushed up off the ground. Then the pain in her knee was almost forgotten as a cramp grabbed her middle. Surely that was just because she'd been kneeling beside Joseph too long.

When Mathena pushed open the door, Bo hobbled out on three legs to bark at Cleo. Mira grabbed the railing by the steps to pull herself up on the porch. "Don't hurt that dog."

Cleo glanced back at her and growled. "Get the mutt away from me then."

"Bo." Mira spoke his name firmly. Bo whined and lay down. "Good dog."

She wanted to sink down on the porch beside Bo and just stay there, but instead she picked up the dog. He yelped and began panting hard. He was heavier than Mira expected as she carried him into the house.

When Cleo laid Joseph on Ada June's bed, the boy moaned and twisted to try to see the dog. "Bo?"

"Keep still." Cleo peered over his shoulder at Mira. "Fetch a towel to staunch the bleeding. And stir up the fire to boil some water."

Mathena looked at Mira in the middle of the floor holding Bo. "I'll fix the fire and get some water."

Cleo frowned at Mira. "What's wrong with the dog?"

"His leg. Connor kicked him."

"I reckon he deserved it," Cleo said.

Rage burned through Mira, but at the sound of Joseph's weak voice, she tamped it down.

"No, Uncle Cleo. He weren't doin' nothing to Connor."

Cleo didn't give any sign of hearing him. He was still staring at Mira. "Stop actin' like you ain't got a lick of sense. Put the animal down and come tend to the boy."

He was right. She put Bo in the bedroom and ignored his whines as she shut the door. She pulled in a sharp breath as another pain grabbed her back and radiated to her front. It couldn't be those kinds of pains. Not this soon. She breathed out and grabbed a towel off the cabinet and limped over to the bed.

Cleo moved out of her way. "Somebody kick you too?"

"I fell." She had no interest in giving him more information.

"A woman in your condition should oughta be more careful."

His words surprised her. She'd never heard a man speak of any woman other than his wife being in the family way. No woman had even spoken about her expecting a baby to her face other than Granny Perry and Miss Effie. Granny Perry out of nosiness and Miss Effie out of caring.

She ignored Cleo as she leaned over Joseph. The wound was still bleeding but not as much. She covered it with the towel and pressed down. "You're being so brave, Joseph."

He grabbed her arm. "Bo? Is he kilt?"

"Don't worry about Bo." She smiled at him. "Your grandmother will be here in a minute."

"Ada June is gonna hate me."

"That could never happen. Now don't talk."

Miss Effie came in and rushed to the bed. "What have you done, Joseph Foster?"

"I'm sorry, Granny. I couldn't let him shoot Bo."

"So you let him shoot you instead?" She sounded cross.

"I weren't aimin' to."

"'Course you weren't, baby." Her voice softened as she stroked his face.

Miss Nicey Jane was there too, out of breath from her run down the hill. "Cleo. What are you doing here?"

"I come lookin' for Connor. Appears I was late findin' him."

"Connor did this?" Miss Nicey Jane said.

"Don't worry about that right now," Miss Effie said. "Come look about Joseph."

Mira let go of the towel and stepped back from the bed. When another pain grabbed her, she gasped. Miss Effie gave her a look before she turned back to Joseph.

"It don't look too bad." Miss Nicey Jane glanced around at Cleo. "You done good, Cleo, slowing the bleeding."

"That weren't me," he said. "Preacher's missus done that."

Miss Nicey Jane nodded. "You need to put some water on to boil."

"Mathena went for water," Mira said. "Where's Ada June?"

"I sent her after Riley. He'll know what to do."

A new worry. What if Ada June came across Connor out in the woods? She might let her temper flare. There might be another fight. One Ada June couldn't win. But surely Connor wouldn't hurt her. Not after this.

320

Nothing she could do about that. Besides, she had other worries. She put her hands over her abdomen as if she could stop the pains and stepped back quickly. She bumped into Cleo. When she jerked away from him, she couldn't keep from crying out as her knee gave way and the pain in her middle doubled.

Cleo caught her. She didn't have the strength to pull away from him.

Miss Effie was beside her. "What's wrong?"

Cleo answered for her. "She says she fell."

Miss Effie's eyes were sharp on Mira. "You having pains?"

Mira burst into tears.

"Don't be givin' up hope yet." Miss Effie hugged her.

"You need to be seeing to Joseph," Mira choked out between sobs.

"She's right, Effie. Come hold this towel proper, and I'll see to Mira." Miss Nicey Jane came over and laid her hand on Mira's belly. "Cleo, pack her into the bed."

"I can walk." Mira stumbled as she moved away from Cleo. He caught her again.

"Do as I say, Cleo." Miss Nicey Jane gave Mira a fierce look. "Off your feet is the babe's only chance."

Cleo picked her up as easily as he had Joseph earlier.

"Don't let Bo out," Mira said when Miss Nicey Jane opened the bedroom door.

"Blast that dog," Cleo boomed, but he stepped around Bo as Miss Nicey Jane pushed the dog away from the door.

Cleo put her down on the bed and was gone as though the room was on fire.

Miss Nicey Jane looked down at her for a minute. "Don't you be gettin' up for nothing."

"Will that make the pains stop?"

Miss Nicey Jane huffed out a breath. "Hard to say. Bein' abed might turn things in your favor." She shook her head a little. "But if the Lord don't intend this baby coming, nothing will change that. Nothing 'cepting maybe prayer."

Mira caught her hand as the woman turned away. "Will you pray for my baby too?"

Her face softened. "Me and Effie, we been prayin' for you already, seein' as how you were carryin' hard." She pulled her hand free and patted Mira's shoulder. "You take your ease. The good Lord hasn't run out of miracles. Else that bullet might have found little Joseph's heart instead of a rib."

After she went out and shut the door, the noise from the other room was muffled while the silence in the bedroom pressed down on Mira until she could barely breathe. Bo hobbled on three legs over to lay his head on the bed beside her and whine.

"Don't give up hope." She repeated Miss Effie's words as she stroked his head. "Ada June will be back soon."

And Gordon would come. She needed him beside her, and not just for his prayers.

40

Ada June didn't want to go after Mr. Riley. She wanted to go see about Bo. People would take care of Joseph, but nobody would be doing anything for Bo. That was up to her. They might even think he wasn't worth helping if they decided he was why Joseph got shot.

Bo didn't make it happen. Connor did. Waving that gun around. Saying he was going to shoot Bo. Poor Bo. He just wanted to get away from him, but he was hurt too bad. Because Connor kicked him.

If Marv hadn't held her, she could have grabbed Bo and wouldn't none of it happened. Connor wouldn't have shot her. Probably wouldn't have shot anything. He was just trying to act big, like as how he always did.

She reckoned Joseph was too little to know that. Poor Joseph taking on Connor for Bo. He could be dying.

Joseph was how come she was running across the hill to find Mr. Riley. Miss Nicey Jane said he'd know what to do for Joseph if there was any way to do for him.

Miss Nicey Jane hadn't told her where to go. She must've figured Ada June knew, and she did know about where Mr. Riley kept his still. 'Course he could've moved it since then if any revenue men had been poking around. Ada June hadn't heard tell of any around Sourwood for a spell. Some folks said Mr. Riley must have paid them off or shot them all.

Ada June didn't think he shot them. She didn't want to think that right now, since she was headed straight up the hill to where it was better not to go. For Joseph. Her heart went to beating hard. Could have been the climb, but wasn't.

Mr. Riley didn't like her. He always turned and went the other way if he saw her coming. She had no idea what he might do when he saw her here.

The path wound around, going up steep on one side and falling almost straight down on the other. She tried to whistle. A person best make some noise if they were somewhere they weren't expected to be.

She couldn't make so much as a tweet. Her mouth was too dry. She started talking. "Joseph. I'm doin' this for Joseph." She spoke the words over and over.

Her heart pounded harder when the birds quit singing. Even they were scared of Mr. Riley. She expected the man to appear in front of her, gun in hand, but instead when she edged around some boulders, Connor was there ahead of her.

Something snapped, and she ran at him with no more sense than Joseph had back at the schoolyard. At the last second, he turned and shoved her back. She lost her footing and slid off the path. She grabbed a root to stop her slide down the cliff.

"Good gosh, Ada June." Connor glared down at her. "What you tryin' to do? Get us both kilt?"

She slid down another foot as the root she gripped gave a little. But she wasn't about to ask Connor Rayburn for help even if she was in desperate need of it. Then she thought of Bo and Miss Mira. She didn't want to be a heap of broken bones at the bottom of this hill. She got a toehold on a rock to climb back up on the path. The rock broke loose and crashed down the cliff. Like she would if the root didn't hold.

"Grab her, boy." A man's voice.

"I can't, Grandpa. She's too far down."

Ada June tightened her fingers around the root and dug her feet into the cliffside to find something solid. Dirt and more rocks slid away from her shoes. If only she was barefoot, she might find a better grip with her toes.

When the man came into sight on the path above Connor, she was back on Pap Leathers' hill running with her ma down the trail. Snow made the going slippery. Her ma's eyes looked wild as she thrust Ada June in behind some bushes to hide. Then she ran on. The man came after them, but he didn't see Ada June.

"Sarai." He yelled again and again, but her ma didn't answer. He came back past Ada June's hiding spot again, his head down. She shook so much the bushes rattled, but he must not have heard them. After he was gone, she clutched her knees against her chest and waited for her ma, but she didn't come. Finally Ada June crept out of her hiding spot and went on down the trail.

She saw where the man stomped around in the snow and then turned back. Her ma's tracks went on. Up the hill now. A good piece farther along, her ma went off the path. Not footprints but a stumbling swath in the snow. Ada June slid down after her. Her ma was chocked against a tree and wouldn't wake up. Ada June cuddled against her in the snow, but her ma just got colder and colder. At daylight the trapper found Ada June and carried her away.

Now she was staring up at the man she saw that night.

"Get on your belly," Mr. Riley told Connor. "I'll hold your legs."

Connor did as he said and slid over the edge of the cliff. When he reached for her, she was scared to turn loose of the root to grab his hands. What if he couldn't or wouldn't hold her? She looked over her shoulder. The cliff went straight down.

"Take his hands, girl. One at a time." When she still hesitated, Mr. Riley guessed what she was thinking. "If he lets go, I'll send him on down the hill after you." He sounded like he was doing no more than commenting on the weather.

"Grandpa," Connor sputtered.

"Naught to worry, boy, less'n you don't hold on to the girl."

Ada June took a breath and grabbed one of Connor's hands and then the other one. He gripped them so tight it hurt, as Mr. Riley pulled him back up on the path and then took hold of Ada June's arms to yank her up. She scrambled away from the edge of the path and tried not to stare at Mr. Riley. Connor sat on the ground, breathing hard.

"What you two doin' up here?" When neither of them answered, he went on. "I ain't askin' twice."

When Connor kept staring at the ground, she figured one of them best talk before Mr. Riley pushed them back over the hill.

"Miss Nicey Jane sent me. Joseph got shot." Ada June didn't know if that was enough words, but she felt almost as out of breath saying all that as when she was about to slide down the cliff.

Mr. Riley must have thought it enough. He looked from her to Connor. "That explains her. What about you, boy?"

"I shot him." Connor looked like he had as hard a time saying his words as she had saying hers.

"You shot him." Mr. Riley's frown looked dark as thunder.

"I didn't do it a purpose." Connor shrank back from him.

"But he's still shot. Bad?"

"I don't know. Preacher's wife was tendin' him. He was talkin' some afore I run off."

"Come up here to hide out, did you?" Mr. Riley blew out a disgusted sounding breath. He turned from Connor back to Ada June. "You know where he was hit, girl?"

"His chest, I think. Not sure. I was seein' about my dog."

"It shot too?"

"Kicked." A tear slipped out of one of her eyes and down her cheek.

"Boy oughta come before a dog." Mr. Riley stared at her.

She wanted to tell him that was why she was there instead of with Bo, but she just nodded.

"Reckon we best go see." He started down the trail.

Ada June stood up and brushed off her dress. She had dirt in her shoes, but she wasn't about to lag behind Mr. Riley to dump them. Instead, she scrambled after him.

Connor didn't follow them.

Mr. Riley must have been listening to see. He hollered without looking back. "Get on down here. A man has to face up to what he's done."

"You never did with Ma." She didn't know where the words came from, but they were out in the air before she could stop them.

Mr. Riley whipped his head around to stare at her. Then he made a sound that could have been a laugh. Ada June wasn't sure. Trembles shook her insides and made her legs weak as she backed away from him and bumped into Connor.

"I figured you'd be apt to remember someday." He gave her a long, considering look. "But we ain't takin' time to talk on that. We have the now and present with little Joey to dwell on. Time could be wastin' for him."

Then he turned and walked faster. Connor gave her a funny look as he pushed past her to catch up with him. Ada June watched a minute before she ignored the trembles in her legs to run after them.

At the cabin, about as many were milling about the yard and on the porch as had been there when they serenaded Preacher Gordon and Miss Mira. But nobody had a look of fun on their faces now. Silence fell over them as they split like the Lord dividing the Red Sea to give Mr. Riley a clear path to the steps.

Connor's pa came from somewhere to jerk Connor aside, but Mr. Riley stopped him. "Let the boy come on in to see what he's done."

When Bo started barking, she wanted to push past Mr. Riley, but she didn't. Not as many people were inside. Miss Effie and Miss Nicey Jane along with Joseph's ma and pa were hovering over Ada June's bed. Mathena and a couple of other women were at the fireplace. Miss Mira or Preacher Gordon weren't anywhere to be seen.

Miss Nicey Jane looked around at Mr. Riley. "Good. You're here."

"I'm here," he said.

Connor tried to stay behind Mr. Riley, but she saw him. "Glad you knowed to go for him, Connor."

"He didn't. The girl come for me." Mr. Riley moved to the bed. "Looks like you got yourself in a pickle, Joey."

"It hurts, Uncle Riley."

He sounded weak, but he sounded plenty alive. That lightened Ada June's heart enough that she could go see to Bo. And find Miss Mira. Surely they hadn't sent her for water.

"Where's Miss Mira?" She pushed out the words.

Miss Effie glanced over at her. "She needed to lie down awhile. Things has her stirred up in ways not good for her condition."

"The baby?" Miss Mira wouldn't be able to stand losing the baby.

Miss Effie didn't answer what Ada June wanted to know. "Preacher is in there prayin' down mercy for Joseph and her too, I'm thinking."

"It'd be a mercy if you would hush up that dog." Miss Nicey Jane frowned at her. "And heavenly days, you have ruint your dress."

"Don't be botherin' her, Nicey Jane." Mr. Riley looked over his shoulder at Ada June. His gaze speared through her. "Boy first. Then dog."

She backed away from him, then turned to run for the bedroom. When she went through the door, Bo tried to jump up on her. He whimpered and fell back. She squatted down to rub him.

"Are you all right, Ada June?" Miss Mira pushed up off her pillow. Preacher Gordon was kneeling beside her. Ada June wanted to whimper like Bo, but she swallowed it down and nodded. They looked so worried. She wasn't sure if that was for her, for Joseph, for Bo, or for the baby. She didn't know much about babies coming except Miss Mira needed a bigger baby bump before a baby could be born.

"Are you?" She peered over at Miss Mira.

Preacher Gordon answered for her. "Miss Nicey Jane says resting can help."

"And prayer." Miss Mira lay back.

"Mr. Riley is here," Ada June said.

Preacher Gordon got up off his knees where he must have been praying. He leaned over and kissed Miss Mira's forehead. "I better go see if he needs anything."

"I'll be fine now that Ada June is here."

Preacher Gordon stopped and gave Ada June a hug before he went out of the room. She crept over to the bed. Bo scooted along with her with more whimpering but surely not loud enough to worry Miss Nicey Jane.

Miss Mira took her hand. "I'm so sorry Bo is hurt."

"And Joseph."

"And Joseph."

"And you."

"And me." Miss Mira smiled. "The Lord will watch over us."

"Will he save the baby? He didn't let us keep Selinda."

"I don't know, but I'm praying he will." She pulled Ada June's hand up to kiss her knuckles. "Put Bo up here in the bed and lie down with us."

"Bo in the bed?"

"He needs something soft."

She did as Miss Mira said and Bo lay right down. She didn't crawl in after him. "My dress is too dirty."

Miss Mira pulled Ada June closer to the lamplight. "What happened? Your face and arms are all scratched up."

"I fell up on Mr. Riley's hill."

"Are you hurt?" Miss Mira sounded worried.

"Not enough to matter. Connor pulled me back up on the trail." She hoped Miss Mira wouldn't ask any more questions.

"Oh. You know I fell too."

"I saw you. You hurt?"

"Banged up my knee. I'm limping like Bo, though not as bad. Poor dog."

"I'm thinkin' Mr. Riley might tend to him. After he sees to Joseph."

Just then, Joseph yelled in the next room. Ada June cringed and Bo jerked up his head.

"I don't care about the dress." Miss Mira scooted over. "Climb in here beside me."

Ada June slipped off her shoes and brushed the loose dirt off her feet before she got in the bed. Miss Mira put her arms around her. "Thank you, Ada June."

She thought on telling Miss Mira about remembering Mr. Riley chasing after her ma, but then she didn't want to. None of that had the first thing to do with her and Miss Mira, excepting the part of making her an orphan so these years later Miss Mira could take her in.

She matched her breathing to Miss Mira's for a few minutes as they lay quiet as water spiders on a still creek. Then she said, "Can I call you Mama?"

Miss Mira looked surprised but pleased. "Please do, daughter mine."

"Thank you." Ada June hesitated a second. "Mama."

Her new mama reached to smooth Ada June's hair away from her face. She picked out a twig and smiled. "But I have to say you smell more like dirt than starlight this time."

Ada June didn't know how long it was before Preacher Gordon came back in the room with a glass of water and some of those crackers he'd brought over from Jackson. If he was surprised to see her and Bo in the bed, he didn't say so. But Ada June slipped out from under the covers to stand up anyhow.

"Mr. Riley got out the bullet. Says Joseph should be fine, though sore for a while with a cracked rib."

"Thank the Lord," Miss Mira, her mama, whispered.

"Can we thank the Lord for you too?" he asked.

"The pains have eased some," she said.

"Miss Nicey Jane said it might take a while of bed rest." He looked at Ada June. "Mr. Riley wants you to bring Bo out to him. You need me to carry him?"

"No. I can."

It was funny going from the dim back room to where daylight still came in the windows. Miss Effie and Joseph's ma were over by Ada June's bed. Joseph appeared to be sleeping. The other women were gone. Even Miss Nicey Jane.

"Come out back." Mr. Riley picked up one of the table chairs to carry with him. "Don't need nobody worrying the dog 'cept me."

Ada June's heart beat a little faster as she followed Mr. Riley outside where the sun had about slid behind the far hill.

Mr. Riley put the chair down. "Sit. I ain't gonna hurt you." He stared at Bo. "I need to muzzle him?"

"He won't bite less'n I tell him to."

"Then best not tell him to." His eyes narrowed as he peered at Ada June a few seconds before he turned up a big chunk of wood and sat on it in front of her.

He made a deep humming noise while he ran his hands over Bo's back and legs. "Nothing broke that I can tell, but his hip's out of joint."

"Can you fix it?"

"I'm thinkin' I can if'n he stays easy." He frowned at Ada June. "Stroke his ears, croon to him, whatever makes him feel good."

She leaned her head down close to Bo's ears and whispered nonsense words as she rubbed his chest.

"I weren't gonna hurt your ma. I was some fond of her," Mr. Riley said.

"You were chasing her."

"You got it wrong. She was runnin' from me, but I weren't chasin' her. I had in mind to keep her from starvin' the both of you, but she were a hard one to help when she weren't in her right mind."

"She wasn't a witch."

He smiled a little. "I never thought she was, though she had a way of entrancin' a foolish man. I just aimed to get her off that hill. For you if'n not for her. But she run afore I could say the first word to her."

Ada June stared down at Bo. "When she fell, you didn't help her."

"I woulda if I'd a known. I hollered for her. She wouldn't answer."

"She couldn't."

"That could be, but I didn't have no way of knowing that. I figured if I let her be, she'd go on back up to that shack of hers. Come morning, I aimed to come again. Make Nicey Jane come with me, and if she wouldn't, get Effie. She would have done it." He looked off toward the trees on the other side of the holler. "But then Otto come packing you down the hill saying Sarai was gone. Didn't see no need stirrin' up more trouble for everybody then."

"What about me?"

"I thought they'd do for you. They did. You were just too ornery to take to 'em."

"They didn't take to me."

"Ain't no wonder, with how you acted like some wild thing. But Effie, she took you in. Let you have this dog here." He put his hands flat on his thighs and shook himself. "Can't believe I'm tellin' all this to a half-growed girl." His eyes narrowed on Ada June again. "But I done said all I'm gonna say about it, understand?"

Ada June nodded without looking at him.

"Now put ever'thing out of your head 'cepting this here dog of yours. Keep on that talkin' you was doin' a bit ago." He put his hands on Bo's hindquarters. "When I think he's easy 'nough, I'll put them bones back in place. But don't you watch. Better for you not to know so's he won't know. Dogs have a way of being in our heads and knowin' what we is gonna think afore we think it."

She leaned down close to Bo's ears again and talked in a sing-song voice. Mr. Riley started his low humming. After a little while, he gave Bo a twist. Bo yelped and twisted to snap at the air behind him.

Mr. Riley sat back. "Keep him inside for a spell. Use a rope when he has to go out. Don't let him do no running. Got that?"

"Yes sir."

"It could happen agin."

"Could you fix it again?"

"Most likely, but better if it don't need more fixing." He stood up and started off.

"Mr. Riley?"

When he turned to frown at her, Ada June somehow knew he was already hearing the question she couldn't push out the words to ask.

"Best you don't ask."

She stared at him, not knowing if he was right or not. But then she said, "I was just gonna say thankee."

41

Gordon fixed Ada June a pallet on the floor in their bedroom. Joseph needed Ada June's bed until he could be carried to his house. Miss Effie stayed with him since his mother needed to take care of his sisters and brothers.

After Gordon straightened the kitchen and banked the fire, he stopped to pray with Miss Effie where she sat in the rocker by the bed.

After they prayed, Miss Effie said, "Poor boy."

"But Mr. Riley thinks he'll be all right, doesn't he?"

"He does. Riley has experience with such things. You knew he's my brother, didn't you?"

"I'm sure someone has told me that, but I admit to not always keeping all the relations straight."

"I reckon that ain't no wonder for somebody brought-in."

Gordon cringed a little. No matter how long he lived right in the middle of the Sourwood people, he would always be brought-in. "I didn't get a chance to thank him for fixing Bo before he left."

"He didn't want no thanks." She rocked back and forth a couple of times. "He ain't a bad man, Preacher Gordon. He just ain't one for church. I figure he worries gettin' too much religion might work agin his business." She paused a moment before she went on. "And I reckon it's better we don't talk none about that."

"Then we won't. I'm not in the reforming business. Just the spreading the gospel business. I let the Lord do what reforming he thinks needs doing."

"Just as well. Me and Nicey Jane done been tryin' with Riley for years without the first scrap of progress." She shook her head. "How's Miss Mira? Pains still punishin' her?"

"They've eased up, but Miss Nicey Jane says she should rest a few days and forget teaching for the summer."

"She won't like that."

"No, but if she taught in the county schools, they'd make her quit. They have a rule against married women teachers."

"Plumb foolishness. Being married don't make your head stop working. You ain't gonna make her stop, is you?"

"Not unless she wants to. Our school isn't part of the county system. We can make our own rules."

"Good." Miss Effie nodded. "When she feels up to being back at it, I'll come give her a hand agin, like as how I did afore plantin' time."

"She will like that."

"Being so little and all, I didn't think she could handle some of the rascals, but they generally pay her mind." She was quiet a moment before she blew out a breath. "I'm sorry she had to give up Selinda, but I'm tickled she's took Ada June to heart."

"We want to adopt her legally to make sure nobody will ever show up to take her."

"That won't happen." She sounded more than sure.

"But she could have relatives we don't know about."

"Don't worry your head over that, Preacher. Fact is, it could be she has kin all around her but none that is gonna bother her chance with you and Miss Mira." She looked up at Gordon. "And that's all you'll ever hear me say about it."

"I see." Pushing Miss Effie to tell anything she didn't aim to tell was useless. "Then good night. If you need anything, just holler."

"I can tend to myself. You go tend to your woman. She's a right sweet little thing."

When he went into the bedroom, the lamp was still burning. He was going to take a saw to the logs tomorrow and make a window. If Mira had to stay in bed, she wasn't going to do so in what folks called a blind cabin. One without windows.

Bo raised his head, his tail sweeping against the floor. Then he lay back down next to Ada June.

"Is she asleep?" Mira whispered.

"Looks to be." Gordon sat down on the box that served as a chair.

"Did she change her dress?"

Gordon looked over at Ada June. "I don't know. Did she need to?"

"Would have been best. She looked like she'd had a tussle with wildcats. Said she fell down the hill, but wouldn't say more than that." Mira looked over at Ada June.

"As long as she's all right." Gordon untied his shoes and slipped them off. "Feels like dirt on the floor."

"Part of the tussle with wildcats." A little frown wrinkled the skin between her eyes.

"Give her time. She might tell you more." He thought again about Miss Effie's words about Ada June. More was under those words, but he wouldn't dig for it. Let the Lord handle it.

"She asked if she could call me Mama." Her voice trembled on the word.

He took her hand. "That's good, isn't it?"

"Very good. But sad too. Sad her mother died. Sad I won't ever hear Selinda call me Mama like I hoped. Sad that I might lose this baby too." She sniffed and swallowed hard.

He tightened his grip on her hand. "That hasn't happened yet."

"But it could happen."

"It could. So much can happen. Like Joseph in there. Another inch or two and we'd be burying him. We don't get any guarantees for our tomorrows. The Scripture tells us that."

"Yet we go to bed every night expecting to see the sunrise."

"I think the Lord intends that too."

"But things don't always turn out the way we think."

"What do you mean?" Gordon asked.

She smiled. "Me having a ten-year-old daughter."

"A blessing."

"That's what Miss Ophelia told me I could be to the children here and look what I let happen to Joseph."

"None of what happened is your fault, Mira."

"I suppose not, but I keep thinking if I'd been outside a minute earlier or I don't know. That surely I could have done something."

"You can't change what has already happened."

She sighed. "I know. Will Connor be all right? He didn't aim to shoot Joseph."

"But he did. He'll have to suffer the consequences, but we can hope he'll learn something from it."

She was silent a moment. "Things haven't been at all like I thought they would be when I came here."

"How's that?"

Instead of answering him, she asked a question of her own. "Do you remember when you first asked me to come to Sourwood? When you said if I married you, the people would accept me quicker."

"I remember."

"And do you remember what I told you?" She was smiling.

"I think you used words like ridiculous, outrageous, impossible. Maybe scandalous."

"I never said scandalous." She gave his hand a shake.

"Right. Could be I was the scandalous one for asking. Not only asking. Insisting. Practically badgering you."

"Then it turned out I was the one doing the insisting on the train here."

"Yes."

"What did you think you were getting when you married me? A schoolteacher?"

"That was my aim. I did want a teacher for our school, but what I got was much more. A wife I love more than I can ever say." He lifted her hand up and kissed her fingers. "My turn. What did you think you were getting when you stood before Pastor Haskell and let him marry us?"

"A teaching position. A place to live. A new life. A chance to be a mother. I have always so wanted to be a mother."

"And now." He started to speak, but she put the fingers of her other hand over his lips.

"And now I have already gotten that with Selinda for those few weeks. With Ada June forever. With this beginning of a child that I pray will continue to grow inside me. But I have even more. I am a wife and I'm ridiculously glad I am. I love you, Gordon Covington. Till death do us part."

Gordon's heart felt too big for his chest. "Thank you, Mrs. Covington."

"Come to bed."

He undid his suspenders and took off his outer shirt but left on his trousers in case Miss Effie needed something. "What is in the bed?" he asked as he got under the covers.

"Dirt." She laughed softly. "I wanted Ada June to lie down beside me earlier. She warned me she was dirty from that tussle with the mountain, but I didn't realize how dirty. You might have to hire somebody to do the wash."

"But where am I going to get the money to pay them?"

"Oh well, somebody will do it for nothing. You're the preacher."

"So I am. And the husband of the schoolteacher."

She closed her eyes and was asleep almost at once. He watched her, glad he hadn't blown out the lamp.

The line from an old hymn came to mind. *The Lord moves in a mysterious way his wonders to perform; he plants his footsteps in the sea and rides upon the storm.*

For that, he was thankful.

Epilogue

October 20, 1910

Dear Julie,

Thank you so much for the lovely baby blanket you knitted for your new little niece. What a blessing it is for her to have a loving aunt like you and even more of a blessing for me to claim you as a sister through more than marriage but through love. It was so good to get to know you when you came to visit in June.

I wanted to write to thank you myself, even though Gordon surely did so already when he wrote about our sweet baby daughter's early entry into the world. Gordon says she just couldn't wait for us to hold her in our arms. Although still very small, she is doing fine. Miss Nicey Jane—I'm sure you remember meeting her when you were here—says that any baby who squalls that loud when she's hungry is better than fine. I can't wait until you come to Sourwood again and meet her. You know you are welcome any time.

I suppose you are curious as to what name we've given her. Ada June was adamant that her name be Amelia. She wanted something that started with A the same as hers. I don't know *where she heard the name, but I was happy to let her choose since she is so excited to be a big sister. Gordon laughed when she told him the name. He said it was quite a mouthful for such a tiny person. Ada June insisted the name is more than perfect and that Amelia will agree when she's older.*

I added Faith because of her hard journey to make it to her day to be born. So often I feared I would lose her, as you know since you were here during one of those times. You were such a help and encouragement then. After you left, Miss Ophelia, my former landlady in Louisville, surprised us when she came to see the sourwood trees blooming. I'm sure Gordon wrote you about how she must have loved those trees so much that she has stayed.

She took over the teaching when school started back up in July, but I will be teaching with her next year after Amelia Faith is a little older. It could be you should pray for the children who will have to deal with two brought-in teachers. I'm smiling when I write that.

I doubt Sourwood has ever dealt with anyone quite like Miss Ophelia, but she's cut out of the same cloth as the mountain women here, even though their lives have been so different. She has become family, a grandmother to Ada June, a mother to me. A stern one for sure, but a loving one under that sternness. You will understand when you meet her.

Gordon is well, busy sharing the gospel and helping the people here in Sourwood. Joseph has recovered completely from his wound and is back trailing after Gordon or playing with Bo. The dog limps a bit at times, but so far his bones have stayed in place, much to Ada June's and my relief. Gordon talked with a lawyer about adopting Ada June, but she is already ours in our hearts. You'll laugh to hear her calling Gordon "Papa Preacher."

Thank you for the hair ribbons you sent her. She especially loves the blue one as do I since it is the color of the little bluebirds that nested in an old woodpecker hole in the oak next to the schoolhouse. I wondered if you purposely chose it after we watched them when you were here. I did love hearing the papa bird sing his courtship song that gave promise of more bluebirds in Sourwood.

Ada June has tied back her hair every day since she received your package. She's nothing at all like that girl I first met in January who seemed to hardly know how to use a comb. Perhaps because she had none of her own.

So much has changed for her in this one short year. For me as well. I am blessed beyond measure with love and family.

I pray that you and your children are well. It will be wonderful if they can come with you to Sourwood next summer. What a blessing that would be.

Amelia Faith is fussing. I best close this letter and see to her. Thank you again for the beautiful baby blanket and even more for embracing me as a sister.

Write me all your news.

Love, Mira

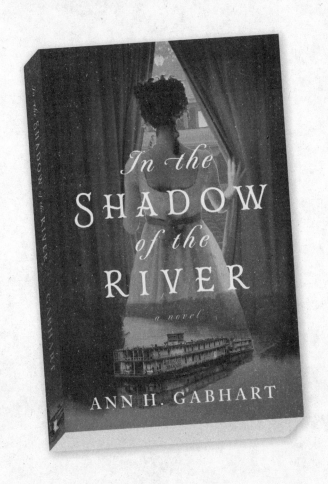

1

Jacci Reed's mother shook her awake, then put her fingers lightly over Jacci's lips.

"Shh. We have to get off the boat." Her mother's eyes were wide in the light of the lantern she held.

Jacci wanted to ask why, but instead she sat up and felt for her shoes with her toes.

Her mother shook her head and pulled her off the bed. "No time." But she didn't fuss when Jacci grabbed her sock doll.

Her mother left the lantern on the table without even blowing it out. At five, Jacci had been warned so often about a candle or lantern being upset and catching the boat on fire that now she feared the room might explode in flames before they got out of the door.

Her mother led Jacci out into the passageway. "Not a sound." She sounded scared.

Jacci's mother never got scared. She was always the one to help Jacci not be afraid when thunder boomed over the river or floods made the steamboat bounce in funny ways. So now Jacci bit her lip and didn't cry out when her mother squeezed her hand so tight her fingers hurt. The fear coursed between their hands and Jacci's heart pounded up in her ears. Maybe the boat was on fire already and they would have to jump in the river to escape.

347

But she didn't smell smoke as she hurried to keep up with her mother's fast steps. Her nightgown flapped against her legs. Her mother never let her go out on the steamboat deck without putting on a dress. Ever.

She couldn't swim. Maybe she wouldn't have to. They were at the dock. She'd watched the crew tie up their steamboat earlier and listened to the roustabouts sing while they unloaded barrels and crates. She'd stayed hidden up on the top deck while the fancy men and women headed out down the gangplank. The women wore hats with ribbons and feathers. The men carried gold-knobbed canes.

Even better than that was the sound of a calliope drifting down the river that meant a showboat was on the way. When it docked right beside their boat, she clapped her hands. She never got to go to the shows, but she loved to watch the actors coming and going. Sometimes they played music and sang.

By the time the river swallowed up the sun, people were streaming up onto the boat to see the show. She did so wish she could be one of them, but her mother would never allow that. Instead she had found Jacci and made her go to bed.

Now as Mama hurried her up to the main deck, Jacci could hear music spilling out of the showboat. Lively music and then laughter.

Sometimes when she watched a showboat tied up next to their boat, she laughed too when she heard laughter, even though she had no idea what was funny. She didn't feel like doing that now. Not with her mother so afraid.

A man stepped out of the shadows in front of them. Her mother shoved Jacci behind her.

"You can't get away." The man's voice was low, as if he didn't want anyone but her mother to hear him. "Just let me have the kid and nobody will have to get hurt."

"No. She's mine." Her mother's voice sounded strained.

"That's not what I've been told," the man said.

"You've been told wrong."

"Lisbeth says different."

"Lisbeth?" Jacci's mother breathed out the name as her whole body stiffened against Jacci. "You're lying."

Jacci peeked out from behind Mama's skirts. She could see the man's smile in the moonlight, and she wanted to jerk free from her mother and run hide. She knew plenty of great hiding places on their boat. But what if it really was on fire?

The man laughed. "I think we know who has been lying."

He was barely taller than her mother and had on fancy passenger clothes. Not what the crewmen wore.

Her mother held Jacci behind her and jerked her small gun out of her pocket with her other hand. "Get out of the way."

The man laughed. "What do you think you're going to do with that?"

"Whatever I have to." Mama's voice sounded so cold, so wrong, that Jacci shivered.

The man rushed toward her mother and knocked the gun out of her hand. There was a flash of metal in his hand.

Her mother made a choked sound. "Run, Jacci."

But Jacci couldn't leave her mother. She dropped her doll and grabbed the gun off the deck. She'd seen men shoot at things on the riverbanks. She knew how they spread their feet to stand steady while they held their guns out in front of them. She did that now as the man pushed her mother away from him so hard she landed against the railing. Jacci pointed the gun at him and pulled back the trigger.

The gun made a popping sound, only a little louder than the plop of a fish jumping up from the river and falling back in. The man looked confused as he turned toward Jacci. Then, still staring at her, he sank to a sitting position on the deck, his hands pressed against his middle.

Jacci shook so much she couldn't hold on to the gun. It clattered to the deck once more. She looked at her mother doubled over against the rail. "Mama?"

As if the sound of Jacci's voice gave her strength, her mother straightened up. Her voice was weak but back to sounding like Mama. "Get the gun."

Jacci did as she was told while she tried not to look at the man still sitting there with that funny look on his face.

"Socks." Her doll had slid over close to the man. She hesitated, then took a step toward it.

"No." Her mother grabbed Jacci's shoulder to yank her back as the man lurched toward her. "I'll make you a new one."

The man said something as he fell back, but Jacci couldn't understand what it was. His voice sounded all bubbly and wrong. She wished the moon would go behind a cloud so she couldn't see his face.

Mama's hand was wet and sticky now and her grasp weak instead of hard the way it had been.

"Where are we going?" she asked as they went down the gangplank to the wooden dock and then onto the grass.

"The showboat."

Jacci wanted to be happy about that. She'd always wanted to go on a showboat and see what made people laugh. But now she wasn't sure she would ever laugh again. Her mother's breath was ragged, and when she stumbled over a rock, she groaned. Jacci put an arm around her to try to hold her up.

They went up the stage plank toward the music. Happy music. Horns and drums and a piano. Her mother's steps slowed until she was barely moving. Jacci wanted to run, but she couldn't leave her mother.

"Do you still have the gun?" Mama said.

Jacci held it out.

"Throw it in the river."

When Jacci started to drop it over the side, her mother stopped her. "Not here. On the other side. Throw it as hard as you can." She pushed Jacci away from her and leaned on a post. "Don't let anybody see you. Be fast."

Applause and cheers came from inside the theater. Jacci ran through the shadows around the deck. She was scared to be away from Mama, but she had to do what she said. After she slung the gun into the river, she raced back to where her mother hung on to the post as if that was all that kept her from falling.

But when she saw Jacci, she pushed away from the post and they went past the empty ticket booth. A few people passed by them, but they were too busy laughing and talking to pay any attention to Jacci and her mother.

Inside a big room with rows and rows of seats, a crowd of people moved toward the front where men and women in frilly costumes smiled and waved from a stage. Some lanterns glowed bright there while others along the wall flickered with only enough light to see the way between the rows of seats. A man came toward them, stopping now and again to turn up the lantern flames.

Her mother followed the crowd toward the stage, but stopped when she got close to the man in the aisle. She called out to him. "We need to see Tyrone Chesser."

The man looked at her and then at Jacci. He took a step back. "Freaking fishworms. What's happened to you?"

Jacci looked down at her gown. It was red with blood.

Acknowledgments

I have been down many story trails, and I am always happy when I find the ending I hoped for when I wrote the first word months before. But a book doesn't truly come to life until it has a reader. I, the writer, and you, the reader, form a partnership as the story goes from my imagination to yours. So thank you for being willing to partner with me as a reader in this storytelling venture.

Once I've written the words, many other people help my story become a book you can read. I'm thankful for an editor, Rachel McRae, who loves books and does all she can to make my stories shine. I appreciate copyeditors like Barb Barnes and Kristin Adkinson who help me tell my stories in the best words. The Revell art department designs fabulous covers for my books that get compliments at every book event I attend. The Revell team and everyone at Baker Publishing Group who works to get my books in front of readers are the best. Thank you all.

I can never thank my agent, Wendy Lawton, enough for her encouragement and help through the years we've worked together. She prays for me, celebrates successes with me, and lifts me up whenever I hit a chughole of discouragement in my writing life.

I am blessed with a wonderful family of readers. Some of them even read my stories, including my husband, who has put up with me an amazing number of years and has been more than patient when I disappear down story trails with imaginary people.

The Lord has given me so many stories to share since I was that young girl with the fanciful dream to be a writer. For that, I can never be thankful enough.

And I thank you, dear reader, for traveling this story trail with me.

Ann H. Gabhart is the bestselling author of *In the Shadow of the River*, *When the Meadow Blooms*, *Along a Storied Trail*, *An Appalachian Summer*, *River to Redemption*, and *These Healing Hills*. She and her husband live on a farm a mile from where she was born in rural Kentucky. Ann enjoys discovering the everyday wonders of nature while hiking in her farm's fields and woods with her grandchildren and her dogs, Frankie and Marley. Learn more at AnnHGabhart.com.

Pick up another inspirational historical novel from
ANN H. GABHART

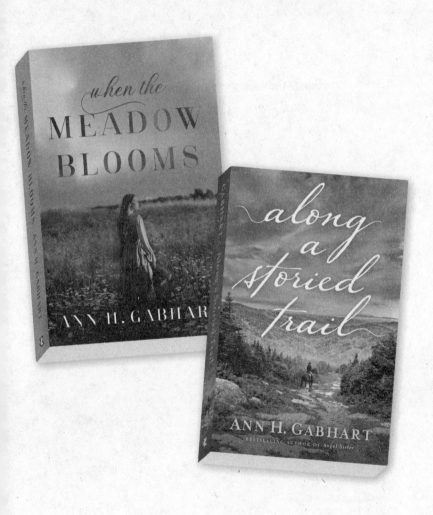

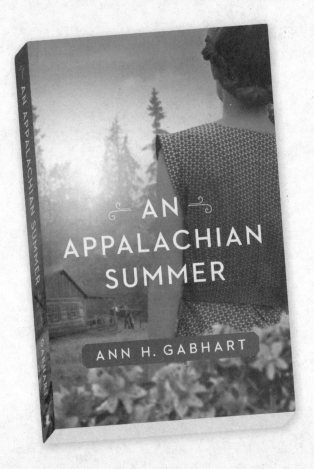

Meet
Ann H. Gabhart

AnnHGabhart.com